Eve's Rib

Nora Hill

TLS

Copyright ©Nora Hill

All rights reserved. No part of this book may be reproduced or used in any manner without the express written permission of the publisher except for the use of brief quotations in a book review. All images within this book are property of The Three Little Sisters and may not be duplicated without permission from the publisher.

ISBN13: 978-1-959350-51-4

©The Three Little Sisters
USA/CANADA

Chapter One

Annabelle Pierce wrapped her eager hands around Molly's heart. Major vessels gave way to curious fingertips, tissue slick against her bloodied skin. The organ was more delicate, more ethereal, than she had imagined. A mechanical whirring jarred against the biologic expanse. Keeping her grasp steady, Annabelle looked at the wall clock. Never enough time. Annabelle freed her prize from its cage, the jostling sounds of her efforts raised the hairs on her neck. If her mother were to burst in that very moment to discover her kitchen-side anatomy lessons, Annabelle might as well surrender herself to the clerk at Ticehust Asylum. But Annabelle's mother hasn't set a slippered foot below the civil comforts of the main floor of the Fernhead House since 1845, when she was a babe in Mrs. Mingle's arms.

Reassured her experiments would at least momentarily remain undisturbed, Annabelle surrendered the organ alongside the liver and bowels nestled into one of her mother's prized ironstone china serving bowls. Surely, it was quite normal for a well-bred young woman to spend the wee morning hours elbow-deep in the belly of her recently deceased household dog. She only could keep on for another day or two. Molly was beginning to smell.

A loud rapping sounded on the door to the housekeeper's office.

Annabelle jumped and straightened from her task. Breakfast was at eight.

"M'lady, yer father's down early and yer mother's up earlier than usual." The doorknob shook as if possessed. "Come now, let us in."

"Sarah, you frightened the daylights out of me." Thank God for Sarah. Annabelle hadn't expected to like her lady's maid so much. She had caught Sarah palming a small gold clock off the walnut grand piano, just before the housekeeper, Mrs. Mingle, bustled into the drawing room for the interview. Annabelle envied the lack of any flush to Sarah's cheeks. Annabelle snatched a stolen kitchen towel and crossed the room, cloaking her sticky hand before she rocked the bolt back from its rest.

The door flung open, knocking Annabelle back a step as her lady's maid burst through the doorway.

"Miss Pierce. I've come to help, in any way I can. Tis my duty, nay privilege." Sarah's gaze was low; a shoddy effort at humility. "To bolt around like a madwoman, in the middle of dressin' everyone in the bleedin' house, to find your careless arse." She broke into peals of laughter and gave Annabelle's shoulder a shove. "Just to keep the peace. Lord knows I can't stomach another one of yer mother's turns."

On her first week at Fernhead House, Annabelle paid for the black space in Sarah's smile to be filled with a soldier's tooth. She questioned that kindness now, for with the improvement to her presentation, Sarah's propriety became nearly nonexistent.

"The clock continues its assault. We've two minutes to clear this battlefield and make yer way to breakfast. No need to chance yer mother coming down early."

Sarah was right. The tyrant in lace typically ruled her kingdom from the comforts of her bed things. Annabelle wasn't in the mood to defend herself today. She was looking forward to some quiet time with her father to discuss her edits for his latest medical article for the Lancet.

"Don't just gawk, then, help me." Annabelle turned back to the disastrous dog and desk.

Sarah chuckled. "Don't know 'bout the bother, m'lady. Everyone knows yer game. There are no secrets at Fernhead House."

※

Grain sacks were Sarah's genius contribution to the morning's adventure. Molly now resembled one of the sacks of root vegetables slumped shoulder to shoulder at the far end of the cellar. The cool damp and sweet mustiness of the room were somehow more inviting than distasteful.

Annabelle perused the army of glass jars brimming with Mrs. Mingle's particular delicacies for the Pierce family, canning was a favorite pastime of the housekeeper's, though she was so much more to every member of the house—confidante, advisor, absolver.

"Your favorite." Annabelle thrust a jar of raspberry preserves toward Sarah. The maid's loyalty was rivaled only by her vast appetite for both sweets and entitlement. Annabelle thought the bribe would taste like heaven compared to the offerings at the prison, gruel, hard labor, lice; Annabelle couldn't comprehend the horrors. "Jam for silence. Memories of Newgate beginning to fade?"

Sarah puckered her face. "No need to bring up the past, m'lady." She snatched the jar. "But see as ye do, and we both like to give t'other a bit of a run." She appraised Annabelle with calculated coolness. "Ol' Freddie's been up to his tricks. He means business this time."

Annabelle knew of Ol' Freddie. Sarah had climbed from a poorhouse orphan to a swift-handed street urchin. Her meeting with Ol' Freddie after her third interview with the sour Old Bailey magistrate was a mixed blessing. For the security his ring of thieves offered, Sarah had exchanged her free will for the security Ol' Freddie's ring of thieves offered.

"I thought we were rid of him?"

"There's no we in this story, m'lady."

Her tone lashed Annabelle's heart. Sarah's offered crass, if wise candor to Annabelle's dreams and dilemmas. Annabelle cherished Sarah's confidence, and Sarah knew it.

"He's plottin' somethin' big. Needs me 'elp. I were the brains behind the whole stinkin' operation, m'lady. He couldn't go this big without me."

"Would you give us up?" Annabelle was hurt. After she had taken the risk to hire her against Mrs. Mingle's wishes. Sarah was more than a maid.

"This?" Sarah's eyebrows raised. "I've got far grander plans than spending me days hauling you in n'out of silks and stays."

Annabelle set her jaw. "Don't you forget—"

Sarah whisked the kitchen towel from Annabelle and wiped at a few suspicious biological bits on her skirts. "Point is, I've nicked several choice letters ye wouldn't want fluttering into the wrong hands. Twenty quid. That's what Freddie's distance'll cost."

Annabelle hands went icy. "What letters?"

"Larkin's, of course." The glee in Sarah's eyes spoke of a mischievousness bordering on cruelty.

Annabelle's stomach cramped. She regretted sharing their correspondence now. Her reputation would be irrevocably tarnished—decimated really. And there was the trouble with Olivia. Annabelle had wickedly enjoyed the element of intrigue when she began a torrid flirtation with her childhood friend's husband.

Sarah thrust the jam jar into a deep apron pocket. It clanked against some previously stowed booty. "I thought I'd help meself to one or two items—on account of me sealed lips and all."

"Jam's one thing. Twenty pounds is quite another. You'd bite the ring off Queen Victoria's fingers for the right price."

"Friggen' hell, I'd take her fingy if I 'ad to. Twenty sovereigns by t'morrow night. Or I'll end up snuggled up to Molls here as yer next experiment."

The hands of Mrs. Mingle's table clock clicked onto eight o'clock and sounded the hour.

It was always something in the Pierce household, Annabelle thought. *Now my supposed confidante is blackmailing me into paying off some lunatic criminal element.* She wondered if she'd rather take her chances in a dark Whitechapel alley with Ol' Freddie. She patted the shrouded dog on the head. "Til tomorrow, lovely."

Sarah shuddered. "You've seen a great deal worse than a dead dog stowed away in the basements of Harley Street."

※

Sarah took the steps two at a time. Annabelle hung back at the bottom of the back stairway. She understood her maid's sense of self-preservation was stronger than any fledgling ties of friendship. Twenty pounds was nothing. Silly really, to give a servant that much trust.

"All's clear," Sarah hissed as she poked her head back around the doorway.

Annabelle wouldn't have minded a few moments to herself. A headache of her own creation to purchase a few hours of peace was tempting. But her father's article was overdue. No rest for the wicked, she supposed. She hoisted her skirts free from her ankles and began her ascent.

Sarah laughed. "You've made this bed yerself, missy. Recken I don't feels sorry for you."

"Just once could you give me the authority to grouse?"

9

"Not from where I sits, m'lady."

"You forget who you are and where you've sat."

"Nay, m'lady, I'll never forget. But me sooty past has always been open for yer inspection."

"An honest extortionist. I don't believe for one minute you'd show anyone my letters."

"Wouldn't I?"

"No."

Sarah drew herself up, brow to brow with her mistress.

"Something to add?"

The soft rustle and squeak of Mrs. Mingle's breakfast cart far down the end of the hall offered her the opportunity to overt her eyes from Sarah's.

Sarah tugged a rag from her skirts and spat. "You'd be lost without me—always cleanin' up the evidence." She scrubbed a rusty streak from Annabelle's cheek. "Like I said, you got no secrets."

Annabelle wished that were true. Thoughts whirred in her mind. The Lancet rewrite first. Then she'd easily cajole the twenty pounds from her father. A new set of gloves and hair bows for the ball would become of utmost importance, never mind the decomposing dog in the cellar and her father's latest article on pulmonary consumption. The thought of deceiving her father gave Annabelle only a momentary hesitation. Remorse and regret were useless emotions.

⸺⸺

She crossed to the breakfast room and grabbed the door handle. She patted the front of her morning dress and loosely contained curls to assure nothing was too amiss before swinging it open. The door slid open silently, giving her the chance to soak up one of her favorite moments of the day. A view of her father at the long dining table, framed by the display of china on the buffet, a newspaper billowing out in front of him, his spectacles inching down his nose. The soft minty walls with the tall windows facing St. George Street offered the sun a standing invitation. The sight of scholarly pursuits coupled with the brightness of the room cloaked Annabelle's heart in contentment. "Good morning, papa, have you slept well?"

Dr. Michael Pierce ruffled his unruly eyebrows to acknowledge the presence of some type of lifeform. He wrinkled his nose to stabilize his spectacles. "Good morning, my dear. I can not say well. This latest submission has given me some of the most intractable ruminations; quite prohibitive to the Land of Nod." He gave his newspaper a crack with the edge of his hand and folded it. "However,' he tucked it beside his plate. "Do you know what offered the relief I needed to find a few hours rest?" His eyes twinkled.

"I'm sorry you've been worried, father. How did you fall asleep?" Annabelle moved by her father's side.

When she had seated herself, he continued. "I thought of the great mind who shares my passions and whose attention to detail far surpasses my own. You're right about the article's weaknesses. I must submit this evening to make it to the Lancet's press for publication next month."

Annabelle's heart leapt at her father's praise. She hoped his esteem surpassed that of a daughter for his offspring and stepped into the realm of colleague; a title she vastly preferred.

"I was hoping we would have a few minutes to ourselves." She reached to find the revised work she had been editing all week from the folds of her dress.

Empty.

Her stomached lurched. She couldn't have lost them. The feet of the chair shrilled against the floor as she jolted back from the table. "Papa, I just had them, I was working on them this morning before I went—" She caught herself. Best not to admit to her bloody early morning activities.

"Now, now, you surely have laid them somewhere."

"I can't remember." Annabelle tossed the events of the past twelve hours back and forth in her memory. But her files were empty. She had fought sleep as she verified concentrations and molecular formulas of the oxidation reactions her father felt were the main physiological duties of the pulmonary circuit. Too vague, the critiques had said. Too little theory, more explanation. Over forty hours spent pouring over every numeral, every statement, and she'd lost it. Now she could not enjoy her toast and jam.

There was a bump at the door before a wide grey skirt backed into the breakfast room.

"Mrs. Mingle at last." Annabelle's father sang out with delight.

The housekeeper's wrinkles and ruddy cheeks spoke of both authority and mischief.

"Tis a brilliant morning." She nodded toward the shining windows. "And nothing compliments this kind of morning better than a cuppa tea as strong as an otter's tail." She bustled the cart over to the buffet and began to unload its sagging shelves. "And a great whack of bread with a thick spread of butter and sweetness." Bustling back to the table, she landed a laden toast rack between Annabelle and her father. "There you be." Ceramic pots clattered behind. "Blackberry jam, fresh made yesterday. I confess I've had a taste—some of my nicest work."

Before Annabelle could concoct a suitable compliment, Mrs. Mingle took a parcel of folded papers from a square pocket of her apron and waved them in front of Annabelle's face. "Now little Madame, you've been scratching at these all week. And there you go, leaving them on the sideboard between the crockery. Any one of the scullery maids could have swept them out with the rubbish."

Annabelle met her father's eyes and sighed. "Mrs. Mingle, you've saved me once again from absolute despair."

"All in a day's work." Mrs. Mingle swept to give Annabelle a quick peck on the cheek. She darted her head back sharply and furrowed her brows.

Annabelle offered a one-sided smile in protest. Mrs. Mingle would understand her silent plea for complicity.

"Well done, as ever, Mrs. Mingle." Dr. Pierce patted the housekeeper on the arm and dove back into The Times, throwing its sheets ajar with great circumstance.

Mrs. Mingle leaned close to Annabelle and whispered. "You smell of the slaughterhouse, lass."

Annabelle shrank in her chair and glanced at the clock, cheerfully keeping the family's countdown. Mother will be down any moment now, her weapons concealed strategically behind mountains of taffeta, a vulture in a sparrow's suit. She rose and moved to the buffet out of earshot of Dr. Pierce.

Mrs. Mingle swept beside her. "You needn't fear him overhearing. When he's reading, I could fire the royal cannons three breaths from his right ear, and he'd take no notice."

Annabelle laid her head for a moment on Mrs. Mingle's soft shoulder. There were days she wished she could spend the entire day with her head cradled by the kind, capable bulk. But she let her daydream pass, she never sat with anything painful for long. The not unpleasant mélange of washing silver polish, cinnamon, and smoked fish filled her nostrils. "Kippers and buns this morning as well?"

"Aye. But don't let the greed take hold of you yet." Mrs. Mingle withdrew a glass bottle from the mystifying depths of yet another apron pocket. "L'eau d'orange ."

Annabelle adored the valiant attempt at worldliness. The housekeepers throaty Northern accent added a humorous coarseness to the words.

"A dabblet or two should cover your morning studies up nicely."

"You're irreplaceable, Mrs. Mingle." Annabelle allowed Mrs. Mingle time to apply the sweetly floral application behind her ears and at her wrists. She mouthed a silent 'thank you' just before Mrs. Mingle retreated. The delicious absurdity of the thing struck her. Moments before the future of her personal medical inquiries stood to be lost. Now things had tidied, she should still have a few moments of precious solitude with her father.

Chapter 2

Annabelle had written her father's articles for years, though under his authorship and subsequent acclaim. But this morning she would face a necessary evil in this next conversation with the renowned Dr. Pierce of 212 Harley Street. Annabelle was glad she only had to call him papa . She gained courage from Mrs. Mingle's preparations, sucked the last dregs of jam from her fingertips, and plunged in. "Papa, how long have I been assisting you with your submissions to The Lancet?"

Her considered her as though he were sizing up a rare jungle creature on exhibition at the London Zoo. "I can't seem to remember a time when I haven't consulted you on my clinical research." A smile took over his face. "I imagine you must have been about twelve, just after you gained an understanding of Darwin's basic principles and the chemical elements."

Annabelle recalled her enchanted afternoons under the lens of a microscope, examining creatures from water samples she took from the dog's dish, puddles, and even, as a crowning achievement, several droplets of scum from the top of Mrs. Mingle's crock of bubbling sauerkraut.

But Annabelle shuddered, feeling the chasm between that young girl and the woman she had become was not as great as she would have hoped. "So it was." She beamed at her father. "We've been at this for over a decade but there's something that's begun to trouble me."

Dr. Pierce's lower lip fell. "What my dear girl?"

"It's nothing like that." Annabelle pushed the ruffled stack that was their latest collaboration toward him. For such a brilliant mind, he could be quite plain on some matters. She tapped her finger under the byline. "Something's missing."

Her father shuffled the papers and cleared his throat. "My dear, there doesn't seem to be anything amiss."

"To have to ask my own father for a place in the spotlight beside him." Annabelle rebuked.

Dr. Pierce distractedly fanned the papers in front of Annabelle. A whiff of metallic caught the air. "There are mysterious chocolate smudges on the pages. Or have you smuggled some of Mrs. Mingle's plum preserves to sustain your intellectual endeavors?" He shot Annabelle a well-known look.

Annabelle wrinkled her nose.

"Or are they perhaps made from something a bit more sinister?" He could no longer uphold his austere expression. "These pages are almost drowning in dried blood. What on this blessed earth have you been up to my pet?"

"Papa, I'm your daughter, not a spaniel."

Her father frowned. "That high horse of yours may throw you some day. Simply a figure of speech." Her father reached for his tea. "Come now. Why have you been reenacting the siege over the Daube across my lovely bit of work?"

And just like that, I'm back in my corner. Her father's kind voice only vexed Annabelle more. She'd play his heart strings to save her skin. "At least it's not human." She sent him her most winning grins.

Her father nodded. "Weak, but go on."

"It's Molly's." Annabelle admitted. "I know I said I wanted to bury her under the rose arch in the north garden."

Her father squinted.

Annabelle pressed on before she lost courage. "I slipped out at night and rescued her."

"Rescued? There was no breath in her, darling girl."

Annabelle braced herself. "I've been following Sisson's veterinary text and confirming with Gray's Anatomy. I wanted to see it for myself. Not just in books and sketches."

"You mean you..."

"Yes. In the root cellar. I labeled everything with those pins and tags you gave me for cataloguing butterflies."

The tip of her father's nose twitched. "You and Molls?" He began to chortle with all this might. "In Mrs. Mingle's root cellar? You are a brave spirit, my girl." He threw his head in total surrender.

Her father's laugh full of abandon, almost childlike in its exuberance, melted the threads of anxiety which had been woven thickly around Annabelle's stomach. She allowed herself to slump in her chair with relief. She had to ask now.

Dr. Pierce finished dabbing at his eyes. "What a sight you must have been." He leaned over and traced the curve of her face. "Beautiful and bright, you are my pride."

For once, just once, Annabelle wished her father would complement her apt mind before her looks. "I'm glad we've cleared up that searing question, P apa. Let's return to mine, shall we?"

"By all means. What question is on that heart of yours?"

When framed like that, her father made Annabelle feel a bit oily, full of dangerous ambitions. But the question had lain so long on the tip of her tongue, she felt as though she would grow mute if she did not free herself. "Father, I'd like,' she swallowed and rephrased. "I want to be a co-author with you. Write my own articles for The Lancet." There, it was said. Let loose like a fox. Free to run, compelling the hounds to bay and the hunting party to chase in mad abandon.

Annabelle's palms went clammy at the look which overtook her father's face. Disbelief or even rage would have been simple for her to placate. But the crestfallen shape of his brows and his downcast eyes were agony. What had she done? She couldn't take her words back now.

Her father finally looked at her from under heavy lids. "You don't want to work with me anymore?" His exhale seemed indeterminable before he finally spoke. "Are you not happy keeping your old P apa in check? You know I'm hopeless spinning my medical musings into sensible literature for my colleagues."

Annabelle's heart snagged again on the possessive my.

"You know my men think quite highly of our articles." His small smile brightened. "Just last week John Pae was telling me how nicely my last piece on the use of nitrate of amyl in angina read. He does not offer praise lightly, my dear."

Bones for the mutt in the corner, sucked dry of their marrow, Annabelle stewed.

"But it's not enough. These are my ideas. I've been finding a ring of causality in your mountains of notes from the ward."

He gazed off into space, as if the best deflection to her request could be found in the swirling scrolls of the wallpaper. "You have a gift for imagining the human impact of my hypotheses. You see the life of medicine from a wider view than I."

"You admit then, I am more than a scribe."

"I would never dream of minimizing your contributions, my dear." He pressed toward her, his face falling again. "You take raw ideas and spin them into a beautiful web of theory."

"Papa!" Annabelle wanted so much more than to be an eternal translator.

He lay his hand over her fingers. "I had no idea this was such a frustration to you."

Annabelle almost caved, slipping back into the tracks of their well-worn dynamic. But his blindness stoked a long-smoldering ember inside her. "Father. I have my own ideas, my own hypotheses. I want to write my own papers."

"On medical topics?"

"No. I thought to submit my musings on microbial properties of honey to Philosophical Transactions. A perfect bookend to articles on the stars and extraterrestrial phenomena."

Dr. Pierce's eyes widened as if considering the plausibility of her suggestion.

"Father!" Annabelle slapped the table, making the teacups shudder in their saucers. "All I'm asking for is to have my name alongside yours. For now."

"The medical woman question polarizes our field." Dr. Pierce was matter of fact.

"It separates the lunatics from the sane."

"Not lunatics, Annabelle. They have a point."

"Pray tell what point is that?" Annabelle's jaw was locked so tight her ears were beginning to throb.

"Medical science, though slightly less repugnant to a women's nature than clinical medicine, still opens the floodgates to a vast array of improprieties. Some things are best handled by men, others yield to a gentler touch."

Annabelle found small delight in the fine rusty rings outlining her smooth fingernails. Badges of honor from the dissection. "I want a by-line."

"Several imminent lady scientists publish on topics of astronomy, education, and even botany. Perhaps you—"

"I have little interest in those topics." Annabelle grabbed the edge of the breakfast table for support. "Will you, or will you not, allow me a by-line for our work in The Lancet?"

"Annabelle, my dearest. My colleagues simply do not have the same respect for a woman's influence in the medical arena, as other areas of study do. It wouldn't be allowed."

"Who wouldn't allow it, Dr. Pae?"

Her father flicked his lip between his teeth.

A stiff smile grew over Annabelle's face. "Or you?"

"Both, really, my dear."

"You don't mean that, father!"

He took on the quality of a Greek bust in the Victoria and Albert Museum . "I do, Annabelle."

"You won't even entertain the idea?"

"It breaks my heart, but no."

Annabelle's hands began to tremor. "Why?" She reached for the sullied papers, sweeping them to her chest as if she were a criminal cornered, knife to a hostage's throat.

"Medicine is not the field for women. It's too brutal."

"I've been reading from your old textbooks as long as I can remember. I practiced sketching the Vitruvian man while other girls were busy with their roses and butterflies."

"You were,' her father attempted to take her hand again, 'are,' he corrected himself, quite precocious."

Annabelle jerked her hand away and sprang to her feet. "I'm more than precocious, father. I love science, medicine, anatomy; all of it." She clutched the papers tighter to her chest. "These articles started with your data and some vague notion of a hypothesis. But I was the one who wove the story."

The corners of her father's eyes twitched, and he nestled back in his chair. He seemed amused with her anguish. "I trained you well. Your brilliant mind has been fashioned in the shape of my own. Your thoughts are an extension of mine. This is really for the best. Pursue the topics you like under the protection of my authorship."

Annabelle's face twisted. "That's absurd."

"I don't want to subject you to criticism for which you are unprepared. My peers can be brutal. There's politics in this profession of which you are totally unaware."

Annabelle rolled her lips together tightly to stave off looming tears.

"Sit down, child." Her father's façade cracked at her emotion. Annabelle hated tears were her most effective weapon.

"No,' Annabelle barked. She wished she had a more damning retort to hurl but rejection had tarnished her resolve.

"Listen to me, Annabelle. A man's intellect is for invention and conquest. But a woman's power is for rule—for sweet ordering, arrangement, and decision. The two complement one another."

In a sick sense, her father's rationale was understandable. But Annabelle scurried out of that wormhole. "I don't want to be your compliment , father. I hate always being one step behind." She waved the crumbled papers at her father. "If you won't put my name alongside yours, I won't let you have them."

His eyes widened but he made no effort to protest.

"If you don't, I'll burn them." She nodded to the delicate fireplace which housed a small fire, its delicate flames licking gently upwards. "I will."

Still no response.

She wished she had never offered the threat. The hundreds of hours it had taken to construct a sensical tale out of seeming rubbish and spare parts. Annabelle steeled her heart. She spun and marched towards the fireplace which seemed delightfully unaware of its sinister quality.

"Now, my dear, no need—"

"I will be taken seriously. As an equal. As a colleague." Annabelle unleashed the papers inches away from their fate. The skin on the back of her hand felt electrified so close to the fire. She could stand it for only seconds more. "The choice is yours, Dr. Pierce."

Her father regarded her, as he had earlier that morning, with a curious mixture of affection and disapproval, as if he were allowing a child's tantrum to run its course.

That was the look. The one that struck chords of primal rage in Annabelle's soul. As if she were not capable of wickedness. Of genius. She moved closer to the flames, the pages a sacrificial offering to her captive dignity.

When her mother burst through the door, Annabelle froze, having not been so glad to see the woman in quite some time.

Mrs. Pierce flashed a wide smile, her eyes widened almost to the point of frenzy. "I've been too excited to sleep. The wedding day is fast approaching!"

Chapter 3

Annabelle locked eyes with her father. "I mean to have a career. One I hope finds its stride aside yours. You know I will not be content to match a man—step for step—from behind."

Dr. Pierce's eyes glossed, as if he were wrestling with great emotion cloaked beneath his waistcoat.

Her mother's interjection saved him from an obligatory response. "What's all this talk of a man's stride?" She cast her gaze to the heavens Annabelle thought were certainly frowning upon her.

Rattle your poor skull any harder, mamma, and your remaining facilities will clatter right onto you plate. Mrs. Mingle would never stand for brains on her menu, regardless the time of day.

Dr. Pierce finally roused himself.

Annabelle relaxed into her chair, certain of her final victory. I knew Papa wouldn't fail me. Perhaps her by-line dreams had not disintegrated into ash after all.

Mrs. Pierce looked at her husband with expectation.

"What I think our ambitious daughter is trying to say—"

"Michael," Mrs. Pierce barked. "We discussed this."

"Not in any great detail."

The quiver of her mother's upper lip silenced her father. "Your father and I have discussed this. We,' she sent a hard look at Dr. Pierce, 'know it's best if you marry."

Refusal had been sufficient before. No reason why this morning shouldn't be like any other. "I won't—"

"Silence, insolent girl."

The vitriol soaking her mother's command threatened to drown Annabelle's heart.

Funny, that word insolence.

Precocious, enchanting, tempting. Those were the soft words Dr. Christianson spoke before he implored Annabelle to call him Horace. Never mind he was her father's oldest friend. And her mother's lover, until Annabelle's youth proved too great a distraction.

It was the lascivious dichotomy of the slow turning of the doorknob on retreats between mother and daughter's quarters. The first hip-splitting thrust and trickle of crimson horror were lost amidst Annabelle's pride at being noticed as more than a little girl by a grown man.

Hindsight and perspective had wisely purged memories of those whispered fondlings—a womanhood too soon discovered. Now Annabelle could just manage to contain that piece of her past. Though she was unsure if she found it shameful or simply despicable, imprisoned in the haunted, cobwebbed recesses of her mind.

"Spinsterhood impends." A dare in her mother's eye grated against Annabelle's soul.

"Spinsterhood implies certain things about a woman, mama ." Annabelle darted a glance at her father still spellbound by his wife and tightened her lips against the truth between them she would never whisper in her father's ear. "I would never be a spinster by any stretch of the definition."

"You are twenty-three. Far too old to behave in so spoilt a manner." Mrs. Pierce's tone rose. "You will marry."

Annabelle chose to address the first condemnation in hopes of evading the second. "You know full well my spoiltness was not of my own doing." She again looked to her father, wondering how far she could continue speaking between her words.

"Time withers even the most luscious fruit."

Her mother's unabashed transparency caught Annabelle across her cheek deeper than the lash of freshly cut leather.

Mrs. Pierce pocketed her whip and drew breath. "It is the way of this world."

The initial flicker of shock when Mrs. Pierce had cracked the door on Christianson's partakings (if that's what one could call them) had been replaced with an indescribable expression which haunted Annabelle since. The closest thing Annabelle had since seen was her father's nod of approval when one of his fine riding horses took a shockingly high gate in stride. Annabelle was horrified to realize she yearned to bath in the rays of such a look. The recognition her mother felt as much maternal feeling for her as a croupier felt for his roulette wheel had hardened Annabelle's sense of self-preservation.

"You should know about withering—a fig overripe—wrinkled from cruel time."

A jolt of emotion flicked over Mrs. Pierce's upper lip.

Emboldened, Annabelle did not let up. "Or a young green thing plucked to soon. Would you advertise me as damaged goods like the bruised cast-aways Mrs. Mingle feeds to the pigs?"

Dr. Pierce hastily ruffled his newspaper as he made it his business to educate himself on the exact happenings of the recent soar of the price of half mutton and corn.

Mrs. Pierce leaned over to Annabelle. "Perhaps by their very constitution,' her voice just shy of a whisper as her spidery grip slowly tightened with surprising strength, 'some goods deserve their place in the swill."

Before her mother's words had completed their escape, Annabelle heard only the crumple of fists on newspaper before she twisted free and cannoned from her seat. The aplomb she had momentarily harnessed, slipped beneath the breakfast table like a dog shamed for begging too heartily for scraps.

Her mother smoothed her skirts. "You will present yourself to your fullest advantage this season. The Foster's engagement is just around the corner. I will make it quietly known you have regained your senses and put your past games to rest. You have until your birthday. By which I expect a formal offer of matrimony to have been discussed with your father."

"Two months then before I embark on the high seas of swill?" Her disguised protest made her pity the foxes she so dearly loved to hunt while safely astride her agile steed.

"Exactly. You will be twenty-four. A ridiculous age not to be settled with a family of your own."

Annabelle took another step towards the door. She prayed Mrs. Mingle would trolley in to release her from the inquisition. Right now, she'd be glad to join the pigs. "But I can answer my own plea, for I know you would not, as you have already turned an eye blinded by ambition to what any sane person would find despicable." She wished she could shout her violations loud but one heartbeat in the room that she dared not break.

As if he were a chained bear in a traveling show, jabbed with a stick for sport one too many times, Dr. Pierce exploded. "Katherine, take hold of yourself." He cast a dismissive look at his wife before he moved on to Annabelle. "Watch your words, my girl. There is nothing contemptable about a mother wanting the very best for her daughter."

"Stay out of this, Michael. This is something between a mother and daughter in which a father has no role." The withering quality of Mrs. Pierce's tone could have eaten through the tempered steel of the London Bridge .

"Shall a whiff of your smelling salts in your room revive you?" Annabelle quipped.

Dr. Pierce's eyes ballooned as he regarded his wife— bracing himself as if he anticipated a secondary explosion.

Without waiting for him to dash to her defense, Mrs. Pierce rose slowly from her chair and drew her final card. "If you have no prospects, I have spoken to Lord Bingley Crispin, and he was more than delighted in the proposition."

"Have your senses taken leave entirely?" Annabelle attempted to calm herself as she gained proximity to the door. "I bet he was delighted at your scheme. A lovely wit to keep his bed sheets warm at night, and to play captain to his regiment of unruly brats? I'd sooner stoke the hearth for Mr. Fellows, take pity now as he's been widowed for just shy of a year."

"Annabelle," Dr. Pierce stepped in. "Meanness does not suit you—
" "Do not make light of our faithful butler's heartache—" Mrs. Pierce trailed off as her eyes and Annabelle's fixed on the single, blood-stained page now resting in front of the fireplace —its starkness made all the more brilliant by the thick, royal blue weave of the rug's mosaic.

Her mother dove and snatched the salvaged front page of her article.

"I was wondering where that had gotten to—" Annabelle attempted to wrestle it from her mother's grasp.

Mrs. Pierce's eyes narrowed—nose to nose with her daughter. A sick jolt of fear speared through Annabelle's core. She knew that look. A look which commanded all feeling and pain be choked down whole and covered with the ashes of dreams. It demanded she play the part Fate had assigned. To be a good daughter. To keep quiet. For the name of Pierce.

Her mother marched back to the table as she surveyed the page. She looked up at Annabelle. "Is this . . . blood?" Her face twisted in disgust. She drew herself up and glided toward Dr. Pierce who sat at attention, his Times surrendered. "Michael." She shook the page in front of him. "I suspect you know about this. Do not spare our daughter. Tell me the truth."

Annabelle tried in vain to catch her father's eye. He held more power than he knew. It infuriated Annabelle he never wielded it.

His words tumbled out. The ease of his confession as to the extent of her perceived wickedness made Annabelle's heart free fall to her feet. In what could have not been more than ten seconds, the depths of their scientific intrigue and Annabelle's course of discovery were flayed bare.

If Annabelle had been taken by surprise on a sundry corner in St. Giles, beaten, robbed, and left for dead, Annabelle thought she would prefer that experience to this.

With his story finished, her father crossed his arms as if in hopes of detaining the last whisp of wind leaving the sails of the SS Pierce.

Annabelle felt her eyes well and her lower lip jut out in honest despair. She would never forgive him for her undoing.

It took Mrs. Pierce several moments to replace her contorted expression with one of supreme conquest. "I cannot comment on what kind of depravity you must nurse to butcher Molly in the way you have. You have a duty to perform as our daughter that has absolutely nothing to do with these revolting escapades."

"How can you call a curious mind a kind of depravity, mother?"

"You call it curiosity; I call it looseness." Mrs. Pierce settled herself back into her chair, so confident in her cause, she no longer made eye contact with Annabelle. "A looseness in the mind, leads to a looseness in the body. Which leads to things only your father has witnessed."

"You must recall looseness is learned."

Mrs. Pierce played with her lips. Annabelle did not know if it was to encourage more venom to flow, or to dispel it back to its stores.

Annabelle took advantage of the pause in her mother's assault. "You call me a wh—"

"Silence." Dr. Pierce stirred from his position of seeming defeat. "Do not soil your lovely lips with such filth."

It was a rare occasion when her mother and father united fronts. This uncommon maneuver drained Annabelle's remaining resolve.

"You have two months." Her mother repeated. "We'll leave your husband to deal with you and your curiosity."

"Deal with me?" Annabelle echoed. Being dealt was not a specialty of hers. Marriage had never sounded so sinister.

"Perhaps you would settle down and find more fulfillment with a family. I believe your mother is right."

"You choose to agree with her now?"

Mrs. Pierce stood, her voice rising. "You underestimate what has transpired between your father and I. Things that have nothing to do with you."

"They have everything to do—"

Her mother plastered a terse smile on her face. "Do you doubt your powers of bewitchment of which I am regrettably all too familiar?"

Annabelle caught her father's eyes for a half-second before his dropped to the floor—leaving her without a life vest in the sea of his duplicity.

"Never."

Defiance, not an uncommon emotion for Annabelle, typically invigorated her. Today it echoed hollow in her soul and make her feel queasy.

Chapter 4

The shock of the cold water tempered the sting of Annabelle's tears and made her breath catch in her throat. She buried her face into a towel and tried to steady her heaving shoulders. As she wiped her eyes, she found solace in a photograph on her scrolled sitting table. In the remarkably sharp daguerreotype, an angelic boy with stick-straight hair and a freckled girl of a similar age perched atop fuzzy ponies. The boy proffered a darling smile, the little girl directed her pint-sized whip at far end of the unsuspecting cherub's mount. The story of Annabelle and Ben on a pinhead.

That grin had warmed her heart and tugged her from the stickiest of altercations with her parents. Annabelle smiled to herself. Ben would be in the midst of chores and would offer her a kind ear, and a bit of a laugh to put her back together.

What a joy it would be to be twenty-four and free.

"Come along," Annabelle yanked her walking coat from its hanger in the varnished armoire. "I can't be in this blessed house for one more minute."

Sarah stood back as Annabelle twirled as she attempted to fit the snug garment over her voluminous morning gown.

"Are you just going to stand there?"

"As a matter of fact, I were ."

Annabelle scowled. "This isn't funny."

"Tis, rather." Sarah smile broadened. "Yer a right sight. Morning gown, afternoon walking jacket, hair all amuss . And a temper just a brewin' ."

Annabelle swallowed the desire to lunge at her lady's maid, fangs glistening. But she was fortunately confined by the exhaust of buttons and numbingly tight sleeves of her coat. She changed her tune. "Help." She flapped her arms.

Sarah chuckled as she pealed her mistress from her restraints. "Shall I go with ye?"

"No. I just need to talk to Ben."

Sarah shrugged. "Please yerself . Nothin' a purse-pinching street urchin like meself could offer a fine lady."

"I hope I won't have to resort to assassination, although the thought is reassuring."

"As much as I like ye, m'lady, I don't know if I'd be willing to take thirty to life to save yer hide." Sarah closed the door of the wardrobe and pushed Annabelle toward the door.

She pulled a heavy fringed wrap from a bureau drawer and neatly coiled it around Annabelle's neck. Its ends remained in her palms.

"What are you playing at, Sarah?" Annabelle went to loosen the brocade folds.

Sarah held fast. "I've escaped the gallows once and shorted me stretch behind bars. Ye know how I'd done that?"

This was the first time she mentioned the gallows. Annabelle's proverbial feline made a step closer to the precipice. "Quite the recommendation indeed. How?"

"By looking out for number one." Sarah arched her eyebrow.

As mercurially as their odd exchange had come to pass, the tension evaporated. "Might be a bit of advice worth taking, m'lady." She released her mistress from her bonds.

Annabelle took the shawl. Sarah's steely eyes stared back at hers with a clarity no other maid would have been so bold as to offer.

"Advice, and silence." Sarah smiled as though she were a molting magistrate granting an undeserved pardon. "Just a reminder of me bargain price of twenty quid."

The barometer of their unlikely friendship ticked deftly to hover over the line between ally and foe. "And what of your duty to me?"

"You've given me a good turn, m'lady, n' I'm grateful. But security's short in gratitude. Like I's said, I like meself best."

Sarah's frankness simultaneously pricked Annabelle's well-polished propriety and evoked a bizarre twist of envy in her heart. "I'll remember that." She swept towards the door. "Twenty pounds is a paltry sum to exchange for a new life philosophy." She could easily exchange a less favored bobble for the sum—preferable to asking her father now.

"And t'keep yer reputation glossy." Sarah smirked. "Don't you forget about the fun ye've 'ad with that dashing doctor." She swayed her hips just enough to make Annabelle blush. "All with his poor wife n' brats at 'ome by t'hearth ."

Annabelle felt the walls of her corner as she offered Sarah her best glare. She raced down the back stairs, wondering what Ben would think of Sarah's opinions on security.

"Ye won't find better words in the stable." Sarah's laugh tinkered down the hall. Her words were a little too loud for Annabelle's liking.

"Where are you bolting to now?" Mrs. Mingle's baritone cut through the din of the kitchen seconds after Annabelle's feet hit the linoleum floor.

Nothing could calm her nerves more than the lingering scent of crackling oil and over-steeped tea from the morning's breakfast. Annabelle enjoyed a heavy breath before replying. "Your kitchen's so marvelously bracing."

Mrs. Mingle grinned. "Off to where now?" Her smile expected Annabelle's honest answer.

Annabelle skittered between between the gauntlet of kitchen maids bobbing back and forth as they transferred knobs of root vegetables into great roasting pans and rolled balls of dough in crystal sugar onto long tins. The younger girls gave her shy smiles in return as she bid them 'good morning.'

Annabelle pressed shoulder to shoulder with Mrs. Mingle and instantly felt a momentary reprieve from her outrage.

"Out with it." Mrs. Mingle gave Annabelle a look as if she had just scuttled away, having pressed her ear to the breakfast room's keyhole.

"Can't you guess?"

"I can. But let's skip your shy bits today."

Annabelle took the bait spilled her tale of woe into the housekeeper's sympathetic ear.

"She has you there, lass." Mrs. Mingle set down her pencil. "Might not be such a bad thing." She squeezed Annabelle's arm. "To make yourself a match, with a house of your own. You could do as you please then."

"Are you mad?" Annabelle jerked her arm away and glared at her confidant. "As much as my husband would find proper."

"Marriage has been the making of many a fine young lady. You're special to me, my girl, but not so different than all the rest."

"I'm not a shade like the rest." She wrapped her skirts in her hands. "Anyway, I knew you'd eventually agree with mama. I need someone I can really talk to." She hoped the slight would land in its mark. "I'm off to the mews to find Ben."

A deep shade of rose briefly shifted over the housekeeper's already ruddy cheeks. "The truth stings to be sure. You're a young lady of merit and worth, but not getting any younger. With your privilege comes a duty you cannot shirk."

"You sound your age." Annabelle snapped. "I've managed to shirk my duties, as you say, for longer than most. And enjoyed it."

"Frivolity comes at a price."

"Are you threatening me with spinsterhood?"

Mrs. Mingle's shoulders heaved and her face softened. "I love you like my own. You have so much to share, do you withold yourself out of spite?"

"Not spite. But I can't stand to be wrapped, boxed, and labeled like a gift from Father Christmas."

"You'd rather spend your life in buried in dog's guts, bounding around a grand house?" Mrs. Mingle swept her arms wide in mock despair. "That'd be a sight when your five and thirty."

"I'd prefer to be a rare bird among pigeons than a monkey on a string." Annabelle snatched the ledger and shook it in front of Mrs. Mingle's nose. "We're not that different, you and I. You had your chance for a free life. That sweet shop in Cornwall would have been just the thing. Your own time. Your own dreams. Not slaving always to fulfill someone else's." She slapped the leather binding back on the long table with a bang.

Mrs. Mingle's expression sharpened. "I stayed because of you."

"Don't use me as your excuse."

"T'was no excuse. You know the rocky tide you faced. I knew it too. With your mother, recovering." The corners of her mouth pulled down, seemingly drawn by a distant heartache. "I couldn't leave you alone. You would have been too much for your father."

"I'm too much for him now. And besides," Annabelle stood tall. "He agreed with momma . Just sat there and let her spill her little opinions all over me. I can't. I won't."

"Marry?"

"Not now. She would have won then." Annabelle shrugged. "Perhaps I'm spiteful, after all." Annabelle found momentum in her righteous anger. "I need to talk to Ben." She bent to kiss the housekeeper on the forehead. The clean smell of her smooth, dry skin tasted both of happier and sadder times. "You know he's got that way about him."

"It's his open heart, girl. Yours is still a work in progress."

"You know it didn't crack closed on its own accord." Annabelle knew Mrs. Mingle saw the looming tear which bulged at the corner of her eye and threatened her resolve. But determined not to give in, she offered Mrs. Mingle a defiant toss of her head and was off.

Chapter 5

Annabelle's feet landed on the uneven cobblestones. As the side door to the kitchen thudded closed behind her, the weight of overwhelming respectability from Fernhead House seemed to lift from her shoulders. She inhaled the scent of sweet escape—and coughed. The gritty dampness of the ammonia-laced air contrasted sharply to the smell of Mrs. Mingle's ovens. The sharp clatter of shod hooves and the jostle of harnesses and wheels of passing carriages stoked Annabelle's internal chaos. Ultimatums or not, Annabelle thought to herself, life will go on. She hoisted her skirts to safe heights and started in the direction of the mews.

Not two hundred yards from the back of Fernhead House, the stables had long been a safe escape. Among the neatly fluffed stalls and organized swatches of harnesses and blankets, Annabelle found a serenity was over her. The gentle thuds of hooves and the rhythmic chewing of alfalfa moved her more than Beethoven's Adagio. The stable floors were kept so spotless, they could have served as a dinner plate, so she took no care to keep her skirts clean as she swept down the aisle towards the back workroom where Ben was sure to be found.

Her hand found the familiar latch before she swung the door wide. "Ben, I need you."

"Christ Almighty." A young man lurched from his stool, a tangle of reins and surcingle in his hands. A flicker of alarm washed over, though he'd been caught up to no good, before a broad smile replaced it.

Annabelle felt Ben always a boy in a man's skin, though he always wormed under hers, to her chagrin and delight. His low voice and broad shoulders were at odds with his mess of sandy hair and eyes as blue as a newborn baby.

"You gave me a right start, Lady." He nudged a pan of waxy goop out of the way. "Shut the door, don't want the wax to chill." Ben pushed his heap of leather workings aside and dragged a second stool across from his. "What's that you said again?" His tone was heavy with mischief.

"I need you." Annabelle wondered if the lye fumes from the stall floors had affected his faculties.

"That's what all the lasses say down at MacAlester's Pub."

Annabelle bit her lip to corral her smile. "You didn't hear them properly, Ben." She brushed off her dusty throne, its base littered with bits of bridles and metal shanks. *He could be such a goon. But one who made her heart both pitter and patter.* With a roll of her eyes, Annabelle began Court . "This morning didn't go as planned. I've been dealt a rotten hand."

"A two of spades in a sea of aces?"

"Worse. Mother can no longer abide by my ways."

The deep furrow between Ben's brows softened. *He has no idea this morning was not our typical cat and mouse—more like Burmese tiger and Tibetan antelope .* "She's demanded I marry."

Ben tipped his head to the side.

Annabelle fought to avoid losing herself in adoring eyes. "I've been commanded to strap myself to the coattails of any gentleman whose address is in the general direction of Piccadilly. Anyone would do, so long as they're worth 20,000 pounds a year. Smash a bottle of champagne across me after the papers are signed and she can die with peace in her heart."

Ben's face contorted just like the first time Annabelle had made him try the imported taleggio from Bologna . "You don't want to do that."

"Of course not. You've missed the point. Her wits have frayed beyond limits I've ever seen. I've exhausted my tactics. I must obey."

"You're serious." His wisp of a smile disappeared.

"As a dead man swinging on the gallows of Newgate Street."

That was when Ben's face fell for good. Annabelle had seen that disheartening look of defeat on only two other occasions. Once when they were no more than ten, they had locked the chambermaid minding them in a closet. In hysterics, they had snuck out and indulged their gruesome fantasy of witnessing a hanging. They hadn't slept well for weeks as the sounds of the dropping platform and visions of the body twisting rhythmically midair danced through their dreams. The other was far less grizzly when in the early hours of her sixteenth birthday. Ben had told her of the inner workings of his heart, and she had refused to kiss him.

"You'd have to leave."

His emotion was purer than she could bear. "Obviously." Her tone was sharp. Damn him. Damn those eyes. Annabelle squirmed in the silence. "This situation calls for an adventure."

Her last word had its intended effect and Ben brightened.

"You're in luck as adventures are my specialty."

If I'm headed for hell, I might as well play the part. "What do you have in mind?"

"It's the fifteenth, right?" Ben too rose quickly.

"Yes?"

"Today's really your day, then." He sent her a wicked smile as he began to tuck away his leather wax and rags.

"Really?" Annabelle could stand for a change in the winds.

"My cousin Bert told me about a rally Sunday last when we went for dinner in Lanchester Street ."

"A rally?" Not the kind of adventure Annabelle had in mind.

"Yes, on marriage."

Annabelle laughed, "Are all Victorian ladies up in arms, perhaps then I might join them?"

Ben seemed charmed by her flustered state, which irritated her all the more. "They're muckin' about with ladies' monies. What's theirs, what's their 'usbands ." He grew shy at his last word. "Bert's of the mind, being a teacher and all, ye've got the right to work and keep wages as yer own,

"I have no wages, only a dowry." Annabelle felt a bit let down.

"As things stand, ye can't touch a penny, but that's changing. Balls bouncing around the Commons. The rally's to push it home. Might be worth a gawk." He kicked playfully at her skirts. "But ye can't go out in this mess. A fine lady and her coachman, taking a turn. I've known you to be a bit of a nutter, but no use thumbing your nose at all convention."

"I'll go out in whatever I please." She hated the topic of money, only slightly less than marriage. But might there be a way to keep some freedoms? Then the soft folds of a coarse work pants and cotton tunic came into sight on a hook just over Ben's shoulder. Crossing the room, she swept the garments into her arms. "Alright. To the rally. Turn 'round . I'll be out of my contraptions in a flash."

Annabelle found he way Ben's eyes bugged out of his skull before he obediently turned to the opposite corner intensely gratifying.

"You can't go out there, striding around like a bloke. You'd be— you'd be—"

"I'd be what? Arrested, tortured, stoned?" She loosened the fastenings of her skirts and bodice. "Better options than the fate currently laid out for me."

The freedom of her legs as she pulled on the baggy trousers was thrilling. She stood for a moment in her corset before yanking the bristly shirt over her head. She shoved the shirttails down and buttoned the front flap. The waistband threatened descent with every breath. That wouldn't do. "Off with your belt."

Ben moved mechanically and handed over the thick leather strap.

"Much better." Annabelle locked the pants in place. "What do you think?"

Ben darted a warning glance over his shoulder before turning fully. From his blush Annabelle knew the answer. Not her original intent, but a compliment was a compliment. She wondered if Larkin would enjoy seeing her in a similar ensemble.

"Will I do?"

"I'd say." Ben almost coughed out the words, but didn't look away. "You need a hat."

"We won't have to worry about that, we'll be running."

Ben groaned. "Does everything always need to be a catastrophe?"

"My future's at stake, Ben." Annabelle feigned seriousness. "We can't waste a minute."

"I can't let you go prancing to Trafalgar like that." Ben reached for a dusty broad-brimmed hat on a wall peg. "You know I'd go anywhere with you."

Annabelle knew his words were true and felt a wave of calm sooth the morning's anger. It was so good to be seen. Words, clothes, status aside. To be known for who one was. She snatched the hat and shoved it over her ears. "I'm off." She kicked her dress to a corner and headed to the door. "Coming?"

Ben shrugged into his short coat. "After you, m'lady. Mustn't forget yourself in that get-up. We're equals now." He brushed past her towards the door leading out to the streets.

"What?" Annabelle sputtered and locked her feet to the ground. Equality was not a virtue, at least in this setting, she was sure she fully appreciated.

"You're a carriage man, now. Wear a wolf's clothes, you hunt with the pack." And with a laugh, he grabbed her hand and pulled her from the safe jewelry box of the stables into the tumbling stench of London.

It was all Annabelle could do to stop herself from letting whoops of joy loose in the now late-morning smog. Not that anyone would have really taken notice The crash of work carts and the clanging of fine carriages would have drowned it out.

With Ben leading the way, they ran several blocks south, towards the less fashionable neighborhoods.

They slowed to catch their breath.

"I don't know if mother could even blow a constable's whistle properly. "

"You two are cut from the same cloth, that's why yer always at it like wet cats."

Annabelle scowled. There was a razor's edge to their history, and she preferred not all truths be told. "That may be, but we're worked with very different tailors, Ben, don't forget it."

Ben shrugged.

"I can't let her win."

"It's not just her, Lady. It's this whole, bloody state of things. The have's and have not's ." He nodded at a dusty little boy struggling with the task of clearing the road of horse matter with a shovel larger than he . "Ye think his sister would balk at a choice between a Hyde Park or Kensington address? Split hairs between the finer points of distinction of Lord Itchy Britches and the Duke of Blathering?"

Her heart missed his humor and winced at the poor lad. "You defend her and mock my misery in one breath?" Annabelle's frown deepened before she glanced farther down the street. "The Smithfield Market should offer plenty of distraction." She shoved her hands deep in the pockets of her trousers and strode off with what she hoped appeared to be great, masculine strides.

"Yer a right corker, l ady."

Annabelle glanced over her shoulder and thrust her hand deeper into the pockets . The crack of a carriage whip made her start just before two horses blazed by, the whites of their eyes straining beyond the confines of their blinkers.

Ben just missed being clipped by the onslaught of carriage wheels as he dodged across the road to meet her. "Come now, Bella." He grabbed for her arm, but she stuck her hand fast, unwilling to concede.

"I was just teasing, you. I don't want you to—"

"I'll figure out something." Annabelle interrupted before he had the chance to dive into sentiment she had no interest in hearing. "You're going to help me think of a way out of this mess. Mother will listen to you." She spun around, and with a new sense of assurance, headed away deeper into the belly of the city.

⚜

Few streets in London so closely resembled a chameleon as those surrounding Piccadilly. With its skins shed according to the height of the sun in the sky, Annabelle's hopes were high for Bert's rally. The change of scenery would offer a bracing jolt of reality to inspire a defense against the tides of the new demands which had so recently rocked her ship.

Not a soul could recognize her. The anonymity of her ensemble afforded her the freedom to stare—never mind the glorious chance to breathe. An egalitarian sentimentality seemed woven into Piccadilly, more democratic than starchy Bond and St. James's Street, and less flashy than the nausea-inducing new regime clubs of Pall Mall. Annabelle drew in a deep breath, missing the acrid, burnt aroma which typically welcomed the early teasing of the sun. The coffee-stall, offering seedy hand pies and mugs of muddy water to laborers with a farthing for the luxury, had vanished with the moon like a witch.

The groaning market carts, laden with produce had been replaced with the less pleasant sight and smell of the overflowing manure wagons on their return journey from Covent Garden. Small processions of overworked and underfed families shepherded their livelihood from the urban chaos. Annabelle slowed as she took in the hangdog look of a mother, whimpering infant slung on her hip—her own defeat echoed from the wisps of hair framing the nondescript unfortunate.

The roadway, cramped to the gills with pedestrians, somehow found the expanse to welcome the herds of carriages and horses of every variety, from the aristocratic private hansoms to the plebeian growlers. This was the time to see Piccadilly—a study of the guts of life. By the by, clusters of clean-scrubbed shop girls tripped along arm in arm as smatterings of aspiring clerks, full of the self-importance of their town calls, flowed between the traffic. Farther on, the Egyptian Exhibition Hall came into view, with its stacked stone trapezoids framing two huge Egyptian figures.

Their furrowed limestone brow made her feel as though her mother had enlisted them in her current army. After they skirted the Wellington, Ben tore their silence with a laugh. "In the mood to share a pint of gossip in the cellar at the New White Horse?" He nodded to the opaque cubed glass window fronts of the landmark coaching inn. "We haven't gotten 'round to your rehearsal?"

Annabelle glared at him as her spirits floated back down to Earth. "It's such a muddle. Why couldn't she let things lie as they are rather than demanding I marry? I've been perfectly content to work with father and—"

Ben broke in with a half-smile. "And parade around as a complete and utter tease, crushing the hearts of unsuspecting dandies and their lady-loves in suit."

"You make me sound like a dragon." Though Annabelle was quite pleased her reputation was discussed in the mews. "Is that all you have to talk about?"

"Don't flatter yerself, Lady. I can see you aren't too ill-pleased that you have a bit of lore to uphold."

The weight of her pride became heavy on her shoulders, tiny rivulets of humility ran from the fresh cracks in her previously polished veneer. Was there nothing more than this? An eternal game of cat and mouse, a fatal bet with dismal stakes?

Her mind reeling, Annabelle pulled from the pedestrian flow and set her back on the reassuring sharpness of a facade. Her temples throbbed. Tears stung. Damn the rally. Things would never change.

"Not like that. You can't lounge there like a damsel in destress. 'Member the trousers, Lady." He fell next to her, his shoulder touching hers. "Like this." He kicked one leg behind him to rest on the building and fell into a repose Annabelle supposed was meant to appear dashing. He turned to Annabelle.

Her lower lip trembled, and tears began to spill from the deepest part of her. "I'm trapped."

"Like that jeweled lioness from Arabian Nights we used to read." Ben's voice softened.

Annabelle felt too numb to do anything but stare back into his calm, blue pools.

"So Mrs. Pierce wants you to marry a grand gent."

Annabelle took a few shaky breaths. "That's her scheme."

"Marriage itself isn't the worst idea I've ever heard."

Her numbness cracked. "It isn't, is it?" Annabelle took satisfaction in Ben's grimace as she elbowed him sharply between his ribs. "You go tether your destiny to some loop of gold." His aplomb irritated her to no end. "Golden noose more like."

"A title and a bit o' gold would buy a ticket in that line then?"

"A fistful of mothballs and a few well-shod brats would set you at the very front." Annabelle's humor returned. Ben had a habit of towing it back from any abyss. "She's offered me to Lord Crispin on a silver platter. Apple's even been shoved in my gullet."

"Christ, he could be yer grandfather." He ran a hand over his brow. "You'd consider 'im, then?" A twinkle ignited his expression.

"Certainly." Annabelle would not be bested. "I never knew what that feeling was—the one that makes my heart flutter and my cheeks warm whenever he walks into a room."

Ben's forehead furrowed as he seemed to take her bait.

"I can see it now. Mornings spent organizing lesson plans for the governess. Then the great work of deciding between a chocolate ice and lemon posset at the ball for St. Bart's Home for the Infirm or Insane." Annabelle drummed her fingers on the bricks at her back. "Evenings spent miles and miles apart in some horrid dining room full of beheaded African beasts,' she paused for breath, 'considering whether my butter knife would be best served hoisting peas to my mouth or shredding my wrists."

"Come now, La—"

Annabelle was a steam engine, its belly full of coal, burning bright. "Our lot is dim, growing dimmer and more dim-witted. As women, we're never actually allowed to leave our nursery, you see?"

Ben swung in front of Annabelle. He left one hand on the bricks to support himself and swung into her, nose to nose. "Don't you ever get sick of yourself? You and your endless, privileged whining."

God save the batty Queen. This was not the Ben Annabelle hoped would soothe her crumpled ego.

Ben caught his breath as if feeling the singe of the sparks between them and pulled back.

Annabelle felt a physical regret at his retreat.

"Back to that line." The harshness dissipated from this tone. "Who's in second place? Anyone I know?"

Annabelle heart warred between the freshly beating heart in her chest and Larkin's secret letters and stolen kisses. "I shan't name names, but I'm sure you've made his acquaintance on more than one occasion." She kept the corners of her mouth upturned, knowing they would tantalize.

With that, Ben seemed to melt, and Annabelle retrieved her crown.

"He must be an alright chap then."

"He is." Annabelle felt it only kind to keep Ben's tightrope taught.

"Do you love 'im ? This second-best bloke?"

"I might."

"Does he coast about St. James' Park in his landeau , letting pound notes flutter from his soft hands for his amusement?"

"Likely not." Larkin was a bit too classist for any outward displays of generosity.

"Not as grand as Mrs. Pierce would like?"

"Not at all." It was Larkin's reputation, but his wife's annual means, which bought them invitations to dine and dance at Society mansions. With the agonizing details of Larkin's books analyzed in the Foster's powder room after Olivia announced her engagement, Annabelle was quite aware of Larkin's paltry five thousand a year. This knowledge offered only mild consolation to Annabelle's bleeding heart as she forced smiles and congratulations.

"But would she like 'im ?"

"Very much indeed." Annabelle let a soft smile emerge, hating herself a little at the encouragement.

Ben cleared his throat. "A few of me pals have tied the knot."

Annabelle again had the distinct sensation of being held, not uncomfortably, within a globe, its snow yet to fall.

"They seem quite taken with their lasses. So much so they more often than not thumb their nose at me offer to get them a pint at the Red Mile." He stuffed his hands in his pockets and looked back at Annabelle. "But they seem happy. Can't be that bad."

"Not bad for the male party."

"They're good blokes—" Ben postured as if he was defending all of mankind.

"I'm sure they are, but it's different for men."

"Why do you make everything such a puzzle? How is it different? Two people meet, fall in love, then show up in front of the clergy on a Sunday morning and do the deed right and proper. Nothin' more to it."

"We're at the mercy of our husband's every whim."

"You make us out to be monsters."

Memories of Christianson's shadow slunk from behind unlocked doors in Annabelle's mind. "Only because some men are."

"But I'm not, Lady!" Ben swung back in front of Annabelle and took both her shoulders in his hands.

Safe hands. Annabelle wondered if Larkin would ever look at her with that much honesty.

"I won't pity you in your ivory tower when the key is within reach. And think of the rally. Things are changing."

She made no reply.

"I won't work for your father forever, you know."

Annabelle mustered a hesitant smile—though a whirl of panic had begun its vortex inside her chest. Seeing a gap in the traffic beyond his shoulder she took flight.

Then they were away, dodging the Sisyphean procession of hansom cabs and growlers, horses slipping in the wade pools of muck. Passing by the white colonnades of Francatelli's at the St. James Hotel, glimpses of the chandeliers, now dull without the prettying effect of the electric light, and stern-looking waiters only highlighted the dullness Annabelle feared was in store for her if she were to concede to her mother's demands and sacrifice her own heart.

They ducked down a side street, Ben's pace keeping time but giving her just enough space to keep the lead. They skirted a farm family with several children, none could have been over the age of five unloading sacks of potatoes and flats of cabbages to the restaurant's kitchens. Ben slowed and flipped the few between motions a half-pence and a handful of sweets from his jacket.

"If your father wasn't the kind of man he is, I might have started out like those little blighters."

She measured the vast escape between their lives and her own. But as she explored their soiled faces, between the children's chattering and their father's directions, she saw they were smiling. "I still don't have my answer."

Ben nodded at the family now a safe distance away. "That lot didn't spell it out for you?"

"But they look happy. That's all I want."

"You could be. If you really wanted."

Annabelle wasn't ready to let him have the last word—or listen to it.

They passed the lawns of Hyde Park where a metalized Achilles keeping a stately eye on the gothic artifice of Apsley House. As they turned onto Waterloo, the crack of a driver's whip and a symphony of panicked neighs drove Annabelle back into Ben's chest with a thud. His closeness was as welcome as a down comforter on an arctic winter night.

Shots of mud and rattling of harnesses took over the street as two horses fought to stay upright as though they were ice skating on the Thames. The crested carriage rocked alarmingly, its wheels faring no better than the horses.

A finely dressed man jutted his head from the window to shout a deluge insults; the driver standing on the footboard wrestled with the tangled reins threatening to unfurl from his hands at any moment.

Inside the carriage, a delicate violet hat feather caught Annabelle's attention. The stare of its owner met hers before the woman leaned forward to her window. "Hold the curb steady now, Jackson. Let them find their balance, then turn them quickly to the right." Her companion dove back into the carriage and slapped her across the face with his open hand, knocking her hat askew. The woman wilted back to the far corner of the carriage, every ounce of daring evaporated as she swept another glance at Annabelle.

Annabelle took the look to heart.

"Turn 'em hard to yer right," Ben shouted.

A large dark clot of questionable composition careened firmly into Annabelle's chest just before Ben pushed her a safe distance from the flying hooves. She wondered what advice Larkin would have proffered in the situation.

The abusive gentleman sent a quizzical look at Ben, then hung once again out of his window and growled the same advice. After several tenuous attempts, the horses and carriage lurched back into the well-worn ruts in the road and continued on its way, mud splattered, but none the worse for the excitement.

Annabelle could not be as certain about its passengers.

Chapter 6

The white crescent of the National Gallery yawned in welcome to Trafalgar Square. A pulsating human lawn surrounded the base of an imposing column of Devon granite. Several steps above, tri-colored crescents adorned a podium where a woman seemed to be inciting the crowd. Annabelle could hear the roarings of support despite the traffic still milling on the road surrounding the square's perimeter.

Their restless energy permeated the air and Annabelle eagerly drank it in. The rally. This is what I've come for, she thought. A longshot at hope.

They wove between the circulating pedestrians and two flanking oblong fountains towards the commotion, cramming their way through the knots of men and women before they settled between the paws of a bronze lion keeping a forlorn eye on the zoo of protestors.

"What do you think?" Annabelle turned back to grin at Ben as the speaker concluded with a hearty crescendo.

With the deafening roar of applause and here-here's, Ben shoved his mouth beside Annabelle's ear. "You might hear some things that'll help you answer a question for me later."

His breath in her ear stirred something sweet within her. But before Annabelle could badger him about the dangling question, another woman stepped to the podium, her serene countenance dominated by a black hat topped with a billowing white plume. She lifted her hand which elicited more wild cheers. She allowed them their revelry for several moments before dropping her hand to her side. An obedient hush struck.

Annabelle had no idea who the woman was, but she dearly wanted to. Even against the underlying turbulence of the traffic, her voice rang quite clearly, with an authority which surprised Annabelle. "Who is she?"

"Gertrude Fawcet. A right force for women's suffrage."

"What do you know or care about suffrage?" Annabelle countered.

Suffrage. The term always conjured images of horsey-looking spinsters with inflammatory propensities who could use a romp around a dance floor to shake the cobwebs from their hearts.

"Plenty. Keep yer pretty mouth shut and listen. There's somethin' I'll be asking later."

Annabelle frowned. "A post rally exam?"

"In a manner of speaking." Ben confirmed before he directed her back to the podium.

The spark in his eye made her question if Ben knew how close she often came to encouraging his affections. She was quickly, and irritatingly so, beginning to realize how seriously she had underestimated his capabilities and overinflated her own.

Ms. Fawcett's congregation seemed to quiver in anticipation before her clear voice set them free. "It is with great pleasure I take this opportunity to speak with you on a matter of great national importance in the name of reform." She scanned her audience before her voice raised a note. "The issue of Parliamentary Franchise and the proposed inclusion of women."

A rebel cry which had been unconsciously lodged in her heart sprang from Annabelle's lips just ahead of the unanimous murmurings of approval from the bystanders. Her head jerked back in surprise. When she found Ben, he grinned and joined in with a few choice joyous hollers.

"I would ask to recall some of the great calamities in our history have involved the distribution and limitation of power. There is rarely a law passed which does not affect women as well as men."

The truth of the statement rang in Annabelle's ears.

Gertrude continued smoothly as if riding the waves of her audience's admiration. "There are some laws involving marriage, divorce, and the custody of children which are of the utmost interest to the female gender. Can it be then deemed just when Parliament prevents women from exercising any influence on these matters?"

A few shouts in the negative gave fuel to the engine of her speech.

"If women share such burdens of the State, and their welfare hinges on the state of such laws, they ought to be franchised alongside men."

"She's serious."

Ben nodded as if she had told him there was a sun in the sky. "And sharp as a whip. Bert told me she's in medicine—like yer father."

"A nurse?" Annabelle felt the word as sour as an Italian lemon. Visions of lamp-totting angels of mercy and gin-soaked aprons clouded her thoughts. Though her father spoke quite highly of the ward nurses at the College, Annabelle wondered how they must tire of orders from doctors. From men.

"Naw, she has a clinic in Seymour Place. For women and children."

Annabelle huffed before she turned back to the fabulous Ms. Fawcett. The epic dullness of combing for lice and treating for worms, with the occasional feminine complaint thrown in to avoid total mental stagnation was all she could imagine. That would not be her lot—not when she had tasted the successes, though anonymous, of The Lancet. "I'm sure she's does good work," was all the kindness she would muster in response.

"Very good, from all I've heard from Bert. And she's quite the spit."

Having no intention of giving Ben any more satisfaction, Annabelle returned her attentions to the unusual specimen speaking.

"I challenge you today to see that while women's suffrage is still within its cradle, our emancipation would only prove testament to our great nation's tradition of progress." Ms. Fawcett trilled on.

When it seemed she was filled to the gills with their boisterous accolades, Ms. Fawcett squared her shoulders and the voices quieted. "Our men and society at large will only benefit from the enfranchisement of women. And think to of our children and generations to come, who will bask in the freedom we can cultivate to support them mind, body, and soul. Later today, I will speak to the Cambridge Reform Club in hopes of receiving their support for the Married Women's Property Act, one of the first steps in our mighty journey to emancipation."

Annabelle's ears pricked at the word 'marriage.' Marriage was the reason for this excursion in the first place.

"As it stands currently, married women under the law of couverture , sign away their independence and are distilled into nothingness as they become little more than an accessory appendage fused to their husband's side, with no function or voice of their own."

"I told you mother's notion of marriage is absurd."

Though they were packed around Nelson's column like Mrs. Mingle's much-prized pickled kippers, the anonymity afforded by the throng gave Annabelle a boldness that the trousers alone could not afford.

"It wouldn't be like that."

Before she could search for a reasonable reply, the buzzing swarm drew closer to the honey of Ms. Fawcett's words, knocking them forward against their neighbours and derailing the train of their conversation.

"There were many instances in which men would deliberately seek to marry a wealthy woman and neatly tuck their wife into their pocketbook—her wealth now his property to dispose of as he pleases. Equally, a woman may seek to marry a wealthy man to obtain financial security—"

"Then marriage is an exercise in futility!" Annabelle burst out.

With unusual acuity, Ms. Fawcett's exacting gaze settled on Annabelle—her subtle power plucked a quiet chord of fear in Annabelle—even the Queen had not elicited such a response. "This damning admission,' a smile quivered on her lips, 'from a gentleman."

As she ran her palms over the knobby grain of Ben's work pants, Annabelle felt the term 'gentleman' was a generous extension of goodwill. "Not at all." Her mouth spread wide with the joy of her mischief.

A cove of the curious formed around her, scanning her person. A tiny flame of panic ignited deep in Annabelle's stomach, but her inhalation extinguished it immediately as she swept Ben's tweed hat from her head and her tousled curls fell down her back.

A collective gasp travelled through the crush.

The woman's magnetic presence drew Annabelle back—her eyes seemed to stream electricity into her very bones as she smiled with approval. "This bill would at least give married women some comparable property rights to single women. Some members of Parliament make the argument our female domestic duties would be neglected if we were allowed political privileges."

The congress swayed like a racehorse in a starting gate.

"They argue,' Ms. Fawcett's voice trembled, 'women remain married for the financial security alone."

Annabelle needed no more encouragement than a wild beast driven mad from hunger. "If women had sufficient resources, they could leave their husbands as they would be useless!"

"Say here—' Ben ruffled.

"From one perspective, perhaps." Ms. Fawcett countered. "But this attitude tarnishes the religious sanctity of marriage to have it only considered as a mere vehicle for a woman's comfort."

"Comfort indeed." Annabelle cried. A pinched look of horror overtook her guiding angel.

"The accusation that a marriage be made for financial gains and corporal security denigrates the love on which all matrimony is founded." Gertrude spread her arms wide. Below the billowing red, white, and blue crescents, Annabelle felt her metamorphosis from dove to falcon was complete. "I mean to no more attack that sacrament than I do my dear husband."

"Here, here!" Now it was Ben's turn to rally.

Annabelle could not smite his grin down this time.

Before the falcon's eyes could return to Annabelle's, a four-teamed coach crossed the thoroughfare and slowed. A frowning gentleman with a wiry beard lowered his window with grave regard.

"Our small gathering has the marked honor of the attention of our grand Secretary for the Home Department." Ms. Fawcett sounded both triumphant and irked as she waved a salute to the carriage. "A pleasure indeed."

Keeping her arm aloft, as if to suspend his attention, Ms. Fawcett turned back to her audience. "You well know this man remains unconvinced of the worthiness of our cause."

Annabelle could almost smell the kerosene dripping from her words.

"Secretary Sommersville. Stubborn old fool. Can't recognize change is inevitable." Ben muttered.

Annabelle wondered why Ben hadn't spoken more of Gertrude—he must have known she'd quite like her.

The dutiful masses responded to Ms. Fawcett with a collective roar. As if drawn into their vortex, the wind picked up, adding an eerie echo to their voices. Bits of rubbish and gusts of ash swirled around their feet.

Annabelle drew closer to Ben. She held the moment in her breath as she took in Ms. Fawcett and the Secretary, his carriage almost at a halt. That was the kind of courage she wanted—and pretended to have. Annabelle had been roused from her slumber in her softly lined existence, not by a kiss, but by moral outrage. She wondered if feminine gall might edge out beauty in the realm of male temptation. "You don't find her less ladylike for her methods?"

Ben shook his head. "All the more, I'd say."

Instantly feeling inadequate, a feline imposter in her trousers, Annabelle looked down just as she felt the jostle of something solid through her work boot. A stoneware Newcastle ginger beer bottle.

"I told you today'd be good." Ben goaded.

She could scarcely sense the thoughts which engineered her next move. Annabelle roped her hair into knot, jammed his hat down tightly, and swept up the bottle. She dove for the bottle and took an instant to gauge her distance from the carriage—the member's sour frown still at his window. "Here's one for the ladies."

Ben's obvious disbelief set her spirits sailing as her grip tightened around the bottle. The country summer afternoons spent, more often than not, lobbing croquet balls at Ben, servants, and unsuspecting guests, came to Annabelle's good use.

Annabelle launched her rather domestic weapon. It soared in a perfect arch and meet the carriage a hare's breath above the Harcourt's crown and shattered into smithereens. The carriage swayed as he flailed his sizable weight back and disappeared from view.

The carriage came to a standstill and the driver stood tall and pointed his whip and blame directly at Annabelle. "He did it!"

Whistles screeched as a shock of terror coursed through Annabelle. It had been fun until now.

"Arrest him!"

Annabelle's mouth formed a pert 'o' as her eyes darted to Ben.

Ben groaned and scanned the crowd. "Your voice comes at a price."

Annabelle shrank behind him, as several constables confronted the confusion of gawking carriages and pedestrians, their whistles now a constant scream. "What do we do?"

"We?" Clocking the Secretary with a lucky near miss was your idea."

The fright of standing with one foot on her self-made precipice made Annabelle's head heavy with indecision and affront. "You can't leave m—"

"I'd never leave you." A smile took over his mouth. "And there's still that question of mine."

The whistles grew louder. Annabelle saw the constables were now at the front of the allegiants but appeared unable to penetrate their ranks. Annabelle glanced to the column to see Mrs. Fawcett had orchestrated a human shield from her audience, purchasing her precious moments of a head start. "Never mind your blasted question—"

"They've not covered the back. We're off." Ben took Annabelle's hand and began to press them through to their escape. She felt pats on her back and heard anonymous praise for her 'jolly good eye' as they pushed through their protectors.

Gasping at the perimeter, Ben paused. A lone sergeant clattered toward them and they took flight. The chilled air searing Annabelle's lungs, as they raced toward the south west corner of the square, next to Napier. Not hearing the rally of accusing whistles after they passed a steely Charles I, standing watch over Charing Cross Station, Annabelle looked over her shoulder. She was almost disappointed there wasn't a sergeant in sight.

Piccadilly's piquant charm dwindled as its individuality was diluted by the roving din of the horse markets of Tattersall's.

"Best to throw them off on my turf." Ben wove them expertly among the striped awnings and prancing merchandise before heading back to the safety of Harley Street by way of Whitfield Street.

※

In the expanse of the mews, they slid through the gate unnoticed and padded back to Ben's workroom. Annabelle was certain things would never quite be the same after that white plume and bottle of ginger beer.

Ben slumped onto his stool. "That the kind of adventure ye had in mind, Lady?"

Annabelle leaned against the wall of harnesses and slid the derby off her head. "Not exactly,' she spun the hat into Ben's lap. "But I couldn't have imagined a better one."

"Yer a corker, Lady." He toyed with the hat, worrying its grain. "You could 'ave been arrested. That'd go down in the books, ye know." He considered a particularly irksome speck on its brim. "No amount of string-pulling or gold-slinging from yer father would have made things right."

"I don't need my father to rescue me at every turn." Annabelle knew her protest couldn't be farther from the truth. She hated Ben's fleeting look of sympathy.

"You could 'ave hurt that daft bugger, ye know, Lady." Ben shoved himself upright. "You don't need that sort of thing on your conscience. It's a more serious charge then the heart-breaking and general harassment ye've got on your record."

Annabelle glared at Ben. "Cover your eyes, if not your mouth. By-line or not, I should really finish that piece for the Lancet ." Her skirts felt heavy as she dragged them over her linen underthings. Her ribs protested as she bound the ribbons of her corset as tight as she could on her own. She tucked her coils into a reasonable approximation of a twist before they walked to the door.

"We're both stuck in the in between. The Harley Street version of the Prince and the Pauper."

Annabelle said nothing, feeling the stickiness of her situation. She didn't want the exhilaration to end.

Ben made as if to say something then halted and Annabelle looked up from her thoughts.

Annabelle raised her eyebrows. "Some last words of wisdom you'd like to inflict?" She couldn't stomach any more commentary on her conduct, person, or flaws at that very moment.

The mechanical rhythm of the horses finishing the last mouthfuls of their morning hay filled the silence.

Annabelle knew he had something to say. She backed up several steps and rested her back on the warm curve of a flank the color of molasses. "Pims and I will wait." Annabelle was enjoying the soft rise and fall of the horse's ribs against her when there the latch of the stable door clattered open.

Ben slipped his hand into hers and pull her into the front of the slip stall. They fell into the front trough. Pims rolled an underwhelmed eye in their direction before continuing an excavation for any last flakes of bran.

"Ben, the cobbler's come to collect the fixings." A voice squeaked.

Ben held his index finger to his lips—a smile behind.

"Albie?" She mouthed the name of the youngest groom. Ben's hand was still intertwined with hers.

Ben nodded.

Annabelle smiled as she heard two footsteps hesitate before they pattered away and the door slammed.

"I've got to get the delivery; he won't wait long." Ben sighed. "There's never going to be a right time for this. I'm never going to be in the right mind for this. So here it goes."

Annabelle was unsure if she was safer to withdraw her hand before the torrent of God-knew what , or to leave it as it was. She let it linger.

"Marry me, Lady."

Annabelle couldn't repress her smile—there were some bits of Ben Fulbright that were coming harder and harder to resist. Dimples. Shoulders. She stopped herself at the muscles pressing against his stock coat. Best not get carried away, lass. Annabelle heard Mrs. Mingle in her ear.

"We could make something of this life together. I've big plans for me own stable. Racing's big money in America. Kentucky. New York."

Annabelle's brain had crystalized at the brusque proposal, she struggled to digest her real feelings.

"I love you, Annabelle. I'm no gentleman now, but I'm going to make one of myself. Stick with me now, you won't regret it."

"My father wouldn't give a dowry."

Ben took her by the shoulder. "I don't want your bleeding dowry. And your father might be secretly pleased at the match. He's made his own way in the world—he respects a bit of grit and wager."

The diverging paths her future could take seemed magically paved for her. Lord Crispin—a resounding no. Mystery gentleman with a title and tidy sum, quite possible, but a Pandora's box to be sure. Ben—possible. If she was willing to eschew every single rung in Society she had so painstakingly scaled. Then there was the matter of Larkin. Taken in name and body, certainly. But his mind and heart she was almost certain were hers. Almost.

The promise of almost, and Annabelle's ambition, won out over the undeniable temptation before her.

Awash of sadness swelling in her soul. "I can't. I just can't."

Annabelle felt Ben's grip on her fingers give and a dull glaze came over his eyes. It would be too hard to explain. But she wanted more. She couldn't quite shake the dejected look of the woman she had seen earlier in Piccadilly. Love was a tricky venture.

Ben squeezed his eyes shut.

Annabelle wanted love, though she wasn't sure if the kind Ben or Larkin might offer was to her liking. But freedom, to do what she pleased, in any manner that she pleased, was the ember which burned brightest in her heart.

She'd risk her fate on Pandora's box then.

Annabelle pulled herself out of the manger and patted Pims. "You really are a dear, you know. To propose in the middle of all this business." The short soft hair along Pims' back reflected the almost midday light. The horse's muscles rippled under the light pressure of her fingers as she ran them along his spine.

"I meant what I said, Annabelle." Ben slid easily from his repose. "I love you. We could leave the titles and the snobs. Make our own fortunes on our own terms."

Annabelle hated the hope radiating from him. "Those are your terms, not mine." She didn't want new castles in the sky, she simply wanted one more to her liking right here. "I am one of those snobs."

"No yer not. You'd like to chuck 'em behind you as much as I would." He followed Annabelle as they walked out of the stall. "Admit it. That's why yer in this fix. It's not in ye to be one of the crowd."

"I hope that's true." Annabelle swatted at stray bits of alfalfa on her dress. His logic was as sure as his heart. "But I can't. Please don't ask me again. Careful what you wish for." She fiddled with one last button on her sleeve. "In a weak moment, I might say yes."

"I'd never take advantage of a lady when she's down."

"A most admirable quality in a man. Many gentlemen would not act as you do."

"Look how far it's got me." Ben reached to brush her skirts before he straightened a hairsbreadth from Annabelle.

"In case it's the last chance I get." He cupped her face in his hands and pressed his lips to hers.

Annabelle didn't protest. Warm oak and happiness. When he released her, it took a few moments for the stars to clear from Annabelle's eyes.

"The Lancet's calling." Ben bit his lip to cloak his smirk. "And I've got work to do."

That night Annabelle dreamt she was again sprinting through Piccadilly. Its glory faded in the evening light with the swells and working folk long gone home. She could hear clearly a second set of footsteps, but could only make out a top hat, bobbing faceless, waving the baton of a wooden stethoscope beside her. She might have been alarmed, but for the laughter that she realized was erupting from her sleep-sweet mouth.

Chapter 7

Annabelle slouched in her dressing chair, wishing she could pause time as she spun one of her pearl studs round and round like a top. She had spent that past week fielding her mother's ill-disguised marital proddings and wishing she could stir up more reproach for her father's collusion. It had been Mrs. Pierce's best ultimatum yet and it rung with the solemnity of a copper Chau gong announcing Annabelle's last supper. Despite years of tutelage and countless bloodlettings at the hands of needlepoint gone awry, the notion of the domestic angel was one Annabelle considered most appropriate when strapped to a coal cart headed straight for hell. But if she could find herself a malleable, though amiable, wealthy man of good social standing, he might prove to be an acceptable adornment to her future. An elegant subterfuge for her academic ambitions.

Once safely married, her father might reconsider the by-line predicament—for what harm was a woman once she had been ' cuffed with a gold ring? The unfairness of the feminine lot almost usurped her reason—a passing flirtation again with Ben's question. She really would have to leave London if she were to accept the Pierce's head coachman—it would be social suicide otherwise. She wondered if the wild brambles of Kentucky, amidst the thundering of hooves and crunch of New World money, would excuse their sin of circumventing classist convention. But wonder was all she would allow. A chord of snobbery, which Annabelle presumed was plucked at birth in all British aristocracy, would not quiet itself.

Her choice was made. The ball tonight would offer a litany of fitting gentleman. She could easily coax out a proposal in the following weeks, with a wedding to shortly follow. Then she could be back to her books and pen, none the worse for her troubles. Annabelle wished she had paid closer attention to the articles on patchwork patterns and household bookkeeping in Beaton's Englishwoman's Domestic. But immediately revoked that sentiment when she recalled the whitewashed history of Julius Caesar Beaton's had presented for delicate minds—the equivalent to intellectual bloodletting for the female humors. The demonstration had been quite a revelation and while her hope was not exactly concrete, at least it had made itself known.

If she were clever, there could be a type of freedom inside the vows of marriage. She was sure of it—so long as she was exacting in her choice. Annabelle gave her pearls one last spin before cutting their gaiety short with her palm as she pushed them aside and pulled last month's copy of The Lancet in front of her. She flipped open the cover. Mr. Charles Ball's Case of Double Hernia in a Man. Case of Popliteal Aneurism, operation by Mr. Lovett. The by-line that started this all. She didn't regret asking. She'd keep asking. Her future husband could ask (even demand) it too. Her finger traced the column of articles. Mr. Husting's Letter to Sir Carly the on the Impropriety of Male Midwifery. Hope was a dangerous thing. But surely some arrangement was possible for Amazons to escape their pearled shackles.

The staircase creaked and assured steps approached.

The door crashed open. "Oy I've 'ad a bit of the run-around today." Sarah announced, a little out of breath. She tossed a basket to the corner and gave Annabelle a quick smile as she examined herself in the oval mirror above the dressing table. After a few pokes at her frizz and a pop of her lips, she looked at Annabelle and frowned. "Christ, I've to get you puffed and mighty and out the door in just shy of an hour." She looked down at the clutter on the table before she chided. "And all yer good fer is to sit here twiddling with yer medical things and bobbles ." Her hand glided over the arrangement.

"Good evening to you too. You do look like the day's given you a turn." Annabelle tugged at the shoulder of Sarah's plain dress to straighten its twists.

"I've got me stays all in a bundle." Sarah stepped back and wrestled with her wayward ensemble.

"New dance you've picked up?"

"Ay now," Sarah laughed. "Be careful now how ye treat yer messenger, or they can go quite dumb."

"Or the messenger can spit her message out or be tossed to the corner." She tapped the vacant plot near the binding of The Lancet. "Really, Sarah. My earrings."

Sarah bent to meet Annabelle's eyes in the mirror as the two earrings skittered merrily back to their home.

"Shameless."

"I know."

"You give me very little credit."

"Quit yer chatter, or I'll say the same about you." Sarah pulled a narrow envelope from her skirts and thrust it ahead of her.

The ambling script of the address made Annabelle's heart skip. "I'll wear the pink tonight and my long gloves." What was Larkin about now? "I suppose there's a benefit to having your sundry talents around."

"Ye bet yer arse there is." Sarah touted before she went to setting out Annabelle's ball gown—the one with the daring shoulders and tiny waist.

Annabelle turned her attention back to the envelope. She withdrew a stiff, rectangular booklet—a slip of paper wafted out.

Dinner & Reception

Given by the Foster family in celebration of the engagement of their daughter, Josephine Helene, to Augustus Beechwort

Monday evening at 7 o'clock
September 28, 1868.

Annabelle skimmed over the featured musicians and a smile spread throughout her body as she saw each of the evening's dances were preemptively filled. Two of the four waltzes having our pleasure jotted in beside them. Bold move. Two dances promised to a married man. She picked up the slip of paper, the ink was smudged from haste.

Angel,
I've got the timing right.
To hold you in my arms is my only desire.
You make me reckless.
Your Devil

Annabelle barely gave thought to the fate which she had been so carefully plotting, so heady was the lush sensation his letter provoked. With half her mind's eye realigned in imagined ecstasy, Annabelle scanned her other partners. All were monied, a Lord or two scattered between. None, Annabelle noted, could compare to Larkin, in intellect or appeal. Could he possibly know her sad predicament? She faintly wondered if he did and if her struggle amused him. Even as her heart melted, she bristled. She'd have to regain the upper hand.

"I'd thought you'd be right tickled yer grand man penned you in." Sarah wedged herself next to Annabelle on the edge of her dressing chair. "Then ye could dance in front of God and everyone."

"He's the only man I know worth having."

"I can respect ye skating above the law." Sarah shot up. "Lord knows I've done me fair share of that," then propped her hip on the table. "Settin' yer hat on the britches of a married man, m'Lady. Takes a special kind of spirit. Sure ye couldn't be content with one of them rolly polly dodgers? Ye could muck 'em about the dance floor fer a lark and they'd fall at yer feet." She crossed her arms. Her look eerily resembled Mrs. Mingle's irritatingly motherly gaze. "Well, take that trip and snatch their pocketbooks, first thing."

"You make it out that I'm mining for gold. I've no other option. I've to marry well, and with top speed. I can't fight my mother any longer. Father's no help."

"Aye now, ain't he the one turned ye on to that right pickle. Where you nearly decapitated some high-steppin' gov'ner? Murder by ginger beer, that's a lark!" Sarah threw her head back in glee.

"I told you that in confidence."

"'Suppose it takes a nutter to know one. I'da paid to see that picture." Sarah flicked Annabelle's shoulder and her elation settled. "But there's ways of getttin' a taste of freedom ye haven't even considered. Aren't you the one with the fancy pants book-learnin'?"

Annabelle never guessed she'd have her stays tied by Minerva herself. "What brilliance have you tucked up your sleeve today?"

"To skirt the system ye need a crook on yer side."

The large hand of the wall clock found its home at twelve and released its chimes.

"Gads, five o'clock, the carriage'll be 'ere at quarter to."

Before Annabelle could protest, Sarah swirled about the room like a dervish—ribbons, pins, petticoats danced to her tune. Amidst her skillful tugs and lacings, Annabelle found her ears filling with Sarah's investigations. "Ye asked me 'bout that lady Fawcett. Ben's got it right. She's got a sweet little set up on Seymour Place."

Annabelle didn't bother to ask how she'd come by her information.

"Sees women and children at 'er dispensary too. Me chap, Patty's missus has gone 'round there for 'erself and when her babe had some spells. That lady fixed her up right as rain—they think the world of 'er."

Sarah meet Annabelle's eyes in the mirror. "A bargain get-up. Tottles down to that place, saves a few lives, then hops in her carriage back to Hunter Street in time for supper with her mister. Sees she wouldn't even need a mister—I know I wouldn't if I was her."

Annabelle thought twice before opening her mouth. A woman practicing a sort of medicine intrigued her. But applying poultices and administering tonics to the unfortunates of the London belly seemed incongruous compared to her tidy, academic affairs with her father. How many bandage wrappings would she have to dole out to keep her in dancing heels and stoles? "She's found a suitable playground, and good for her. But I mean to take a more scientific approach."

"Keep yer hands clean then?"

Annabelle didn't look at Sarah. She didn't know what she wanted. Aside from that blasted freedom. And money could buy that. Money found on the path which ended in marriage.

"Look 'ere." Sarah ducked her head next to Annabelle's. "Tis a simple thing, m'lady. Ye either fold n' catch yerself a rolly polly — with the right sort, ye'll talk his smitten brain into your scribblings with yer father. If ye do it right, he might even take credit for the notion." She pressed her check to Annabelle's. "Or ye take the knife by the blade, swallow yer blasted pride, and take Lady Fawcett's line o'work."

"Father won't give me authorship." Annabelle couldn't escape the cool gaze of Sarah's reflected back in the mirror. "Ms. Fawcett might be a gentlewoman, but she's not a lady."

"Now yer wantin' your afternoon sponge with sugar, berries, and cream? I'd forgotten I'm in the presence of royalty,' Sarah chortled. "Keep up the lady bit then if ye must. If yer safe and married, with yer mother off his poor back, yer father might surprise ye."

After Annabelle slipped into the sumptuous rose creation from The House of Worth , she felt certain of Larkin's undivided attentions tonight.

"My brassy lady's a right picture, let's set our argument aside. On me way back, I found a few posies that might be just the thing." Sarah went to the corner and withdrew several small bundles of brown paper. "I thought as much ye'd wear the pink." She tore at the paper to let a cascade of tea roses, sweet peas, and honeysuckle fall out.

"Those are perfect, Sarah, how thoughtful."

"Mister Lateda Larkin won't know what to do with himself," Sarah went to work adorning Annabelle's curls. "Or will he?" She winked.

Annabelle again kept herself from meeting Sarah's eyes—she didn't like anyone being so candid with her heart of hearts. But at the suggestion, she closed her eyes and let herself drift into Larkin's waltzing arms.

"M'lady?" Sarah cleared her throat. "I 'ate to mention it, but I must beg yer pardon for me late arrival tonight." She looked to the clock. "Though you shan't be late."

"Not a worry, Sarah."

"I didn't want to 'ave to tell ye this, m'Lady , but—" Sarah swallowed. "Ol' Freddie is turning the screws on me."

Annabelle turned. "I thought ye were through with him."

"No lass is ever though with Ol' Freddie. I've got need to chare a right fee fer me services."

"That business again?" Curse her posies.

"Another twenty quid. Or it's me head."

"Couldn't you just ask rather than play this game. "

"I always like to 'ave a bit of bait in me pocket for 'ard times."

Annabelle figured if she wore Sarah's shoes, she'd have done the same. Ignoring the insulting slap of her maid's blackmail, Annabelle figured she should take notice of Sarah's calculations and put those lessons to use. Every kiss had its price. Larkin and rolly-pollies alike wouldn't stand a chance.

Chapter 8

Crystal pyramids of light beamed from the ceiling, offering sun to the pastel collections of blooms bordering every arcade as Annabelle entered the Foster's gallery. She smoothed her bodice. The spring strawberry satin pulled the same tones from Annabelle's exposed skin, setting her aglow.

She felt like a cloaked hawk, poised to plunge its talons deep into the soft down of an unsuspecting creature. She had never regarded domesticity as a weapon. An Achilles heel, surely, but the idea of strength because, rather than despite, her womanhood, was a delicious revelation. She soared into the ballroom, charging directly into the swirls of waltzing couples.

The looks she received from the women in the room, laced with jealous admiration, were just as precious to her as the unabashed looks of approval from the male members of her circle. Now she knew the coordinates not only of her final destination— one husband, of suitable temperament and means, but just as importantly—the most pleasant of side trips—Cassius Larkin. Where was Dr. Larkin? Playing the part of the sickeningly devoted husband, no doubt.

And there he was. Standing apart from the orchestra and the colorful kaleidoscope of dancing guests and black-coated waiters.

As if he possessed a sixth sense, Larkin lifted his attentions from his conversation and pointed himself at Annabelle. Their eyes met. Annabelle tipped her head to one side. An arch of her brow would have been too forward, she couldn't risk even a whisper of discovery. Though just the touch of their sleeves could be counted on to set her skin into an electric blaze with—

What?

Desire.

Annabelle could not deny this instinctual response, the way she assumed many women did. It was not something acknowledged— between mothers and daughters, sisters and friends. Presumed to be man's emotion, Annabelle believed she knew better. She credited her past education with her witnessing the many faces desire could take. It was not so simple and primal, or sordid a thing. It was a thing infinitely more complex which now accelerated her fluttering heart.

Power.

She was sure she could read Larkin with as much ease as she sailed through the pages of a novel. Keeping her eye on her prey, Annabelle slowed her pace—both allowing others the pleasure of a longer stare, and herself time to think. Now what to do about Olivia?

Olivia Blackbloom, the sound of Olivia Larkin was too hateful for Annabelle, was her oldest friend. They had shared carriage rides in Hyde Park and giggles over Miss Milner's nasal butcherings of French conjugations. Annabelle's heart tore—there had scarcely been a time when one little girl would been seen without the other. After their terrified trippings up to Queen Victoria for their presentation into correct society, Olivia had gushed for weeks following about the austere magnificence of the reine. Annabelle couldn't overcome the remarkable resemblance the Queen's bore to a hog. Then the ax of circumstance landed and Annabelle felt a chasm cleaved between them.

Out of the corner of her eye Annabelle saw Larkin turn back to his wife. Annabelle congratulated him on the move—not a whisper of suspicion. She was pleased when she saw Olivia kept her in full view for a moment longer before the corners of her mouth tipped down in a delicate pout.

Annabelle glided from her post. Larkin turned around and strode to meet her as they both reached the foot of the swirling staircase.

"Good evening, Miss Pierce." Larkin's formal address was anything but. His eyes dragged down her body and he bowed. "Have you misplaced your chaperone?"

Annabelle commanded her cheeks to stay at a polite half-mast

"Doctor Larkin." She both loved and hated his lack of propriety with her. "Not at all, but my dance card—"

He moved in closer. "We'll sort that out, Angel."

Annabelle shied away, his amorous candor being too bold. "Perhaps." Her voice flitted over the word. "But I've not come to squander my attentions on a devilish, married man."

When his eyes tempered as if she had slapped him with a kid glove, she let her smile reassure him things weren't over between them and continued on her circuit of the ballroom— before he could protest.

The first part of the evening proved mortifying. Having conducted her social research as thoroughly as she had the treatment of organic nervous afflictions for an article several months back, Annabelle marked her targets. Not quite aristocracy, though she hated to admit, there were young ladies whose funds and titles would usurp Annabelle's more corporal persuasions for the most ambitious single young men. So she had settled on one Sir Jonathon Hastings. A member of the landed gentry in Devon. Amiable enough on paper, though his face reminded her of a Vermeer butcher. Unfortunately, Mister Hastings was a pedantic young man who tread grossly on her toes. His release was heaven.

Her other interest that evening was Lord Murshum, born Samuel Cuncliffe, bequeathed a title as a wool-combing magnate who had amassed thirty-five thousand acres in Sussex. Though he held the most tempting bank book, Lord Murshum bore a startling resemblance to a long-eared owl and found it refreshing to discuss the agonizing mechanics of the textile industry. When those sufferings concluded, Annabelle requested she be deposited at the refreshment table, ready to sit down at her drawing board of potential husbands. Not only that, but a bit of punch would ease her anticipation as the first waltz—Larkin's waltz—would follow the quadrille.

As soon as Annabelle had brushed off Lord Mushum's request for the second quadrille of the evening, there in front of the silver lagoon of bright slices of citrus fruits, Annabelle found herself cozied right next to Mrs. Olivia Larkin.

"This is a joyful note of happenstance."

Annabelle's falsely bright declaration did not appear lost on her friend though she snuffed Annabelle's rancor with her saccharine reply. "Darling Annabelle, your cheeks do look so pretty after your exertions on the dance floor."

Annabelle eyed Olivia for her deeper meaning.

"You perhaps have forgotten a lady should never promenade the ballroom alone, nor enter it unaccompanied." Olivia's once kind eyes exposed volumes over the rim of her cut crystal punch glass from which she would only wet her lips.

"But I am accompanied, Olivia, darling." Annabelle fought her inclination to sneer. "My Aunt Maude—Baroness Maude Pearle—my father's sister has been kind enough to attend with me tonight. Mamma was overtaken with one of her headaches and Papa was called out for a patient."

Olivia's demure expression twinkled.

"She was detained momentarily by Lord Archer in the reception room."

"I had forgotten she had once been married to Baron Whitehall. She does not use his name any longer—most proper—and very kind."

Annabelle's knuckles whitened around the slim handle of her punch cup in defense at her aunt's character. Maude Pearle was publicly recognized as one of the most alluring woman in Victoria's empire. Privately she was known as the well-compensated, former lover of the Earl of Newark, and more recently the Duke of Lancaster—leaving the Baron's bed undecidedly cool.

"She is married to Baron Whitehall who is a bore. She knows her own mind." Annabelle contemplated further defense but realized she was slipping into a treacherous debate.

"She has taken you under her wing. I would take care not to become too comfortable nestled to that vulture's breast. Or I would say you are not the Annabelle I know."

"The truth is you do not know me at all. You knew a child. I am a woman." Annabelle took a fierce sip of punch. "I also know my own mind and listen to it. Perhaps you would be in a better position if you had yours."

"Make no assumptions. We seem to no longer know one another at all. I have three beautiful children, a lovely home—homes counting the estate in Kent—and a dutiful husband. I am complete."

"Children, a home, and a husband. An equation for a complete life? Funny your husband falls lowest in the rankings. A life, perhaps. But one complete, I can hardly agree."

With smoldering pleasure, Annabelle watched her dagger sink through the coffee-colored silk screen which could not veil Olivia's wounded heart. The quiver of her friend's upper lip pulled Annabelle over the finish line. Annabelle smiled with ill-concealed satisfaction. Serves her right. Annabelle told herself she had every right to hold this grudge with Olivia. The lies she told sweet Larkin about that aristocrat in Brussels when I was away with father. She had those engagement bans slapped to press so fast the damage was done. I returned to a neat little invitation to their vows. The little minx.

"You might scoff at me, never mind might, I know you do. But we are both twenty-three. I have a husband, children, and am well-esteemed by Society. What do you have to show for these years since we were presented at Court?"

Annabelle would have preferred if the floor would swallow her whole. These moments where she was caught, exposed, with no weaponry were so few and far between, she could count them on one hand.

So many years ago, packaged in the recesses of her subconscious, it was a moment like this which spurred her to crystalize that black event into a seed of inherent confidence which would propel her, rather than destroy her.

Annabelle would not be undone. Not today. Not ever. And not certainly by Olivia. "I have my freedom and self-respect. And the admiration of many men." Annabelle bore her meaning into Olivia. "You married to please everyone else. To fulfill your duties. We dreamed of so much more."

Olivia's stare flooded and almost made Annabelle forget her animosity. Almost.

"At least I thought we did. Perhaps it was just me all along?"

"I hope you enjoy your own company. Twenty-four is a lonely number."

Her friend's sharp reply thrust Annabelle back to her previous animosities. If she could have throttled Olivia with the side of her bone fan, she would have taken grotesque delight in doing so. "Though I never find myself alone for long, the joy of breath on my own two, unshackled feet will never grow old." The truth of her sentiments made her decision to fold for a band of gold waver pale.

The well-kindled tension between the two women was snuffed momentarily as a spittle-filled stuttering voice boomed from behind them, "S...s...s—simply captivating is the word I'd use to describe the two of you ladies this evening."

Annabelle could have kissed little George Gosling, now not so little, as he lumbered up to them, blissfully unaware of the battle he was postponing.

"Miss Pierce," he cleared his throat and repeated himself. "Miss Pierce." He drew himself up to his full height, his top-heavy torso perched precariously on oddly slim limbs, as though he had just taken first prize in a spelling contest.

"Good evening, Georgie, but the phrase 'simply captivating' is actually two words," Annabelle couldn't help herself. She had known him since he wore short pants and suffered only a lisp. "You are generous, but I have not yet had the punch, I can recall my own name."

This second barb sent Olivia's hand to Annabelle's elbow; her fingers vice-clamped into its tenderest bits.

Annabelle's breath caught as her arm jerked reflexively away from the sear of Olivia's grip but she could not lose her.

Olivia released a laugh bursting with allure and rebuke as she ignored Annabelle's scowl. "George, you know Annabelle well enough to understand her wit. You are the kindest there is."

The poor man simpered sweetly in her graces.

"I was just telling Annabelle I have not had the pleasure of your company in far too long,' she cast Annabelle a pointed look. "Your hard-won fortune has carried its whispers into Society's ear only to your credit." She released Annabelle's elbow like a schoolmarm satisfied with a pupil's rebuke. "Do congratulate our old, dear friend on his successes in the world of confections."

Annabelle thought wisely against commenting on the carnal successes she noted in terms of little Georgie's circumference. Instead she murmured something faintly kind and did not protest when Mister Gosling expressed his desire to take the next waltz with her. She found her spirits lofted by his good-natured, if mundane, chatterings . Just as she wondered how she could, as a lady, broach the number figures his esteemed bank accounts could boast. Annabelle felt a touch she knew gently lift her hand from Georgie's shoulder.

Spontaneously she twirled underneath her now lifted arm into Larkin's broad chest—the obligatory tile's distance between dancers ignored.

"Thank you, Gosling, you've done your part. I simply must cut in."

Annabelle felt the small of her back sway beneath his touch.

A stutter of protest formed on Gosling's lips.

But Larkin reassured, "Her father's orders, my good man. I dare not argue."

And the two whirled away, leaving George Gosling partnerless and dumbfounded.

"Olivia's gone off to be sure the children haven't eaten too much cake." With time ticking down, Larkin kept Annabelle close as they painted the expanse of the ball room. There was nothing Annabelle wouldn't have done for him. The thrill of being enveloped by another's longing, and echoing it, made her breath catch in her chest as she swung in his arms—unsure if they offered a lifeboat or a noose. The truth was, Annabelle didn't care.

The incredible muskiness of his being, melded with the faintest trace of fruited tobacco, made the colored blobs of dancers in her periphery blur. The precarious struggle between authority, propriety, and abandon were the only things keeping them upright.

At last Larkin turned to look at her. His waxing smile shone down more strongly than the beams of the noon sun between the leaves of the chestnut trees in Greenwich Park. Annabelle's mind flew back to that afternoon, with a bottle of champagne and a worn book of Keats—which would rest softly in her heart until her last breath. That was when she knew she could say how falling in love felt.

Heady, exhilarating, devastating.

Annabelle pretended she hadn't seen the champagne's vintage—1864—the year Larkin and Olivia wed. She became addicted to the unworldly highs and crushing lows of their unconsummated affair.

"If only you knew the depths to which you move me." Larkin confessed.

Shocks shot through Annabelle's core; her soul devoured his equally hungry gaze.

"You've made a Devil of me."

Annabelle felt as if she could exist on the tailcoats of a Chinese firework cannon and explore the cosmos hand and hand with her pirate. "You have made an angel of me."

In the gusto of her pure emotion, Annabelle forgave every grudge as Larkin's fingers kept one-two-three time along her ribs and allowed herself to slip into gratitude. For tonight she was a vision in rose-colored satin and neither of them seemed to be in the mood to be inconspicuous.

She wondered if she were to feign a fainting-spell—as her mother had on countless occasions to great effect—if it would expedite a polite exit to a clandestine corner where they could answer the question they had both not dared pose.

It would be a delicious evening.

As Strauss's strings climbed to a rigorous crescendo, matching the wordless electricity between their hearts, Annabelle felt, for a second time, another familiar touch on her shoulder—though one which brought no pleasurable jolts to her senses as she was pulled from Larkin's embrace.

On landing, she recoiled, but a firm grip kept her close as she continued across the dance floor, leaving Larkin nodding to his senior colleague, Dr. Horace Christianson.

Annabelle opened her mouth to protest, but Christianson's arms was already around her. He wore the same smile she remembered, but always tried to forget.

"You are bewitching tonight as usual, Miss Pierce."

The hairs at the nape of her neck stiffened where a wayward curl cascaded. Her breath caught.

"Do not look so struck, your Uncle Horace has come to your rescue just in the nick of time. You looked as if you were going to expire in that dottering Gosling's arms."

Annabelle hated herself as she found she only possessed the strength to hang limply in his arms, finding empathy for the downy rabbits who had taken much the same stance in Molly's jaws, as if praying for a timely execution.

"Your same tricks and magic have spun your web tight around poor Larkin too." Christianson cooed.

The symbols crashed, making Annabelle start.

Christianson pulled her to him. "I'm afraid your favor has transferred?" His question trembled with the uncertainty of a lad though his fingers curled—his nails biting her skin beneath her satined back which caved in agony, rather than pleasure.

Repulsion brewed in her veins. His wiry beard grated against her breasts and she took stock of the waxiness around his eyes which betrayed his age, though his hair was still full.

"Have I lost your favor?" His grasp from their outstretched hands clammed shut over her knuckles.

Annabelle swallowed a wince.

His tone softened as his grip tightened. "A silent Venus, my favorite kind."

Annabelle remembered when once she had been flattered by dear Uncle Horace and his attentions. Why had she righted every other ship, dampened every eel of a memory into a slithery recess of her brain? But face to face? A snifter of arsenic would have proved a Godsend.

A shattering of strings erupted. Christianson continued to spin them in three-time with such ferocity Annabelle's shoes barely graced the floor.

"I've contented myself to enjoy you now from a distance, but I've found it necessary to remind you of what true desire feels like. Or at least keep you in the family."

Annabelle could have let her tears fall for a century. She saw a thirteen-year-old centaur, a woman-child, who did not recognize an uncle for what he was, starving for a taste of adult validation, believing it tasted of him.

"It was yours, not mine." Annabelle pushed back only inches in his vice.

Christianson's expression became sallow as if he had been found dead, floating face-up in the Thames. Year-old seaweed at his throat.

The blur of dancers against the light paneling of the room made something somersault in Annabelle's throat—wild bluebell and honeysuckle petals, deflowered in a windstorm.

She could not take her eyes from his now—uncourted magnetism. She closed her lids, shielding her soul from theft.

"Look at me." He hissed. "Do not make out I misconstrued your coy invitations."

Her knuckles cracked together. A spear of pain rode up her arm as a silent cry hovered on her lips.

Annabelle found a sliver of anger came with the pain. "Good parents do not let children play with fire."

"In your bed, there were no children, my dear."

"Only violated hearts."

Her knees buckled as she felt a bone in her hand move in a direction God did not intend and she slid from him—lightheaded, the violins seeming to celebrate her demise.

"My, my, I never would have given Johann enough credit to take one's breath away." An arm of surprising strength stretched under Annabelle's. A vial was thrust under her nose.

A putrid punch righted Annabelle, her mind trailing footsteps behind. A vision in burgundy came into view. Her dangling earrings on any other woman would have been considered declasse.

"Vipers belong in the garden." Maude Pearle removed the cigarette holder she had clamped in her teeth. "There'll be no exchange of darlings tonight." The grande dame blew a perfect dragon's breath of smoke into Christianson's face as the dancers eddied around their standstill ménage. "Or ever." She finished with a grin that could have crippled all of Grimm's ogres and evil stepmothers before releasing Annabelle's hand from his.

A twitch of his nostril and puff of his cheeks gave way to a sputter before Christianson replied. "They must start teaching the boys that Prometheus was a cunt."

Maude flicked the end of the holder, dusting his evening coat with white ash. "At least I can be sure where my Hercules resides." She let out a trill before arranging herself in Annabelle's still limp embrace and turning them out into the floor, as the horns entered into the fanfare.

⊗

As if her glass carriage had rolled in from the lamplight, fully equipped with her own fairy godmother, if not a prince and slipper to match, Annabelle felt a twinkle of herself come alive. She blessed Maude with her entire heart. Just as she had the day her mother cursed Maude's name as between torrents of sobs, she told Annabelle her dear Uncle's heart no longer belonged to them. Though incapable of completely snuffing out his lechery from afar, her aunt's orchestration of a luscious distraction had ended his midnight tyrannies for good.

Chapter 9

Their espionage went smoothly, just as Larkin planned. A switch of a datebook, an indisposed aunt, a clever lady's maid, and it was done.

Now Annabelle stood with Larkin in a private galleria off the Royal College of Surgeons lecture halls at Larkin's invitation—to be educated and to marvel at the wax works of Susini. They were not carnival sideshows, but anatomical models used as a morality tale for the weaker-willed citizens of London. And for entertainment. The footsteps of the onlookers echoed from the high ceilings. The electric lamplight threw a blanket the color of grassy butter over the labyrinth of anterooms. The damp air seemed to intensify the mood of academic sensationalism.

Annabelle heard of the busts of syphilitic fallen women that drew the judging throngs. She wondered why male busts were woefully unrepresented; men were afflicted in equal proportion. But this exhibition, Larkin had told her, would be entirely different. Twelve life-like female wax works—a mystical synthesis of art and medicine: beauty and intrigue.

"I see the Mona Lisa behind those schoolgirl eyes."

Annabelle jumped—wonderfully on edge from anticipation—from what she hoped might follow the exhibition—and general air of intrigue that pervaded the galleria. Larkin edged towards her, though his closeness was unfortunately thwarted by her heaping skirts.

School girl indeed. Annabelle softened and shifted her gaze back to his. Curiosity—and an altogether different beast—thrashed inside her. At once at ease in his native habitat of formalin and books, Larkin was as attractive as ever—an academic Adonis. The headiness of their attraction easily suppressed any pangs from her pesky conscience—hadn't Olivia betrayed her first?

Annabelle had not felt the part of a schoolgirl when she had lain in Christianson's arms. "A schoolgirl would catch quite a fright if she could see through these Mona Lisa eyes."

The crinkles at the corners of Larkin's eyes spoke only of his high esteem before his lips turned up. "You take offense so easily and find malice when there is none." He offered his arm.

She took it. "Watch your words, you are not the poet you fancy yourself to be. You know I prefer Pasteur to Yeats."

"I'm glad of that. I hope my education continues."

He lead them towards a wood-framed glass display case. "I'm delighted you were able to accompany me today. This will prove a remarkable experience, my sweet."

"I would expect nothing less than an extraordinary day with you, Doctor Larkin." Annabelle blushed hard at her boldness.

"Naturally. We have a long history of the enjoyment of each other's company, have we not?"

"My fondest memories—" Theirs had been an early, quiet flame, breathing new life into her broken heart. He arrived the autumn after her summer in Brighton with Mrs. Mingle, into her father's tutelage, and her heart. Annabelle's voice evaporated as she caught sight of the subject housed inside the case—a female form, human hair cascading down the sterile white pillow embracing her long white neck and head. A section of rib had been fileted, upturned to lay on her wax shoulder, her heart in full view.

Annabelle gasped. The model's carved intestines extruded down over her wax flanks to meet the sides of the case as her knees bent in a curiously casual angle. The model's wax hands rested gently away from her trunk as if caught in a moment of repose on the banks of the Thames after a picnic luncheon. Annabelle marveled at the intrigue and disgust which collided in her own guts as her eyes coursed down the rest of the lifeless replication.

Feeling the reassuring flutter in her chest, she heard two bearded gentlemen behind them conversing about the collaboration between the artist and a famed Cagliarian anatomist. But the question of how was of much less interest to her as to why the artists had created this duplicitous exhibition.

"Quite a feat." Larkin remarked, sounding both a statement and a question. "Beautiful and grotesque."

Annabelle understood well the repulsive curiosity she felt. She scanned the room, searching for similar reactions. But the stern nodding and pointing of the clustered attendants divulged nothing. Was no one else disturbed by this butchering art? This resplendent nightmare in wax? The woman's expressions were other worldly, almost blissful. The somber expression of the departed, lids mercifully closed, or at least the caustic fumes of preserving fluid would have appeased Annabelle's cultural catch-safe of gentility—but her mind whirred on. "Horribly beautiful."

"Well put." Larkin nodded in the direction of the anatomy labs, in the far wing of the college. "The modeler procures real specimens to ensure the work of art is as exacting as possible."

Annabelle had visions of Michelangelo-type artists clad in robes and pudgy velvet hats juxtaposed against masses of rotting corpses. Intrigue peeked ahead of her afront . "A painstaking process, no doubt."

"Spitzner has truly outdone himself with a very special model, the first of its kind." Larkin beamed as if he could take credit for the artist's genius. "She's over there." He nodded to a corner of the gallery where a group huddled in front of a tawny port-colored velvet chaise lounge.

Without waiting for Larkin, Annabelle let herself be swept along in the swells of the crowded gallery towards the chaise, the murmur of their voices crested as she approached. She rounded to the head of the display. Unsure what her eyes would discover, she drew her belly in tight—leaving a modicum of space between her chemise and the whalebone ribbing of her corset. Her eyes rested on another woman, standing a respectable distance away from the spectacle. The angle of her nose matched the pert angles of her hat, both of which tipped delicately away from the Venus, as if acknowledgement would be too much for the day's allotment of smelling salts. A quiver set in Annabelle's jaw as she searched for another compatriot.

Larkin nestled next to her. "Are you shocked, Miss Pierce, to be a unicorn?" His eyes circled her and a softness around his lips make Annabelle's knees catch. "It is a role you play with such distinction."

"I suppose I always can say you dragged me here against my ladylike wishes, as your wife would not accompany you, and you felt I at least might appreciate the work."

Larkin touched the tip of his tongue to his upper lip. "Let us keep our conversation to the two of us." He let his gaze fall for a moment. "Real life and its memories have no place this afternoon."

Annabelle swallowed before she turned to peer at the chaise. There was nothing different between the first Magdalene and her wax sister. Both held the same disarmingly contented, close-eyed expression—limbs peaceful, ankles enchantingly crossed.

Annabelle's eyes traveled down the form. The wax figure's abdominal contents were splayed open a level or two deeper and draped onto a delicate throw, exposing her plum liver and knitted small intestines. "Ah!" The wax figure seemed to shutter as her plasticized chest rose, shifting her organs a few centimeters to accommodate her human breath.

Annabelle'sh and flew to her mouth to swallow the cry that escaped. She pushed past several suits, not a bustle in sight, but Larkin's broad chest stopped her flight. She turned her forehead to meet his tweed frock coat. The smell of smoke and allspice soothed her. "She's alive." Annabelle realized his chest was heaving as he chuckled.

"No, no, my dear. She has never and will never draw breath of her own accord. She houses a mechanized respiratory system. A true Sleeping Beauty."

Annabelle pushed away from Larkin and sniffed. "Pigs' lungs, no doubt."

"As perceptive as usual, my angel."

Annabelle blotted her temple with the back of her gloved hand before she took a second look.

Now her eyes registered the intricate webbings of violet and cranberry-colored vessels feeding her vital organs and the swells of the lobulated liver. Yes, Annabelle could name these well. She had not sat idle during those late nights with her father and Larkin, hidden behind an angelic gaze of childish ignorance, her brain neatly cataloged the medical jargon and disease processes.

"My Sleeping Beauty has awoken. I see your glorious gears churning." Larkin appeared to mistake her breathlessness for an altogether different emotion. "You are perfection. A face that is such an invitation to an even more startling mind."

The clarity in his regard for her made Annabelle's eyes water.

"Know you are adored." His husky breath revealed his unsaid intentions plainly "You are just like her. Regal, an ideal. You both even wear a single strand of pearls." He leaned toward her and brushed the tip of her ear so slightly she wondered if it was imagined.

But the thrill of contact, actual or imagined, eclipsed the sting of his patronage in the moment. Warning bells tinkled in Annabelle's mind. On the Venus' neck a single strand of pearls with a singular sky-blue cloisonné portrait hung delicately in the hollow at the base of her throat. Her chest rose and fell again, haltingly, as if the model had been holding her breath for Annabelle. Annabelle reached for her own necklace, almost identical and drew back.

"There's no use resisting, lovely girl,' his tone became muted at these last words, 'you are meant to set up house on a pedestal, drawing admirers from the far reaches of this empire, nothing to do save to accept their adoration." Annabelle rolled her eyes and remembered their beginnings.

After a dawdling season at Mrs. Mingle's spinster sister's cottage on the Brighton dunes, Annabelle had returned to Fernhead House revived, full of fairytales, candy floss, and oyster shells—shining. But the salted seaside she hoped would rinse her innocent of Christianson's tarnish could not compare to the sheen of Larkin's posies and limericks over chemistry lessons.

But today his pedantic praise rang hollow. "I would never surrender, strung up in ridiculous positions, a disemboweled casualty of war. An unfortunate."

Larkin shot her an incredulous look. "Must you always have such a disastrously contrary opinion?"

"If it allows me to self-preserve, then yes. No one will do that to me. I would do my worst to them first."

Larkin chuckled. "Why must you run through life, barbs raised? Don't your arms tire?"

"It's the only way I know how." Annabelle found she could not hold his kind face in view and found herself fiddling with the loose clasp.

"You are an unstoppable force, Annabelle. Perhaps an alternate perspective might be a welcome relief?" Larkin wrapped his hand over hers. "There is no need to defend yourself on my account."

It would be pleasant to let her armor clatter to the floor. But she could not relinquish her shield.

"Do you not see the smile of her lips, her eyes heavy with rapture?"

"I do not." She replied sharply before she took a turn to consider the Venus. There was a certain arch to her wax neck, and a delicacy with which her fingers graced the valley between her breasts. A corporal glimmer of comprehension landed in Annabelle's core and she blushed, new parts of her awakening under Larkin's spellbound attentions.

"Surrender can be of the upmost sweetness." Larkin tucked his hand in hers.

As their eyes met, Annabelle returned his grip with equal feeling.

In the aftermath of Olivia's betrayal, Annabelle had half-heartedly attempted to disentangle their ties—distracting herself with her father's research had proved fruitless. She wrested her eyes from his to regain a modicum of self-control. "When did you first discover me for my mind, Dr. Larkin?" She wanted to laugh at her diversion.

"From the first moment my eyes met yours. In your father's study." Larkin tantalized her as his grip remained strong. "From the very beginning."

Even the gentle tides and seagull songs had not assuaged her ghosts entirely. Until Larkin crashed into her father's library and her fifteen-year-old heart, she felt doomed to bear witness to her own destruction as she played a bit part in Society's genteel freak show. A figment of an idea crystalized in Annabelle's mind. "My mind is my most alluring quality then?"

"Without a doubt, my sweet."

"So perhaps there could be a,' she searched for the most delicate of words, 'a collaboration of sorts, between our minds? And an understanding between our hearts?" Could the stars have aligned? Annabelle knew men who kept house with their wife but left their hearts in their mistress' hands. And if she were to marry, so be it. Arrangements could be made, to keep every pawn content.

In the midst of the milling exposition attendants, awareness to their impropriety was nonexistent. The murmur of voices played melodic to the staccato of her heart as she searched his face for his reply. Finding none, she attempted to wrest her hand from his as her heart sank. No, she could not have read him so poorly.

Larkin's eyes drifted to their knotted fingers before catching hers tight.

Annabelle's heart swelled so, she worried briefly for the safety of her bodice. Could fulfillment of this fantasy allow her to have everything she ever wanted, expunge the tarnish she still carried?

The cold tap of a walking stick rapped sharply close by, steely above the soft din of the gallery as more onlookers swept in.

As if her skin was made of hellfire, Larkin dropped her hand. His other hand went to his top hat in greeting. He nodded. "Lord Darborough."

Annabelle found a sudden enthusiasm for a non-existent spot on her skirts and scrubbed it violently with her thumbnail. Annabelle knew to worry of discovery was ludicrous. But— their paths always seemed to cross at the right time—enough to allow the regular love letter—an impassioned kiss in passing.

Larkin pursed his lips and shook his head. "An acquaintance from Edenborough. Not to worry, my angel."

Annabelle felt suspended at some metaphysical fork between one road, and one of lower elevation. Having never found a bit of muck and wobble to bother her, she took the latter. Damn the consequences, it would be her choice, this time, to light the fuse.

Annabelle hooded her gaze before aiming a practiced look at Larkin. "I suppose if worship at my alter is inevitable, you might as well be the first to surrender at these holy gates."

Her lie tasted as sweet as the answer in Larkin's eyes.

But not as sweet as vengeance would taste. Her tears would not stop after she heard of the engagement of Olivia and Larkin. Within days of his anticipated proposal to her, Annabelle had the first of her papers published in The Lancet. She had never seen her father so exuberant as he galloped the two of them around the house, declaring them a duo for the ages—just weeks after her eighteenth birthday. She was so proud as she sat quietly in his study, entertaining congratulatory visits from his colleagues, never questioning the credit shone only in his light. The sensation of success outside her ribboned birdcage was more succulent than anything else she had ever experienced, even Larkin's kiss. Accompanying Dr. Pierce to a conference in Brussels, their stay extended when discussions over the conductivity of the heart had blossomed. When she returned home, flushed with the exhilaration of expanding horizons, Annabelle was met with an equally blushing Olivia who shyly told her of her acceptance of Larkin's proposal.

Polite conventions, fragile pride, and a sympathetic, pretty face conspired to tilt the gaming table which Annabelle had meticulously arranged.

The horridly captivating wax models lost their appeal to more pressing matters of form and pleasure, as the two trailed off away from the exposition galleria. Annabelle wondered if a casual observer might speculate on the intent of their hasty venture. Would she offer herself against the disapproving spines of Hippocrates and *Grey's Anatomy*, to a married man? Annabelle looked back and could hardly bear the broadness of his shoulders and narrow hips. Indeed. She would.

They breezed through the arched doorway between the exhibition hall and the catacomb-like hallways leading to the classrooms, laboratories, and hospital wards. The pleasant, musty scent was balm against the dewy perspiration gathering on her upper lip.

Determined her private humiliation would not be made public, Annabelle, appeared to forgive her oldest, if no longer closest, friend. But a nugget of jealously remained wedged in Annabelle's soul. From then on, she took pleasure in Larkin's wistful glances and abashed half-smiles as she twirled along on the arm of some suitor or another. Until one evening a tearful confrontation, between the two women in a shielded opera box in Covent Garden, pulled the curtain back on Olivia's cruel charade.

Annabelle could have forgiven her friend for a besotted play at Larkin's heart, if Olivia hadn't highlighted Annabelle's previously unmentioned feelings for a Swiss ambassador with a dashing moustache. Though Annabelle quickly clarified the unfounded accusation on her swift return, Larkin was a man of his word. He and Olivia were engaged. Annabelle was too late.

Her mind flicked back again to Olivia as her fingers pressed into the outline of Larkin's wedding band as their feet clacked and her skirts swirled, intent on their mission. Eye for an eye, heart for a heart.

Larkin nipped at her heels now. "This way," his voice, husky with intent. He took her hand and pulled her near him as they took a hallway to the right. "There's a room off the archives, we should be quite alone."

Alone. The word was delicious to Annabelle. She thanked the heavens for her bloodied underthings last week. The stench of milk and the glisten of snot would not be part of her undoing.

They came upon a nondescript cherry-stained door, which Annabelle guessed must be adjacent to the private offices of the medical professors. "We have arrived, mademoiselle." Larkin looked like a small boy just before he breaks into the sweets jar. He rapped a knuckle on the door before he cracked it open. Keeping her hand in his he peered in. "Empty."

Larkin opened the door—its creaking welcome adding to their intrigue. The crackling of a blazing fire bade them enter the pleasant room, walls paneled in rich, deeply stained wood, floor-to-ceiling bookshelves tucked into the walls. Annabelle felt as though if she could see the inside of her heart, it would look like this.

The warmth from the fireplace enveloped them as Larkin shut the door behind them. No sooner than their cocoon was established, Larkin pressed into her, his lips dove for her neck.

Unadulterated current coursed down her body. "What are you doing?" She struggled with her words as she recovered from the exquisite shock.

"Exactly what you've asked of me." Larkin's words were muffled as he continued to press his lips around her ears until they found hers.

She let his kiss lead her back to soft memories. Tucked into a corner of the study's Chesterfield sofa, Annabelle had whiled away the most contented periods in her life. The sooty smell of the fire and the musty vapor of the books warmed Annabelle's heart—the complex vernacular of human physiology, the low octave of masculine voices, and even the acrid bite of redolent cigars. Those times wove themselves so deep in her subconscious, they became permanently entwined with her definition of happiness. That was what Larkin meant to her.

Though Larkin's hands grappled with her welcoming skirts, the sharp scent of burnt cedar pierced her nose. Annabelle's eyes opened, reeling her into the moment. Logs cracked as flames lapped the stone grate.

A languid tendril of smoke wove from a cigar propped in a silver tray on the bare mantle.

Her mind intent on her prize, the question of the cigar's owner did not pierce her psyche. Annabelle channeled a bit of her Aunt Maude. Urban legend whispers of hushed exploits and tasty tidbits dropped from her aunt's lips after too many glasses of French champagne, served as a veritable how-to seduction manual. She had heard a lady's lips around the thick barrel of a cigar would drive men to all depths of misdemeanor.

Annabelle pushed Larkin away, then strolled around the perimeter of the room, running her gloved hand lovingly over the books. "Set just for us." She glanced around the room before she met Larkin's now stoic gaze.

His facade cracked at her lilting suggestion. "The gods have smiled."

She must have him. Or she would burst. The thrill of a shackleless choice spurred her on. "Have you mustered your courage, Doctor Larkin?"

"Courage for what?" He was suddenly all wide-eyed innocence.

Boldness took over. Perhaps she could satisfy her heart and her head. Many married couples had arrangements outside their vows. Perhaps freedom from that golden noose gave love space to blossom? Theirs could be a love that spilled from their bed into their work. Of course Larkin would allow his lady-love a by-line, and even more. "A gentleman wouldn't force a lady to answer such a personal question."

"A gentleman wouldn't be found alone with you." He reached to touch her cheek. "And a lady wouldn't bring a supposed gentleman here with the promise of her charms."

Annabelle loved the rakishness which threatened to usurp Larkin's stately demeanor at this most opportune moments. Her prize in sight, she crossed to the fireplace and picked up the cigar—it was a less elegant suggestion up close. Gentleman , as such, were overrated in her date book.

"I've never truly aspired to be a lady." Annabelle frowned as struggled to manhandle the thick cigar into an artistic pose. "I'll take that as a compliment."

"It was meant as one." Larkin came to her and launched the cigar through the grill as he tossed his top hat on the side rail with a muffled clatter. "Nothing's coming close to those lips but me."

His kiss was full of more passion than Annabelle anticipated. She kept his hand in hers as she stumbled back to catch her breath and heaved for a moment or two.

A bust of Socrates loomed down from its perch just below a high window across from them. The sun streamed in, adding an effervescence to the air that matched their mood. Annabelle regarded his sanguine expression. *Watch me. I dare you.* She tipped her head back as Larkin encircled her waist with his hands and hoisted her alongside his hat on the side rail.

The rest was child's play.

Chapter 10

Annabelle wriggled her bare toes against the starched sheets then rolled over to stretch long on her side. There really wasn't a more marvelous sensation on Earth. Her eyes found Larkin's latest unfurled letter and she smiled. Catching the letter between her fingers, Annabelle propped herself up for optimum enjoyment of her umpteenth read of yesterday's news. Over a month had gone by since Annabelle had given herself the not unpleasant title of adulteress. She adored having a secret. Larkin's touch had brought her body to life, as if for the first time. But there was more to their liaison than a simple dalliance, Annabelle was sure of it. The way they holed up together for an afternoon at that little inn, on the wrong side of the river, but quaint and clean, with an innkeeper as quiet as a church mouse. Weaving through medical complexities, and reading the latest medical journals, the ones from the States were shockingly pioneering, had been simply heaven. Their heads and hearts were conjoined, and human law could not stop or separate them. Annabelle traced the letter's salutation and realized she was thoroughly happy.

⚭

Dearest Angel,

I am seriously concerned over the state of my chest. The alarming fact is it may no longer be able to contain my heart which has expanded to such a size as of late that it threatens the confines of my thoracic cavity.

His attempt at humor. He really was such a dear.

Our latest conversation regarding Lister's germ theory, and its application in almost every, if not every, sector of medicine, has not left my head. Your mind is really so nimble—despite my training, I feel as though I may never be able to keep up. I wonder if you would consider collaborating with me for a submission on our theories to The Lancet ?

Annabelle's beam expanded. A professional collaboration with the man she loved. And she had only gently hinted at her frustrations with her father's lack of academic acknowledgement. Larkin had taken the bait and run.

I don't want to make things difficult between you and your father, but darling, he really must be made to see your value. Perhaps I'll drop a hint at the club, we're meeting Wednesday to discuss the new chap from Edinburgh, interested in sanitation and smallpox I believe. I think his work is quite valid, though I suspect your father feels otherwise...he really must awaken from his cobwebbed dreams.

Regardless, my dear, no one can stop you shining, I'd just like to be the one with the steel wool (and bouquet in hand, of course.)

I can no longer sign in my typical fashion, as over these past few weeks, you have reformed me. I'll send a carriage for you Thursday, we can lunch at that tiny inn in Castlebluff, charming with its discrete side entrance.

Your reformed rake, Cassius

⊗

Annabelle considered herself exceptionally lucky to be a woman of democratic morals and little remorse. She could have the very best of Larkin without the quotidian frustrations of residing under the same roof. There would be no discussions of household tribulations or discovering he was slightly less dashing in his flannel nightshirt every night. There was a place for women like her, and Olivia. Both could be equally happy, if one remained blissfully unaware, and the other kept her conscience subdued.

It was this. Or the tempting articles Aunt Maude had paraded within Annabelle's reach—an heir to a soap fortune, a weathered though still distinguished sea captain turned salt merchant, and a cool dark thing from Bombay, with an exotic turban and black eyes. But she returned to Georgie Gosling. There was a certain something about his boyish lisp and gargantuan stature Annabelle no longer found so unappealing. His monstrous fortune, amassed in the pursuit of rotting the teeth of every soul in the Empire, had much to do with her change of heart as well.

Their marriage would provide quite a satisfactory arrangement for Annabelle—a cover for her multitude of dalliances—with a person she could actually stand—if only for several hours in succession.

Annabelle allowed herself one last shiver of self-satisfaction before she kicked off her bedcovers and sat up to fully greet the day. She held Larkin's letter to her nose and inhaled, the faintness of his musky aftershave teasing her nostrils before she leaned over and rang the bell for Sarah. Life surely has a funny way of righting itself. Annabelle refolded the letter and stuck it between the pages of Wuthering Heights before weighing it down with the newly published Middlemarch for safe keeping.

No use tempting her. An occasional twenty here or there was of no matter, but as much as Annabelle had warmed to Sarah, she felt it was time Sarah's games were cut short.

※

Annabelle had shooed Sarah away before her hair had been properly plaited and the row of cream fabric buttons completely fasted at the back of her sky-blue confection that made Annabelle think of Royal Copenhagen china.

It was as if her fingers had been replaced with toes, Annabelle had never seen her maid in such a state. Sarah hadn't even cracked a corner of her mouth at Annabelle's well-executed impersonation of Georgie's impending proposal. Annabelle couldn't be sure what bee had blown under her bonnet. When humor failed, Annabelle tried a honeyed approach, but her gentle questioning had only made Sarah bristle.

"Take the afternoon off. I won't need you. I'll speak to Mrs. Mingle and then I plan on spending the day with father."

"Won't need me," Sarah huffed. "That's the thanks I get for me mum's word on all your little affairs—dead dogs and love letters."

"I was just trying to give you the afternoon in case you needed it to yourself." Annabelle almost wanted to laugh—her criminally-inclined lady's maid a sentimental streak. "You seem rather flustered but won't say why."

Sarah's sullen expression remained.

"Do what you like. But mother has found out about Molly and you've been well-compensated for your silence on other matters. No need to put your guard up."

"I'm sorry, m'lady. It's just I've got a lot on me mind. There's talk of Ol' Freddie wantin' to have words with me."

Annabelle thought she recognized an almost imperceptible wash of fear in Sarah's face. Sarah, who would have told the Devil himself to shove off.

"Likely all poppycock, but it gave me a right scare."

Annabelle sighed. "Proper poppycock indeed. You're safe here. Come now." She took Sarah by the shoulders and led her to the door. "Do as I say. Take the afternoon. Pack a picnic and take a stroll in St. James. Clear your head. You'll be as right as anything by this evening."

Sarah worried the edge of her lip before offering a small smile. "If Freddie don't find me on the way. His boys are clever."

"You better take an extra slice of treacle if you're going to sound like that, Sarah. You're the most wickedly clever person I know. You have absolutely nothing to worry about."

⋙⋘

Annabelle bounded down the back stairs. Funny Mrs. Mingle had raised a multitude of questions over the menu for her father's colleague dinner tomorrow night. Her mother's magical migraines often pulled her from her domestic duties into the comforts of her well-blanketed bed and piles of milk toast. But truth be told, Mrs. Mingle sat solidly at the helm of Fernhead House, mooring her ship with the firm hand of an open-hearted country woman. Mrs. Pierce was simply the decorative figurehead, easily assaulted by rough waters.

As Annabelle descended into the malty kitchen air, her stomach let out a roar that would have put Sanger's circus lions to shame. Skipping breakfast had not been wise. She had heard her father rise early, likely for a house call, and did not prefer to share the table with her mother for sole company.

The usual culinary pandemonium was in full swing. Great pots set on the black stoves bubbled mercilessly, sharp knives danced as they made short work of great piles of roots, and a rack of lamb lay glistening on a side table. The earthy scent of cabbage and carrots hung in the background.

"Aren't we blessed to see you in the light of day." Mrs. Mingle chuckled as she finished grating nuggets of nutmeg over a bowl.

Annabelle laughed and swept into a deep curtsy.

One of the scullery maids giggled, Annabelle hated she couldn't remember her name.

Mrs. Mingle nodded at Annabelle. "Well then, yer Highness, can ye do us a favor, and put on airs over in that corner so my girls don't take a spill over you?"

"I'll do anything you ask of me, my sweet,' Annabelle rose and leant over the workbench to give Mrs. Mingle a kiss on the forehead. "As long as I can commandeer an enormous slice of bread and jam. Momma has been taken with her unfortunate afflictions and with Papa away, I spend the morning counting my blessings in bed."

"Blessings a-plenty indeed." Mrs. Mingle crashed her great whisk down, sending a cloud of flour across the workbench. "Your momma's fed her migraine troves of milk toast and honey tea, so I've used the last of yesterday's bread." She twiddled her fingers as if conjuring a bit of universal ingenuity. "But I've some dough rising now. It'll take ages to bake a loaf. . ."

"My greed will manage without. I'm sure that's a wedge of seed cake or—"

"I hadn't finished, my love." Mrs. Mingle eyes twinkled. "I've not had a bite myself." She scrubbed her hands on her apron. "I'll get the iron ablaze and we'll lob off some of that dough and make us some wee jacks. It'll be a great treat."

Mrs. Mingle was three steps into her task before she turned to look at Annabelle who had hiked herself up on a undirtied corner of the workbench in front of the stoves. "Did you think the kitchen needed a bit of adornment this morning my dear or could you help a woman out?"

Annabelle jumped guiltily from her post. "You know I'd burn the poor buns to smithereens. Don't you remember when I tried my hand at making a spotted dick for father's birthday?"

Mrs. Mingle hooted as she set pads of butter blistering in a cast iron griddle. The salty smell of instant hunger permeated the kitchens. In unison, the heads of the scullery maids popped up, their necks craning at the stove. "Keep up your choppin', the lady and I have some business to attend to, but don't you think I'd forgotten you—I'll set a plate out for when you've finished with those veg." She nodded hugely as their knives stepped up their tempo.

"Now, my darling, I've masses of eggs to whip for the Pavlova tonight. Cook leaves those delicate things to me."

"You're hinting there's a job for my incapable hands?" Annabelle looked around the kitchen, ladles and spoons and tins could have belonged on the moon for all she knew. She felt a small surge of delight as she realized she was much more at home eye to a microscope or in the depths of her father's medical bag.

"There's a sharp lass." Mrs. Mingle poked her chin to a waiting clean bowl and whisk. "With all those muscles you make toting poor Molly to the cellar, you can beat those until they near jump over the top."

"You really shouldn't be using my curious mind against me."

"That mind o' yours sets you up against yourself, my love." Mrs. Mingle began to flip the disks in the griddle, their perfectly browned tops sent even more heady aromas into the room.

A sudden urge to spar overtook Annabelle. "How would you say?"

"Before I take that bait—" Mrs. Mingle gave Annabelle an appraising look. "Take to beating those whites. Get a good bit o' energy outta you."

Annabelle acquiesced and began to drag the whisk through the gelatinous lake.

"You'll be here 'til next Tuesday if go about it like that." Mrs. Mingle gave her griddle a warning gaze as if to command it to remain on the perfect flame. She crossed to Annabelle and snatched up the bowl. "Like this." And her forearm began to turn at such a rate Annabelle feared it might dislocate from her humerus. She made a move to rescue the bowl from Mrs. Mingle, who clung fast. "Your social activities have certainly picked up since that grand blow-out with your momma. "

"Meaning?"

"Nothing especially,' the house keeper's eyes swept over Annabelle's face. "I just wonder with your brains, healthy load of ambition, and that face, if you've been making ladylike choices as of late." Mrs. Mingle's whisk stopped and she pushed the bowl back to Annabelle. "There, I's got ye started."

There was absolutely no way she should know about Larkin. None. Or could she?

She winked before hustling back to her stove. "A culinary masterpiece." She pulled the hot disks from the pan and lay them to cool on the grates as she proceeded to make a second batch. "Five minutes. The tea's been on. Whisk away."

"As much as I love you, my choices are simply that. My choices. And are of no business of yours."

With more butter sizzling happily in the pan, Mrs. Mingle looked back at Annabelle. "You're no longer a girl, my love. There's weight to your actions. Take care. Think carefully over the hearts you handle—those you squeeze, and those you release."

The corners of Annabelle's mouth trembled. She knew. But how? "Sarah said you needed to speak to me about the menu for papa's dinner party tomorrow?"

"I was just getting to that." Mrs. Mingle's tone was as soft as kitten fur. "It's a mess of your father's doctor friends from the College, the folks to impress, tomorrow night?"

"Yes, and yes."

"Right. I was wondering about the change your father made to the wine. His latest delivery from the wine merchant was for a cask of tawny port rather than his typical claret."

"That's odd." While a bit of port or even currant would have suited her father just fine, for her mother, only claret would do—a defining line between the gentry and the upper class.

"And he's requested only a red Burgundy with the lamb, completely gone away the broiled oysters and champagne, his particular delight." Mrs. Mingle's expression held no trace of disapproval, only a questioning, which appeared to be more feigned than truthful.

"And lamb, not even butchered into cuts?" Annabelle looked at the great side of meat. "He typically likes to serve them something a bit more high-brow—or at least mother has taught him that. Scottish salmon or at least St. John's fish." Annabelle would have to find a gentle way to ask father about his unusual changes as of late—completely unlike him to be less than effusively generous. Thankfully Mrs. Mingle knew that the truth would not always set one free and could be counted on to keep more than a handful of family secrets.

"There we are now." Mrs. Mingle dampened the fires before taking the remaining brown, yeasted beauties from the pan and shuffled them to a platter.

Annabelle hoped she could stop this infernal whipping soon, her arm felt like it might like to murder her. Though the rain cloud in her bowl appeared to be more pert—perhaps at the notion of a sunny day. Not bad for a brain, Pavlova indeed.

"Tea break with flap cakes," Mrs. Mingle hollered to the kitchen.

Just as a round of thanks cheered the place, the sound of what seemed to be a scuffle and echoed behind the kitchen's side door. The door flung open and Ben marched into the kitchen wearing a long heavy apron, four stout plucked chickens, heads bobbing, hanging from his fingertips. "Chicken fricassee a Chez Mingle,' he announced, thrusting the birds aloft. "Along the Champs Elysees in gay Paris, you will find no finer dish. Zee Madame is a genius!"

Annabelle burst out laughing at his rather accurate mid-Parisian accent.

Mrs. Mingle applauded, basking in the compliment.

Ben whipped around, chickens nodding, to face Annabelle. His impish grin, which she hadn't seen much of these last weeks, made her happy.

"Your accent is impeccable, Ben. Are you certain of your English blood?" She tipped her head, not minding if she felt just a touch flirtatious.

Chapter 11

"I always wondered about the carriage with four black horses that passed slowly by the back lane of Hatsfield House every fourth Tuesday. The woman inside casting forlorn gazes at father. One never knows the goings on at the backsides of Longchamps." He barely managed to conceal his grin as he released the birds into the sink.

Annabelle laughed at the notion of Ben's kind but plain father carrying on with a mysterious French madame and wondered, not for the first time, how a stable boy could have unearthed such a nimble imagination.

"Sit your fancy pants down here with me and our girl for a bit of a breather." Mrs. Mingle slid the piled plate onto a rough table meant for chopping. "We got some menu items to blather about for a wee bit, then she's yours."

Ben settled himself down with the ceremony of a minister and began to baptize one of the biscuits with a sticky sweet, indigo spread. After the last gobs blueberry jam were licked from their fingers and the details of Dr. Pierce's dinner party were sorted, Mrs. Mingle left Annabelle and Ben swirling the dregs of their tea in front of the fireplace.

Ben tipped back, balancing on one of his chair's legs. "It's been awhile, m'lady." His eyes seemed to luxuriate on her face as he clasped his hands together and tucked them behind his neck. "You look well. Perhaps the scent of chocolate—and money—suit you better than the stench of the stable clothes and old ginger beer bottles?"

"Mister Gosling and I have discussed the purported health benefits of the cacao plants."

"Among other things." Ben nodded.

Annabelle gave him a look, but Ben's smile only widened.

"He is quite certain if every British citizen consumed one of his chocolate bars each day, we could cut the costs of our nation's doctoring bills in half."

"Ahh, a great benefactor you have on your hands, m'lady. Healing the British, body and soul—and his pocketbook simultaneously. How convenient."

Annabelle narrowed her eyes. "Cacao could be a great area of research." She could not imagine how.

"You know another great frontier for scientific research?"

"Yes, I likely do." Annabelle snipped, though she liked to spar. "I doubt you are aware of a new bound I am not."

"Lady Love, some days there's nothin' I'd enjoy more than takin' a pot shot at the hocks of that high horse of yours." Ben released his propped feet and clattered back to the ground and he dove in close to her.

Annabelle could smell the sweetness of the blueberries on his breath and liked it.

"Ye won't bother to guess, so I'll tell ya . The new frontier is Kentucky."

"You're of a confederate persuasion now?" Annabelle felt a flicker of worry in her stomach—or heart—she wasn't sure—but kept her expression mischievous.

"Naw,' Ben leant back. "Slavery' bollocks—nothin' to tease at. It's the racing I'm after. I'm bound out there Winter of '72, to set up proper before foaling. Little mound smack in the middle, called Versailles. Guess I'll be keeping up with the Frenchies after all."

"A teaming stable of your own?" Annabelle had never given the idea of Ben leaving service a thought. It was something his father had done, and his father, and so on. He talked great talks. Othello really had nothing on him. "You'd leave then." This war between things inside her was almost too much.

"Of course." His voice was quiet against the din of the tea break wash-up—clayware splashing, maids chattering.

She smiled, no sense of the gamine this time. "I'd miss you. You're one of the only real friends I have." Somehow honesty didn't hurt with Ben.

Ben turned red, the look of a pickpocketing chimney sweep overcoming him, displacing his sincerity.

"Swallowed your fat tongue?' Annabelle chided, breaking the spell.

"Almost," still red-faced, Ben eyed the rest of the kitchen, then reached for her small finger with his. "I wasn't planning on going it alone. That day in the stable after ye nearly murdered that official, I told you I'd keep asking and I will, m'lady. You know I will."

Annabelle let the warm of his fingertip warm her heart. Surprising how much more she had given to Larkin and still could make herself feel quite like this with Ben. The sensation strengthened to such a ferocity she started back, sending a green glass bottle and a spray roses tumbling to the ground. The empty rattle reminded her of her rolling earrings as she bent to rescue the flowers unscathed. She took a deep breath before rising, wits collected, to meet Ben's gaze and changed the subject. "Something's deeply the matter with Sarah."

"What's she been up to now?" Ben crossed his arms.

"I know she's not your favorite person on Earth. But she's in trouble."

"She's been in trouble since the day she was born."

"Meanness doesn't suit you." Annabelle glared at Ben as she set their empty mugs on the crumb-speckled plate.

Ben shook his head. "It's the plain truth. She's a right criminal. Did jail time with Mother Parker. A baddie to the bone if I dare say such a thing 'bout a woman."

"I bet Sarah's been called far worse than a baddie—but she'd claw your eyes out for the comment on principle alone."

"That's her problem. She doesn't have any aside from save her own skin. She's shifty. Always watching, turning up in places she don't belong." Ben thrust back from the table.

She had to tell him about Ol'Freddie . And the necklace. Annabelle swallowed hard and tapped the table with her palm. "There's more."

Annabelle told Ben about Ol' Freddie and Sarah's request for the filigree emerald necklace. Though she hadn't mentioned the twenty pounds for Larkin's letters.

Ben, as usual, brought up some very good points. "That ratter must be slick. I 'aven't seen any lowlifes hanging around. I would 'ave introduced myself right and proper if I 'ad ." He ground his fist into his palm for good measure. "But I just don't believe they'd recognize you dressed as a bloke. I mean they must 'ave , but there's no way to prove it." He put his hand on Annabelle's shoulder. He felt of self-reliance and trust. "Yer lucky I'm your alibi. We were muckin' about fitting Dexter with that new saddle of yours all morning. Never left the mews of Fernhead House." He shot a glance over his shoulder, then pulled her close and landed a kiss on her head. "Whose word are they going to take? A stand-up, respectable chap like myself, or a scavey criminal? Keep yer necklace. Sarah's just rustling up a bit of scare for your sympathies. Nothing more to her tale than that."

Reassured, Annabelle cut back through the kitchen, aiming to catch the side stairway up to the main floor so she could lightly jostle her father about Larkin's proposed collaboration. Though, she had to admit, its sparkling promise was slightly hampered by Ben's Kentucky departure—although still two years off. She'd be Mrs. George Gosling by then—renowned scientist, wife of a chocolate mogul, and society matriarch.

How could the hard-tacked life of a racing stable compete with that? Unless Ben were to breed a continuous flow of winners.

"You two were in some serious conversation." Mrs. Mingle cut through Annabelle's inner debate. She bustled across the kitchen.

"Not really." Annabelle lied to Mrs. Mingle's back.

Mrs. Mingle fiddled with her apron strings. "Something's afoot. It's those excursions of yours. Then your father's menu. Then those whisperings. I can only guess at the truth, but there's one article I know for sure, my sweet. I know you. Brains and S ociety aside, could do a good deal worse than that lad. Simply pining for you—with 'is good heart and handsome face." She gave Annabelle's arms a squeeze. "And he's clever. Mind me now, he'll make somethin' of himself. You don't want to meet him back someday and remember 'I knew him when' and recall you had the chance to say 'I know him now.'"

The truth in the air made it impossible to look back into Mrs. Mingle's eyes. A multitude of 'if onlys' tumbled through her mind as she let the silence between them drown out the bustle around them.

"Now my girl," Mrs. Mingle brushed her warm lips to Annabelle's cheek and released her. "Weren't you planning on spending the day with your father, now we've his affairs sorted?"

Annabelle allowed herself a half-smile. "That I was." She tilted her head and appraised the housekeeper turned cook turned mother and keeper of the family heart. "We don't need words to speak. I've my own mind, but I do value yours, more than you know."

Mrs. Mingle flushed and grappled for a corner of her apron—bringing it to the corner of her eyes. "You are my heart, my girl."

With a rush of contentment, only known when her heart was full, Annabelle wrapped Mrs. Mingle in an embrace. Even with sentiments running as high as the Thames after heavy Spring rains, Annabelle couldn't stop herself from whispering in her ear. "It really is quite scrumptious to have so many options—so many hats—so many men—so little time."

When Mrs. Mingle swelled up like a lit cannon, Annabelle skittered out of the kitchen with a gleeful shriek before she could feel the swat of well-aimed kitchen towel.

Dr. Pierce stood at the long windows in his study, his spectacles pushed low on his nose, examining the journal gripped in his hand with singular concentration. Annabelle detected a quivering energy about him, the rippling of a house cat about to pounce on a mouse nibbling blissfully on the stalk of daisy. Today it seemed, the plotting feline was in a cheery mood to swat rather than kill. Perfect, Annabelle thought to herself. I know just how to tickle under his chin—then I'll find out what Larkin and he have discussed.

"Ready for some kind of merriment I see?" Annabelle trilled as she swept into the room.

Dr. Pierce tore his eyes from the pages to his daughter and grinned— as if he had just taken first prize in the sailing competition or shot a much younger man in a duel. "Merriment indeed, my pet." He shook the journal. "For my, ney , our , article has been made the prime feature of this month's Lancet.

Annabelle crashed into her father with a hug, rumpling the journal between them. She could hardly decide what was more wonderful— having written the feature or having her father acknowledge her contribution. Oh heady day indeed!

After a few moments of generalized jolliness and jumping about, the two disentangled themselves from one another laughing.

"I'm sorry to have crushed the pages, papa ." Annabelle fingered the now rather pathetic looking publication.

"No matter, my darling, I've ordered extra copies so I can gloat with the boys over dinner tomorrow night. Nothing seems to go quite as well with an earth claret than a good boast about our family genius."

Annabelle flopped onto the sofa—a rogue wire from her bustle prodded her sharply in an uncouth locale. "I quite agree—' she pressed up onto her elbow. "But we haven't any claret. Mrs. Mingle told me just this morning you requested tawny port instead." She let the sentence take the shape of a question.

"Fool's choice on my part. Harrison and Sons sang some song about only having subpar claret in stock, so I settled for their best ruby port."

Annabelle made sure to keep her face bland. They had been ordering from Harrison and Sons ever since she could remember. But Harrison always kept a selection in stock, as she had learned when her mother was taken away from the drudgeries of menu planning with her convenient migraines. But with Dr. Pierce's demonstrative mood, and her own agenda, Annabelle felt it was best not to press the matter, though a stir of worry remained.

"There's another reason why I'm riding heaven's beams, you know." Dr. Pierce settled himself onto the couch beside her, assaulting the tufted upholstery, with this month's Lancet, now rolled into a tight cigar.

"There could be no other news to bring you to such heights," Annabelle turned and propped her chin on her hand. There was no better company on Earth than her father when he was like this.

Her father released the journal and brought his fingers together, tips touching, over his chest—a bit like a laughing Buddha. "I think you'll be quite proud of your old Papa. Things should smooth out quite nicely for you, as I always hoped they would."

Could things get any easier? Annabelle couldn't imagine how much more could fall into place.

"I'm glad you've come up to me as you mentioned over poached pears last night." He blinked slowly, in obvious enjoyable anticipation of his news. "With one word from you, my darling, many suffering issues with be resolved."

"What word?" Annabelle was enjoying the guessing game. "Battyfangler? Hornswoggler? Wopperwagtail?."

"No, no,' Dr. Pierce's smile dipped momentarily before he found frivolity with a chuckle. "Monosyllabic. A baby could manage it. I'll say no more. As in truth, this bit of good fortune is not really mine to tell."

"Come now, papa ." A quiver of vexation tinged Annabelle's words. "Out with it. There'll be no secrets between us." Her words hung thick, as if wishing to highlight the multitude of things—old and new—left unsaid.

"It wouldn't be fair to steal the pleasure from your Uncle Horace."

Annabelle felt as if she has been struck down by a North Ayrshire gale force wind. She could almost feel her teeth chatter. Her eyes settled on the intricate geometric diamonds and scrolls of the Oriental rug, as if a reply would appear from beyond their dizzying illusion. She hadn't thought of Dr. Christianson since the Foster's engagement ball, when Maude had swept in with her scathing remarks which had brought such a satisfying silence to his thin lips.

"I've invited him up to tell you the good news himself, any minute now."

Each of Annabelle's vertebrae came to terrifying attention. If she had been a cat, her fur would have stood as tall as the spines of the Hylaeosaurus skeleton at the Crystal Palace.

The sound of a metal knobbed walking stick rapped on the study door with no warning footsteps. There was a brief flurry of voices before the door breezed open and their dark-headed, ruby-lipped Irish maid, almost fell into the room as she announced, "Dr. Horace Christianson, Dr. Pierce," a bit breathlessly.

"Michael," Dr. Christianson nodded at Dr. Pierce. "I'll tell the doctor, Kitty."

Chapter 12

Christianson's eyes steeled as if he could devour Annabelle's soul.

Annabelle met him with a saber-raised gaze. "Uncle Horace." The twisted euphemism of 'uncle' with its many unspoken meanings felt sour on her tongue as the room hung in silence. Some sins could never be forgiven.

"Horace, my friend," her father was on his feet, hand extended. Annabelle despised his honest amiability. He shook Dr. Christianson's hand as if priming a reluctant water pump.

A lift of a brow brought crinkles around Dr. Christianson's eyes, leaving the trace of evil doings to splinter onto the rug. To a casual observer, he appeared the most pleasant of men—and had been, for that short while, so long ago. "Annabelle, my dear, is it possible you have become more ravishing since the Foster's ball?"

His compliment with subtle unseemliness took her off guard. Her eyes flicked to her father, still beaming.

"I couldn't agree more, Horace, I have noticed an extra glow around her cheeks and prance in her step. Quite a picture you are, my pet."

Pet. Collared, leashed, caged. Annabelle acknowledged, with a sigh of defeat, it summed up her situation disgustingly well.

"You know, Horace, Annabelle deserves a great deal of gratitude for her assistance with my Lancet cover article." He took Annabelle's hand high and sent her twirling beneath his arm before depositing her back in her seat—a little breathless at the public acknowledgement.

One small step towards that byline of hers. But now any subtle probing regarding Larkin's involvement in shifting her father's opinion would have to wait. Annabelle spread her skirts wide and settled back into the couch. "What do you think about that, dear Uncle Horace." Annabelle hoped her 'dear' cut.

"You must have seen it this morning. Fresh off the presses." Dr. Pierce snatched one of the copies from the glass coffee table and handed it to Dr. Christianson with the solemnity of a page presenting the Crown Jewels to the Queen herself.

"The Use of Chloride of Ammonium in Chronic Affections of the Liver. Rather well done. You dropped so many hints, Michael, I expected nothing but an engrossing read. I'm glad for you, both,' Christianson nodded at Annabelle. "I wish the same success had followed your philandering over that blasted recording machine." He seated himself in a delicate armchair, its frame accentuating his similarities with a well-shorn grasshopper.

"Siphon recorder, rather. Science is moving with such exhilarating speed. We must gather the best minds from many disciplines to create inventions which would have seemed extragalactic even ten years ago." Dr. Pierce settled into the other arm of the sofa opposite Annabelle. "It is a Renaissance, Horace."

Annabelle loved when her father clambered onto a philosophical pedestal—she could image her mother falling helplessly in love with his shameless idealism. Too bad it hadn't been enough.

Dr. Horace Christianson's chuckle sparked Annabelle's bones as he settled himself stiffly into the straight back of his chair.

He was never natural. Always so calculated, mechanical—so different in life than he had been in her bed. She hated she had begun to take on similar tactics—though hers she credited to self-preservation.

"You're a dreamer, Pierce, with little to boast of by way of Da Vinci, always gets you in trouble. A constant toe over the ledge of reason, slips you to an abyss of hurt. Isn't that right?" He sent a mournful look, reminiscent of an archbishop summoning a sinner's pardon—without the clear eyes of an empathetic soul.

Annabelle shot up from her seat. She artfully dodged the coffee table with an angry swirl of her skirts to hover over Dr. Christianson. "We find progress only through the eyes of dreamers, Horace. There have been difficulties in silvering the quartz fibers and the cost of cathodic bombardment has been astronomical." Glancing over at her father, though she wished she hadn't been looking for his approval, she found a new north wind for her sails and continued. "We just need to sort out the complexities of a sustainable alternating voltage in the oscillograph. We'll have a portable protype for Smithfield's by the end of next year."

Dr. Pierce sputtered at her aggressive unfounded, timeline , but she barreled on. "Bedside diagnosis of abnormal rhythms, lung disease, liver afflictions, all will be possible. And you preach on the dangers of dreaming." Annabelle stormed around the coffee table and collapsed beside her father.

To her surprise, Christianson clapped slowly, shoulders trembling, though his laugh held a rare genuine note. "Your beauty may be eclipsed by the stunning capacity of your mind. And what a perfect soliloquy to set the tone for our announcement."

He had never been so forthcoming in praising her academic propensity, but Annabelle maintained her guard. "I'm delighted to ease your delivery." She looked sideways at her father, hoping for a clue, but found none.

"May I do the honors, Michael?"

Her father bobbed his chin eagerly as he sat up. "By all means."

Annabelle smoothed an imaginary wrinkle from her skirts and settled on an expression of artful anticipation, hoping it came across as such. "It is ungentlemanly to keep a lady waiting, Uncle Horace."

"You have questioned my status as such in the past, but I will disprove your unfounded chastisements."

Dr. Pierce shot Annabelle a rueful glance. She detected a hint of jest in his eyes. How little idea her father had of the truth. And she'd let it remain so. "Then suspend social niceties and speak forthright."

"It's been many years since you've seen my son, Thomas."

Thomas. Thomas. Annabelle drummed through old memories. Vague recollections of a hawk-nosed, lanky introvert crystalized. A thin sense of revulsion from memories of a corn snake dropped down the back of her dress settled into her mind.

"He's done rather well for himself. Graduated with top honors from L'Ecole Polytechnique in Palaiseau. Then joined her Majesty's army. After he was moved by conditions he witnessed revamping the irrigation systems for the Sutlej Valley Project, he made his way to Berlin to study at Humbolt with one of his idols, Dr. Rudolf Virchow. He's just been promoted to Major-General—though I must credit his engineering rather than surgical talents on that account."

"Like father, like son." Dr. Pierce nodded at Annabelle in approval.

I sincerely hope not, Annabelle thought to herself. She recalled the rakish look on Thomas' face as he denied harassing the swans who made their home on the back lake at their estate in Derbyshire. This despite the plum-sized rocks which deposited themselves mysteriously at his feet one-by-one with each chord of their gardener's rebuke. No, pretension was not a word which came to mind as she stretched to remember Thomas. "He must take after his mother."

"Annabelle—" Her father sent her a look full of thunder.

"A sharpened wit is the true sign of an active mind." Dr. Christianson lauded.

Annabelle clung to reason, if only by kite strings. "Dear Uncle Horace, I jest gently among close company." She lowered her chin in an effort at gentility.

Christianson returned the gesture with ceremony.

"You see, Papa, I have not drawn blood."

Dr. Pierce seemed to question the validity of her statement, scanning Christianson's face.

"I see I mustn't keep this tigress baited any longer, Michael." Christianson rose and sat beside Annabelle in the manner of old chums.

The soft clarity in his eyes was so new Annabelle could not bring herself to retreat.

"My dear, your father and I have come to an arrangement. One benefiting all parties involved."

Her mind leapt to images of efficient wards full of patients, mass-produced galvanometers, recording pens hopping in time to the beating of their hearts, now diagnosed and healing. "You've helped papa find a new collaborator? Has there been a new development?"

"Always work on your mind, Annabelle." Christianson laughed. "Take work out of your precious equation. This is of a personal nature."

We've been there already, Annabelle thought.

"With all his successes abroad, Thomas has had little time in Society to find a suitable match. Now he is to be returning to London, he will need to do so—for both his own happiness, but professional standing as well. He has amassed quite a tidy fortune on his own with investments in the British Raj and is quite well-regarded by the ladies of the division."

"Come now, Horace." Dr. Pierce chided.

"You know I'm putty when it comes to Thomas, Michael." Dr. Christianson placed a firm hand on Annabelle's shoulder. "Your father and I discussed possible mutually beneficial arrangements and decided a union of our two families will be just the thing."

The syrupy looks on the men's faces felt like pegs pounding realization into Annabelle's thick skull . Recent compliments be damned. Her eyes darted to her father. "You've sold me then." An instant throbbing settled behind her eyes—her dreadful statement sinking in.

Dr. Christianson had the gall to snigger as her father patted her arm like a small child who had just witnessed their scoop of peppermint ice cream plummet to the pavement.

"Papa, you don't deny it?"

"My dear girl, that is no way to put this matter of your marriage."

Christianson's laughter dwindled and his irritatingly frank demeanor returned. "We've taken your best interests to heart. Everything has been arranged. He's due to arrive from Bombay tomorrow. We will be dining together before the opera Saturday night."

Execution in an opera house. Not what Annabelle had in mind for her untimely end, but she could imagine worse. Her disbelief stilted her outrage. She was riding astride Neptune—orbiting their sphere of dysfunction, an uninvolved observer rather than a bloodied contestant. "I am to have no say in the matter?"

"No." Christianson's declaration sounded incongruent against his honeysuckle tone.

Her father chimed in, eyes widening at Dr. Christianson. "You have quite a way of putting things." He leaned over and kissed her cheek.

Annabelle wished his affection would have brought her any semblance of reassurance. But she now realized she could trust no one.

"You've done a marvelous job spinning that hapless chocolate monger around your finger, but he's no match for you." Her father rolled on.

Annabelle preferred a pliable, simple husband rather than having a relatively unknown commodity forced upon her. Her work would occupy her mind. Home would be for show. "George Gosling may be educated differently than I, but he is kind. His proposal is certain."

"Right you are my love. He requested my blessing last week—which only spurred our discussions of Thomas."

Annabelle groaned. How had her beautiful day suddenly gone so horribly wrong? "Congratulate yourself then, on saving me from marrying a fool, and forcing me to marry a stranger."

"Aren't dark, handsome strangers to most young ladies' liking?" Christianson added. "Right out of The Ladies' Cabinet."

"A mutual interest outside of science, my girl." Dr. Pierce beamed widely at Annabelle.

Annabelle began to tick through the possible ways she could wriggle out of this catastrophe as the two men carried on. She decided to play the vapid gentlewoman for now, she'd get to the heart of things after lunch.

A blessed lull came over the study as the men paused for breath.

"I think this momentous occasion calls for a toast." Dr. Pierce announced.

"And a eulogy, perhaps?" Annabelle suggested.

"There may be a place for you on the stages of Drury Lane yet, my girl." Her father replied as he rose and headed towards a brass cart with several cut-glass decanters decorating its surface. "Perhaps a thimbleful of Royal Lochnager to mark the future joining of two great families?"

Christianson clapped his hands together. "Excellent idea."

"Are you sure Harrison's has stocked it, and you've not replaced it with gin?" Annabelle layered her voice with thick innocence.

Her father's brow wrinkled.

Christianson slapped his thigh. "Pierce, with this excitement I forgot to tell you. Mrs. Blackbloom sent a note just before I arrived. I'd told Kitty I'd relay the message. Mrs. Larkin had unexpected troubles overnight. Expecting mid-March. She wondered if you'd go 'round to examine her." His voice was rinsed with a trace of menace. "I suspect it may not be a small trouble."

Dr. Pierce sadly poured the contents of his snifter back into the decanter. "She's had me worried for a few weeks now. Never had easy terms, but this was altogether a worse matter." He returned and handed a glass to Christianson and set a diminutive serving in front of Annabelle—not before taking a moment to wet his lips and send her a wink. "My patient beckons my dear. I'll leave you with your Uncle Horace. Ask Mrs. Mingle to hold lunch?"

"I will, Papa, please give her my best wishes." Although Annabelle wasn't quite sure what those were, but she certainly wouldn't wish Olivia ill. "By all means. This Saturday then. I'd best put the order out for more port."

"Enough with the port, my love. A comment, ridden too hard, just like a horse, tires. I'll speak to you about that later."

There was an edge in his statement to which Annabelle was unaccustomed and she acquiesced. "Alright papa . Love to Olivia."

<hr />

After the door closed behind her father, Annabelle sat, dazed on the couch, thoughts too muddled to follow any one course. "You're very much a different man than the one I've met on so many varied occasions in the past."

"My son softens my edges. He's the one thing who can truly bring a lightness to my spirit. Although you have had that ability as well in the depths of my despair."

"Yes. Despair and desire. Opposing faces on the same coin. You've made that point quite clear." She had briefly peered down the shadowy corridor of the past. "Now you find my despair appealing?" The acrid whiff of smelling salts—the hateful way she had slipped into her familiar role of submission at the ball. Venus would not be a victim today. She'd ring her own wedding bells. There had been too much hard work and delightful happenstance over these past few months—chocolate fortunes to amass and the bubbling field of medicine to upend.

"I will not catch myself on your barbs this morning, Miss. Pierce."

"Pity. They've been sharpened most adequately since we've last spared."

"I'm glad to hear it. At our last match to Strauss, you were not yourself."

Annabelle had no interest in commentary on her foibles. "Thankfully I'm in my right senses today. I don't remember Thomas well. He sounds like a genuinely perfect specimen of manhood with an equally handsome bank account." She ran her fingers pointedly along her neck—blessing the wide neckline of her dress—as she kept her eyes locked with Dr. Christianson's. A point of her anatomy which had been one of his preferred. A bastion of hope waved through her as she caught petals of blush touch his cheeks. "Why has he not been snatched up by some debutant's talons? With his resume, he should have a doting, well-bred wife and children, a warm seat at White's Gentleman's Club, and a landau outfitted with four Frisians."

Christianson's flush flashed ruby before he snorted. "I've been saving him for you."

"That seems at odds with your past sentiments."

"This is the best of all possible situations. Everyone will benefit."

"Will I? Benefit?"

"Do you not recall one well-aimed ginger beer bottle? The skirted country rendez-vous with a dashing young doctor?"

Annabelle drew in her breath tight. She knew her face matched the knot in the pit of her stomach.

"There has been cause for you to deserve a cage, Miss Pierce, but out of the kindness of some," Horace put his hand to his chest, "and the ingenuity of others, you have enjoyed the freedoms of a virtuous young woman."

Annabelle set her jaw.

"You make no effort to deny your dalliances?" He appeared rather delighted. In the way a small child might be as a soil-coated worm recoils beneath jabbings with a sharp twig.

Annabelle let uncried tears drip down the back of her throat and found empathy with prisoners as the words of their unpardon echoed in their ears. She was caught but didn't allow a wrinkle or a blink expose her terror.

"Your lady's maid offered up these choice articles in hopes of saving her own neck. Your fate came rather cheaply if I do say so, my dear."

Desperation had made her maid a traitor. Perhaps Sarah's new fears were founded?

"And if I refuse?"

"You'd leave me with no alternative. Your father would be heartbroken."

Now a known scarlet lady. Annabelle's heart fell to the very depths of Hades, joining other condemned souls.

"You would resort to blackmail, rather than rely on your powers of persuasion?"

"But this is a kind of persuasion." The flinty shimmer of his stare evaporated. "You'll see, Thomas will be the very making of you."

"I've heard that promise before." Annabelle said bitterly. "There is a theme then—like father, like son?"

"In intelligence and looks alone. In personality and tastes, he is his mother's son."

"Thank Christ for small blessings. Perhaps my happiness still stands a chance."

"The sculpting I began I will now turn over to him to finish. Sometimes paternal responsibilities usurp carnal desires." Christianson seemed to allow himself a pleasurable dalliance into their past before his expression became more transparent. "He's a good man."

"He must decidedly take after Mrs. Christianson." She chewed on his comment. "Why wait until now?"

"It was not the right time before, for either of you. Thomas was taking on the world, and you were refining your charms."

Annabelle shook her head.

"We have had differing memories, that I allow you. I have known every part of you, Annabelle. Make no plans for arsenic-laced tea, you'll be pleasantly surprised with this match. A late winter wedding, in the height of the season. You'll be the envy of London."

Annabelle looked down at her free will, laying like an amputated appendage, on the dark-stained floor panels. She'd expected more blood. She stood, a dizzying ache setting at the sides of her eyes. She needed Mrs. Mingle's warm embrace. "I must tell Mrs. Mingle about Olivia and lunch." She brushed past Dr. Christianson's outstretched arms as she broke from her gentile Coliseum—unsure if she was running from her past or future.

Chapter 13

Annabelle was quite enjoying herself on Doom's Day. The mother of pearl face of the mantle clock glowed the time, 6:25pm.

"Our future lies in education of the masses. Women are shackled by an inexcusable paucity of the stuff."

It had been a very long time since Annabelle had been in the line of Mrs. Beatrice Christianson's torrents of social reform rhetoric.

"A formal education is not considered vital to a woman's domestic role. Thus she is cast aside to allow a herd of males to fill Britain's classrooms." Beatrice's formidable crown of curls formed a likeness to a Roman ivy crown. "Worse still, some feeble-minded of our political brethren doubt our capacity for critical thought."

Thomas Christianson was due at 6:30pm and the final link in Annabelle's chains would be soldered closed. Her fate tethered now to the whims of a man. But what kind of man?

The loose skin framing the soft crevices between Mrs. Christianson's nose and chin trembled with the matriarch's passion. "Men are fools. We must accept that as a God-given fact."

With her experiences of late, Annabelle ascribed to the same view.

Annabelle's mother let out a shrill yip at the comment. The chatter of the other Pierces and Dr. Christianson in the drawing room dwindled, as if the gas spigot of polite inspiration had been drawn closed.

"Most of them, anyway, current company excluded." A murmur of comedy tickled Mrs. Christianson's cheeks. "I find it so difficult to contain myself, my dear. You're lucky, Annabelle. To have a father who has raised you to be well-schooled and vigorous."

"We share a common temperament, Mrs. Christianson."

Mrs. Christianson let out a breathy laugh as guttural as the singsong frogs serenading a pond on a sticky, July night.

"I can't agree with you, Mrs. Christianson." Mrs. Pierce objected.

Mrs. Christianson whispered huskily to Annabelle before shifting herself to bring Annabelle's mother into view. "You must call me Bea. I haven't time for all that twaddle and formality."

"To what part of my assessment do you take offence, my darling Mrs. Pierce?"

"To both assessments, darling."

Annabelle exhaled. Her mother had never once been original in her conversation.

"Indeed. Annabelle has been given far too much liberty. Her father's liberal hearth-side education has led her to quite too vigorous a stride for her status."

"I say—" Dr. Pierce protested softly.

Annabelle felt it an appropriate moment to enjoy a sip of the much alluded to, but presumed absent, sherry. A few of Dr. Pierce's private bottles had been brought out for this occasion. The significance of which Annabelle was quite certain only she and the two men were aware.

"There is no such thing as too much female vigor," Mrs. Christianson chorused. "On my eighteenth birthday, after the candles were blown, my mother announced to the party she refused to have any daughter of hers sitting around with her mouth gaping open, waiting to be married."

Annabelle swallowed her laughter, and the sherry, at Mrs. Christianson's candor. The inky folds of her indigo skirts, and her dignity, remained unscathed.

"Here, here ." Dr. Christianson raised his near-empty glass. "To feminine virility, intellectual and otherwise." He winked at Annabelle.

"Here's to the majority,' Beatrice Christianson held her full glass aloft, 'to the vim and vigor an education brings. We must look for is a healthy dose of courage and a propensity for growth in our populous." Mrs. Christianson gazed off into the distance as if communing with her muses, "I have complete faith in the capacity of the British people. If they have education and leadership. The ladies at the COS have these jackabald notions that fecklessness and a hopeless incapacity for thrift and planning are the downfall of the London poor."

Annabelle questioned just how bad Thomas could be—with a mother like this. She felt a momentary pang as she briefly considered how different her life would have been if she had grown up under different wings. Another pang followed, as she immediately felt disloyal to Mrs. Mingle.

"That is what Mrs. Foster always says." Mrs. Pierce chimed. "Poor slatterns, muddling through their days."

"Diane Foster has spun sugar for brains. The notion that poverty is a character flaw to the degree of Shakespearean villainy makes me crazy." Mrs. Christianson looked at the two men. "You cannot disagree."

Annabelle, finding a pleasant space in the silence, whispered to Beatrice she also agreed the moral taint of pauperism was utter rubbish, and left the group to stare awkwardly at each as she went to freshen her drink. Halfway to the brass drink cart, Annabelle looked down to find Christianson's glass in her hand as well and wondered at her occasional subservient regressions. Her father's glass remained empty in front of him, as her quiet commentary.

During her slow journey for refreshment, Annabelle recalled her father haltingly relaying the news he had lost more than half his worth in his (and her) ideological pursuit of bridging academic science and clinical practice. Such a devastating reduction in funds could send the family plummeting from their hard-earned rung in the Upper Ten Thousand. Not to mention destroy his marriage, though the thin tethering of which Annabelle believed he remained unaware. Thus Dr. Pierce had set his sights on his protégé to right his wrongs. If he had requested Annabelle don scarlet boots and promenade the harlot streets to bolster his accounts, Annabelle would have been less offended, for at least an occupation in evening sales required some skill and forethought. But all he requested of her was to accept the offer of one Thomas Christianson.

It would be a private partnership between their fathers. An act of patronage on the part of dearest Uncle Horace. Despite his remarks, his sustained confidence in the ultimate success of her father's machine would save the family from financial ruin, provide a sounding board for her father's revolutionary ideas, and a real opportunity for financial gain for all parties involved.

Her father sealed the crypt of her future with his final sentiment, "I have never asked you for anything before, and have allowed your every whim. Come to me in my hour of need."

She reached the drink cart and returned to the present. Her hand clutched the octagonal stopper, shaking in anger at the memory, as did the amber sherry, which she streamed into the two glasses—though no drops landed away from their mooring. The clock let out a mechanical chirp as its hands pointed to her destiny at the number six. Without a thought she lifted her glass and downed its contents, its temperateness at the back of her tongue bracing her spirits.

A rap on the door of the drawing room sounded before Kitty breezed in, her cheeks bright, a treacle-sweet mien made the giddy tone of her announcement melodramatic. "Dr. Thomas Christianson, sirs and ladies."

Annabelle almost lost control of her fingers, glasses in tow, as she drank in the charms of the man who strode into the room, beaming with the confidence of a practiced Adonis. The idea of flesh-and-blood Prince Charming falling into her lap was almost as overwhelming as the proceeding notion that her happiness might not have gone extinct after all.

"Dr. Pierce," his smile was as sincere as a Newcastle greengrocer's, though his pristine teeth belayed his privileged upbringing. He crossed the room to meet her father, who rose to his feet.

"Thomas, my boy, I haven't seen you since you were shipped off to Eton." Her father turned to acknowledge his parents. "Could you be more proud?"

Annabelle's knees went weak as Thomas brushed aside Dr. Pierce's handshake, and almost picked the smaller man up in his embrace.

From over her father's shoulder, his eyes met hers, with what appeared to be a kindly question. When she started at the acknowledgement and her blasted knees threatened to take leave, he flicked a wink her way.

Her heart winked back. Most like his mother, Annabelle thought. She feared the same sticky countenance Kitty had worn was beginning to creep accross her face as well.

Thomas kissed Mrs. Pierce lightly on the cheek, and his mother more heartily, eliciting from both women a sigh of pleasure and the happy maternal chortling respectively. He made his way to his father, slapping him on the back, before the latter wrapped his arms around his son, his face ignited with genuine affection.

The effect Thomas had on Annabelle was almost as remarkable the second time he caught Annabelle's eyes. But she commanded her legs to carry her towards him. They met just to the side of the gathering—all heads snapped to witness their exchange.

"Miss Pierce, I must offer my sincerest apologies."

Annabelle blinked. "Goodness, why?" He was even more marvelous looking up close.

"I'm afraid on our last meeting I had the disastrous impulse to cast a slithery friend into parts unknown, and cement my very first, and I hope only, enemy." He placed both hands over his heart with a mischievous downturn of his mouth. "I hope you can find it within your heart to forgive me, and we can be friends."

Annabelle was quite sure she could. "Eve was spiteful with her appetites, and in these uncertain times, a union of feminine wiles may be most prudent."

"Then I offer my hand to the Lady Eve, and to you, Miss Pierce." He extended his hand with an easy smile.

Held by his magnetic gaze, Annabelle offered the sherry glass in her right hand to Thomas with unladylike gusto. She wove, he dodged. But her dancing skills, of which she had been previously rather proud, failed her. She watched in horror as a shimmering arch of sherry sailed to meet the artic white teardrop of his dress shirt exposed between the dark lines of his long-tailed coat.

Her target did not miss one beat of their new tune. He took the empty glass, released the widest smile of the evening thus far, and kissed Annabelle's hand with sweet ceremony.

"Your shirt—" Annabelle sputtered.

"The latest in Parisian fashion. Patterns are the thing this season." Leading her back to their parents, he dropped his voice. "In truth, this damn straight jacket's a bit large. There's a hidden button so I can tighten the panels, it will cover your decoration beautifully." The conspiratorial twinkle in his grin made Annabelle, along with the rather heaven of the past several minutes, forget the smattering of romantic involvements she had found herself intertwined with as of late.

Annabelle expected the cannon to be let off somewhere between Mrs. Mingle's foie gras and her salmon mouse. But it never did. Frankly, she couldn't detect even a hint of a fuse. Mrs. Christianson began a diatribe—to her right—on the nebulous nature surrounding the status on child labor. To her left, Thomas offered the perfect foil to his mother's stimulating but exhausting energy. He smiled (as was his resting countenance) and offered soft 'here-here's' of praise but let his mother salute her soapbox. Her parents and Dr. Christianson skipped lightly over common political topics, leaving Mrs. Pierce to play peek-a-boo with her reflection in the cutlery when the discussion moved into medical topics.

Annabelle thought she heard Olivia mentioned. She'd have to ask father later. Her own woes (now with this wonderful change of face) had pushed more than superficial niceties from conversations with her father. As no mention of the arrangement between the two families came forward, Annabelle found herself much less prickly on the matter, and was content to enjoy herself in present company.

Mrs. Mingle had outdone herself for the occasion and escalated the gastronomic joys of the evening with her rendition of a Neapolitan opera cake. When Kitty wheeled in a second cart, small dishes of ice cream and flaming cherries jubilee, Annabelle was at a loss. How could she downplay the desperation the excessive offerings smacked of? And how could she stow portions of each? She intended to exhaust her appetites tonight.

Dr. Christianson offered a toast which spoke of warmth and family, though Annabelle continued to focus on his recent shapeshifting. Over raised glasses, Annabelle could make out her father mouth, "Thank you." Despite the wonders of the evening, Annabelle had not forgiven him completely, but allowed him a gentile bob of her head in reply.

When their desserts came around, Annabelle hesitated, torn between greed, manners, and nerves.

"One of each, to share?" Thomas offered.

Annabelle sent him a grateful smile as Kitty cozied two plates and spoons between them. "Mrs. Mingle knows my weaknesses."

"Weaknesses," Thomas scoffed. "That word would not have the audacity to find itself in the same breath you are mentioned."

If only you knew, Annabelle thought. "Very chivalrous, Dr. Christianson." She speared a triangle of the tri-colored cake. "Perhaps to a fault?" She held his gaze and found his melted her efforts.

"I have many faults, Miss Pierce. Though chivalry is one only when sweets like these are not involved."

Before Annabelle could blink, he snatched the morsel from her fork.

Annabelle looked at him, unbelieving. He was leonine, equal parts charm, propriety, and imp, balanced by a puckish intellect. She well may have to truly thank her father—someday.

At the same time, devil met devil and the two collapsed into each other, shoulders heaving at the shared joke.

"Truce then?" Thomas offered her the last spoonful of creamy cherries. "A token of my reform as my fondness for corn snakes has significantly diminished?"

Annabelle accepted the scarlet orbs as a peace offering before Mrs. Pierce made a comment on their two bright offspring, apparently oblivious to the sparks beside her, and launched into her thoughts on the shortcomings of the proposed Married Women's Property Bill.

⚭

The Covent Garden Opera House was the first place Annabelle ever carried out a long-distance flirtation. The neat lines of penguined members of the Upper Ten Thousand served as a perfect backdrop for coy bats of her fan and pointed manipulation of her opera glasses. These maneuvers had begun as a method to evoke a reaction from a newly married Larkin. Annabelle had found Olivia's nuptial glow most vexing. Finding her ruse successful, she continued her coquetteries to the curiosity and distress of many a male, and female, heart. The brocade drapes, gilded ceiling, and arias of the operatic divas provided a perfect milieu for her successes. Annabelle, neither speaking Italian nor finding much in common with the weeping sopranos, found this a most agreeable pastime indeed.

Tonight, it all seemed fresh on Thomas' arm. Nestled in the back corner of the box, Annabelle and Thomas explored the varied corners of their minds in muted whispers and silent laughter. During the hansom drive to the opera, they had discovered their mutual unappreciation for the libretto itself, improved regard for the orchestra, and highest esteem for the bevy of human nature spread at their disposal for review and critique. Thomas secured another rung in her heart after he offered rather astute observations on the inverse relationship between the diameter of a woman's ear bobs or the size of a gentleman's protuberant abdominal luggage, and their general propensity towards Tory persuasions.

Saccharine looks from their fathers sent them into silence.

Thomas eyed Annabelle. He produced two pairs of mother-of-pearl clad opera glasses and after joyously flipping the binoculars right-round on their handles, he handed one to her. "A diversion."

Annabelle wondered if Thomas knew of their plans. He seemed a bit too familiar—though this was something she would continue to encourage—but had made no reference to them. She sighed. All Annabelle knew was she could decidedly feel the heat from his body again now and she would give herself the luxury of another viewing. Leaving her opera glasses in full salute, she slowly turned her neck towards him. She started when she encountered two twin eye pieces just inches from her own.

"Shall we remain like this for the rest of the evening?' he whispered. "A masquerade?"

"I much prefer to converse with an unmasked stranger." Annabelle withdrew her glasses.

"The lady's wish is mine." Thomas lowered his. Their eyes remained fixed on one another.

"Much better," Annabelle handed her glasses back to him. "I've tired in my examination of the upper crust. I'd rather be in papa's library, elbow deep in something more meaningful."

"What could be more meaningful than art?" Thomas looked crestfallen.

Taken aback, Annabelle found she wanted immediately to remove the clouds settling over his face. "I'm finding myself in need of some refreshment."

"Of course. An ice, champagne, port?" Thomas was half-way from his seat.

Annabelle took him by the arm and shook her head. "Simply some air. Will you take me?" She hoped her doe eyes would have their historic effect—and they appeared to do just that. Without regard for their parents' pleasures, they swept from the auditorium but instead of continuing down to the piazza, they skirted the grand staircase, Thomas guiding them past the flickering gemstones and pomaded hair. Crossing a small foyer, they arrived at a barely perceptible door within the expanse of embossed wallpaper. Thomas drew her through a storeroom full of theatrical clutter and stage furniture. He flung open a pair of French doors, an icy winter draft sweeping the blush from their cheeks. They sucked in the fresh, biting air. The twinkling of the streetlamps and the London Tower made the city appear to have been overrun with fairies and lightening bugs—the daily grime of Old London swathed kindly by the night.

Annabelle let her breath and heart refresh, appreciative of the Thomas' proximity—and silence. Christianson's threat had deflated any hopes she held regarding control over her destiny. But Thomas, independent of his paternity, was rapidly edging into her heart. Even Larkin seemed expanses away with him so near.

She turned to Thomas who, for the seeming first time that evening, appeared to be lost in his own thoughts, gazing out beyond the dusky cityscape. "What's brought you back to smoggy London from the exotic corners of India?"

Thomas seemed to relinquish his reveries to the night with some regret. "The climate, among other things, finally became too oppressive. At least here my lungs can filter the soot and I know where I stand."

"That sounds ominous."

Thomas laughed. "It wasn't meant to. Politics to be dealt with abroad, from the Queen's military, and the locals, alike. I'd enough and asked for leave to return home."

"It was that easy?"

"My whole life I've followed my heart and it's never led me astray. A few months ago, it told me it was time for a change. My reputation eased the transition and last month I found myself on a steamer from Bombay to London."

"And your feet weren't on dry land for but a second before you tumbled into our sitting room." Annabelle hoped her tone sounded mischievous rather than accusatory.

For an instant, the moon polished Thomas' temple, before he took her gently by the shoulders out of the line of the doors and swung them shut in harmony. His face became more somber.

Annabelle was not sure if the sound of the latches sliding into place was the opening of her heart or the closing of his.

"You know then?"

"Know what?" Annabelle played oblivious in the delicate moment.

"Of my ,' a shot of worry flashed across his face.

"Of the arrangement?" Annabelle would have done anything to erase that look.

Thomas cocked his head. "You know of our father's intentions." His faced smoothed perceptibly. "I wasn't sure until now."

"Yes, that." Annabelle suddenly felt shy; any trace of her flirtatious battalion had vanished.

"You're not opposed?"

Her eyes darted up to meet his. She hadn't expected such a direct question. She swallowed. "I was, vehemently, I suppose."

"To all marriage then? Or ours in particular?"

Annabelle pushed her shoulders back, amazed at the openness in Thomas' face, beautiful and invigorating. It invited her unfettered truth. "All. It is too confining, too limiting for women. Everything we are is absorbed into our husband and we devolve into a remnant of our former vibrant selves."

"I couldn't agree more. It's a kind of legal slavery."

Instinctively Annabelle reached for his arm. "You're not a proponent of the institution?" Her voice sounded a bit more doe-eyed than she hoped. "Then why are we about to embark on such foolishness?"

"Decorum." Thomas said breezily as he took her hand and swept her spinning under his raised arm. Her skirts brushed heavily against the chaise and scattered a row of candlesticks, clattering on the floor. Annabelle laughed and they stooped to set them upright.

"Our marriage will advance my career and offer financial steam to your father's work." After pushing the clutter a safe distance away, Thomas held her in regard, his elbows resting between his knees.

Annabelle's satin slippers slipped on the wooden floor. Suddenly our was the loveliest of words.

"I find it hard to believe, despite your beliefs, that some well-trussed gentleman hasn't swept you off your feet by now." He gave her the slightest of prods on the shoulder, "Most of your debs have fallen into the abyss years ago."

Annabelle fought to maintain her balance, but the weight of her bustle won, and she toppled back into a heap of skirts. "Now you've done it, I look like a smashed meringue," she giggled in spite of herself, finding only humor from her vantage point on the floor.

Thomas collapsed next to her. "I'll join you then. I have a terrible fondness for meringues."

Annabelle blushed at the memory of their instant chummery at dinner. She thought of something she might say to Larkin, with his arms wrapped around in her their forbidden bed, but words didn't come. She stared back at Thomas, realizing that for this breath, she was happy.

"How have you kept the troves of suitors at bay?"

"I simply boot them aside, one by one, as they stream by, like railway cars tipped off the wrong track." She waved the tip of her shoe.

"That's not an answer."

"The unladylike answer is I simply told myself to become more and more invaluable to my father, and he would subconsciously be loath to let me go."

"Then what?"

"I was caught almost red-handed elbow-deep in the entrails of our family dog." Annabelle declared airily. And crimson-skirted with a certain Dr. Larkin but we need make no mention of that. "Mother went berserk and formulated an ultimatum. One I had hoped to outsmart in a manner until you came into the fray."

Annabelle could not tell if the look on Thomas' face spoke to a new obtusion of his frontal cortex. "It wasn't vivisection. She was ancient and I found her one morning. I was desperate to check a few points from Grey's and thought no more about it."

Thomas's smooth cheeks cracked. "Eternal damnation for the want of a cadaver?"

Annabelle propped herself up against the back of a dusty, upright piano. "You're not shocked?"

"Seems perfectly reasonable. Diving in elbow to elbow with the lads at the Royal College wouldn't have won you much—"

"Father wouldn't allow it." The sting of his repeated refusals still sharp. "I was tired of researching second hand and wanted a bit of gore under my nails so to speak."

"I admire that." Thomas pushed over beside her. "But a bit of wizardry with a boning knife bought you this sentence?"

"I used father's set of scalpels." Annabelle narrowed her eyes, both to scold him, and avoid his question. Ignorance on occasion could be a beautiful thing.

Thomas's smile grew wider by the second. "It matters that much then?"

"My work? Obviously."

"Yes. And that secret of yours."

"I have no secrets," Annabelle pursed her lips.

"That's a stance I can respect." He sat back, stretching his legs long. "And second."

The high C of the Queen of the Night's Vengeance aria—the opera below rather muted before—fractured the still. They looked at one another.

"It is quite pleasant to sit in amicable silence." Thomas remarked as the aria returned to a less jarring octave.

Annabelle swam in his deep irises for a moment longer. "An appreciation for silence is something I look for in any person with whom I spend my time."

Thomas laughed. "For having become reacquainted only for a few short hours, I am finding we share more things in common than we do not, am I wrong?"

"Without a doubt." Annabelle hoped her attraction was mutual.

"Father had mentioned you had turned the drawing room of Fernhead House into a hotbed of clinical research. How did you become so interested in your father's work?"

"Frankly he could have been an expert in the mating rituals of the Cantonese mongoose and I'd have been interested." Annabelle played with the gold buckle on her evening slipper. "It's cruel to open a person's mind, then with the top fully lifted, command them they put it to rest. Father saw my general nitwittery in all things domestic and began my scientific education."

"Boredom is the very worst torture."

His empathy was more seductive than any ploy Annabelle had previously encountered. "I intend to continue my collaborations with my father. What do you think of a wife who wants a professional life?"

"I would celebrate her."

"Celebrate or credit. I would forgo every ball forthwith if I could make a name for myself among men. As an equal, for my intellectual contributions."

"Credit is the critical word there, Miss Pierce." Thomas pushed himself aside so he could face her squarely. "You played a heavy hand in your father's most recent success in The Lancet?"

Annabelle's heart jumped. "Yes. He brings me his observations from calls and hospital rounds. Together we tease out patterns and hypotheses and I string them together. My writing is stronger than his."

"Remarkable connections you've made without a medical education. The concept of a connection between the mind and body in a disease state and review of the clinical applications of electricity were ingenious."

Annabelle feared her smile had taken on an alarming similarity to a Piccolo puppet.

"But your name was not in the by-line."

"I have pursued that elusive beast but have lost the scent each time."

"Too many elusive beasts appear in your corner of the woods, Miss Pierce. Perhaps I can offer you more than a padded bank account and companionship." He offered his hand palm up to her. "If I were to propose a lifelong safari? Would you join me?"

His joviality lifted her worries altogether. "I'd been opposed to the idea." She looked down into the pitch floor. "But I've warmed to the idea over the evening."

"That's as good as an acceptance, then." Thomas enveloped her fingers in his. "We'll be revolutionaries—reinventing the trodden tradition of marriage."

Annabelle caught his steam. "Pioneers then."

"In the manner of Percy and Mary Shelley, though without the ridiculous nuptial trappings of lace and butterflies. Rooted in intellectual exploration and service to humanity, and the pursuit of happiness."

"Haven't you pilfered that from the American Declaration?"

Thomas leapt to his feet; their fingers still intertwined. "Do shut up, Miss Pierce." He pulled her to him. "Beautiful lady, tonight is the very beginning of our ruse."

Annabelle could feel the heat of his breath and she wondered if he noticed hers quickening.

"Free to follow our hearts and inquiry of our minds as individuals, and as a collective reckoning." His linguistic caress made Annabelle feel as if a proper swoon would be appropriate.

Thomas' eyes roamed over her face, as if searching beneath her joyful expression for signs of reluctance. He leaned in. His eyes batted down for an instant. She wondered if this is what a first kiss should feel like—glorious anticipation. Allowing electricity to surge through her body, Annabelle stood suspended in the balance.

"This is new for me." He smiled quickly before settling a light kiss on her forehead. "Shall we go back, they'll be wondering."

"Let them wonder." She wondered too. Her lips were still aching for his.

As he swirled them out of the room, the conversation turned to his excitement over the International Exhibition of India in London, a most civil and stimulating ground to officially begin their impending courtship. Was two months a respectable length of time before his knee met solid ground and his voice posed the question?

The looks of regard from other men and women finding refreshment outside the theatre temporarily snuffed Annabelle's yearnings as they charged back to their box and waiting parents. Her future now seemed as open as the salty expanses of the Atlantic rather than the uncharted, gloomy waters of the River Styx. Every time Thomas looked at her, Annabelle could have been catapulted to the stars.

What was at the very core of her lifelong dissonance—which Thomas so seamlessly seemed to tune? Was it the desire to do something definite and make something out of her life, was it the desire to achieve independence, or to find love? What if her soul cried for all three—was it possible to have them all?

Chapter 14

There was always a period of time after Thomas said his sweeping goodbyes when Annabelle felt as if he had unknowingly stolen a vital piece of her.

Dr. Cassius Larkin's assault at her heartstrings ceased after Thomas had swept Annabelle's heart gently into his palm that night at the opera. Larkin's letters piled high until one day, Annabelle swept them into the blazing grate with supreme satisfaction.

Over the following weeks, luminescent debates with Thomas over the smarter brushstrokes of Cassatt or Degas and the waning validity of phrenology cloaked her memory. The aching anticipation of more sweet remembrances pulled Annabelle from bed with an ease with which the intricacies of electrolyte metabolism and statistical equations could not compete. Annabelle felt she now knew how Elizabeth Browning penned those sweet words to her Robert. Her earth indeed had recently become a particular kind of heaven and she ran happily through it barefoot.

※

One morning, Annabelle awoke from a darling dream. She and Thomas had sailed around the newly opened Suez Canal. After releasing herself from her sleepy wonders of his India, she noticed the shape her body took in her bed. She would certainly relish the day when she would follow the curve of his. Mischievously insisting the proposal would be a surprise, if not their marriage, she had begun counting the days.

When his hand went for his pocket, only to draw out a cellophane encased pear drop, her heart beat faster. When he crouched to read her his favorite lines from The Woman in White, she wondered if a loop of gold would appear between his fingers. But she commanded herself not to press. Electrified, Annabelle bounced from her bed. Sarah still had made no appearance. With the latest happy developments, Annabelle had kept quiet about Sarah's defamation of their friendship, congratulating herself on her magnanimity. Left to fend for herself in the wilderness of combs and pins, Annabelle found it no small triumph to mound her hair into a semblance of reform.

Thinking her silhouette would be enhanced by a dangling ear bob, she perused her vanity. Its top was strewn with a clutter of journal articles in revision, a few tubs of rouge (applied only with the lightest touch per Maude,) and a scatter of her weekday jewelry. Strumming over its offerings, Annabelle plucked a pair of silver pendants—pear-shaped, tipped with rubies—and jammed one to her ear.

The clock chimed eight o'clock. She'd cut into that precious hour with her father before her mother overtook the breakfast room. In her haste, the post missed its mark and fell with a refined splash into the water glass below and bobbed in the tiny sea.

Annabelle fished the floating earring from the glass, then tossed it back in its pool. It bobbed a second time. Gems would sink. She rummaged for one of her heavy opal claps and gave it the same opportunity to swim. It did. Over and over, Annabelle tossed each treasure from her jewelry box with growing alarm. Only paste would float.

She watched the pearl brooch her father had given her on her sixteenth birthday confirm Sarah's corruption. Every one of her jewels had been replaced with cheap imitation. If the water glass hadn't been positioned just so, Annabelle doubted she ever would have discovered the crime. But the pearl brooch was a step too far. Sarah knew how much she treasured it—desperation held nothing sacred.

※

Dr. Pierce chattered between great gauges of marmalade drizzled toasts and herring at breakfast that morning. Uncle Horace had been good to his word. Some revisions to the galvanometer blueprints and plans for a production line were beginning to gain traction. But now Annabelle was in search for solace, and Sarah, as she descended into the heart of Fernhead House.

"How'd you find that bitter orange sap this morning, my love?" Mrs. Mingle's workspace, likely just tidied of crumbs from the morning, was strewn with papers and pencils. "A special treat—a shock of bitter, tempered by smoothing sweet. Sums up the last few months I'd say."

Annabelle climbed onto a stool in front of the housekeeper. Agatha Mingle would have appeared quite at home with her pitchfork held high aloft a straw heap, but for the wisdom which lit her irises into dark orbs of truth. This quality kept Mrs. Mingle's position safe for life. And allowed her to say her piece without fear of retribution.

"You seem very free with your tongue this morning, dearest Mrs. Mingle."

"Shame to make this morning different than any other. I doubt you'd have me any other way."

Annabelle eyed the housekeeper for a moment before swinging over the tabletop and kissing her cheek. "No other way, indeed." She contemplated revealing the paste exchange to her but decided against it. Annabelle might consider it leverage against Sarah.

"Have you got something for me, my love, or else I'd best be back to the books. We're back in with Smithfield's." She reached over and patted Annabelle's hand. "Ye've done this family right proud, my girl."

Annabelle radiated in her motherly praise.

"But I don't see it's been much sacrifice to hold up your end of the bargain. Dr. Christianson, the Younger, is a fine man."

"I couldn't agree more, but that's enough of that. What has Sarah been up to this morning? I had to tumble myself into my stays and bastion my hair into submission."

"That girl's been stewing about something for weeks. Going about like a black cat on All Hallows' Eve. Tight-lipped as a corpse." Mrs. Mingle filed her papers aside. "Then last night after a bit of jam trifle around the fire,' she ruffled in her aprons and pulled out a folded square of paper, 'she stuffed this into me apron and asked me to give it to you today before she was off like a flash. Truth told, I didn't give it a second thought 'til now." She pushed the letter towards Annabelle.

Annabelle took the letter.

"Take a look now. Perhaps she'll explain herself in that lot."
Annabelle unfolded it, pressing the creases flat against the coarse grain of the table. The script was thick and careful. Her hand was elegant. Annabelle wondered if forgery was among Sarah's many underworldly talents.

※

Dear Miss Pierce,

Annabelle couldn't remember Sarah ever addressing her so formally, her m'Lady's had always been offered with her tongue tucked close to her cheek.

I write this piece to give you some explanation for the things that, as you read this, you may be hating me for. With your big head, you know by now, how I've managed to keep Ol' Freddie at bay during my time at Fernhead House. For that, I do feels some pangs, but as I always told you, I look out for number one first. That's what kept me a hair's breadth from the gallows. But as you will soon find out, Freddie, as I always expected he would, has had his last laugh—God, if you'd hear it, you'd think Satan sounded like an angel.

As you know my story, I'll jump in as my time is short. After I did what I had to do to get out of Newgate, I vowed to go straight. And what could be more respectable than a ladies' maid? I'd learned some la-tee-da ways from some of the jessies that lives above Ma Raddler's and I can cop quite an uppity accent. The only trouble was the references. But Mrs. Raddler reminded me of how's my mum knew your father and his lot and I got to thinking.

I finally gussied up my truss and hauled my best hat and smile to Harley Street and banged on the door. Mister Bainesworth was a bit of a blighter but I got by him and into that big room of books. A few words in with venerable Dr. Pierce, and I knew I'd hit gold. So there I was, with more black marks on my record than pages in the Bible. Mind you I never offed anyone, mighta messed them about a bit to keep me in body and soul. But there I was, rubbing shoulders with the likes of you.

I'll admit, I didn't expect to like you. I fancied I'd call you the Lady Cherry Strumpet or something far worse, but you were kind to me and looked me in the eye. You know how long it's been since someone did that?
By now I would guess you know how well I repaid your kindness. But as I says, I'm out for number one. Always. Forever.
  But now, that motto's bit me in my cheeky ass, and I reckon I'll be sunk down to the bottom of the Thames with an anvil cast around my ankles. Likely a better way to go than the way I'd planned. Though I hope not, for your sake.
  As I know I will be dead and gone within a fortnight of writing this, I want to make you the solemn, very solemn, gift of my flesh. The way you dove into Molly, like a tiger, bloodthirsty for knowledge made me proud to be a woman—to know your type exists. I can't say I've spent a breath making another soul's easier for having known me when I walked this Earth.
  But I'd like to know perhaps more persons—through you— would be better for me having been a murdered wretch. I ask, no, demand, you make me your next Molly. Rip me to shreds as you must. Tear the meat from me bones, leave nothing unturned. Suck every bit of knowledge you can from my sad corpse and put it in your writings. Think hard, think long. Let that giant brain of yours flex itself and let me be the key to one of life's mysteries.
  Just a simple bastard twat from Dorset Street hoping to leave a little legacy and mend the only friendship I ever had.
  Love from the grave, S

PS. Go in for that nice bloke Thomas. Larkin's a prick if I ever saw one.

⚜

  My father and his lot? The other way she'd planned? Annabelle underlined the damning words with her finger, feeling as if her face could slip off her skull in shock. And her bizarre legacy?
  "You look as if you've seen the seventh hound or Judas himself,' Mrs. Mingle nodded at the outstretched letter, "May I?"

119

My father and his lot. Annabelle relinquished the letter. "How could my father have possibly known Sarah?" She wondered if she was prepared for the answers. "Before her coming to work here." She hoped she had been on the payroll of a patient or had been a patient at the College's charity infirmary. But the acid boiling in her stomach told her their connection was anything but cursory.

The ruddy apples of the housekeeper's cheeks blanched, as if Artic winds suddenly pervaded the kitchen. "Must've." Her eyes flicked around the kitchen. "Must've."

"You're a hellacious liar, Mrs. Mingle. There's nothing my father doesn't keep from you. His skeletons are safe in your closet." Annabelle smacked her hand on the table, sending the ledgers and lists to cascade to the stone floor.

Sad Bassett hound eyes met Annabelle's.

Annabelle would have quickly offered kisses and apologies in the past, but dread and a distain for ignorance drove her on. "Start from the beginning, I want to know everything."

As Mrs. Mingle obeyed, setting her story in the days Michael Pierce and Horace Christianson were eager and reckless medical students at The Royal College, a determined scratching sounded against the back door of the kitchen. A plaintive whine accompanied more hurried pawings.

Mrs. Mingle pulled herself from her seat with what seemed like relief. "They've a new hound, special trained for Lord Crispin. Nice-looking pointer but his manners aren't set in yet." She ambled towards the door, pausing mid-way to take a reed carpet beater from the wall. "He could jump the walls of London Castle. Now you furry bugger—" Her voice hushed into a gasp as she slammed the door behind her.

Annabelle heard a few blunted mutterings, but before she could move to investigate, Mrs. Mingle pressed through the door ajar only far enough to allow her to pass. Her face was stony.

"Lock that staircase door and the one to the main."

This was the voice she had used before sweeping Annabelle off to her sister's seaside cottage. Annabelle rose to follow her commands—her fingers feeling of ice as they drove each bolt into its home.

"What are you about?" Annabelle hissed; the kitchen now barricaded.

The whining and pawing of earlier recommenced.

"Shall I have a go at him?" Annabelle crossed to the housekeeper and reached for the reed cleaner.

"No." Mrs. Mingle whisked it behind her back. "We've had a development, Annabelle. With Sarah."

Annabelle gave Mrs. Mingle her best withering look and brushed past her, throwing the side door open wide.

Her feet met with a rumple of muddied skirts. The movement dislodged the heap and a limp hand fell from the jumble. Annabelle recognized a head as it rolled in her direction.

Sarah's very dead eyes met hers.

Annabelle had encountered human death before without much pangs, but the glassy expression of terrified defiance caught in her soul.

❈

After Annabelle allowed herself a private storm of grief in her rooms, she collected herself and made her way to the gardens of Fernhead house to think. If one could disregard the small matter of Sarah's criminal departure, and the questions Annabelle had yet to ask her father, she could have considered it a beautiful afternoon. She sat in her favorite garden chaise, a thick afghan cloaked about her legs, the rest of her swaddled in a tartan wool coat. But the only thing that felt solid to her was the steaming mug of tea in her hands and the drip, drip from the eves. The unseasonably warm day for February, turned January's snow into joyful tears in anticipation of Spring.

As with other messes the Pierce household had encountered, Mrs. Mingle took to the helm of her ship with the panache of a navy captain. The ludicrous idea of involving the police was pushed aside. Annabelle would not deny Sarah a chance at redemption—or turn down her own cadaver. Old sheets had been spread and the root cellar of Fernhead House once again became Annabelle's private anatomy lab. Though the question of what to do after she and Sarah turned the final page of *Grey's Anatomy* lingered.

A fat robin sang a merry song, as if imploring Annabelle to desist the line of questioning she would soon aim at her father. The fact that a relative stranger knew more about her father than she unsettled Annabelle. Almost as equally as when she dragged Sarah into the kitchen, her head lolling in the most unnatural angles, her poor throat had been cut clean to her spine. The thought of the expertise needed to inflict a blow with such depth turned Annabelle's stomach in the worst way. She sent up a silent prayer, to a god she was not altogether sure she trusted, that her death had been quick.

Annabelle pressed the heels of her feet into the garden path and twisted the gravel beneath her. Her father would be back from his regular Thursday afternoon call on Lady Addley's famed biliousness. She sipped her cooling tea, bergamot and lemon played lightly on her tongue. Unsure how she would make it out the other end of the dreaded discussion, Annabelle questioned if she should include the small detail of the body in the pantry.

※

Annabelle and her father approached confrontation very differently. Annabelle regarded a clashing of minds as an opportunity for clarification, evolution even. She delighted in a round at the table of discord—never shying from an intellectual cut and thrust over a splash of blackberry cordial and Brahms. The fact that she typically walked away from these matches victorious, colored her perspective favorably.

Her father, on the other hand, could keep his tailcoats upright with respectable vigor on topics of local and even international significance, political, medical, or otherwise. But in matters of a personal nature, he shied from discussions as if he were a horse, nostrils blowing, body arched, veering from suspicious entanglements.

Annabelle sank her teeth into a rich slice of pound cake. The task of broaching Sarah's connection with the Pierce family was becoming arduous. She'd been too nervous to eat anything at lunch besides a few leaves of watercress plucked from the middle of Mrs. Mingle's lusty version of salmon and cucumber sandwiches.

She nestled back into the sofa, resisting the urge to kick of her shoes and tuck her feet up. Despite her garden musings, Annabelle had unconsciously kept her tone singsong as she waltzed into her father's study earlier that afternoon. It had taken some coaxing to convince Kitty it would not be too improper to let the young lady of the house bring her own father his tea.

But thirty minutes into a playful tête-à-tête regarding the asinine use of cocaine by Dr. Helmsworth for the treatment of angina, Annabelle was still no further in her quest to coax the conversation around to Sarah and yet another dark Pierce family secret.

With her fuse centimeters from detonation, Annabelle, still too tense to join her father's afternoon epicure, leapt from her chair, wrested the crumbling shortbread and milky tea from her father's lips, and slammed the lot on the table between them.

Her father, aghast, took on a semblance to a baby bird, his crumb laden tongue visible between his lips.

"Father, Sarah's taken all my gems from their setting and replaced them with paste."

Dr. Pierce chased a few lingering bits of shortbread before he dusted himself free. "We knew of her nimble fingers. Clever. How'd you discover the exchange?"

"That's what you have to say, father? It's our fault she's lost any sense of reason—and loyalty for that matter?"

"We knew of her past."

"I can't imagine how many hundreds of pounds ran through our fingers into hers."

"It doesn't matter. Her behavior's not entirely her fault." His eyes downcast, Dr. Pierce leaned forward to recommence with his tea and biscuit.

Annabelle snatched the laden cup and saucer from his reach.

"She betrayed our trust."

123

"Hers has been betrayed time and again, early instincts are difficult to disobey." His voice was weary. He half rose and reached for his tea.

Annabelle pulled them away. "You have nothing else to say on the matter?"

"She was a consummate professional until her recent sojourn at the Bailey. She'd have sold them the instant they were pried from their settings. Nothing to be done now." His fingers settled on the saucer.

Blazing, Annabelle jerked them away and crumbled the biscuit into the tea, relishing the crestfallen look on her father's face, and tossed the sludgy dregs into the grate with a hiss. "Nothing to be done now?" The dishes met the mantle with a crash. "Now her throat's slit by some gangster and has been delivered to our kitchen door?"

Her father rocked back heavily in his chair.

"She left me a letter with the oddest request." Her father didn't move. "She wants to make her own bodily contribution to our work."

Not a whisper in reply.

"How did you know one Mrs. Raddler and Sarah's mother?"

At her last question, his eyes finally dragged up, if not quite to meet hers. "She'd mentioned her dangerous associates. It was why she wanted a fresh start. No one save for ourselves will even notice she's gone."

This was a father she could not read. "How did you come to know those women?"

"Charity wards in medical school." He gave the impression that Sisyphus's plight would have been a lark compared to his current one.

A reasonable enough explanation. But even at the remote connection, Annabelle had expected shock, horror, outrage. Her father's typical sense of social responsibility was absent. A surge of righteousness fury for Sarah blazed within her. "She's asked me to start at her head—and Chapter One of Grey's—and not rest until I reach her toes and the index."

At last their eyes met. "A very noble gift, my dear. May I suggest you begin immediately? Decomposition begins the moment life ends."

Annabelle crushed herself into the arm of her chair. "Should we not ring for the police? Do we not owe her justice?"

Now Annabelle could see emotion flicker in her father's eyes. "You are still quite young in many ways, Annabelle. Justice, like truth, and love, are relative. Would you have the trappings of a murder inquiry brought on this family? She's a convicted criminal. We would expose ourselves and for what? A limp-wristed investigation stamped 'perpetrator unknown' to be tucked away in the Queen's files. There will be none of that." Rising, her father straightened the lapels of his fawny tweed jacket. "But I will offer you this, my dear. You've not left her for all the world to see, I presume? I've heard no shrills or shrieks to inform me otherwise."

"You give me little credit, Papa."

"You play that tune mercilessly, my pet. I propose a private room for you. One week, no more, at the College. My own anatomy notes are far better than Grey's and will be yours for that week. Take upon her like only your rabid mind can and memorialize the poor chit's memory."

"But how—" A gruesome vision of herself, draped in a rust-speckled coroner's apron materialized as the reality of her proposal set in.

"I'll take care of the details, even look in on you if I can—though I doubt you'll need it."

Annabelle barely recognized the shrouded compliment.

"We'll call it an appropriate wedding gift."

Chapter 15

The London streets spoke of early spring crocuses as the morning mist fell on Annabelle's umbrella. In her other hand, she held a small basket which she swung in time with her step. Each day, before beginning the half hour walk between 212 Harley Street and the Royal College, Mrs. Mingle packed her a cannister of sweet tea and a wedge of almond tart wrapped in a tea towel. "Do me a good turn and please set away from the blades and fumes for your supper. I couldn't bear the thought of you dribbling bits over poor Sarah."

Annabelle passed through the gold-tipped iron fences guarding the pillared exterior. A few wizened glances from clusters of passing students made her feet quicken. After all, she was a woman treading on hallowed ground. Finding her way to an unmarked door, Annabelle let herself into a small passage bordering the Great Hall, moving by the rotunda-shaped lecture halls, without a second glace down the hallway which had led to her undoing under Socrates' watchful eye.

Ben had jockeyed to take her in the carriage with the irritating sincerity of a boy, jealously in love. The fact that a chaperone of sorts was expected played in his favor. But she had forbade it. The chance to be alone with her daydreams was too precious to be fractured by conversation. She wasn't ready to answer the questions lingering between them and had taken care to avoid the stable these last weeks.

Her footsteps echoed loudly into the corners of the large dissection auditorium as she passed the rows of white-sheeted cadavers. Death en masse still unsettled her. The gross anatomy lectures for the rowdy, tuition-paying students were held in the afternoons, so Dr. Pierce had arranged for Annabelle to have her mornings in the almost secret single room off the back to herself. Free to page, cut, and hum to her heart's delight.

After wrestling with its lock, Annabelle slid the slatted door open. The peeling walls of the whitewashed room shone with a tinny glow as the grey of the rainclouds came through a rectangular skylight. Her own murdered azalea bush of flesh and blood lay on a thin-legged metal table at its center. As the heavy door clanked shut and she slid its bolt into place, a calming solemnity seemed to fill the small space in contrast to the eerie chill of the auditorium—like a confessional full of forgiveness and hope.

Two days ago, tears sprung as she made her first pass with her father's scalpel from Sarah's manubrium down to her pubic symphysis. The very humanness of the thin line of fine hairs following down Sarah's belly made Annabelle's cut too superficial. It had taken three passes to reach the layer of subcutaneous fat.

Pouring the steaming breakfast tea into the lid of the cannister, Annabelle planned her attack on the thoracic outlet as she let its balmy cedar organize her thoughts. Thomas would be here soon.

⊗

Another glorious evening at the London Philharmonic the previous week, allowed the couple a quiet interlude.

"May I ask you a very ungentlemanly question, Miss Pierce?" Thomas' expression was full of the kind of jolly only an all-knowing deity would likely have enjoyed.

"Most certainly, Dr. Christianson. I'd been hoping your perfect manners might give way. Perfection can lead to a certain dullness."

He set his cup of black coffee down on an arm table beside the settee and moved closer to her before picking up her left hand as delicately as if it were a butterfly's wing.

Annabelle's heart waltzed (and may have backflipped a time or two.) *It's coming. He's going to ask.* Her other hand moved to push a loose strand of hair from her face. *He's ungodly handsome.* She wondered about the enchantments of their marriage bed. "Go on then."

His lips went her hand.

She shivered stilly in expectation.

But before his lips made contact, his fingers found hers and he held her hand back for his surveillance. "Do I detect a line of rust around your nails?"

Annabelle went to rescue the evidence from his hand. He held her steady, meeting her alarmed eyes with smiling ones.

"I didn't notice you had any other four-legged household friends who may have left this earth too soon? Although with Mrs. Pierce's historical sentiments, perhaps you kept them in a secret wing?"

Annabelle wrinkled her nose but didn't fight his grasp.

He bit his lip in a poor attempt to cage his grin. "Nothing dark asunder, I hope?"

There was something liberating in his joviality (and even regard) for her previous endeavors, Annabelle decided to plunge straight to the sordid truth.

Thomas took her tale with the same lanky stride she had become accustomed—making trips double-time around her heart. "You are most certainly the most interesting young woman I have ever met."

―――――

After deciding the best method to access the brachial plexus through the interscalene triangle, Annabelle heard a postman's knock through her thoughts.

No sooner than she had lifted the bolt, Thomas bounded into the room, a light breeze in his wake smelling of Spanish leather and moss. "It's not even nine o'clock and already it's a brilliant day."

Annabelle drew the sheet over Sarah's face before dunking her soiled hands into a bucket of now icy water by her side. "You're in better spirits than I've ever seen you." She dried her hands on the coarse apron protecting her morning dress, "If that's possible?" She felt an impulse to pat down the back of his coat to check for angelic wing roots for he seemed to practically levitate off the block floors.

"I suppose it is, my dear, Miss Pierce." Thomas moved like a colt, bridled for an early race. He lapped around the small room, his head turning this way and that, assessing its wares. He descended next to her, chest pressed to the dissecting table. His grin was wide.

Annabelle squinted. "Isn't that the same tie and waistcoat you were wearing yesterday. " She had admired the particular check of navy silk over an indigo base. It had made his eyes even more piercing.

Thomas dropped his chin to survey his suit. "So it is." With a deep inhale, and an even deeper exhale, he removed his coat. Slinging it on a wall hook, he shot Annabelle a sheepish look, she was certain he knew was devastating.

"I haven't slept a wink. One of my best chums just arrived in London,' he looked down and seemed to savor a deeper, private smile. "An unexpected pleasure. We took to the club last night and didn't leave 'til after hearty noshings this morning."

"With other nefarious activities included, no doubt." Annabelle imagined Thomas indulging in one too many cigars or even a nostril's breath of opium. This picture of him with slightly less reserve made her bodice feel excessively snug.

Thomas let out a chuckle that spoke of card games, scotch, and bay cigars. "Men. Will be men. But a proper lady would not know of such things."

"I've never made that claim, Dr. Christianson." The tips of Annabelle's ears burned, though she was enjoying their light spar, and suddenly thought Thomas might have more in common with the soot-tinged rivulets of early spring than the freshly fallen snow of the New Year. "I am unlike other women. You seemed to enjoy me all the more for it."

"Truer words have never been spoken. And I assure you,' a smooth arc of pink grew over his already peachy cheeks, 'no hearts were broken during the night."

"Well you are one of the rare individuals appearing the better without their forty winks." The musky undertone to his cologne was quickly affecting her concentration.

"You are a rare gem, Miss Pierce." Thomas swept her a kiss on her check, his full lips hugging her skin. She longed for him to linger.

⚜

When they uncloaked Sarah, Thomas was quick to compliment. "You've made jolly work, Miss Pierce. Taken a modified radial approach to expose the submental triangle."

Annabelle beamed. Pleased with the extent of her success armed only with a moderately dull scalpel and her father's anatomy scrawled notes.

"But look again. Your appetites have blunted your powers of observation."

Annabelle, unused to critique, peered into the cascade of Sarah's mauve insides, the internal reams of her oblique and inner abdominal muscles spread open like covers of an immense book. Cracking her ribs had been an effort with the bone crushers she had pinched from a set-up labeled Unknown William Tell in the main lab outside. But she hadn't gouged Sarah's heart or torn the lacey lung tissue. "I see only high marks here." She hated meeting his gaze empty-handed.

"Come back,' he said before guiding her a few steps from the table. "Start at her head. What do you see?"

"We discussed the matter of her throat, did we not?"

"Farther down. It's there if you look."

Thomas led Annabelle around the table. He pressed her fingers to frame the ugly inverted nipple she had glossed over hours earlier. Annabelle let her fingerprints find the dimpling of the skin encircling Sarah's inverted nipple—now a telltale clue to her other fate if she had not chosen to stand against Ol Freddie. At first sweep of the body, Annabelle had given the anomaly little thought.

Thomas shifted down the table and lifted the transversus abdominus back and teased the clusterings of shiny oblong masses scattered over Sarah's intestines and liver. "Take a guess, now."

Cancer. Sarah had known the gift her diagnosis offered.

Thomas fished in his pockets and produced a slim leather sheath. "Ol' Freddie or not, Sarah was not long for this Earth. We owe this to her." He slid two glistening scalpels from the case, and handed one to Annabelle, handle-first. "Come, my pioneer, unchartered territory awaits."

The rest of the week, the two moved layer by layer through the mysteries of humanness, making Annabelle want to free her own heart from her ribcage, leaving the shards to be swept into the rubbish bins by the nightly cleaning crew.

With each passing hour, words poured between them like the waterfalls of Caping Gill crashing into North Yorkshire caverns. At each anatomic landmark, new layers of the physical (and non) yielded under Thomas' sure hand, with Annabelle's growing steadier alongside his. Over short breaks for tea, in a tiny garden plotted prettily in the outside corridor, their minds met at that pithy crossroads of imagination and logic. Among the buds and butterflies, the two hatched plans for research projects and the construct of their revolutionary pairing took shape.

On their final day, with only the lymphatics and vasculature of the lower extremities remaining, the pair sat in the sunny corner of their secret garden. Between healthy mouthfuls from a sugar-crusted shortbread wedge, Thomas broached the topic which had laid dormant for the week. "Let's be serious about this marriage."

"Do you feel I've taken it too lightly?" A smile danced at the corners of Annabelle's mouth.

"No." Thomas brushed his cheek on his shoulder to rid evidence of his indulgence. "It's just I'm not in the business of roughing up young ladies' dreams."

Annabelle reached to sweep a rogue crumb away . Lucky crumb.

Thomas eyed Mrs. Mingle's basket. "No more then?"

"You've eaten five to my two."

"I nibble when I'm nervous. It's just there are various things which I must honor." He looked down and rubbed his palms on his pant legs. "It's just,' he mashed his lips together. "I've promised I'd live my life for me, I can't be any other way."

A draft of pain passed over his face as softly, and quickly, as a distant lightning bolt.

Annabelle snuggled into his neck. "I made myself that same promise." Today he smelt of clove and cedar.

His fingers found hers on the stone ledge they rested against. His lips parted but his voice kept shy in his throat.

"I'm not like other women. You know that."

"Yes. I appreciate that more and more." He shifted his weight to look at her directly. "You are much like some of my mother's friends at the Kensington Society. With those fearsome ladies to reckon with, suffrage will not be long to come."

Annabelle enjoyed the comparison to what she considered revolutionary minds. Their appeal had been diluted in the past as there was no place for them in the polite conversations held by the Upper Ten Thousand. But she was yielding to a new regard for this free-thinking band of women whose esteem for tradition was fading in this new dawn. "I can't wait to be introduced to their stimulating debauchery."

He grinned; any trace of concern absolved. "They'll find you as much of a delight as I do."

Visions of sparkling conversations by a roaring fireplace and ballrooms filled with the finest intellects London could offers spun Annabelle into orbit. If she were ever to fully forgive Dr. Christianson, now was the closest she'd ever been. And without any conscious effort on her part, Annabelle felt a tiny bubble in her heart rise to its surface and pop, with the delicacy of Ardennes champagne.

"Have I said something wrong?"

"Of course not,' Annabelle blotted at the corners of her eyes. "You just always seem to say the right things at exactly the right time."

Thomas' face grew long, but a telltale twinkle brightened his eyes. His hand left hers as he fumbled with his breast pocket button before he retrieved a poesy ring. Its gold band studded with diamonds before they ascended to a large, square-cut emerald.

Annabelle rested speechless as Thomas fell to one knee, his lips forming the loveliest of letters, 'W,' and asked the loveliest of all questions.

Chapter 16

Happiness can begin with the most confounding of circumstances, Annabelle thought to herself.

She had believed herself immune to the kind of love she now felt for Thomas. This love filled her up, unlike any emotion which has called itself by the same name before. It lacked the perverse appeal of illicit trappings and the sickly pining of maiden hearts; both now only made her stomach turn. This levity carried her heart high beyond the balayage of April clouds set against an azure sky. Annabelle supposed the certainty of a lifetime in Thomas' arms safely elevated her to this precious loft.

The hours of combing infinitesimal details into place ensured no wedding, even those at the Mayfair Millennium Hotel , could compare in taste and beauty, at least in the eyes of one Mrs. Pierce. Over the last weeks, scraps of lace, rose petals, and pearls gathered into a furious cyclone of quivering, feminine anticipation. With a now unusual (for her) wry assessment, Annabelle wished for one day, the handful of men in her acquaintance would acquiesce, without protest, to the blissful insanity propelling the families to the pinnacle of the morning, when she and Thomas would wed.

Annabelle had attempted to quell her fractious nerves with tisanes of passionflower and lemon balm sipped over the pages of Jane Eyre. But this morning, Aunt Maude prescribed something stronger. After sniffing at Mrs. Mingle's preparations, Maude dashed off in search of sterner stuff, poppy flower tincture from the Orient.

Enjoying the calm of the drawing room at Farleigh Court, save for the gentle creak of the floor beneath her ivory heels, Annabelle plumped herself onto the window chaise looking out to the mossy Somerset lawns. She untucked the last snippet of Jane Eyre, handwritten for delivery at a moment's notice. Annabelle slid into the familiar lines as if slipping on her favorite silk dressing gown.

I have now been married ten years. I know what it is to live entirely for and with what I love best on earth. No woman was ever nearer to her mate than I am: ever more absolutely bone of his bone and flesh of his flesh. I know no weariness of my Edward's society: he knows none of mine. . .We talk, I believe, all day long an audible thinking. All my confidence is bestowed on him, all his confidence is devoted to me; we are precisely suited in character — perfect concord is the result.

The quiet description of like hearts seemed to be sole key to slip between Annabelle's ribs and find its way home to unlock her soul. To that end, she swore her festivities (at least on the holy day) would not resemble Sanger's three-ring circus. Feeling true to the role of dutiful daughter, never mind the convenience of her own unforeseen happiness, Annabelle had stood firm as her mother attempted to cajole her into a more elaborate affair with white-robed bridesmaids and poesy-tossing flower girls. A sole venture suited Annabelle quite well, she told herself.

The echoing of clipped footsteps heralded Maude's return. A vision in a shade of chartreuse only she could carry off, the wide brim of her hat was tipped at an angle which spoke of clandestine whispers. "By the by, I had my suspicions Lady Audrey would have a dram or four of laudanum on her person for occasions such as these, my dear." Maude seemed to wriggle in pleasure at her cleverness as she undid the tiny silver bottle. "A few drops under the tongue now should last you through the vows." She wedged the dropper past Annabelle's lips.

Anise bitterness pooled at the base of her mouth. Annabelle shuttered. "That's devilish."

"Takes like to cure like, my love." Maude winked and tucked the vial into her handbag. The angular bright birds embroidered on its sides made ferocious guardians to its contents.

Feeling a gloss, like melted butter, smooth over her, Annabelle moved to the dressing table, pulled from one of the guest rooms in the east wing, for her finishing touches. She preferred to think her own poise, rather than the laudanum, was having its intended effect. In keeping with the Queen's preference, her torso was swathed in light satin the color of oyster shells. A wide sash of oceanic blue nipped her waist into impossible proportions which the wide bustle and flounces of the tiered skirt accented all the more. "Thank you, Aunt Maude." She motioned to the nape of her neck. "Be a dear and fasten the last few buttons beyond my reach."

"You are as perfect as a picture, Annabelle." The sentiment in her aunt's face spoke of the age she never admitted before her typical beam returned. She moved and began with the buttons. "It's much more cumbersome to do these up. I'm much more skilled at their undoing." Their eyes met.

Annabelle rolled her eyes at Maude's sly grin.

"Don't you have a lady's maid for such things?" Maude smoothed her row into place. "Becky or Mary somebody or other?"

"Yes. Sarah." Annabelle hoped she sounded nonchalant. She rose as she pinched her cheeks for a final touch of color. "She's moved on, pity, I was fond of her."

"I'll find you a replacement on the double. A good maid is hard to find. Especially one who can attend to one's hair." Maude took her handbag from under her arm and removed a small pot.

"The laudanum was enough."

"Rouge, my dear." Maude dabbed coral stain at Annabelle, standing back to assess her work as if she were Michelangelo's best apprentice. With each motion, trickling tales of her own happiness both under the auspices of a respectable marriage vows, and even more so outside them, came forth. "Fall in love, but for Christ's sake, don't lose yourself in the process."

At times, Annabelle had found her aunt's exploits dangerously appealing. But the appeal of anything but the simple (and deep) desire for Thomas made Maude's existence seem as transitory as a butterfly, with a known expiration date. "It's different for you and I."

"How so?"

Time was pressing and Annabelle recognized the tangled construct on which Maude tiptoed. While Maude savored the preoccupation, and validation, she found in her liaisons d'amour. "Just the timing, the circumstances,' her voice fluttered like the rose petals that had drifted softly to frame the temporary aisle she would soon walk down, 'the men."

"On that last note, we are in agreement, my dear." Maude wrapped Annabelle in her arms. "Just know, there are many definitions of a marriage. I prefer the dynamic variety. Come to me when your static one breaks free and you wonder about joining my spectacle."

Annabelle found herself grinning at Maude's kind-hearted persuasions as the door crashed open, the inside knob thwacking the neat wainscoting. Mrs. Beatrice Christianson bore into the room, the stodgy briefcase in her hand at odds with her starched navy day dress. "What have we here?" She announced as if the idea of her son's wedding had only headlined The Times that morning. Her head craned right and left, her sharp eyes gulping in every detail. "Rose at four this morning, finished off my personal amendments to the Municipal Property Act, and delivered it personally into the hands of the Chief Justice. Their idiocracy won't last for long." The coffee-tinted bows trimming her flounces seemed swell in applause.

Annabelle faintly perceived a sigh escape from Maude before she released her.

"A blushing bride,' Maude met Annabelle's future mother-in-law with a kiss two inches from her right cheek. "You've cut things quite close,' she slid a Faberge lid from a trim bangle to expose a clockface. "The procession's in fifteen minutes."

"Early to bed, early to rise, lost time is never found." Mrs. Christianson spouted, "And so on and so forth."

Annabelle adored the idiomatic assault.

"I also ascribe to that philosophy, but likely to very different ends." Maude gifted the room with her widest smile of the morning. "Ravishing, my love. Think of husbands as well-appointed accessories." She collected her bag, blew Annabelle a kiss, nodded at Mrs. Christianson, and swept out the door, leaving a lingering trail of lilac scent in her wake.

Curiously the room felt smaller without Maude's presence.

Mrs. Christianson tossed her briefcase onto the chaise with a heavy thud. "She's a bright star to be sure." She jammed edges of her bodice down— as if she was a knight, adjusting her armor for battle.

Taller than most London men, Thomas' mother achieved a spot-on pantomime of Mother Goose, although she avoided ridiculousness with the depth of her sage expression.

"You are so lovely,' she said, approaching Annabelle, 'without out all this monkey paint." Taking scrubbed at Annabelle's checks with her thumb. "Time is funny with minds and faces. Kind to one, cruel to the other, or the other way 'round. Remember that inquisitive mind will never droop, unlike other faithless, unmentionables we prod and hoist with the years. An hour at a book, rather than the dressing table, is never a waste."

"Your clandestine education will last you a lifetime, my son is the luckiest of men."

Annabelle felt as if the ends of an electric cord had traced its way between their hearts with a subtle jolt, only slightly less of a sensation than she experienced so often with Mrs. Mingle. The word 'mother' formed at her lips, but its acrid wash made it stick. She contented them both with a shy smile, anything else would have brought on a faucet of tears.

"Lord take me away,' Mrs. Mingle trilled, standing at the threshold.

Annabelle feared the East London Water Works might break way.

"I've never seen such a grand picture in all my life." She hurried into the room, shoved aside the wanton briefcase, and plopped beside it on the chaise. She rummaged in her drawstring bag speckled with faint worn patches. She blotted at her eyes and nose savagely. "My nose's running faster than Eclipse's four legs at the Prix."

"Thomas is the luckiest of men and I am the luckiest of women to soon call you my daughter." Beatrice squeezed Annabelle's hand before retrieving her briefcase, patting Mrs. Mingle affectionately on the shoulder, and striding out the door, quietly closing the door behind her. A faint scent of starch and fresh soil lingered.

Her face now a nicer shade of peach , Mrs. Mingle settled in like she was in a great box at the ballet, gazing up at Annabelle with a rapt expression.

After a stretch of silence, Annabelle broke in. "Will I do?"

"You'll more than do, my love. And what's this drivel about our day? You're the one in white frock."

"If you hadn't whisked me away to your sister's that summer, my heart might have crystalized completely. I might have found myself an old maid with whiskers as long as my collection of cats, rubbing my father's chilblains not long from now."

A roar spilled from Mrs. Mingle. "That would have been a vision. Quite a different setting than today, to be sure. You aren't the type to have your heart whither . I had nothing to do with that, my dear."

Annabelle sat beside the housekeeper.

Mrs. Mingle pulled her close and Annabelle's head fell to her shoulder. "It's in your sweet nature to love, my girl."

"You think mother would notice if I escorted you in my wedding chest to 17 Berkeley Square?"

"That is a bit of finery I wouldn't be used to."

"It is a bit pish posh, but it would just be us. Grand fun really. Us cozily at work in the library after feasting on your delectable . Rounding out fearsome academic interludes with your miraculous dinners." Annabelle eyed Mrs. Mingle, knowing her weakness for culinary pomp and circumstance.

"You do know how to tempt me. But ye know I can't."

"I know you won't say it, but Fernhead House would collapse in a heap if you weren't there to weave walls together." Annabelle righted herself.

"With all this mush, I clear forgot to give you this." Mrs. Mingle withdrew a thin box from her bag.

137

Annabelle wondered if there were a full tea service set and new puppy in its velvet folds, perhaps even a new lady's maid. She took the box. "There really was no need."

"Not sure what's inside, but my present will greet you at Berkeley Square. This is all Ben's doing."

Annabelle's stomach clamped painfully. Ben. She had become accustomed to avoiding the stable when her attentions had turned foursquare to Thomas. Then with Sarah, and the wedding plans. To her regret, she had never been able to right, or at least smooth things between them. The last look he had given her—part hurt—part hate—plunged into her mind's eye.

"I'd had a word with him. About your father's affairs—general-like. He knows why ye did what ye did." Mrs. Mingle motioned at the box. "He wanted me to see you open it and report back. Thought best not to make things awkward giving it himself."

Lifting the lid, Annabelle blinked at the unexpected treasure inside. On a small rack draped in current -red silk, lay neatly arranged scalpels, rakes, scissors, forceps, and a thin saw blade. Annabelle traced the outline of the enamel handles as if they followed the same curve of Ben's square jaw. She smiled as her finger encountered fine slats—textured for better grip. Affection, sadness, and a quiver of conscience overtook her. Ben had that effect on her. She didn't like it. Her stomach flopped like a hooked fish.

"There's a wee note there too."

Annabelle plucked the triangle of paper protruding from below the saw blade and unfolded the note.

Something to remember our ol' days by, Lady Love. And to make yer new ones shine. There won't be a day gone by...
Forever and always, Ben

He was cleverer than she had given him credit for. There couldn't have been a gift she would have treasured more. And not another she would use so well.

She hung in indecision for an instant, as if mesmerized by his bright blue eyes staring back at her from the blocked print.

"There's a better part of half his year's wages."

Annabelle scanned Mrs. Mingle's face unable to decipher her implication.

"With him saving for his big adventures."

The elusive push in her voice caused something wound tight inside her to snap. She was right to be Thomas' pioneer. "It is the perfect gift from the perfect friend." Annabelle hoped her smile was wide enough to disguise any trace forlorn lingerings and dismiss her housekeeper's personal perspective.

"Ah, Mrs. Mingle, Georgia's in need of your guidance in regard to the place settings and the arrangement of the fowl mayonnaise and the wedding torte."

Annabelle stiffened at her mother's voice. Mrs. Mingle swept the surgical set back into her handbag and pushed to the opposing arm of the chaise. "I'll keep them safe. As the Lord says, to thine own self be true. Not me own words, but they fit the moment,' she whispered. Rising she dusted her skirts. "Georgia's in need of more guidance than I can offer this morning. But as for the torte and sandwiches, leave it to me." Reading Annabelle's face, distressed at the threat of imprisonment with her mother, and sent her a wink. "Be back in a jiffy with your veil in tow. We've only got minutes to send ye down the aisle." She eyed Mrs. Pierce before bustling away.

"Good morning, mama . Today's the day."

"It certainly is, my sweet girl."

Annabelle couldn't recall the last time her mother had called her anything with such affection. The sentiment could take a place next to her fondness for handmade Valentines and giggling bridesmaids.

"Your life can really begin now." Her mother moved adjusted an oversized brooch at her throat before clearing it. "Just when all hope was dwindling—"

"Yes, mama , just when spinsterhood loomed around the bend—"

"Thomas came to your rescue, sweeping you off your feet, and the ball room floor you'd so long trod." Her mother let out a tinkling laugh as she eased herself onto the chaise with an exhale of contentment. "And now you'll shortly be Mrs. Annabelle Christianson of the smartest block of Berkeley Square with five thousand a year and three rigged pair of carriage horses for as long as your good health endures."

This morning's tone was as liquid and sugary as wildflower honey, causing just as much unease as Ben's unexpected gift.

"I do have the best fortune indeed, to have the hand of a wonderful man, with thankfully, the constitution to match." Annabelle wondered if her mother's past vitriol was really no more than self-centered thoughtlessness rather than aimed barbs.

"A wonderful man who should be easy to please." The pleasurable silence lasted only a moment before she sat up with a start. "You will keep him—happy—won't you?"

The extent of the concern on her crumped face made Annabelle want to laugh. Taking pity on her mother, she returned her saber to its sheath. "Of our eternal bliss, I am very sure."

"Equal parts?" Mrs. Pierce shifted upright. "That's a calculation I've never been able to pencil correctly." She tapped her knee with the thin satin clutch which had never left her fingers. "Your father was never my equal. He was so handsome. And kind. He thinks I'm empty-headed. He's right, of course, as learned men always are. That's why I fought so hard for Fernhead House, invitations to the right parties, to make a place for the Pierces in the right society."

"Father wouldn't be where he is now without you." The acknowledgement stuck in Annabelle's throat.

"Or you. I see that now. You're bright—his equal. I suppose I envied you that." Her voice dropped to a whisper. "I've made unkind choices too." Mrs. Pierce turned her eyes, now red-rimmed and watery, to Annabelle. "I am a spiteful woman."

Annabelle searched for a way to end this conversation, feeling she might drown in the overwhelming sewage of her mother's long-trodden shame. "You've made this family what it is." Words which could be digested in any which way. "Are you pleased with the dress? Monsieur Clautilde worked around the clock for it to be on time." It was an effort to moor their ship to a safer landing.

Mrs. Pierce cleared her throat a second time and the more recognizable sharpness of her features returned. Her eyes seemed to dry as if beaten by desert winds. Rising to her feet, she approached Annabelle with a starched smile. "You look just as pretty as I did when I married your father."

A compliment without comparison, that would be the day, Annabelle thought to herself.

"I am glad, then mama, I hope you are proud." The last word brought a sting to her eyes though she was certain it would never be wholeheartedly felt. She stared into the mirror, only bringing herself to meet the outline of her mother's silhouette. A direct stare would have undone her. "It'll be time now." The clock couldn't tick fast enough.

"I brought you something." Her mother sounded as hopeful as if she were begging for an extra hour to play among the shells on the Brighton dunes.

"Really?" The unpredictable vacillations of her mother's mood really could be nauseating.

"Yes." Her mother held out two trembling bobbles —their sapphire facets caught the morning light with a fierceness which Annabelle preferred over diamonds. "They're borrowed, blue, old, and new to you."

"Very clever, mother." Annabelle said, meaning it.

"I wore these on my wedding day. I was so proud." Mrs. Pierce's gaze thickened she spoke of past happiness. "Like I said, you are every bit as pretty as I was." She held the earrings to Annabelle's ears. Up close, the glimmering chandelier shape seemed a bit gaudy against the simple lines of her dress' neckline. For an instant, their faces seemed blurred as one, so similar was their contour. Annabelle would wear them gladly. It was the closest thing to an apology her mother would offer. She hoped her father would notice her beneficence.

"Now isn't that a sight for my old eyes." Mrs. Mingle brought with her a joyful levity as she hustled into the room. "Let me take it in." She paused, letting the yards of creamy tulle swell around her like still afternoon clouds. "Enough dilly dallying, two minutes 'til ye best be perched on yer father's arm."

"Then I'm off, my dear."

"I never doubted you were." Annabelle left her mother to interpret her sentiments, as she turned to Mrs. Mingle. "Do me up, Mrs. Mingle, please." She caught her mother backing out the doorway in the mirror. "Until our breakfast then, mama ."

"As pretty as me," echoed back as Mrs. Pierce took her leave.

Mrs. Mingle pushed pins and arranged layers, her eyes darted between Annabelle's reflection and Mrs. Pierce's earrings. "Wearing those today, are we?"

Annabelle looked back at her. "Yes, to keep the peace."

"Head up."

"Yes, Sargent ." Annabelle righted herself. "Do you not like them?"

"No, no. They're a fine bit o' gold." Mrs. Mingle couldn't seem to decide on a direction to nod her head. "It's just—"

"You had another idea?" Annabelle took the lingering pin from the housekeeper's fingers and shoved it home into a last curl.

"They're not near so grand as those bobbles . But they were my grandmother's. I'd hoped to wear them myself but never had the chance." Mrs. Mingle searched the folds of her dress before producing a neatly cut square of quilt backing with two silver oblong earrings pinned through. Annabelle picked them up, shifting them back and forth, the engraved pattern as intricate as an Egyptian obelisk.

"My grandfather fashioned them himself for her rather than an engagement ring. Finest metalwork 'e ever done. Far cry from the horseshoes and gates which were his daily bread."

The patience and love put into the pieces made them feel alive in Annabelle's hand. "Would you really let me wear them?"

"Don't be daft, my girl, that's the idea." She ogled the sapphires. "Though the style doesn't match your grandness. Your mother gave her best effort." She shook her head violently. "It wouldn't be right. Perhaps on your anniversary in a year's time." She reached for the backing, but Annabelle withdrew it.

"Too late. I've set my heart on your grandfather's handiwork. You shouldn't begrudge a bride on her wedding day." She merrily slipped with earrings into her ears , admiring their happy nodding in the mirror. "Much better."

"But what about your mother's?"

"My sash is a bit plain on its own,' Annabelle palmed the sapphires and fiddled with their backings. "If I arrange them just so, they'll give me just the gleam I need." Job done, she patted her creation and rose.

"It would mean the world to me, my love. You sure you'll catch no flack from your mother?"

"It was a hollow gesture. She'll be too busy thinking all the guests are here for her to notice."

"I'd not want to hurt her precious feelings, but if ye don't think she will, I'll leave ye be."

"Please do. Now isn't there one lonely arm waiting for me?"

"Yes, yes. I plum forgot myself—as I tend to do at weddings, making me full of nonsense and blubber." She kissed Annabelle lightly on the forehead before leading her toward the door. "Remember love, to thine own self be true. Nothing changes at the other end of the isle."

Annabelle, at that moment, believed she was following her truth straight to the change she was certain awaited her in Thomas' arms. That change smelled distinctly of hope, freedom, and steel.

Chapter 17

Annabelle plucked an orange blossom from her bouquet, twirling its reedy stem in her fingers, considering its symbolism of purity and fertility. One an ideal to which she could not ascribe, consideration for the second she would postpone.

The day still felt unreal as she glided on her father's arm beneath the garlands of eucalyptus leaves and orchids. Pastor Hendricks stood as master of the assembly. To keep her nervousness at bay, she reminded herself how everything would be different with Thomas. Previously experienced nuptials evoked images of post boys with huge favors, smirking servants, and wretched tipsy speeches from the men (and even more wretched tears from the women) in attendance. Then more champagne, a great wallop in the head from an old shoe for luck, and away the happy couple would go. Off to damnation.

It stood to Annabelle's reason, as nothing about her and Thomas' union would be traditional, the day to mark the occasion should hold none of those moth-eaten trappings. Gone were the tiny flower girls, trails of supportive maidens, and an adoring crowd salivating in the reception line. Theirs was a small, simple affair at Fernhead House with only the Pierce's very closest Society acquaintances and their short list of extended family in attendance.

Her father looked even smarter than his usual fastidiousness allowed in his mulberry frockcoat. That morning he became a man of few words and Annabelle did not press him. The gentle pat of her hand before the chords of the wedding march rang out said it all before they made their way slowly down the parted sea of wicker chairs for the intimate gathering of like hearts.

Thomas had simply asked his father to stand in as best man, lingering after the ceremony to give Pastor Hendrick's his due fees. Annabelle wondered if the price for a pastor and an executioner were equivalent.

Down the aisle, Thomas in his black top hat, a jaunty rose the color of late summer raspberries in his lapel, made Annabelle steady herself against her father. She scarcely felt her father's kiss on her cheek as she centered herself before Thomas, soaking up the warmth of his smile.

"Bless you my dear girl." Dr. Pierce's voice was hoarse. He shook Thomas' hand and patted him on the shoulder a few too many rounds before Mrs. Pierce hissed for him to remember himself and join her in the first row.

Ignoring the quiver in her knees, Annabelle almost choked on the words to honor and obey. But her cheeks were full as she agreed to cherish Thomas as his voice, as smooth as polished crystal, sounded, "With this ring I wed you, with my body I honor you."

When the final salutation rang out, Thomas let his lips linger over her cheek as he whispered. "To honor my pioneer and obey our hearts, that is my promise to you."

⚭

In the reception line Thomas fielded the onslaught of congratulations. As Annabelle expected, she was never acknowledged. Society dictated the honor was inferred upon her by marrying the groom. Thankfully her overflowing heart couldn't be bothered the trouble of offense. The cutting of the fondant-robed monstrosity and small talk among the guests following breakfast would have proved just as tedious. But she was saved by the never-ending wedges of a less ostentatious, but far superior confection, slid onto her plate by a beaming Mrs. Mingle. "I know you're never been one for fruitcake, my love."

Much revived by the jolt of sugar, Annabelle found it easy to keep her silver tongue to herself.

Then the Larkins approached the receiving table.

Annabelle reluctantly lay the tines of her fork across her plate.

The trio in question stared at one another for a long moment, stupefaction mixed with politesse strewn across their faces.

"Larkin, my good man, thank you for coming." Thomas sounded as hearty as a Cornwell coal miner .

Larkin's expression turned instantly convivial, outside his typical aloofness.

"And the renowned Mrs. Olivia Larkin, I presume?" Thomas kissed Olivia's lace-fitted hand. "You never mentioned a loveliness quite like this, Larkin."

Olivia looked like she might collapse into a puddle before them.

Not quite vetted to her best behavior, Annabelle considered an unpleasantry, but reconsidered. She was now Mrs. Thomas Christianson after all. Then Larkin turned to her. The furrow of his brow and searching expression were those of a man who'd lost his lifetime savings at the Monte Carlo tables. It would be improper to be quite so demonstrative in her victory.

"Olivia, Dr. Larkin." The history between them, with Thomas' ring hugging her finger, seemed as distant as her memories with Olivia, dolls strewn on summer lawns, and just as childish. "It has been far too long. I hope you are enjoying yourselves."

Olivia flittered Annabelle the briefest of looks, before fluffing her feathers underneath Thomas' complimentary wing.

With Olivia safely captivated by Thomas' attentions, Larkin gave a salute to her new groom before rounding the end of the table to meet Annabelle. He stood at her side as if he were Isaac Newton, contemplating gravity after being knocked unceremoniously in the skull with a Bramley apple .

Annabelle found he stirred nothing inside her, then sent a longing glace at Thomas, still merrily flattering Olivia. As if he could feel her affection, he shot her a quick wink. Annabelle contemplated ignoring Larkin and returning to her luscious half-eaten cake. But his nervous shuffle compelled her to turn back. "Dr. Larkin, how have you been?"

"I've been better."

"I am sorry. When we last met, I believe I left you rather well." The tomfoolery of their exchange made her want to explode in hysterics. At least she could amuse herself for the time.

"I have not been so well since, Miss Pierce."

"You forget, I am Mrs. Christianson."

"You'll always be my fierce Miss Pierce." Larkin leaned in. "It's the end of an era then?"

"Definitely." Annabelle was amazed at how her current love had made old infatuations wither like unharvested grapes on winter vines. "Perhaps my husband may have a solution in his surgical bag to rid you of those nagging discomforts."

Larkin had the good grace to let a quiver of amusement touch the corners of his eyes. "The good surgeon could search to the depths of that bag and find no cure for my ails."

The words had no sooner flown from his lips then Olivia swooped to the open place in front of them.

Thomas broke the procession of congratulations to peck Annabelle's cheek. "Mrs. Christianson." He nodded with false solemnity.

"I am." Annabelle returned their shared mirth before, with unsurprising reluctance, turning back to Olivia.

"I can't tell you how it warms my heart to now call my dear friend, Mrs. Thomas Christianson." Olivia trilled, as she swung on Larkin's arm. "I admire your brazen thwarting of tradition—no weekly banns, a sparse wedding party—very chic."

Annabelle squared off, not opposed to one round in her old ring. She made a great show of extending her left hand, Thomas' emerald seeming to catch every ray of daylight in the parlor. Her eyes hovered over Olivia's plainer stone. "There's no need for all that show when love is true and sure."

Larkin pulled Olivia close. "It's the beginning of a new chapter for you, then, Miss Pierce." His face set into a charitable smile. "There is no need to follow the footsteps of your Aunt Maude. For your path seemed very much cemented in that questionable direction." He tapped the brim of his hat and nodded curtly. "I bid you good-day."

Annabelle wished she could smash her remaining cake into his smug face. But alas, that would be a waste of a perfect confection. And speaking of which, the perfect confection to her side was coming in for another kiss, and she decided to live for the day.

⸘

And live for the day, she did. The couple left their wedding cards to be arranged and posted by their mothers. Thomas and Annabelle, keeping with their air of marital rebellion, allowed rumors of a grand tour to southern Italy rumble. Though the expected month-long honeymoon, as such, was deemed unnecessary, considering the recent positive developments on their combined research efforts. Rather theirs was nothing more than a pleasant jaunt up to the Lake District.

The wisened inn mistress slipped Annabelle a sachet of herbs, 'for the family.' The chipperings of mid-afternoon swallows, the muggy scent of tilled earth, and her general satisfaction made Annabelle tuck the offering between her bracelets and bobbles, still paste, in her traveling case. She wondered if indeed it might prove more useful in the future than she had foreseen.

The room was strewn with more orange blossoms, their citrus muskiness perfuming the space. Thomas elatedly tossed Annabelle over his shoulder and leapt over the threshold. T hough she had imagined a slightly more dignified entrance, perhaps laying across his arms in a manner fitting of Lady Guinevere. Assuming it was only proper for any nuptial ravishment to take place after the dinner hour, Annabelle preferred to leave afternoon sheets to those outside the luxury of wedding vows. So when Thomas opened a small door with a cut glass knob, and presented her with the stately air of a museum curate an adjoining room, she assumed priority had won out over lust.

When his tender looks and caresses brought them to a dignified parting at eleven o'clock that evening, Annabelle, disappointment stagnating, told herself it was on account of his gentlemanly nature. She told the ache in her heart the wedding night was a myth before she fell into a restless sleep where she dreamed of nights she hoped would come.

On their return to London, Annabelle penned her Aunt Maude, congratulating her on her extrication from the tizzy of the Season's start, and wondering when she would return for her first of many grand entrances that year. As after scrawling several descriptive paragraphs on her current bliss-state, she let her pen tell the tale of the proverbial pebble in her slipper—their still folded marital sheets.

Maude's reply came with timing as impeccable as the Duke of Wellington at Waterloo. Annabelle had settled in to open her last wedding gifts from Mrs. Mingle and Maude. Sticky crumbs from toffee cakes sent over by Mrs. Mingle, left one hand out of commission as Annabelle tore at the wrappings. Mrs. Mingle seemed to chuckle from the pages she peeled back the folds on the malted rust cover of Miss Beaton's Book of Household Management. Its binding the width of two stacked bricks. Her note read, 'Til I get my schedules straight, or you're your mother's eyes,) I thought it best if you had some tutorial, my love. Thomas is an easy man—start with the chapter on eggs. xx'

Maude let her literary preferences be known. A copy of the Karma Sutra. Its illustrations so shocking (the content of their muted hieroglyphics Annabelle estimated to be anatomically accurate) she jumped a mile before sending the small novella between the chaise cushions when Kitty, on charitable loan from Mrs. Pierce, paraded in with the afternoon post. There would be much research in that department to be done quite soon.

<hr>

Dearest Mrs. Christianson,

Annabelle could almost hear Maude's titters escaping as she wrote, knowing she would always be Annabelle to her aunt.

It cheers my cold heart (a condition diagnosed by the Mrs. rather than the Dr. Pierce,) that you considered me an apt resource on which to devote your marital woes.

Marital woes were a far cry from what Annabelle considered Thomas' simple overestimation of her ladylike sensibilities. She smiled, imagining Maude gleefully plotting the quick demise of her recent nuptials and foray into the Bohemian folds of her experienced skirts. All with the best of intentions of training a new society courtesan, no doubt.

In my estimation—with Lord Bartholomew batting so temptingly at my elbow at the lovely hotel on Rue St. Germaine in the 78th arrondissemont—Thomas may be more inexperienced than his age would allow one to assume. And that is where my expertise will shine. Seduction my dear, is the very thing. Granted, I must nod at your naïve successes with a certain C.L. but now you've climbed even farther in Society, a certain sheen has gilded your reputation which is not something you'll want to tarnish. But, as you do seem very happily smitten with the good Dr. Christianson, rather than his evil beast of a father, I'm certain you'll retain your polish. As to the handful of tricks I keep for gentleman of the shyer variety, I am your eager tutor.

Annabelle laughed at her aunt made even the sacrosanct acts in a legal marital chamber seem illicit.

As I can recommend the sentiment in regards to absence allowing the heart to pine, if you could make the journey to Dover with your father (a dear chance to catch up now you are no longer under his roof,) and catch a packet, I would be delighted to meet you at the Calais station. We can take the Club train back into the folds for a ladies' Paris holiday. You're due for one as the strains of your academic mind so soon after becoming a Mrs. have taxed you more greatly than you anticipated. (I know you may bristle at this my dear A, but some pigeonholes are worth lining for your convenience.)

No need to reply. I've sent a note to your father with an itinerary. I suspect you'll start off this next Wednesday to arrive on Friday evening. We'll have a quiet night at the hotel with a larger city excursion on Saturday before an evening at the Opera. What fun!

Her thunderous applause—in anticipation and self-accolade —rang in Annabelle' ears.

Tout haste my love, bises galore, M

⋈

Annabelle admitted she could use a bit of frivolity. The tinkerings over their most recent article on a theory linking afflictions of the heart and liver had her seeing double. She liked the ring of Mrs. Annabelle Christianson, seasoned seductress of mind and body.

⋈

If love was the poetry of the carnal senses, as Balzac claimed, Annabelle felt she could chase his sentiments throughout the bohemian cultural capital of Europe, The City of Lights, with no limit on her desire for corporal satisfaction.

The epic construction of the Paris monuments gave the city's baroque elegance an electric edge which kept time with Annabelle's quickening heartbeat.

True to her word, Maude swept Annabelle, from the Gare du Nord, to an awaiting carriage. The location of La Reserve was best described as 'in the thick of it' with the Avenue Gabriel overlooking the Grand Palais and Place de la Concorde's immense obelisk, moments from the boutiques of Avenue Montaigne.

Over cocktails kissed with guava juice in the jewel-toned salon that Friday evening, Maude took no time in jumping into Annabelle's recent conundrum. Watching guests stroll the courtyard, her worries seemed to evaporate like flash-point evening dew, as Maude made seduction seem as simple as Euclidian geometry (for Annabelle that is.) She was assured Thomas, an altogether different specimen than the infamous C.L., would find a bit of gentile forwardness quite appealing. At first, Annabelle protested at the idea of a role reversal.

But Annabelle soon warmed to the idea as her aunt spelled out a game plan for love which she had used failessly (and most recently in the acquisition of Lord So-in-so's heart—and carriage.) Images of Thomas' sweet surprise filled Annabelle's head as she lounged in her sumptuously appointed room. Stars sputtered in the warm June air, thick with the mechanical scent of the city and the first lightings of bakery fires. In her dreamy state thanks to the gin, Annabelle easily conjured the image Marie Antoinette (head wonderfully attached of course,) leaning over the wrought iron balconies, gazing up to the heavens. With a start, Annabelle wondered why absolutely everything returned to the physicality of human nature, before she dragged the blankets languidly over her legs and fell into a cottony sleep.

The following evening, the Follies-Bergere dichotomized the exquisite and the vulgar. Box seats kept them at a safe distance from the rowdy provincial crowd in the pit and to enjoy the evening's diversions with a panoramic view, free from the dust of seat cushions and carpets. But the raconteur-filled salon bursting with electrified conversation at an unmarked club nestled in the rose-light hills of Montmartre, took hold of Annabelle's senses by their roots. She was pleased everyone seemed to understand her French, which she felt sounded too studied against the nationals, though she could barely concentrate enough to perpetuate a train of thought as her eyes devoured the sea of humanness.

Snuggled arm in arm with Maude, Annabelle forgot herself amidst the fashionable shops of Rue du Faubourg Saint-Honoré and the bustling gardens rimming the Champs-Élysées. Maude revealed more professional secrets. Annabelle, shell-shocked but enlightened, followed her aunt into back rooms of a nameless establishment to be fitted for the most luxurious personal garments Annabelle had ever seen.

With a fine mist surrounding them, stuffed boxes in tow, Annabelle now felt more powerful and sure. Thomas' proper sensibilities would be no match for her newly practiced allure. Maude's tutelage would not lead her astray. Her spirits revived, she considered an early return to London, feeling she would split if she could not rejoin Thomas and make their union official.

Over tiny cups of thick coffee, she slid the thought onto her plate for consideration, aside croissant flakes and a pool of strawberry preserves.

Maude chewed pensively on her own croissant; her eyes closed. "There are few tastes as sweet as butter and yeast my dear." She purred like a cat on sun-soaked pavement. "At first I thought better of an enthusiastic invasion d'amour, but you know,' she patted a swath of grease from her lips, 'I'm inclined to think that may be the precise method to approach the matter of Thomas. The elements of speed and time may serve your course, my dear."

Chapter 18

From the brightness of Paris, Annabelle feared London's gleam would cheapen by comparison. But the warm embrace of the familiar rose to the occasion. Her father met her again at Dover. Between periods of companionable silence on their return home, Annabelle rehearsed her performance, carefully choreographed with Maude. Her father, occupied with the puzzle she had found in an oriental shop on the Left Bank, twisted the mobile rows and columns this way and that, attempting to line up similar characters along each face of the cube. Annabelle did feel sorry for him. She had completed the puzzle on the return train in twenty minutes.

To ease his frustration, Annabelle offered tales which included only the polite sections of her trip. Her tour into Paris's demi-monde was only reviewed in whitewashed snippets. Annabelle was sure the lady in the tuxedo and the certain, white substance she had been were best not mentioned.

The carriage wheels barely halted in front of 17 Berkeley Square before she alighted with a parting brush at her father's cheek. She dismissed his protestations to help her with her bags, and tucking her hatbox under her arm, assaulted the front door with its heavy knocker.

When the door opened, Annabelle sailed past Kitty, letting her bags fall in a heap by the hallway's grandfather clock. "I couldn't wait a minute longer." She knew her smile spoke of the Pigalle naughtiness she would soon put into practice

Kitty had the good grace to blush and take interest in her shoe tips. "Dr. Christianson's not expecting you 'til Tuesday. Today's Sunday."

"You've retained your razor-sharp powers of comprehension, Kitty." Annabelle attempted to breeze past her, wondering why Kitty seemed uncharacteristically daft.

Kitty caught her arm. "He'll be at his offices 'til at least five."

Annabelle wriggled free. "As you cleverly pointed out, Kitty, it's Sunday. Unless he's out on a private house call, he's loathe to work on his one day of rest."

"That's it, a private call." Kitty trilled as she leaned away from the staircase where Annabelle was heading.

Annabelle didn't appreciate Kitty punching holes in her sails set on romance. Thrusting the brown paper-wrapped packages at the housemaid, Annabelle looked at the hat rack tucked beside the front door. There was Thomas' everyday bowler, his weekend Homburg, and a jaunty straw boater with a checked blue ribbon around its band. "A new boater, Kitty. He'll look marvelous when we take to the boat in Long Water." She wondered if he'd bought it with her in mind. "Take these, will you. From Paris. For after." Perhaps she shouldn't be so forthcoming with Kitty—but she didn't care. She was married. She was home. She was ready.

She reached for the valise with the dressing gown tucked inside, which would have put anything from the pages of Queen to shame. "I'm straight to my room for a quick change."

"You'll need my help." Kitty sounded relieved. "I'll be there away after these packages."

"Kitty, I've become delightfully independent. Aunt Maude and I went without a lady's in Paris. I've become quite competent at simple chignons and button-fastening."

In seconds Annabelle was in her room. She slipped into her ethereal muslin and lace, its unexpected silkiness against her skin reminded Annabelle she was a woman. As she adjusted her dressing shoes, she could almost hear the joyous brass and strings of the Follies . A suggestive note on an imaginary trombone blared. She was just as happy as on her wedding day. Pictures flicked through her mind like an automatic stereoscope: Thomas' bright eyes, the opera, the proposal. Their story was just beginning.

Annabelle padded down the hall to Thomas' apartments on the opposing side of the house. Though they had a large study on the main floor, Thomas had refurbished a small anteroom into his own private lair full of dusty engineering and medical texts, travel trunks, and the odd cigar butt, mashed into a stray teacup saucer. On Sundays, after a late breakfast, while Annabelle usually strolled through Green Park, free to roam as a married woman, Thomas would retire to his second-story study to flick through his current academic journal, alternating with excerpts of Lord Tennyson's best wisdom.

Without knocking, Annabelle thrust his bedroom door wide. Sunlight blazed through the glass in the over-sized French doors. As her eyes adjusted, she heard a chair skid across the floor and the shear of sheets drawn abruptly.

As her vision sharpened, the forms of two nude men came into focus. She blinked. One was her Thomas. The other man of similar build had sharper, more rigid features. Their eyes seemed to lock on a central point before the man reached for Thomas' hand, his smile making him instantly handsome. "She's stunning, just as you described, Tom." The look of absolute adoration he gave Thomas—her Thomas—before releasing his hand, could have only rivaled Annabelle's in its intensity. Annabelle's stood motionless as the other man swept a sheet around his hips and crossed to meet her.

Annabelle flicked her eyes at her husband. She could seem him swallow hard, but Thomas made no move. Her stomach heaved as if she were back on the Dover ferry.

"Mrs. Christianson. The Mrs. Annabelle Christianson." The man made an elegant little bow, "Simon Lygonwood, at your service." He took her hand and kissed it. "Tom, has told me what a remarkably progressive woman you are." He let her hand fall limply back by her side. "That gown is divine. A perfect compromise between lady and harlot."

The fine crevice of a scar passing through the borders of his upper lip would have made his aristocratic features accessible attractive if the timing of their meeting had been altogether different.

"The three of us will be very good friends indeed." He cocked his head as if he had uttered an obscenity. "Well, four of us. I assume you have some lovely thing in the wings. Someone who would very much appreciate that ensemble."

"Good friends?"

Thomas made a move towards her. "Annabelle, I so wanted to tell you—"

Her disbelief bubbled into rage before her screams drowned out his protestations. For all Annabelle cared, they could have been alone in the house. Her soul's sorrow echoed through the walls of 17 Berkeley Square.

That first night back in London almost killed Annabelle.

Her evening shrieks subsided into a mourning rumble. Her bowels felt wrenched inside out by a sadistic monster. All she could see was Thomas' face, saddened she realized now, that first night in the light of the moon at the Opera. That first night they met, he had stared across the twinkling metropolis lost in reverie. His enthusiasm had been infectious, like the plague. Now she lay dying from the worst kind of broken heart, despair rotting her bones. She flatly refused to sleep; fearful her subconscious would conjure more cruelties than consolation.

The next day she tried to study, write, do anything to reroute the down-spiraling tracts of her mind. But vision and logic blurred until she found momentary relief in hauling beloved texts against the papered walls, the rose heads bent in subdued silence shuddering against her wrath.

Following a particularly well-timed launch of a bounded poetic collection by Keats, Kitty bolted into the room without a cursory knock, eyes darting with a breathy, "Effing Jesus, Mary, and Joseph." But the poor maid scampered away like she had seen Cleopatra's corpse when Annabelle turned to face Kitty, her face swollen and wet. Feeling as mad as Carroll's Hatter, Annabelle let out a shrill, "Bugger off,' before letting a first edition of Alice in Wonderland fly a safe distance above Kitty's head.

Annabelle was grateful Kitty had enough sense to leave her wallow until later that evening when Kitty scurried in and shoved a tray in front of Annabelle.

Feeling as empty as the polished fireplace in front of her, Annabelle picked her head up and sniffled apologetic thanks.

Kitty crouched by her mistress. "You know I'm not much of a cook, m'Lady, but I scratched together a few fixings that make me smile when I'm low, seeing Mrs. Mingle'll be away for the week."

As she chattered, sulfurous bangers and colcannon steaming as merrily as a Christmas goose, wiffled Annabelle's mind back to awareness. "Come off it, Kitty." Her stomach burst to life with a growl. "I'll always be Annabelle. You've seen me at my worst."

Kitty made no effort to either confirm nor deny Annabelle's assumptions.

"Mrs. Mingle's away? She doesn't take holiday until August."

"Aye, she's gone up to Sussex. Her sister's been taken with the great sick. Night before last. Yer father's taken her with his own carriage and all his boxes. He'll 'ave her right as rain."

Joyce Mingle, at least twice as large and loud (and just as kind) as Mrs. Mingle. Annabelle glanced longingly at the tray, feeling both compelled to action and defeat in the face this news.

"Sit ye down, now." Kitty pressed a fork into her hand. "They'll be naught fer you to do."

As much as Annabelle wanted to disobey, her body overruled her head, and compelled her to acquiesce. Minutes later, with her plate clean, and a honeycomb crunch between her teeth, Annabelle allowed herself to be put to bed to the thin notes of Kitty's Gaelic melody.

※

Annabelle entered the land of the living late the next morning, making her way down the spiral stairs; the ones she had envisioned herself sweeping down in a satisfied state of bliss. Kitty was dusting the wainscoting and light fixtures but jumped to her feet when she realized her mistress had descended. With a bright smile, she dragged Annabelle's stony frame to the drawing room. Throwing the door open, she announced Annabelle with a happy gleam in her eye, before shoving Annabelle into the center of the room and scampering away. Annabelle was stranded, bare to face her husband. Thomas was already to his feet, striding towards her, his smile one of his most magnificent.

She wondered what and who he saw when he looked at her.

To avoid his eyes, Annabelle took in the room. Its minty walls with light-reflecting mirrors multiplying the scattered vases (too many to count,) cornucopias of blooms exploding from their mouths.

"Kitty had the good sense to commandeer my floral attempts at reconciliation."

Annabelle walked the far way around the table, as far away from him as she could get. Her love for Thomas was still a palpable thing. Outside the long, second-story windows, the street was bustling, full of freedom, and here she was, having willfully stepped inside yet another unforeseen cage. Now its door cheerfully banged shut, the key tossed away.

Thomas did not return to his seat. But the clang of a metal lid against its platter, and the sharp scent of rye and smoked fish drew her attentions away from self-pity. Their breakfast table overflowed with an unctuous spread, dishes of thinly sliced smoked salmon and red onions, dark lobs of caraway-crusted bread, and a stack of pancake pillows. Finding her nerves had steeled against her sadness, she felt a solidarity with Sampson, Thomas as the scheming Delilah, and contemplated her narrowing palate of options. One, a debasing tantrum, not unlike her mother's, might gain her some sympathy, if not access to Thomas' bed. Two, a well-aimed tray might offer some crashing relief; her mark had improved with her recent book hurling. Three. Three. She wracked her brain for a more desirable option. What would Maude do? She would never lose her aplomb. She would get even to come out on top. Annabelle found the latter to her liking and without any course to attain that goal, she gave Thomas a slashing glare and plopped into her chair.

His shoulders eased, as if taking her acquiescence as a sign of forgiveness. Striding forward lightly, he slipped three ballooning blintzes onto her plate. A strident 'thank you' hissed from her lips, as Annabelle helped herself to the quivering lox. When Thomas sent a sputtering stream of coffee into a dainty china cup, its bracing aroma was heavenly, Annabelle barked, "Leave it."

Thomas had the decency to return to his own seat, hands in his lap, like a chastised student who had spoken out of turn.

Despite the humanity which the breakfast coaxed forward, she still felt as if cement filled the gyri of her brain. Taking one sensation at a time, Annabelle inhaled deeply and allowed the rich peach of the salmon and the contrast of the drizzle of berry sauce across her plate to hold her attention. "Why have we not had this before?" She scanned the spread again. "And rye? You prefer the light white loaf from Warren's or Mrs. Mingle's oat slice?" Her heart winced, pulling those details from their past seemed too intimate. She had envisioned drawn-out breakfasts in bed, full of kisses and more.

"I do, but I thought a change would be welcome." Thomas took a slurp of coffee. His face was somber but the twinkle in his eyes was irrepressible.

A brief rap sounded on the door before Kitty burst in. The unfettered expectation in her face could only make Annabelle smile.

"You knocked, what a charming consideration, Kitty." A half-smile whiskered across Thomas' face as his eyes met Annabelle's.

Kitty bobbed her head up and halted mid-stride, clutching a plate and cutlery to her chest.

"Come to make sure a certain someone has not been appropriately murdered this morning?" Annabelle let out a grimacing chuckle.

Kitty's gaze fixed on Thomas. "Not exactly, m'lady."

Annabelle looked over at her husband who nodded at Kitty.

Kitty's abashed expression told Annabelle her Irish heart had a secret to keep before she came to the table and began to fill the plate.

"I'd forgotten Mrs. Mingle's away." Annabelle felt a pang of worry as she recalled her sister's sudden illness. "I should go to her." She reached for the tongs and dropped a slice of toast on Kitty's plate. "But first, you'll need your breakfast. You've not eaten, this morning. You must be starved."

"I did, m'lady." Kitty continued to assemble a hearty arrangement but did not look at Annabelle. "Very kind of you. But Dr. Christianson insisted on treating the staff as well." She shot Thomas a hesitant smile and returned to her task.

"For someone else then?" Annabelle brightened, assuming her maid was doing a kind turn for one of the other girls downstairs. Feeling Kitty's construction was lacking, she took a slotted spoon and scattered lemony capers over the salmon. "You really are such a dear, Kitty."

Kitty kept her head low but did not confirm Annabelle's question with a nod.

Taking her first bite of the blintz. "These are divine." She looked to Kitty's plate. Finding a bare spot seeming to cry for company, she scooped up a second blintz and nudged it into place. "Who's going to be enjoying this loveliness, Kitty? I hope they're ravenous."

Kitty almost leapt from the table; a caper bounced from the plate onto the floor.

Her eyes shot up, now glaring at Thomas. "It's not my place to say, m'lady."

Thomas rubbed his chin and found great interest in removing what Annabelle presumed was a stray seed from between his teeth. "Take it to him, Kitty. You've only done as you're told."

Kitty obediently darted away.

"Him?" Annabelle wanted to hear the thunderous echo of her betrayal, but only managed a terse whisper. Her wounds were still too fresh. "You've let him stay on? Under the same roof?"

Thomas let out a breath. "This has been quite the catastrophe. Far from what I'm sure we both imagined of our pioneering marriage."

Annabelle refused to let the morning's whiff of buoyancy deflate and took another hearty bite of her breakfast. "You've actually taken the contrary turn, not I."

With her tilting of the tables, Thomas sat up in his chair, his eyes defiant. "There was a great deal of misleading and assumptions made on both our parts." He pushed back from the table and crossed his legs elegantly at the knee. "I spoke in code. You did not read between the lines. I misconstrued your talk of an abhorrence of marriage and a taste for freedom to mean something quite different than you intended."

"What could you have possibly misconstrued?" Annabelle felt as if she were the director of a play, watching a flawed production go down in flames in front of a leering crowd. "I thought with you it was possible to have freedom of both heart and mind." She was quite sure she knew what Simon meant to her Thomas, but she wanted him to admit it aloud. "Who is Mister Lygonwood to you?" She took a sad sip of her cooling coffee.

"He is my freedom of heart and mind." Thomas' eyes welled. "I'm not sure how things became so twisted between us." He began to wring his napkin in his hands. "Our love has been hard won. I adore you Annabelle, but I cannot, and will not, give him up."

Chapter 19

His admission felt like the final stone of a burial vault had been mortared and slid into place. "You are lovers." A fist wrenched deep into Annabelle's insides. "You cannot adore me. You are a liar." She began to doubt her voracious decisions moments before. "I detest liars." Even as the words slid viciously from her lips, she knew they were not true. Sarah had been a liar, and Annabelle had tucked her memory into a sacred heart space.

"Please don't say that." Thomas' knuckles turned as white as marble around his hapless linen napkin. "You are not like other women. Headstrong, determined. I believed you held similar proclivities. Sought a companionship. An arrangement behind which you could live out your days with whomever you pleased."

Annabelle had never seen Thomas so distraught. "I am as such."

"Then why the fit when you came in on Simon and I?"

"Unfortunate as it may be, Thomas, I am in love with you." The admission felt like a handicap.

Thomas' face fell. "I thought you had your own companion, who I would, at some point, meet."

"Well, I—" Annabelle wavered. Was he speaking of Larkin?

"A lady friend, Annabelle. Like my Simon."

Annabelle's thoughts retreated to the dusty club in Montmartre. The female couples dancing to double-time beats, the ladies in tuxedos. Comprehension struck. Taking stock of her broken heart, its executioner in front of her, she exploded in boiling tears.

❦

Rage, though exhilarating at first rush, had an aging effect on a body. Every inch of Annabelle was raw, like a gypsy doll stuck full of rusty pins in a traveling exhibit at the Victoria and Albert Museum. She packed a trunk and slunk to the safety of Fernhead house. Dr. Pierce would be well on his return from Sussex late that evening. Her mother had been carted off to the Foster's for safe keeping.

Sadly Harley Street no longer felt like home. Annabelle contemplated whiling away her sorrows to Ben. She had yet to thank him in person for the scalpel set, though a note had been penned a quick note from Lake District. But he had accompanied Dr. Pierce. Mrs. Mingle's sister had passed and there was much packing of Joyce's Brighton cottage to be done, aside from funeral arrangements. Annabelle slunk down to the kitchens, hoping kitchen maids would not question her return. To her surprise, they yelped their welcome, nearly capsizing her in their efforts to wrestle a wedge of Leicester and plank of soda bread from the larder at her request for a simple supper. A thaw waved over her as she tucked in front of the fire with a triangle of cheese speared on a grilling fork and the spine of Pride and Prejudice between her knees.

With Austen's gentle introduction, her despair shifted. Sympathy for Mrs. Mingle's loss reined. Between paragraphs of balmy prose, Annabelle distracted herself for the evening thinking of a pretty trinket to bring a smile to housekeeper's tear-stained face. She settled on a journey to High Street the next day, an occasion for a smart bonnet and gloves to match. Annabelle gave small thanks she could now come and go as she liked, being a married woman.

The following morning, she tripped down the stairs with a bounce in her step as if she were still Annabelle Pierce. She'd not give Thomas another thought until after Mrs. Mingle's gift was bought.

A ripple of glee seemed to shake Dr. Pierce as she breezed into the breakfast room as if she wasn't settled in Berkeley Square. He propped Annabelle in a chair by his side and piled far too many pieces of toast on her plate. "I can't think of a more excellent surprise to greet my eyes this morning. Mrs. Mingle's uncanny knowing. She's baked a veritable fortress of bread, just the night before her sister." He paused. "You've heard."

"Yes, Joyce was a kindred. Cut from the same pattern as Mrs. Mingle." Preferring action to soundless sadness, Annabelle reached for the glinting tea pot. "Kitty's told me you were up to Sussex to help with the arrangements. How is she?" The sound of the tea swirling steadily into her cup was so wonderfully reassuring.

"Better than one would expect, my love." Dr. Pierce sighed, as if readjusting the weight of the world across his narrow shoulders. "Bless Kitty then, your timing is perfection. I'll be heading back for the funeral and wake this afternoon. I assume she pulled your black frock and veil from the attic. You didn't take that to the Square?"

Torn between her own selfish sorrows and a deeper grief for the woman she considered a mother, her father presented a brilliant guise for her sudden arrival back to Fernhead House. Annabelle snatched at it with both hands.

Annabelle feigned shock. "I'd forgotten completely."

"I'll send a note, Ben can go 'round to collect them."

Her mind latched. Ben. Annabelle had stirred over various excuses to explain herself that morning as she dressed. A married woman, running back to her family home in a moment of weakness, was nothing to be proud off. Now further embarrassments could at least be stalled. She hadn't considered the other casualties she'd have to face. But she'd Mrs. Mingle's hat and gloves to purchase. No time for awkward conversations, at least until the afternoon journey. "That affords me time to slip down to the shops. To bring Mrs. Mingle something to make her smile." She lifted a piece of toast to her lips. Butter swam in its browned crevices. She sank her teeth in and let the fat and crumb coat her tongue.

"Kind girl, you make me so proud to be your father. For many reasons." Dr. Pierce's expression lifted. "Will Thomas be meeting us? I suppose he'll be coming from his rounds?"

Annabelle almost choked on bite, the butter feeling instantly curdled. One small detail forgotten. "Surgery." She coughed. The word felt like an expletive as it flew from her mouth. "Crush injury. Slate factory." She swallowed. "Horrid burns as well. Called out just as I left." She put the half-eaten triangle of toast on top of its glinting companions. "He'll be in the theatre the better part of the night."

"I'll send word in the morning then. The funeral's set for half past one. An early morning, but I know how much it would mean to have him there."

Epic misperception. Annabelle wiped her fingertips on her napkin and threw it to the side of her plate. "He didn't know Mrs. Mingle very well."

"Annabelle,' her father's tone became cajoling as he sat back in his chair. "Even I can tell you, he'll do anything to be by your side."

"I highly doubt that," Annabelle snapped.

Confusion twisted her father's face. He sputtered, but no words came. Instead he reached for his tea. Perhaps an attempt to wash down his muddled thoughts Annabelle thought to herself.

But sympathy for him won out, as it would on finding a kitten caught in a rainstorm. "I just know he's was set on saving the man's leg. Reconnecting the tibial vessels. Brilliant in theory. He'll not leave the theatre until he's used every trick in his bag. I don't want to add our woes to that pressure."

"Your Thomas is the best of men."

Annabelle was forced to agree. But the devil inside her took ahold of her chain and rattled it like a rabid dog. "You are correct on many counts, father. But how well did you know Thomas before?"

Dr. Pierce took another sip of tea and trained his gaze on Annabelle. "I'd not seen him since he was a lad. He had quite the shining reputation, not only from your Uncle Horace, but from the other medical men at the College. No need to repeat about the troubles I've had. Your uncle came to me in my hour of need. He's a very old friend, and I extend that regard to his son. From my perception, he's been a royal success, if I do say so myself."

"You may say that."

"Are his finances not in the order we supposed?"

Her rage came faster and louder as the comprehension of the interchangeable role of daughter and pawn took hold.

Has he laid a hand on you? Is there another woman? She spat slicing retorts to her father's questions and could have choked on his achingly superficial concern. When his inquiry shifted to her and Thomas' medical research, his probings spoke of professional rivalry rather than fatherly intent, Annabelle's pride rallied. She'd not give him the satisfaction of knowing her failures as a woman, for that was still how she regarded Thomas' proclivities. There was at least one arena to be considered sacrosanct. She could have fallen into the comforting repose of a damsel but did not, finding scornful bitterness far preferable.

The carriage ride to the outskirts of Sussex was as tense as a tightrope. In no mood for warm reconciliations or could have-beens, Annabelle gave Ben no more than a curt nod before she flung herself into the coach across from her father. Ben moved his mouth in protest. But seeming to think better of it in the moment, instead giving her a good-natured grin and a shrug before scrambling atop the carriage to coax the sleepy steeds to full throttle.

The cottage stood at the end of a rocky lane which wound into infinity on the lower cliffs of St. Genny's. Several carriages, with droopy-lipped horses napping between posts, stood in front of the wavering picket fence. Smoke poured from the cottages' two chimneys. The Mingle family's sorrow was expressed with a handshorn spread and blistery cups of tea, pushing disgruntled musings into a far corner. Almost an exact replica of her arrival ten years before. Amidst the chaos of a broken heart and a clueless father, she had arrived at the Brighton cottage after her mother, deranged from the discovery of Dr. Christianson's transgressions had been sent to a sanitarium in the outskirts of Paris. Joyce's kitchen spoke of the warm hands and hearts who pieced Annabelle back together between seashell hunts and Victoria sponge eaten in the sand.

Once inside, Annabelle and her father were shuffled to a place of honor at the head of the kitchen table. Other mourners ducked below the low-slung beams of the drawing room. In the company of so many strangers, Annabelle forced a civil expression towards her father, which he irritatingly seemed to take as reparation for her earlier animosities. After the last lemon tarte , Joyce's favorite, was settled to cool on the uneven stone windowsill, Mrs. Mingle allowed herself to be persuaded to pause for a refreshment. Her first bite made her eyes wet. "There's no amount of tea I could gulp down to refill these wells."

After Dr. Pierce offered what she had to admit was a very lovely impromptu eulogy, Annabelle rushed to blot the tears from Mrs. Mingle's face and pushed the daintily wrapped box from Whiteley's in front of her. The look of shocked delight which overtook her ruddy face made Annabelle question her gift. Perhaps it was too ostentatious against the irregularly bricked utility of the cottage kitchen. But Mrs. Mingle, perhaps in a superhuman effort to reconnect with her sister's joyful spirit, set the bonnet atop her heat-frizzed topknot, and bustled about the place demanding everyone take note. Annabelle, in a better humor, held back the disgusted glare she had saved for her father.

At The White Swan the next morning, Annabelle felt deliciously rebellious as she dressed herself without the assistance of a lady's maid, and descended the slanted stairs in search of tea. The scent of tapped ale, hearty fry-ups, and laughter burst from every coil in the wood-planked walls of the inn's public house . The chatter of customers had not yet ground the place to life. The quizzical look from the innkeeper at a proper lady taking breakfast matters into her own hands didn't make her blush. This wisp of freedom proved too heady to disregard. When he saw the goldware on her left hand, he regained his senses; the damning privilege becoming Mrs. Thomas Christianson bestowed.

"You'll 'ave a cuppa ?" His drawl boomed around the room.

"The tea's strong and hot." A man's clear voice rang from over her shoulder. "I'd swear Mrs. Mingle baked the scones for our good Mr. Jaffrey herself."

Annabelle's stomach tightened. She spun around. Thomas rose from a high-backed booth by the low fire. His hair, wet and dark, swept away from his face, making him look not yet twenty. Her heart clanked. She sucked in her breath and prayed she'd find the nerve to stay upright.

"Good morning, my love. I've had flowers sent from your mother." He kissed her, just shy of her lips. "She's well enough at the Foster's, distracted with shopping and tea. No need to drag her in into reality."

Their eyes held one another for a moment. Annabelle could feel his question as he scanned her face. She let her eyes fall to the floor, next to her still-broken heart. So it wasn't only out of respect for Mrs. Mingle that he'd come.

Thomas's fingers on her elbow relaxed, reading her likely better than she could him. As he shepherded her towards the table.

"You look like ye've seen the ghost of Marley Manor," another man's voice, a few notes higher than Thomas' chorused with a snort.

Annabelle shifted her gaze.

"Allo , M'lady." Ben's scampy grin met her stone face with the brightness of a comic about to deliver a punchline. "I see the same cat has kept the tongue he stole from you so egregiously, yesterday afternoon."

To Annabelle's horror, he sent Ben a look of shared camaraderie. On what cold day in hell?

"He taught me that word. Egregious. Quite a bloke, m'lady."

Annabelle wanted to spit at the both of them.

Ben clambered from his seat in the corner of the booth.

Annabelle peered down her nose, hoping to find another inch of pride to sustain her shredded aplomb. "Ignorance can provide one small comforts."

"Annabelle." Thomas sent her a sharp look and lightly pinched her arm before he pulled her down beside him in the booth. "Ben's an eager student, quite sharp in his own right."

"I bet with the right books, me brain'd be as big as yers , m'lady." He tore a corner from a scone, crusted with sugar, from the plate mid-table, and stuffed it into his mouth. "Bigger likely,' spare sugar crystals stuck to his lips, 'as a man." He whiped his mouth with the back of his hand. The corners of his mouth appeared electrified as they twitched.

Annabelle turned to her husband only to discover a similar affliction had taken over Thomas. "I hate men," she declared, wishing she had something substantial to launch them simultaneously.

As if her anger were a fresh cut match and kerosene had been doused over their party, Thomas and Ben burst out into raucous laughter.

"I'll take tea in my room if you're going to behave like Neanderthals."

Shoulders heaving, Thomas put a hand on her knee.

Annabelle regretted his touch still felt like heaven.

"Number one. Have the cries of hyenas ever put fear in your bones laying in the sweltering sands of the Thar?"

Between cackles, Ben choked out, "And number two. You, most certainly, do not. Hate. Men." He met Thomas's eyes. They shrugged. "At least not the pair of us." He waved his hand between himself and Thomas as if the two were long-lost brothers.

"Don't you have stalls to muck, or leather to strip?" Annabelle wondered how she had ever found him in the slightest bit appealing.

"Nope." Ben gave her a satisfied half-smile before diving into his mug of tea.

The rogue-wind in his eyes reminded Annabelle why certain attachments were best forgotten.

"We're only having a bit of fun, my darling."

Annabelle lifted his hand from her leg as if she were forced to pluck a dead fish from a hook. "I'd say it's a fair share more than a bit." She slid to the far end of their bench. "How can you be in such a humor on the morning of a funeral?"

"Truth be told, my love, you trolleyed in here like a lark."

"Really more like Queen Victoria, in the midst of a hearty romp of hide and seek with Prince Albie at Buckingham." Ben winked at Thomas.

Annabelle removed herself from the booth and stood before half the population of the men, other than her father, she'd loved in her twenty-three years. She hadn't expected these articles to join forces. "Your cheek, Ben Fulbright, is unforgivable." She turned to Thomas. "And your silence only adds to your collusion." Even in the throes of her anger, Annabelle thought with sadness of the pleasure she had deprived the London audiences for never having pursued the stage.

"You know very well of my regard for you both as a walking brain and a woman." Thomas tipped his head across the table. "Ben here thinks the world of you too."

"Mostly of your right arm, and deadly aim."

Annabelle put her hands to her hips. "You've nothing better to do in the early hours than gossip like aging biddies who smell of mothballs and carbolic?"

"I happen to have a particular liking for the right amount of carbolic behind the ears." Ben protested.

"Your tongue flaps rather freely for a groom." Annabelle snapped.

"Head coachman now. Even though he knows of my plans for America, yer father promoted me with Evans retiring. The extra fiver a week hasbought my tongue a bit o' bail."

Thomas shrugged. "That seems to be the general state of things. The larger the bank account, the louder the opinions."

And she was a woman. With neither of her own.

Thomas settled himself back into the booth as if he were in a sunny garden chaise. "Speaking of carbolic and scrub." He poured himself some tea and thoughtfully sifted a spoonful of sugar into its depths. "Wicked accident at the one of the tiling factories. With one shut eye and a pop of a belt, a man's life and livelihood were laid in the theatre before us."

"You mean you operated overnight? It was his leg then, pinned in the machinery?"

Ben whistled. "Still gives me the willies."

Thomas looked to Ben. "I felt the same as I stood there, poor chap just given some ease with the chloroform, a mangled mess." He turned to Annabelle. "How did you know? Your father?"

"Yes." Annabelle was stunned.

"I sent late night word."

A poor man's misfortune became her fortune, then in turn his. "It perfused well then?" The skill of his hands and good intentions made her heart ache for a future that never was to be hers.

"Pinched his pink toes myself moments before Ben rolled to the college gates as the clock struck three."

"I 'and't been up before the rooster in donkey's years." An admiring smile came across Ben's face. "But to hear you jabber on about flaps and tubes and tibias." He leaned back in the booth and appraised Annabelle. "The best man has won, m'lady. Congratulations for ye's both."

"I was unaware of this sainthood when we exchanged our vows." Annabelle begrudged them a smile. "All uncharted waters with my Thomas." Powerless in the instant, she felt the corners of her eyes wet at this truth—Thomas still held her heart in his hands.

Thomas wicked a budding tear from her eye before changing the subject. "Your friend Olivia's husband is in favor of chloroform, as is your father. But the kinks in administration haven't been worked out."

Annabelle stiffened. Larkin. Funny how that wound instantly opened.

Thomas rambled on in his passion for anything of medical importance—a reprieve from their emotional strain. She didn't bother to listen. Her heart, tattered though it was, had wrestled her mind mercilessly into submission. She kept time to his intonations with nods of her chin, though visions of Larkin between the bedsheets only came to mind.

"We can speak more of this later, but when I was over for some discussions with Larkin Thursday last, Olivia poked her head in and wondered if you'd call on her this week."

Annabelle started blankly back at Thomas.

"Olivia. You haven't seen her in ages. About to burst any minute but still done up in satin and bows."

Annabelle could not think of anyone whose company she would prefer less than Olivia in her smug and satin.

"Perhaps I spoke too freely. I thought you'd go 'round next week."

With Olivia expecting, it would be proper to visit. Annabelle recalled her early months hadn't been easy. A sudden skein of worry wheedled into her conscious. Then Annabelle felt as though she had seen a lightning bolt shatter a star-strewn night sky and was counting the seconds until reality was claimed by the requisite thunderclap.

"Tea with Olivia." She rose, straightening her skirts. "You'll have some breakfast sent up? I'll write her in the room before we leave at half-past." As she leaned to kiss Thomas—in true affection and for show—though her rattling thoughts she tried to recall what afternoons Larkin might be caught at home.

Chapter 20

Circumventing the past was impossible. But she'd be damned if she wouldn't take her future in both hands. Annabelle's heart clapped in her chest, at odds with her reluctant feet. The blood-flowing organ was alight with hopes of rekindling an old flame, her heels heavy with misgiving of the disservice she would pay that flame's holder. She hated Olivia had been the larger person to extend a kind hand to Annabelle's bared teeth, though desperation won out. She'd wheedled Larkin's whereabouts from her father and had planned a serendipitous tea on a Thursday when she counted he could be found pouring over reports and research at home.

But her plans spiraled from her grasp when she received a note from Olivia that morning, requesting her presence that very afternoon. The early hour of its delivery spoke of the early rise of its writer, an hour Annabelle presumed the grand Mrs. Larkin rarely encountered.

Still unable to digest Ben's magnanimous acquiescence of her marriage to Thomas at the inn, she'd insisted on walking to the Larkins' Park Lane Georgian abode. The paucity of Olivia's invitations over the past few years amused her. Her old friend's grip of disapproval had loosened now Annabelle wore Thomas' gold band. She found it even more amusing Olivia was naively knighting Annabelle back into her good graces, when she should do nothing of the sort.

Perhaps luck would sort out all her troubles after all.

A butler, new from her last visit over a year ago, ushered Annabelle into an exquisitely decorated front hall. Its poise, like that of its lady, seemed unattainable to Annabelle, domesticity remaining her Achilles' heel. It occurred to Annabelle people might serve as accessories to Olivia, easily exchanged if they did not suit her mood. She resented being on the receiving end of a sentiment she preferred to routinely hold. The similarity to Maude's matrimonial cues surfaced. Her attentions drawn by the new man's appeal, Annabelle thought he was not a bad upgrade in the least. Maude would have whisked him to the butler's pantry in a jiffy. She wondered if Olivia contemplated the same, post-baby of course. She hoped so. It would make the taking back of Larkin all the easier.

With unexpected thoughtfulness, Olivia had set tea, rather than in the parlor, in the Larkin's expansive library. Annabelle found the entire floor to ceiling set-in bookcases to be delightfully reassuring. She took pleasure in the young butler's lingering eye and took her time settling into a plush armchair. After murmuring his mistress would not be long, he bowed himself from the room leaving Annabelle to her insecurities.

Annabelle juggled several conflicting thoughts. She wondered why she believed a dalliance might heal her broken heart. To be wanted. Not as a companion. Friend. Or mind. But as a woman. It seemed ages since she had felt as such. Annabelle trained her eyes on the soothing rows of books, hoping to find steel against her conscience amidst the gold scrolls and jewel-toned bindings.

Soon Annabelle found herself engrossed in appreciation for Elliot's heavy-handed metaphors of Middlemarch, but the jostle of the doorknob pulled Annabelle back to her current intent. Still elegant in a faint steel blue gown, Mrs. Olivia Larkin made her best attempt to breeze into the room. But her carriage was hampered by her generously protruding belly and lessened the effect. But any meanness of comment and wavering glimmer of duplicity evaporated when Annabelle registered her face.

Jutting brow and cheekbones, and petal-shaped lips had been cruelly replaced with a cloak of swollen skin. Annabelle sat astounded in the chair as Olivia barreled towards her. Annabelle was familiar with the typical expandings of an expectant mother, but this was extreme.

Plastering a polite look on her face, Annabelle rose from her chair. The women gave the appearance of bosom sisters as they leaned in to kiss one another's cheek, a long-overdue nicety. The two hovered in indecision before Annabelle offered a hurried smile and plunged towards Olivia with a hasty brush to her soft face. Olivia returned the gesture with unexpected vigor. Subdued by Olivia's sincerity, Annabelle fell back into her chair as her friend eased herself primly, or as primly as her current state would allow, on the sofa across. Her eyes, still sharp, took in Annabelle from head to toe. A quiver of a hope for approval took flight in Annabelle's stomach; a long-time acquaintance to their relationship. Without a word of wit or a scrap of science to shield her, Annabelle hated this juvenile dynamic from which she had never managed to disrobe.

But Olivia's smile was warmer than Annabelle remembered. "Marriage certainly seems to agree with you." Olivia smoothed her dress as she shifted her seat. The blink of a grimace teased her upper lip. "You look positively radiant."

Annabelle was sure a typhoon of disbelief crashed across her previously poised expression. Fresh out of salty tears from funerals and infidelities, Annabelle wondered if the days of anger had left her awash on the banks of docility—make her appear more demur . Or perhaps she simply glowed from still smoldering embers of fury. But she managed a contrived smile. "Furnaces too radiate when confronted with icy blasts."

"Is that really all you can offer to my simple compliment? Can you not stop with this tremendous charade of metaphor and sighs?"

"Charade?" Annabelle was unsure how to defend herself.

A wash of tightness flashed across Olivia's face. The hope for a treatise between the two seemed to be frayed only minutes into their exchange.

Dear Lord, where was the tea? Though a tipple would have been more to her liking. Annabelle would have given anything to have been back in Maude's Paris with her very unusual friends, feeling prim and backwards, rather than to be here. The source of Olivia's exasperation.

"Let's cut this defensive match off before it takes a nasty turn." Olivia's voice was soft but not defeated. She rocked in a great effort to right herself. A dark shadow again crossed her face.

Annabelle who had leaned forward instinctively.

"Be a dear and ring for tea, my enormity and I are at constant odds."

Annabelle rose and tugged at the brass bell pull, glad for the chance to escape. It was odd though. Olivia, even in her state, did not look as a woman should. Though no delicate words came to mind to broach the matter so she held her tongue.

"I've brought you here for a reason." Olivia laid her cards on the table and blinked, as if Annabelle could read her mind and further discussion was obsolete.

"Oh." Annabelle was so surprised at her bluntness she was unable to attach a question mark to the sound.

Olivia's previous warmth was replaced with mineral stone. "This time. . ."

Annabelle could see her shoulders heave.

"This time has been the worst. None of the others were easy. Downright miserable in truth. I had to keep to my bed these last few months. Right after your wedding." She thrust a stocking foot from under her sea of skirts.

Annabelle had seen ankles the size of late summer sapling trunks before, but never on a person so young, or in otherwise relatively good health. She moved to sit by Olivia's side. There was a quality to her old friend's frankness which seemed to dissolve the patina of their past.

Olivia took Annabelle's hands in her own clammy ones. "I'm frightened, Annabelle."

Annabelle squinted, unsure of Olivia's implication, but returned her grip in support.

"Everything I could have handled, even the blood-letting."

"Blood-letting?" Annabelle doubted the validity of that ancient practice with every neural fiber she possessed.

"Something is amiss. Your dear father has done everything possible for me."

"My father's prescribed blood-letting?" It wasn't in his usual store of tools. Clinical heresy. Foolcraft. Worry began to churn.

"Things will right themselves once the baby arrives. But I have this dread." Olivia pressed Annabelle's fingers in hers.

"I'm sure."

Olivia brushed past Annabelle's attempt at reassurance. "I fear when this child takes its first breath; I will take my last."

The clarity of her statement shown in her friend's eyes. Annabelle leaned towards Olivia so their foreheads could rest as one. "That's an awful thing to say—and to feel." She wanted to offer inflated niceties to dismiss this locust cloud stifling Olivia's portrait-perfect sphere. But now the thought seemed to have taken on its own pulse and breath, free to crash about the room. And the bloodletting. She'd be having quite the stern discussion with her father over supper that evening. Her mother remained at the Foster's, self-barricaded against reality in a bunker of lace and smelling salts. She'd not inquire on that topic today.

"I know. You're the only person I've told."

Annabelle regarded Olivia's waterlogged features. "You haven't told your husband?" Cassius would have slipped wrongly off her tongue.

"I couldn't trouble him with this. Dear Cassius has so much to attend to. I know he finds me a bit silly. Dramatic."

Annabelle was prone to agree to that sentiment, but Olivia was not guilty of over-embellishing her current woes.

Olivia picked herself up. "There's nothing to be done. What will be will be."

"That's ridiculous. Defeatist. With modern medicine."

"I'm only being realistic, Annabelle. I've fed myself no lies." Olivia released Annabelle's hands slowly with a smile. "That's why I really asked you to come today. I need your help."

Annabelle thought better of a counterargument considering Olivia's almost dictatorial tone "Of course." Annabelle racked her mind for what she could possibly offer.

"Before Thomas surfaced as a delightful turning point in your story, I had hoped, with your history, Cassius would make his way back to you. After I was gone."

The suddenness of the suggestion caught Annabelle off-guard. The fact that he indeed had was a second matter. "Our history?" Of course there had been a history, long ago as girls, surely was not aware of more recent affairs. "This is absurd. Too morbid."

"But it's not, Annabelle. I've not been sure of many things in my life. But this is one of them."

Annabelle felt it wise to leave their shared history to the winds.

"I have no doubt is of Cassius' love for you." Olivia's gaze was more commanding than her condition otherwise might have allowed, daring Annabelle to deny her declaration.

Words stuck in Annabelle's throat as her eyes were kept hostage. "I have Thomas,' finally came out with effort. Slim consolation it offered now.

Olivia mustered a smile she might have given one of her children at their request for a fourth slice of birthday cake. "I know you're very happy with Thomas. The picture of you and him together brings my heart untold joy."

Annabelle knit several nagging thoughts together. "How do you know I'm very happy with Thomas?"

"Just the very state of you. Now. At your wedding." Olivia wove her arms over her belly. "He's a dream, Annabelle. If an old married woman may be transparent in her approval."

"I thought your approval was obvious the way you carried on at the reception. You nearly tripped over your skirts at his every word." Annabelle sniffed and sat up straight, despising her cued pettiness.

At first, Annabelle felt a surge of triumph—Olivia called out at last. But her eyes seemed to look right through Annabelle.

But quickly the look retreated and Olivia patted Annabelle's knee. "Perhaps you could offer some sanctuary during the mourning period. Offer invitations to the right parties. With the right ladies of the Season." She snuggled back into the arm of the sofa. "He has his looks and name. I've written the deeds and papers all over to his name. My money has become his. He'll not want for a new wife."

"Papers and deeds?" Annabelle knew the Foster's accounts were at least twice as fat as her father's.

Olivia let out a tinkling laugh that sent Annabelle straight back to the sweet times before they were debs, politely at odds for the prize of a husband. "Cassius never lost sight of you." Her hand hovered over her heart. "He married me for my money. He had his charms but was penniless gentility. And would have remained so unless he made the proper match. Archibald Larkin is not a man to mince words nor spare feelings."

Annabelle realized her shock must have been quite plain as the wrinkle cracked Olivia's upper lip.

"Don't look so stricken, my dear. My husband's greatest flaw is his insatiable need to please his family. His fate was at the mercy of his father's demands. He saved his family from ruin. My father didn't mind the Larkin name giving his business wings." The previous twinge of avarice left Olivia's face. "Do you not remember the dreams we had, you and I? We are not that different, Annabelle. But there is a freedom in the hallowed place you sit in Society. Quite moneyed and respectable, but only just. You can afford to balk at convention. To study. To learn. To defy." She licked her lips as if to grease the words to follow. "I envy you, Annabelle."

The sweetness of the admission had no chance to seep in for a split-second later, Olivia cried out and crumpled into a heap, clutching her side.

Annabelle dove to catch her friend's shoulders and pushed her back to rest in the crook of the sofa. Beads of sweat had cropped over Olivia's brow, her eyes darted wildly in a face now the color of freshly milled flour. "I'll get father. This can't go on." She swept her palm over Olivia's forehead. "Your butler's name?"

"Fredrick."

Annabelle propped Olivia securely between two tasseled pillows. "He'll be just arriving back from calls." She dashed to the door ready to storm the foyer. But a sixth sense must have drawn the young butler to the hall, where Annabelle conveniently collided with his brass buttons and starch. "Your mistress is very ill." She gripped his arms. He looked down as if a rabbit in a trap at the unladylike gesture. "My father." She almost shook him. "Dr. Michael Pierce. Send for him. Its life or death." She released the stunned Fred, expecting him to bolt to action. When flames did not light beneath his feet, Annabelle barked her orders again. "Two-one-two Harley Street. Dr. Michael Pierce. An emergency," and pushed him in the direction of the foyer. "The maids can help to get her upstairs. Tell him to bring his bag." She shouted as she headed back to the library, relieved as she saw the bewildered butler streak out the front door, not wasting precious time ringing for a footman.

Back by Olivia's side, having rung for extra arms, Annabelle's fingers found her friend's pulse at her throat, it has been too faint at her wrist. Bounding, though the rate was terrifyingly slow. Annabelle's eyes settled on the pink petal of a bruise forming over Olivia's radial artery. Easy bruising. Bradycardia. Hypertension. Annabelle cursed her lack of interest in obstetrics. Still it all pointed toward shock. These were no ordinary labor fits. But why?

"Bella?" A whisper escaped Olivia's lips.

Tears stung Annabelle's eyes at the endearment. One she hasn't heard in so long. "Livy, we've got to get you upstairs. To bed. Father's coming. He'll know what to do."

"Yes, he'll know what to do." Her voice was as trusting as a child's.

Vulnerability goaded Annabelle's fear into terror. Her father had always had a distaste for obstetrics too.

Olivia refused the hospital. Selective prejudices from the medical profession and classist beliefs forced Annabelle to wave her white flag and honor her friend's request to remain at home. Propped up in Olivia's bedroom, Annabelle wondered if her friend wasn't looking just a bit better. A smudge of rose graced her cheeks. But hot water was always the thing. She glared at the clock, as if the unsuspecting object were the antagonist in their vignette. Back at Olivia's side, a sick, plummy hue now permeated her face. Her lips fluttered as a convulsion traveled up her torso.

Annabelle snatched a terrine and balanced it between her legs, clamping her hands around Olivia's temples to support her heaves as she wretched .

Blistering hot skin met Annabelle's touch. Ice to fire. With each heave Olivia braced arms against her belly. A quarter of an hour later, Dr. Pierce barged onto the scene.

Relief and love blended into a seamless emotion. Annabelle rushed to take his bag and overcoat. Rapid fire details spewed from her as she wove around him. But the reassurance she expected did not soften his expression. "She'll be alright." She did not know if it was a question, declaration, or command.

Her father's face took on a sadness that seemed ageless, too heavy for a mere mortal. "Eclampsia. The only cure is delivery. To give the child the best chance to survive." His voiced trailed off. "Perhaps I've made a mistake."

"It's an impossible choice, Father. You've made no mistakes."

"I'm not the man for this." But even as her father shook his head, he continued to remove his cufflinks and unbutton his sleeves. "I make no claim to sainthood."

Having sent for Larkin, against Olivia's protestations, Dr. Pierce and Annabelle began the business of delivery. Despite the alarming introduction to her labor, Olivia bore into her contractions with the ease of an ox in its yoke. The natural order of things seemed to take over as Dr. Pierce positioned himself with awaiting arms for the newborn anxious to enter this world. Even Annabelle was able to dust the dread of the afternoon from her shoulders, glad to witness the birth, even with Larkin soon to join them. Annabelle felt reassured the wayward events of earlier had righted themselves.

The baby let out her first wailing cords moments after the air settled on her skin in early welcome. No concerto had ever sounded as sweet to Annabelle. Her hands were quick as she inspected every centimeter of the perfect human and wiped vernix away to reveal luminescent skin. Her father busied himself coaxing the placenta into an awaiting basin. Little blood. No tears. Delivery by the book.

"Let me see her," Olivia's voice was strong, her expression bright.

All would be fine, Annabelle thought, as she swaddled flailing arms and legs before resting the little girl into her mother's arms. An ancient connection, as if a thousand microscopic bulbs had simultaneously been switched on, transformed Olivia's face into the Madonna's. "Well done, Livy." Annabelle hoped her smile hid the sliver of pain that jabbed her heart—sharper than desire, larger than jealousy.

But Olivia's adoration was short-lived. Her face knotted. She pushed the infant to Annabelle as she spewed bilious fluid over the linens. As she lay back to find comfort, the blood drained from her face as if a white shade were drawn over a setting sun.

A polite tat-tat sounded at the door. "Do let me have a look at my angels."

Olivia didn't seem to have registered her husband's request. Her father was still occupied with his fingers at her throat and belly. He nodded solemnly.

"There's been a turn. We could use your help!" Annabelle could not spare niceties of congratulations now.

Larkin barged in, his smile slipping to the floor as he took in the room.

"Something's amiss. Much more than the eclampsia we had been treating." Dr. Pierce continued to palpate Olivia's abdomen.

"She's refused the hospital." Annabelle protested quickly in her father's defense. Gently bouncing the whimpering infant, she crossed to Larkin. But before she could rest her in his arms, Olivia shot up from her repose, her hands clenching her sides. An unnatural sound erupted from her lungs.

Instead of reaching for his patient, Dr. Pierce took several steps back as if Olivia were Euryle, bellowing her death cries.

Larkin stood transfixed; his chest did not rise or fall. Annabelle cradled the baby in one arm and reached for his. At her touch, he crumpled to the floor, cracking his head on the slate border of the grate. Her screams brought two maids running. Annabelle sent one away with the baby. Dr. Pierce staggered into the corner where he perched on the arm of a chaise, rocking and moaning, his head in his hands.

Annabelle and the speechless maid rolled the unconscious Larkin against a side wall. She peeled back his eye lids. His pupils shot wide at the insult of light. His pulse was firm against her fingertips. Simple sympathetic syncope. Reassured he was no worse for his lack of chivalry, Annabelle righted herself and strode to the bed.

Sarah's blanched face seemed to hover over Olivia's for a moment, a haunting reminder from beyond the grave. "She's lost very little blood. But all the signs spell shock." She looked hopefully at her father. "Father!" Quivering lids blinked several times over glassy eyes, but he did not respond. "Have you lost leave of your senses? She's dying." The truth of the matter rang cold. "I don't know what to do."

Dr. Pierce's eyes finally whispered , "I don't either."

Her studies in the anatomy lab and Lancet articles now seemed nothing more than childish pastimes.

Annabelle's inexpert hands found Olivia's sides. Even at her light touch, Olivia flinched. Annabelle found sweet, empty nothings on her lips. A port-colored swatch began to surface on her flank. Annabelle whispered Olivia's name, but no recognition registered on her face.

"My husband." Her voice tracked thick in her throat. "My husband."

Annabelle locked eyes with the maid. "The College. Run. Shout. Find Dr. Thomas Christianson. Mrs. Larkin needs an operation. He'll need his box and the chloroform."

The maid's eyes drew wide. Annabelle was not to be questioned. "University College. Christianson. Box. Chloroform. Your mistress' life depends on you."

With a clatter, the poor girl shot from the room repeating her commands to someone on the landing. But her footsteps continued as her voice drifted away.

"Mrs. Christianson?" A far too silky a voice followed a proper rap on the bedroom door.

It was the young butler.

"She needs a surgeon. That's what the maid's about." Annabelle heard a sputter from beyond the door. "In here."

He glided into the room, his eyes downcast.

"Remove Dr. Larkin. Set him up with some salts and whiskey. Be quick. Bring more hot water, as much as the fires can take, and clean sheets."

Annabelle turned back to Olivia. Only a faint quiver around her breasts hinted at remaining life. Small bubbles caught in her flakey lips, inflating and regressing in time. Scooping her friend into her arms, Annabelle fought to recall any verse of the Lord's prayer as she began to rock Olivia as if she were the newborn who had so recently arrived. "We'll get through this, Livy." She declared before cursing a god, any god, for not the first time in her life. "As the Lord sees me now, never again." Olivia shuttered softly as if begging Annabelle's pardon for her troubles before the last bit of resistance in her body gave way and she surrendered to her passing. "Never again."

Chapter 21

Annabelle stood at the threshold to the breakfast room. She had stormed down, having practiced her interrogation as she dressed, still without a lady's maid. Olivia was dead, and her father had done nothing. Damn his sensitivities. Annabelle was in no mood to offer penance for her father's withering inactions. He hadn't even had the courage to join Thomas' cursory post-mortem. Reflection and regret rode high. Human limitation reigned. Nothing in truth he could have done. Olivia had died from a rare, ruptured liver, bleeding the majority of her humanly allotted three and a half liters into her abdomen. The crisis confounded by her pregnant belly and the urgency of her delivery. Thomas had been all kindness and an open ear to her father's stuttering explanation and had taken it upon himself to break the news to Larkin.

Though Larkin's emotion was authentic enough at his loss, Annabelle could not help but notice the lack of effuse heartbreak she felt was due. Perhaps Olivia was more perceptive than Annabelle appreciated.

Beyond the door, a teacup clattered angrily into its saucer. "That's no excuse." A woman's voice trilled. "She's a married woman. Her place is at Berkeley Square now." Annabelle heard shattered glass cascading across the hardwood. Mrs. Pierce had returned, apparently much revived by her sojourn at the Fosters. Annabelle was unprepared to attack her father and deflect her mother's blows simultaneously.

"Hello love," Mrs. Mingle's rattled in with her cart. "You look as right as rain, considering the whirl you and yer father were up to yesterday." She shook her head. "Tis a right shame about that lass. I'd counted childbirth as Death's right to our lot, not a Society queen bee." Her load was full to the gills: boiled eggs in their cups, bacon, and the obligatory basket of toast. She wrapped her hands over Annabelle's hands in prayer. "We come and we go, as they say." She offered a half-smile before nodding at the door. "Be a dear and get the door. I'll be as quick as a flash and get you set down to something hot."

"But mother."

"Was always bound to come back, love. Face her with a bit o' grit and sass as you always do and you'll make it to tea without a scratch." She patted Annabelle's arm. "The door if you please."

Annabelle obeyed and slid the door open. Her father was at his usual place at the long dining table, his newspaper billowing out in front of him, spectacles perched halfway down the bridge of his nose. It was one of those perfect spring mornings full of inviting sun and promise, deeply at odds with Annabelle's tumult. Mrs. Pierce hovered over a pen and well, scratching lines out as if she were a hell dog, marking the inferno's accounts. At the clang of the trolley, her head popped up, like she had smelled fresh blood.

Mrs. Mingle was all smiles. "Aren't you looking like a spring maid. No different than when Dr. Pierce swept you through our doors as a bride."

Mrs. Pierce's expression switched from angst-ridden to full electric glow.

Annabelle, still safely behind the grey battery of the housekeeper's skirts, saw her mother's eyes flit in her father's direction safe behind his Times.

"Mrs. Mingle, you have no idea how your kind words lift my spirits."

Mrs. Mingle played into Mrs. Pierce's carefully laid snare for sympathy and parked her trolley, leaving Annabelle stranded in the sea of oriental carpet. "I can't believe your spirits are in need of lifting?"

Mrs. Pierce's lips smeared together in an angry line. "That one,' she bobbed her chin at Annabelle. "She's put a hole the size England in my sails."

Mrs. Mingle's eyes widened.

The corner of the Times folded down.

"Happily married to the most charming man this century has seen with a house and bank notes to rival. And yet here she is. Slinking around my house like a wonton shrew."

"Now say here." Dr. Pierce cast down his Times.

A windy protest blew through Mrs. Mingle's lips.

"You've been released from the Foster Asylum early I see?" Annabelle fought to keep her ground. "For good behavior? No biting the guards this time?"

Her eyes found her father's and she dared him to correct her.

"We are all on edge. No good will come of words exchanged now. Let us keep the peace so we can sit for a civil breakfast. We've all been coming and going, frayed at both ends." Her father drew his arms wide as if a grand puppeteer demonstrating a tightwire. "Sit."

Mrs. Mingle's snapped to attention.

The weight of the turmoil of the last week settled abruptly over Annabelle and she gave in to his request. "Even shrews need to eat." She caught her father's gaze. He reached for his paper. The piercing accusation of her mother's eyes clashed against her father's limpid ones, daring her to take her seat. Nevertheless, she did just so.

Mrs. Mingle found the opportunity to trundle to the buffet and unload the breakfast things.

"You'd deny me a wedge of toast and tea, mother?"

"You do are ruled by your gluttonous appetites and this constant ravishment of my nerves." Mrs. Pierce put her angst-wrung hands to her temples for effect.

"I cannot deny either charge."

"Now if an empty plate isn't one of the saddest things in the world." Mrs. Mingle hustled around the table, shuffling boiled egg cups to the feuding trio.

"And a daughter's empty room can in contrast, be one of the happiest." Mrs. Pierce beat the top of her egg mercilessly with her spoon.

"I forget you were born without a sentimental streak." Annabelle realized the glimmer of sweetness her mother had unveiled moments before her wedding had been contingent on her marriage.

"Not born without but warn ragged with your antics. You've not been married four months and yet you've not slept at 17 Berkeley Square this last week. Its grossly improper. I'm sure tongues are waving already." She violently cleaved her egg in half, its top tumbling onto the plate in defeat. "I have had much cause for humiliation as of late. I was sure a reprieve was in hand with you safely in Thomas' care. You will go home at once." She jabbed at her quivering yolk with a thin soldier of toast. "Finish your breakfast. Pack your bags. Ben will return you before the noon hour. I'll hear no more on it."

"There are many things of which I would dearly love to think no more. But some are worth mentioning." Now she cast a hard look at her father.

He avoided it and tucked into his own egg with the precision Thomas approached the tattered edges of stellate laceration on a young laborer's cheek.

"I think none can be more worthy of mention than your dismissal of your wifely post." Mrs. Pierce spat. "And the unfortunate state of your stays."

Annabelle stroked her waist. She had always been proud of its perfect flatness, but now it only taunted her. A reminder of who Thomas was and wasn't.

"Olivia Larkin was married at nineteen and welcomed the Larkin heir almost nine months to the day after the church bells rang." She snatched a bite of her dripping toast. "An exam might be the thing for you. To be sure you are not,' she chewed and swallowed. "Defective."

The word landed, blade-first, into the gaping depths of Annabelle's wound. "How dare you." Annabelle smote her egg with her knife, decapitating it with one blow.

"Take it easy, lovey." Mrs. Mingle's warm, hand pressed into her shoulder, offering an unreasonable amount of relief to Annabelle's steaming pride. "Your mama didn't mean—"

"How dare you, Miriam. I'll not be spoken for. I said defective and meant it."

Mrs. Mingle's fingers gripped Annabelle like a depraved lobster.

Having unfortunately finished the operative note on his egg, Dr. Pierce pushed is crumpled Times aside. "Did we not just agree civility was to reign this morning? Our darling daughter is by no means defective. She's been married sixteen weeks. She and Thomas have made great strides in their studies. Perhaps their focus has been outside the realms of human fecundity." He reached to lay his hand over his wife's. "How can you be so unkind?"

Mrs. Pierce snatched her hand from under her husband's as if his were a cast iron pan, having spent the night bedded beneath smoldering coals. "She's never spared my feelings. I feel no need to spare hers now." She scooped the remains of her egg delicately into her mouth. Her expression was all innocence.

When her father's face hardened, Mrs. Pierce's resolve was wrecked and she went to pieces. Instantly her face streaked with tears. "After everything I have suffered through with her, I would have thought she would have the decency to make amends—"

"By offering you my first-born before the stroke of midnight?" But the question regarding her feminine capabilities stung. "I've found the need to define myself outside the constraints of motherhood before I'd inflict myself on an unsuspecting being."

"Despite the joy an heir for your father would bring this sorry family, you do mention a point I hadn't considered."

"There is time." Dr. Pierce's expression eased.

"Olivia Larkin has four children with the fifth soon to be here." Mrs. Pierce quipped.

"You are incorrect, mother." Annabelle sprang from her chair. "Olivia Larkin had four children. Her fifth has arrived. But Olivia died last night." She could not hold back, though anger and sadness seemed to have become one tumultuous emotion. "Olivia's dead." She hauled the accusation at her father.

Gasps and wailing ensued. Mrs. Mingle took charge, dapping Mrs. Pierce's eyes before hustling her from the room, tucked beneath her compassionate wings.

⚜

Annabelle seated herself. Her father was right. No good would come if she continued. She patted her lips with her napkin and wondered where to start her inquisition.

Her father offered her a smile reminiscent of one she imagined a professor would offer to pardon an over-zealous student who had blurted out the disordered roots of the brachial plexus. There was no light of anticipation in his face, he looked oddly and totally at peace. But it was a peace which Annabelle would take pleasure in fracturing.

He reached for his paper and prepared to settle in for the morning.

Annabelle contemplated hurling a teacup over his shoulder. But she held back and cleared her throat.

The Times crinkled. "Yes, my love?"

Annabelle almost wished she could chase time back to before her life had imploded. Back to the safe expanses of libraries and textbooks and ghost writing. But that would be a journey back to a living death and Annabelle was in no mood for mortuaries. "We have to talk about Olivia."

"Very sad business. But it couldn't be humanly helped."

"Thomas assured me of that. But you were not yourself yesterday."

"With the sadness of the circumstances. . ."

"No." Would he not admit anything? "After she screamed, her liver must have ruptured." She paused, hoping he would take the lead.

Her father's head quivered, as it did only when he was absolutely livid. She had seen that quiver aimed at her mother before.

The words tumbled out. "After she screamed, you went to pieces. It was as if you had forgotten your abilities and left me to deal with the chaos."

"You accuse me of incompetence?"

"I did not call it such. But as you do, I will not call it by another name."

"Silence!"

Tossing her napkin aside she stood to meet his height. "You cowered and did nothing."

"Insolence!"

The echo of his protests rang dull; Annabelle pressed on. "You should have done something"

"There was nothing to be done."

"She was bleeding. You could have stopped it."

"With my bare hands? I'm no surgeon."

"But you've had the training."

"Some forty years ago."

"You could have looked for the source."

"Enough! You find it logical that I would have ripped the poor woman open and swum beneath her insides?"

Annabelle nodded.

He slapped the table, the dishes skipped over its veneer. "Her liver fractured Annabelle. A critical organ. She could not have lived. Fate intervened."

"Damn Fate. We give its ill-will too much excuse when the plain fact is you did nothing." The trickle of illogic dawned but she stuck her course. "I could have helped you. I know the anatomy."

"You've lost your senses." Dr. Pierce marched around the long end of the table. "Perhaps I have esteemed your precious senses too greatly?" He grabbed Annabelle by the shoulders.

She had never seen her father like this. She had always left meanness to other men. Visions of dearest Uncle Horace Christianson flickered. Her throat went dry.

"A week in training on a corpse does not make you a surgeon. That is murderous arrogance." Her father was so close she could see a faint smear of egg yolk at the tip of his moustache.

"But it is also arrogance that saves. Otherwise we would be overtaken in a world of cowardice." Annabelle dared a quip.

"I am no coward!" He shook her.

Annabelle felt like a porcelain-headed doll, rag body stuffed and limp. She jerked from grasp. "Don't hit me!"

"I didn't hit you." Her father tried to smooth her crumpled sleeves.

Fragments of memories surfaced as if released by the pressure of his grip. Soft kisses, deserving slaps, fear sifted with pleasure. But never at her father's hand. Annabelle felt the world might go black. She braided her arms around her waist to brace against the escaping sobs. "It would be easier if you had." She sputtered as salt spread over her tongue.

"I've never struck you in my life and do not intend to now!"

Annabelle held her breath to ease her fiery sides. A hiccup erupted and she tucked her chin to her chest, steadying herself against the table.

"Don't be dramatic, my girl, I can't stand it when you cry."

"I've spent a lifetime holding back my tears on your behalf." Sniffling, Annabelle righted herself, finding strength strangely easier than becoming a causality to her past. The shadows of which he knew so very little.

"How could ?" His expression melted into hurt.

Despite everything, it was an expression Annabelle could not bear. "Never mind that." She pulled a chair out. "Right here father." Seating herself she wiped her tears away. "Tell me the whole story. From the beginning."

He sighed, as if it had been repressed for a lifetime. "I had hoped to leave some tales to the sands of time, but I fear I must come clean." He gripped the edge of the table. "Perhaps we should move to . . ."

"Out with it, father."

His tale began, as many of his did, with an exacting setting of scene and character. His third year of medical studies at the College. Early Spring 1839. March the 15th, to be exact. Annabelle gritted her teeth at the details and could almost hear the early robin chirpings and the trickle of melting snow. But it was useless to hurry her father, and she let him choose the pace of its unfolding.

He and Horace Christianson had joined forces two years prior as they cut their newly pointed incisors (and scalpels) in gross anatomy lab . The academic stress and weight of their chosen profession yet to hobble them. Times were fine and carefree. As their years and courses progressed, they rose to the top of their class. At these heights, their confidence grew so as they entered their third year, and the wards, they first put their learning to what they supposed was good use.

None of this was news to Annabelle and she fought to hold from the whip in hurrying his plot's journey.

When her father began to weave in some of the lesser behaviors of his over-confident (and educated) classmates, Annabelle expected him to exclude Uncle Horace and himself from that fray. But it seemed, they, or at least Uncle Horace, were more rogue than Annabelle had previously assumed. After a few hesitant coughs, her father finally picked up his knife and fork to get to the meat of his tale.

To ward off the stressors of the more experimental aspects of their clinical education, and the haunting cries of the unfortunates who clogged the hospital rooms, Horace had taken a mistress. Phillipa Walters. Known on the streets as Honey. Hair like the setting sun and lips like a bow. With the natural progression of their affair, Horace confided late one night over pints of cider his mistress was with child.

With his story paused, Annabelle gently goaded her father. "He must have paid her off then. Sent her to a place in the country. A yearly stipend for her and the child."

"I wish those times were as kind as your heart. Sadly, she declared herself in love with Horace and would not take his money. In her infatuation, likely flamed by a few tumblers of gin, she agreed to rid herself of the child. If it meant he would continue to keep her."

"An abortion." Annabelle knew vaguely of the acceptable butchering of unlucky women for the sake of propriety. Her stomach somersaulted. Bitter herbs. Hooks. Infection. They never ended happily. "He conned her into an operation."

"Conned—perhaps not. But strongly persuaded, yes."

Annabelle noticed a minute tremor of his hand before he anchored it to the table. "Did she survive? What happened to Fannie ?" She felt suddenly protective for the poor woman.

His other hand began to shake. He regarded them as if they were separate entities as they trembled before him for a moment.

"She died?"

"Yes. But more than that." Her father moaned. "I killed her." He wrapped his hands into his face and wept openly, without restraint.

※

Annabelle felt deeply for him as she wove her arm around his shoulders. After a few moments, he found his voice as he blotted his tears with the heel of his hand and continued.

After a blessedly unsuccessful attempt at an abortion, Horace was convinced he could support Honey and her child, though their affair could be no more than what it was. She had seemed happy enough with the compromise and life settled back to right until the night she began to labor.

Have been dealt a poor hand in life thus far, Fannie had drawn the Ace of Spaces . Holed up in a rented room, away from the inquisitive eyes of the questionable establishment when Honey usually entertained visitors, it had started as an oddly cozy affair. The two young men and their patient, hot water, towels, scissors, and a bottle of whiskey (for nerves and pain respectively.) Horace had been quite sweet. R etelling dirty jokes to make her smile between labor pains.

Annabelle's father kept time of her contractions and all in all, felt there was nothing much at all to the whole birthing process. Then her progress stalled. The head was jackknifed against her pubic symphysis. The baby's shoulders caught on the angles of her pelvis. At first, Horace yipped, proud to have fathered such a strapping child. But as the minutes ticked on, their efforts to reposition the child in her canal proved futile, and Honey began to fade. It was no use; they could not take her to hospital. Honey was the worst kind of slut (per Horace,) and he could not risk either his social or professional reputation.

Her breaths hanging in the balance, Annabelle's father offered a possible option. A Cesarean section. While not a common place operation, they had assisted in three thus far this year, a fourth would surely make them experts.

A quick jaunt down the darkened streets. A jiggle of a loose window frame, and the treasure chest of the College's wares was theirs for the taking. Back at the rooms, a flask of chloroform and bunting in tow, the men constructed a drip from the inverted basket of a stovetop coffee percolator. Pleased at their ingenuity, a drop or two eased Fannie's pangs (of pain and doubt) just enough for the pages of Grey's to be consulted and surgical scalpels laid out.

When their first pass was made between her jutting iliac crests, she moaned. A few drops more and she quieted like a rescued pup. With the baby extracted, it was left to the young Dr. Pierce to take over the closure as Horace bounced around the room, juggling his freshly arrived daughter in his arms.

Lofted with their sense of accomplishment, Dr. Pierce made several ties, bringing the edges of the rectus muscles, when he realized it was all too simple. There was no trembling rise and fall of the abdomen to confound the throws of his needle. Frantic searchings with blood-stained fingers make the scene appear more murderous than either of the players ever intended. But Honey was lost, her life sucked from her bones by fatal chloroform and zeal.

Her father stared through Annabelle as he concluded his tale, his past upset overtaken by a mask of detachment, as if he were reading a sad headline from his precious Times. The man had spent his entire life atoning for his sins, encouraged by her Uncle Christianson. The cracks in Horace's character, though only tangentially obvious to a young, awestruck Annabelle, gaped wide, making the grown Annabelle cringe. Her thoughts began to bound. What would Thomas have become without the normalizing influence of his mother? Who knew about this child?

"Where is Thomas' sister?"

"Half-sister, my dear. You've met her actually. I'm not sure it's the time to tell you more."

"I'll take the truth any day over propriety."

"As you wish, my dear." He kept his eyes from meeting hers. "You've more than met her. You knew her."

"Knew?" Annabelle latched onto his past tense. The first person she could think of who had been most recently placed into the past tense was Olivia. "Olivia?"

"No, she was a Foster through and through. Horace's bastard child was Sarah Bramley, your lady's maid."

All sensation vacated Annabelle's face. Sarah's charmingly abrasive chiding, her devilish laugh, and her cold, dead body crashed back into the present. "But—but I—the lab—the knives—Thomas." Her tongue lost its usual elocution.

"He knows nothing of this tale." Her father's eyes took on a metallic quality. "Nor will he. Ever."

Despite the past quarter of an hour, Annabelle nodded her solemn promise. "Never." She wished she had never wrapped her hands around a scalpel handle. A flush of shame at her brazen rush to disembowel Sarah's secrets came to her face. "How could you let me—"

"How could I not? What purpose would it have served then?"

Annabelle did not envy her father's moral entrenchment. But he had heavily nicked her esteem for him. She wondered if she would ever look at him with quite the same childish adoration again.

Annabelle stood. Her father looked smaller, almost shriveled now. "I don't know, perhaps to provide some kind of dignity?" She cocked her rifle. "Then again, that kind of fiber is not for the faint of heart."

Her bullet cracked through his ribs and lodged deep. She left him uttering a few last agonal moans as her feet skimmed lightly out of the room, down the stairs into the din of the late morning kitchen. She flew over the cobbled mews to the stable.

To some kind of sanity.

To Ben.

Chapter 22

Annabelle burst through the stable doors, unsure if she craved Ben's irritating logic or simply his open-hearted admiration. His wide grin hit Annabelle like a beam of much-needed sunshine after a few days storm. The stars and planets, so recently knocked from their familiar orbits, seemed to find their proper axes.

"What brings you galloping in here like a Kentucky Thoroughbred, Lady?" Ben spat out a tuck of tobacco. "I thought you were still sore with me after the rub Tom and I gave ye up at The White Horse." He gave his push broom a few good thwacks before hanging it on a hook. He sent Annabelle one of his infamous looks, dimples arose in impossible places around his cheeks and eyes. "I am forgiven then?"

Of all things holy, did that man have something about him. Her young gelding Dexter took a few kicks at his manager as a reminder that it was nearly noon and he was due for a flake of hay to tide him over until the evening feed. His neighbors followed his instigation and began to echo his protests.

"Hold yer knockers y' impatient glue sticks,' Ben growled before he nodded at Annabelle. "Not a day goes by I don't look at that stall there with a bit of pleasure."

Right. Annabelle sensed unwelcome crimson apples rising on her cheeks. She looked down the slip stall. A kiss and a proposal. What if—But that was then. "You do have an uncanny knack of setting a scene."

A dry, green square arced in her direction. "Aye, ye 'member then?"

Annabelle caught the hay; a fine powder of alfalfa powdered her skirts. She shrugged as she held back her smile, cheeks cooling.

"Nice it was."

She rolled her eyes as she sent the hay sailing to the gelding now dancing in place with anticipation. It had been positively delightful. She turned. With her hands on her hips she countered, "You really are shockingly familiar in your references to the past which has very little consequence to a now, very married woman."

"Well, yes." Ben scratched his head as if waiting for an epiphanic explanation.

Her visit's agency surged strong in the clumsy silence. "Despite the fact I am a very married woman, I've come as a friend in need of counsel."

Ben dropped his arms by his sides and stood at full attention. "Lieutenant Colonel Benjamin Fulbright of the Harley Street Brigade. Champion of Needy, Wedded Women at your service."

As he continued to click his heels together and salute her, like a deranged nutcracker, Annabelle rushed and gave his shins a few teasing japs with her shoe. "It's a sorry day indeed when you, in all this glory, are the best Harley Street can offer for psychiatric consultation."

Ben broke from his foil and stilled Annabelle, his hands on her arms. "I am sorry I offended you at the White Horse. You know I think the world of you, married or not."

"Totally forgiven." His disastrous blue eyes made her see how easy it would be to fold. To fall into his arms in that moment. But she was not so foolhardy. Her discontent would not be solved by a scandalous divorce and a life of domesticity—no matter how lovely the fireplace (and heart) she would stoke. "Yes, yes. The world, I know." Her hands found his as she pushed gently from his grasp. "I need to talk."

Ben dipped his chin. "Olivia. I'm sorry."

"Yes. How did you—"

"Their butler showed up. Speaking in tongues. Must 'av run the three miles here. Covered nose to toe in muck."

Annabelle didn't make the connection.

"Sit down,' Ben pulled them towards the harness room. Inside, he threw a cooling blanket over a stack of hay bales and they sat down, side by side. "Their carriage was out, something 'bout a cracked axel. Their parlor maid, Bridgit's my second cousin. She sent him over here, seeing we're on the way to the College. Good thing too. With the happenings these last few weeks, I knew whereabouts I'd find your Thomas." He seemed pleased at his ingenuity. "I'm just sorry we couldn't have gotten there sooner."

"Time wasn't the problem exactly. If we had guessed earlier. S he should have gone to hospital. An operation might have saved her."

Ben sat up, eager to defend his lifelong champion. "But your father isn't—"

"I know he couldn't have done anything else." Annabelle wasn't ready to forgive her father.

"What gives then?"

Annabelle leaned back; her head cushioned by a knot in the pine planks. Her thoughts were so jumbled and her dreams so vast, it seemed impossible to distill them into any kind of reason.

"Out with it, Lady."

"I can never be that powerless again."

Ben looked at her as if she had requested wings to fly to the moon. "You did everything you—"

"But I didn't. If I knew more, I could have done more. Father froze, making me useless. At least, if he had given me some direction, I could have—"

"Could have's belong in the bin next to guilt, regret, and yesterday's news."

"Your comprehension is shockingly accurate, but easier to preach than follow."

"Aye now." Ben swiveled and propped a knee, facing Annabelle. "Just because I'm me and you're you, don't mean I can't toss my chips on the table. You really can be a snob."

Annabelle didn't dare ask if he'd read Thackery's book on the topic—she really would be one if he had. Annabelle acquiesced. She had few players in her court and could not afford to offend him. Nor in her heart of hearts did she want to tarnish his luster.

"That's why I have such a high regard for your Thomas."

Annabelle realized she must have made a face as Ben blushed and cleared his throat. "Ye know. As a man. Me better. A man's man." His eyes caught hers. He looked as if he were about to choke on a bullfrog. "Not as a man. Not a man's man like that. No funny business."

But it was funny business indeed. Annabelle couldn't stop the laughter escaping from her insides, full more of shame than humor. If only the dear man knew Thomas' secret. The words to give shape to it now would still be too painful.

Between chortles Ben kept up. "You know what I mean. He's a good person. Don't seem to mind if a chap's got a quid to 'is name or 'as never been to school."

"Thomas has many attributes. Having an almost untarnished character is his most admirable."

"Almost untarnished?"

"It's just. . ." A sweep of sadness swooped over her. Thomas who had never really been hers. And would never be. She could not turn him 'round. It dawned on her Ben might hold her in the same regard.

Her resolve softened and the words tumbled. Her frustrations with her privileged but stymied position in the upper crust had not grown stale in the warmth of marital bliss. When she tiptoed about the topic of their quiet marital chambers, Ben caught her eye and put his hand over hers. He opened his mouth, caught himself, then looked down at his knees. His hand didn't move.

"What?" There was a thickness between them that was pleasant. An understanding that was warm and true.

Ben looked sideways at her again. "Tarnished is a bit unkind. I 'ave a second cousin. Good bloke. Different. Like Thomas."

Annabelle caught his wind. He knew. But how could he? "You've got an awful lot of cousins,' was all Annabelle could choke out before she looked away. She tried to take her hand back, but Ben fingers grew softly tight over hers.

"All's I'm gettin' at Lady, is some things don't need to be said. They just are. No explanations. Best left that way."

"But I don't know who anyone is anymore. Everything I know is a lie."

"Ye can only know a person when ye really see 'em—not look for yerself in their eyes."

His gaze was so steady. Too steady. Annabelle felt like a High Brown Fritillary, suspended beneath a magnifying glass, a pushpin poised and sharp, to seal her fate.

His grin split the intensity of the moment. "The truth isn't always a good idea." He shrugged, as if playing a Pickwick Plato was part of his new responsibilities as head coachman.

He was right. Lately the truth had only cut rather than set her free. But where could she go from here? Her questions must have been scrawled across her face.

"So things weren't—aren't—quite as they seemed. Yer lot isn't quite as grand as you'd hoped."

Annabelle wondered where he was going on this perceptive jaunt.

Ben grabbed her hands. "Why ya think I gave you them blades, Lady? These hands make cruel work of embroidery and lace, though I'm no expert."

"Blades?"

"Those bleedin' razors n' handles fer yer weddin'." He shook her hands as if he could stir her memory. "Look. When you're cornered, you've got to come out swingin'. Sometimes swingin' blind is better than takin' one on the cheek."

"What are you on about?"

"I don't think it'll come to this, but you know somethin' yer Thomas'd not like the world ta know. Am I right?"

"He told y—"

"I 'ave half a brain ye know. It don't take a high-flyin' to go from A to C. Between blokes, ye needn't say much. He can get you into school. To be a doctor. It's what you want."

"Women aren't allowed to attend medical school." Even with a twinge of defeat, she loved his declaration was without question.

"I've got you there. Women are allowed in America. And taking me from your equation, consider Thomas. From the sounds of it, he's one of the best. Our regard can't be wrong. He could be your school."

The improbability of Ben's suggestions kept her lips still, but her mind clicked on. Annabelle recalled the intense, bright young men who had been her father's pupils, like Larkin, and the equivalent ranks who were dimwitted and crude. The absolute ridiculousness that women had never joined their ranks (only to likely outrank them of course) speared her skull. Hope flickered at the corners of her lips. "But I wouldn't qualify here. I couldn't practice here."

"You're stuck on this bloody island I see." But Ben didn't stay down for long. "Well you have a year before I leave. How much could you crush into the year, if you studied from dawn to dusk every day?"

What was he plotting?

"But think outside the shores of this bloody island, Bella. The world's bigger than these London Streets. Lady doctors work freely in the States. 'Ave done for the past twenty years."

Tears pricked her heart. "You've done your research, haven't you?"

"Aye, m'lady. We all have dreams." He let her right hand go. His traced the top of her left ring finger—it seemed strangled now by that blessed band of gold. "There are ways."

What seemed like a million emotions coursed through Annabelle. Ben was a constant. He'd never given up on her. Despite teasing, refusals, class, and even marriage vows—snobbery aside, who was she not to be swept away by his tenacity? She tapped her ringed finger, "What have you been scheming, Benjamin Fulbright?"

Suddenly Ben was on his feet, pulling her with him. His flirtatious energy flicked into high voltage candor. "Would you?" He waved their woven hands and skipped them around.

His unabashed joy made tears well and a great drop fell to Annabelle's cheek.

"Would you join me? I could even go first to settle things. Give you more time to study."

He made a new life seem so easy, right within her reach.

Ben kept up his waltz. "One of me backers, he's got some kind of ties to Harver in Boston. The school there."

"Harvard?"

"That's the one. I'm sure when they see how brilliant you are, you could set up your own rooms. See you own patients. Study whatever you'd like."

"In America." It seemed so far away. And even with New York and Boston, it still qualified as heathen.

Ben stilled their dance. "You're unbelievable, Lady. Yes. America. You and me take on their stripes and thirty-seven stars.

The immediacy of his ask made a quiver of panic erupt in her core. "Yes. Yes. Of course I did. Have." Annabelle tripped over the words.

Ben raised his eyebrow. Annabelle was not sure if it was a simple request or a tempting dare. "I've saved and saved. Planned to book me passage on The Athena next month. I'll book yer fare then too. We'll sail second Monday in July next year." His dimples deepened as he smiled. "Mind you, Lexington will be beastly hot in September."

"I'll have to find some means to cope. Seems you have it quite settled then."

"I'd settled on our story quite some time ago. There 'ad been some developments which made me doubt, but not for long. Now all's left is to sort out your training with yer Thomas."

"Stop calling him that." Annabelle nipped. "You know he's not mine." She added softly. "Never was." But in the utterance, she realized the sting was less sharp, the sentiment less bitter. Hope had a funny way of transforming a situation.

"Mind 'yerself, Bella. You know what they say 'bout a bird in hand." He brought her hands to his lips. His eyes found hers. "And I have no intention of letting go."

The melody of the stable door hinge interrupted Ben's soliloquy.

"This is where you two've been hiding!" Thomas careened through the stable door. "Mrs. Mingle said you'd gone to the shops, but she looked a little minxy and I was right." He beamed victorious.

Ben kept Annabelle's fingers knit in his for a beat before he let her go.

"Hallo mate." Thomas strode forward. Ben met him and they embraced, thumping one another's backs as if they had grown up just down the lane from one another.

Annabelle thought she heard him mutter something about enough time and the job done as she thumbed through a list of probable conversation topics to excuse their previous intimacy. Olivia. Ben had known how close she and Annabelle had been. Simple. "Dearest husband,' Annabelle crooned. "You've come to collect me?" It was best to maintain the front of a happy wife, though Thomas' elephant did seem to have lumbered, half-deranged, into the stable.

Thomas matched her stride. "Dearest wife."

Her heart gave her ribs a sound wallop at his address.

"That is precisely what sent me on this wild chase after your father and I wrapped up some discussions."

"Olivia. Yes." Annabelle couldn't hide the sharpness now in her voice. "I gather there was nothing we could have. . ."

Before she could turn down a bilious route, Thomas wrapped her in his arms, murmuring his reassurance there was nothing on this earth that could have prevented Olivia's tragedy. Her blades, so eagerly raised, melted in his warmth and she gave herself, and her multitude of protests, to him.

A shuffle and a cough brought Annabelle back.

"Crikey, look at the time," Ben threw the solitary bale back to its home in the stacks behind them. "I've got loads of pieces to shine before I collect the carriage at Brightman's."

Annabelle gave Thomas a cashmere smile and released herself from his embrace. Thinking it best to avoid comment on the lack of a time-keeping device in the stable, she gave Ben a hooded look. He could take it as he'd like. "Quite right. I trust 17 Berkeley Square is still standing, having withstood the chaos of the last few weeks?"

Thomas had the grace to turn the faintest shade of crimson. "Barely, but yes. It will be a delight to have the lady of the house reseated in her throne."

"Dear God, please don't make me seem I'm like my mother."

Ben snorted. "Not quite there yet."

Thomas laughed in agreement.

"But if you keep yer ' hopes n' dreams all crammed up inside, ye might have a real danger of turning out like 'er ." Ben's damning brow raised again.

"Well I hope you haven't done anything of the sort on my account," Thomas sent Annabelle a look of real alarm.

She shook her head, pleased he might be persuaded to her aims quite easily.

"But she 'as a few ideas. Good 'uns too. On how she could. . ."

"Shhht!" Annabelle could not let him force her hand.

Ben bobbed his head, as if excusing the rowdy emotions of a schoolchild. "I'll say no more, Bella. But just so the good man knows there are things to be said." He gave Thomas nod in respect.

"I can think of nothing more delightful than a proper crashing of Annabelle's plots and plans in the library over tea." Thomas took Annabelle's arm and touched his fingers to his hat brim at Ben.

"You well know we all have plots and plans, dreams and hopes, near and far."

"That's what keeps the human heart beating—dreams and fresh air to fuel them." Thomas smiled. "You'll have to catch me up on how things are sorting out for Kentucky."

"Indeed." Ben beamed. "There have been some developments. Rather smacking ones if I do say. But my dreams are hatched." He looked at Annabelle wistfully. "This lass 'ere just needs a golden goose to settle over 'ers now."

Annabelle didn't like him so dangerously close.

"Then it's your lucky day, my love."

Annabelle winced—for numerous reasons.

"I'd love to play at being your golden goose."

Golden goose. Golden noose. It was all so confusing, Annabelle thought as Thomas swept her away from the stables to a waiting hansom.

※

On the carriage ride home, Annabelle experienced a heart-pounding interval of panic that Thomas had indeed forgotten the insane twists and turns of their jostling journey to date. Seated cozily side by side, he told her of the Persian carpets he'd purchased for the dining room and the Louis XV walnut armoire he'd shipped from Normandy. Other minor purchases and adjustments were rattled off as if he were afraid he'd miss one if he didn't maintain his neck-jarring pace.

When he had exhausted his lists, he settled back, her hand wrapped in his. "If you can think of anything else, just say the word. Your wish is mine." His smile was as fresh as dew quivering on spring blades of grass.

He was as bright and appealing as that first night in the opera when Annabelle had so unexpectedly, and devastatingly, fell in love with him. Then his charming lightness had pushed new winds under her wings, but now it made her heart creak. The poor organ having grown sea-sick from the hopeful crests with Ben and heavy swells with him.

"You really are unbelievable." Annabelle jerked herself from him.

Thomas' rapt expression slid from his face.

"You say any wish I have is yours and that couldn't possibly be farther from the truth."

Question marks scattered over his face.

"My wish is we were to wake from this hellish dream. That you were to have a severe case of amnesia regarding a certain Simon Lygonwood and would find yourself helplessly in love with me. Then we could start our life over at Berkeley Square." Her tone withered. "There were so many things I wanted for us."

"I do love you, my dearest. I've never met a woman quite your equal,' his eyes shifted in consideration. "My mother has a similar luster, but she is altogether quite different."

"You do?" Promise dripped from the two syllables.

"I could never have married you if I hadn't."

"Then what have we been going on about?"

"I love you. Am in love with you in a way. But not in the way I love Simon."

"You cannot love me if you love a man."

"There are so many different kinds of love," Thomas protested as Annabelle slid to the corner of the carriage to sulk.

"There's only one that matters to me." She saw Ben's kind eyes when she closed hers.

Thomas pushed over to her. "Annabelle, like it or not, I can never be the kind of husband you hoped I would be. I was wrong. I heard the words you spoke, but only listened to the ones I wanted to hear. It was my story, not yours. For that I am deeply sorry."

"You've ruined me. I'm caught in another, larger, prettier cage, but a cage nevertheless."

"You are bound in name alone. I will allow you anything. However we are in this together and must maintain the semblance of a devoted marriage for Society." His resemblance to her father vanished as easily as it had appeared. "But behind closed doors, absolutely anything."

Annabelle had thought herself too tired to support another siege of anger, but she had underestimated herself—a rare occurrence. "Am I to live a life behind closed doors?"

"Not quite in the manner you're thinking. We all lead double lives. One for the blessing of Society, and another, sometimes quite a different tale, beyond its prying eyes."

"You know what I mean."

"I'm serious. As wise as you are in some ways, you don't read between written lines very well."

His smile sent another wedge of irritation through Annabelle's inflamed heart. "How dare you!"

"But I do." Thomas pressed on firm, without a hint of anger to match Annabelle. "Many people find happiness outside the marriage to the betterment of their vows. We promised to have a pioneering marriage and I stand by that promise."

"Obviously, we each had our very different definitions. Pioneering. Manipulating." Annabelle enjoyed the sliver of pain her last word dug into Thomas's face. "I want happiness inside our marriage."

"I've done you a disservice which I regret. But do not forget the service I have done for your father and your family." A brief flicker of flint struck through his eyes.

For a few pleasant minutes, Annabelle had enjoyed her righteous anger, having forgotten her life, as a woman of a certain standing, was not hers alone. She was little more than a privileged pawn. She shrank back to her corner, her purpose punctured by his reason.

"Don't play the compliant damsel, Mrs. Christianson. It is one of the only terribly unattractive things you do. A shame as you are so terribly lovely."

"You have both a wrong and a right in your accounts, and I can only register a right in mine."

Thomas broke into a laugh. "So rather than calling it a draw, your aching to find a wrong to put in your council?"

"I can't see why not? "

"I suppose I could find it in my good nature to allow you the deliciousness of a wrong if you'd like?"

"Good." Annabelle shifted closer to him and looked out the carriage window as they turned onto Charles Street. She'd not have trouble convincing him of her plans. She wondered about America. If she could like the rolling hills and sticky summers of Kentucky. In her daydream, she decided she very well just might.

Particularly as one Dr. Annabelle Christianson.

Chapter 23

One rule was never to be broken in medicine. His medicine. An ego was lethal.

When Annabelle nodded in agreement, Thomas sharpened their blades and led her into their dangerous ruse.

Annabelle hated the rough fabric of her nurse's uniform and the way she followed Thomas around the wards like a pet goose. But for the privilege of her clandestine education, she swallowed public subservience to enjoy private freedoms. She learned quickly how to balance administering anesthesia and monitoring vital signs in smaller surgeries. Away from inquisitive eyes, she absorbed all she could assisting Thomas in larger operations without raising doubts of her true aims. No one suspected a starched sister of such eminent aspirations.

They were never caught.

Annabelle favored procedures in private homes of Society's fortunate Ten Percent who disdained consorting with the masses in London hospitals. In their private chambers, with family members dismissed, Thomas instructed with Annabelle free to cut and sew over her anesthetized textbooks. Each week, she found her mind expanded, cataloguing the surgical knots and techniques. With time, her hand steadied.

After Mrs. Mingle's dinner feasts, ever faithful, she'd found excuse after excuse to lend her hand at 17 Berkeley Square. Annabelle and Thomas would settle into the library, surrounded by a sea of notes to review the day's lessons.

In these hours, Thomas gave form to the chaos of her unchartered education. As the months passed as quickly as a comet flaming across a velvet sky, Annabelle found the artifice of convention and disappointments falling away. Even Simon Lygonwood had begun to augment his previously unseen presence with regular appearances by their night fires. At first Annabelle squirmed at his handsome nature, never knowing where his attentions were directed (she did not believe herself vain at the glimmer she saw in his eyes as they traced her form.)

But now she looked forward with immense anticipation to the jolly evenings when he stayed to pleasantly offset her otherwise habitual medical conversations with Thomas. Though at times the shared moments between the two men made her feel a stranger. S he felt she should look away in primness, but never did.

With Thomas and Simon, she could grumble and shout. Romp and be silent. And so her fractured heart splinted, eager to heal for the promises of an unknown future.

⧈

In a cosmic twist of events, Annabelle found herself confronted with a request she was unable to deny—to resect an enormous fibrous parotid tumor. With the carotid artery involved, the thing, the size of a grown meat rabbit, had a pulse of its own. Having grown insidiously over the past decade, Thomas had been distraught the family had not sought a surgical opinion sooner. Now the appeal of an early death over a life of disfigurement shone.

Tuesday, three weeks prior, Thomas reviewed logistics with the patient's family; the dining room turned operating room, the anxious wait sequestered in the front parlor. Annabelle could hear him drumming over the risks of the surgery—paralysis, difficulty swallowing, even death. Annabelle found Thomas' caveat quite irritating as his patients always did well. A fact which he attributed to Lister's inspiration rather than his God-given surgical skill.

As his agonizing litany of perils concluded, Annabelle flickered a reassuring smile to the mass of humanity seated across from her. Corpulent as a bacon-pig at Martlemas was the charitable description of Cornelia Greville. Aunt Maude had once declared the only occasion on which excessive leanness ever proved beneficial to a lady was in an encounter with a cannibal. A sentiment which Annabelle found no hindrance to share.

Annabelle had only been moments alone with the regrettable daughter of the third Earl of Northumberland. The poor woman's observation had yet to shift from her lap. But just then, she offered Annabelle a glimpse of her eyes. Though beady and hooded with flesh they were a stunning azure blue. A mazurka of sorts resulted, between breaths and shifting of silks. Annabelle wondered how a nurse, albeit a well-dressed one, should converse with high society.

Exasperated with their games, she tossed convention over her shoulder, and broke their silence to politely inquire about the safe subject of Miss Greville's left foot.

As if Annabelle had removed a lifelong gag from between her jaws, Miss Greville offered a simple mew, affirming great improvement in her comforts and beckoned Annabelle to her side.

No sooner had Annabelle's hips found the upholstery, the trembling woman clutched her hands and implored Annabelle to remove the hideous growth—to revive any last breaths of humanity to her face. Pity had not been a frequent resident in Annabelle's heart, but in that instant, she acquiesced. No wonder Cornelia Greville had fallen into the habit of examining the wormholes in the floorboards as if answers from hell would come seething through their cracks. Annabelle found herself powerless to stop reaching out her arms as a net to catch Miss Greville's fall. It was that spark which placed one woman's fate in those of another's.

Thomas loved the idea. Annabelle had trained under his hawk eyes for eight months, surgeries during the light hours, the intricacies of medical management by tangerine electric light at night. Now she would wield the scalpel primarily, with Thomas as her assistant, she the surgeon.

The following week, Thomas bounded home to recount his recent investigations into the legal state of medical ladies, incapable of disguising his eagerness to make amends with Annabelle. Between bites of succulent roast capon with currant jelly, the cozy trio at 17 Berkeley Square tore apart a legal loophole where Annabelle could practice medicine. Lagging language in the charter for the Societies of Apothecaries was quite clear. They did specifically not exclude women from the practice of medicine. If she could sit and pass their examination, she could attain the degree of Licentiate, and be free to hang a shingle in Harley Street, blade to blade with Thomas if she liked.

At first, Annabelle laughed, her heart tied to his kite strings. Even Simon swept her up into a celebratory turn around the dining room. But later, contemplating Mrs. Mingle's damson tarts, a wheedling whine came into Annabelle's head. "I would be an apothecary. Not a medical doctor."

Thomas had no choice but to confirm her judgement.

More protests followed. Annabelle would not stand to qualify by means of the scullery door. It was a medical doctor or nothing at all she declared as she morosely tucked into her third tart. Its ability to sooth her affronted ego was remarkable.

Thomas leveled his eyes and logic at her. A look she knew well—and hated.

She narrowed her eyes, ready for the humanitarian reason to come.

"Change is the only constant we know. Title or no title, they can't take away your education. There will come a time. The vote won't be far off. At least not if mamma has her say. And why not lady doctors? There is a genius of sensitivity which our profession very much lacks, and a feminine ingenuity we need. Let's proceed with our plans, my love."

"You excel at ruses, don't you?" Annabelle couldn't help herself, though the shimmer of a smile at the corner of her mouth was genuine.

⚭

In the shimmering hours between twilight and dawn, Annabelle finally grew weary over Grey's and her notes—anatomic landmarks and surgical approach. Wide exposure through horizontal incisions. Reflecting the mastoid muscle and pulsating jugular vein. Onward with gentle blunt dissection of the carotid branches, taking supreme care to preserve (identify first,) the cranial nerves, and finally teasing the tumor off the carotid itself.

The saving of a life in five easy steps, Annabelle thought to herself. All in a day's work. But no amount of study or discussion with gods could steady the trembling of her hands. Annabelle Christianson realized in unrooted horror; she was human.

⚭

"Breathe out." Thomas commanded.

Annabelle exhaled. Despite how often she had sliced into another living being, the simultaneous feelings of fear and loathing poked their repulsive heads from the mire of her subconscious. Thankfully exhilaration cast a rope to safety as soon as the fine swell of blood rose to welcome her blade.

Thomas' long-time morgue assistant, Rodger good-humoredly stood at Annabelle's former post, as chloroform supplier. Their surgical instruments, dipped in carbolic, had been placed carefully beneath borrowed linens, where knives and oyster forks had lain the evening prior.

The evening prior, the Grevilles held a celebration dinner to toast the following day's smooth operation. Their optimism charmed Annabelle before the reality of their undertaking set in her gut like slow-drying cement. Apprehension made her chase the perfect tournedo about her plate, hoping her lack of appetite was perceived as sympathy for the Miss Greville. Their patient, commanded to refrain from food for twelve hours before anesthesia lest the risk of aspiration, followed the tines of Annabelle's empty fork like a hawk tracking a field mouse. The foremost question in Annabelle's mind as she offered her comforting smiles remained. Will her face move afterwards? The small space, the webs of delicate nerves, there was a good chance it would not. But, as Miss Greville had confessed to Annabelle in her final pleas, she felt her life extinguished decades ago.

Silently Annabelle agreed.

But now, the morrow was today and there was work to be done. Her work. Her case.

Annabelle peeled back the membrane which sheathed the lobular tumor. Tiny vessels coursed along its surface like the haphazard intersections of the London maze. At each pass of her scalpel, tiny ruby rivulets flowed. Thomas followed Annabelle dutifully with a thin wire, heated in a candle flame.

Sizzle, smoke.

By the time the mass was almost freed, laying gelatinous on the white sheet draping the dining table, a watercolor stain formed a halo around it, peppered with evidence of their cautery.

In its way, the work was pleasant. Thomas remained true to his word and dutifully assisted Annabelle in her task, never usurping her role as first surgeon. Their hands persisted with their bloody needlepoint and Annabelle grew bolder under Thomas low tones and reassurance, teasing the last bits of fascia tethering Miss Greville to her past,

With one last protest, the tumor succumbed and spread fully onto the table. A wash of calm confidence draped over their scene. It had been easier than either of them could have anticipated. "Well done." Thomas murmured.

Annabelle knew the real test would follow.

Scrape. Retract. The last three cranial nerves.

Expose. The superior laryngeal nerve.

Tease. Slice. The sympathetic trunk.

She reflected the eight branches of the external carotid—nymph-like octopus arms in a sea of red flesh, the thrill of the case intensified. Bit by bit she made quick work of the offending mass. Just as Annabelle withdrew a particularly satisfying triangle of tissue, she saw it. A remaining quivering lobe of the tumor, hidden behind the bifurcation of the carotid. Its pulse taunted her. The tumor would certainly return if every last bit was not plucked from its nest. Miss Greville's artery bulged, as if begging for a fight.

"May I? I may have chosen your first case very badly indeed."

Annabelle scanned Thomas' face and the weaving point of her scalpel. Do no harm. Compassion over curiosity. She held fast to her tool—wary to surrender so easily in the face of this righteous battle. She appraised the pulsating vessel and the derisive remnant of tumor. If she retracted just so and cut at a forty-five-degree angle. She looked back to Thomas whose expression left no question to his demands. She conceded and tipped the scalpel in his direction.

"You've been brilliant, but here, at the bifurcation. In such close quarters. Let this be on my shoulders." Thomas narrowed in on his target.

For once, Annabelle felt a relief on relinquishing the reins. She hadn't appreciated the exhausting power it took to wield a life. Appreciating a breath of lightness, she took over retracting the obliquely stretched stylohyoid muscles. Thomas settled into his work as if pulling on a well-worn overcoat. He could make time, like her heart, stop. His unshakable belief in his skill. He seemed to know how each patient's story would end, even if they only professed the halting knowledge of its beginning.

Small spheres of the mass slipped easily into her awaiting hands, more precious than beads of the finest Russian caviar. Their chests and their patient's rose and fell narrowly in time. Rodger continued the inexact art of anesthesia as he kept the cone filter dredged in chloroform. Annabelle drank in the contours of Thomas' face, in awe of this man who sat down to dinner with her every night and what he was truly capable of. He seemed too perfect, too handsome, to be capable of the brutal majesties of these last months. This juxtaposition had made her heart hang in the balance. But these days her head and soulistic ambitions won over sentiment.

"Another minute and I'll be satisfied." Thomas drew back to assess his progress then returned to his mechanics.

Having sucked every last dreg of learning she could from their surgical field, Annabelle's thoughts turned to the closure. They had planned a second surgery. A muscle flap. The pectoralis exactly. A wedge threaded back on itself, to fill the defect left in the wake of the tumor. A third and even a fourth surgery would be necessary to attain restoration. Anabelle had sketched the woman's face what seemed like a thousand times. At the anticipation, her fingers twitched. She was anxious to regain the reins. She tapped the toe of her shoe to be sure Thomas took note.

"Last bit there." Thomas righted himself for a final survey. Relief laced his words.

Annabelle threaded the curved surgical needle with waxed catgut and armed her left hand with forceps. "I'd like to take it from here." She invaded Thomas' surgical field, arms drawn for the final victory. She never should have given up her scalpel. Thomas was a fine surgeon indeed, but then again, so was she.

In an instant, hands and instruments tangled, flesh against steel. Instinctively Annabelle held her ground. If she backed down now, a precedent would be set and she would be back to riding on Thomas' coat tails—as an assistant, nurse, scribe, but never an equal.

In an equivocal reflex, Thomas released his instruments with a dull clatter onto the linens. "I've told you to never. . ."

"I'm the surgeon here," Annabelle growled, like a lioness, keeping a pack of bone-thin hyenas at bay, defending her stance with a desperation which frightened her. Her hand jabbed forward ever so slightly in emphasis.

So slightly. But it was enough. Now scalpel in hand, its blade pressed as easily through the carotid artery as a butter knife would pass through butter left out on a June day. Annabelle started. At first there was no angry spurt of blood.

As they peered into Miss Greville's fileted neck a healthy gurgle of bright blood oozed from the wounded internal carotid artery, the branch providing sustenance to her eyes and brain.

"I—I," Annabelle's jaw clattered but the words would not come. To be undone in a rash moment. Exactly what Thomas had warned her against.

As if to question her trust in Annabelle, Miss Greville let out a muted moan. Instantly Rodger was at attention in an instant. "Too conservative on my pacing, sir."

"Five drops." Thomas ordered, as he pressed his thumb over the lacerated artery to staunch its flow. "And not in the least, my poor observation's to blame."

Rodger dutifully dredged the gauze mask soak with chloroform, within seconds, their patient's lips softened, her eyelids sealed, and she fell back to her intended dreamland.

"Arrogance kills, Annabelle." Thomas' look of disappointment made Annabelle wince. "Compress her neck with both hands. Above and below. The wound is not so large."

Annabelle obeyed numbly. She had no choice. Submit or allow a patient to bleed her life onto the carpet. She turned mechanical as Thomas conducted the repair, as if it were the opening night of Wagner's Symphony in C Minor.

One throw. Tie. Two throw. Tie. Three. Knot.

Annabelle slid her scissors down the ligatures. Snip. A tight seal. Success, no thanks to her hands, Annabelle thought, as she withdrew from the field.

"We're not finished."

Annabelle jumped, Thomas' words a spray of darts peppering her ribcage. But he had said we.

"A platysma graft for dual compression's the thing here."

I'm a fool. Annabelle handed Thomas her scalpel to sculpt a wing of tissue from the flat muscle. It wouldn't be missed. Encasing his repair, it would prove a tidy suit of armor against the risk of an aneurysm, or worse, a rupture.

Thomas scanned the slumpering Miss Greville. Her breath was rhythmic and shallow. He shook his head. "You started this. And you'll finish it. Reinforcements were simply required in the midst of battle." He offered her a turn of his lips and returned the scalpel.

Annabelle realized her expression must have twisted as he smiled openly now at her.

"It's no drawing room art we're playing at now."

Reluctantly Annabelle, a stranger adrift in her sea of self-doubt, snatched the offered scalpel and continued on her fated masterpiece. A rhomboid section of platysma muscle seemed to ease itself from the plane under her hand. She paused after sheathing the bedraggled vessel in its cloak, an ideal fit. Another blot of gauze, several whips of her needle. Snug. "You are giving me something not even my father has allowed." Thomas' face was wiped clean of his suffering at her smile. "What do you think of my contrition?" She tipped her head at the salvaged artery.

Thomas nodded.

Only closure remained. Then the proud flesh would bubble up, like the tufted surface of an early summer strawberry. In truth it had been the work of moments. Annabelle completed a circuit of dressings around the neatly sutured arc at Miss Greville's throat. "Right." She looked to Thomas. Rodger could slowly withdraw the chloroform now, inviting consciousness back to the table.

"Slow your drip," Thomas instructed. Moments later Miss Greville stirred. Her fingertips fluttered. Then her eyelids. Above the bandages, her forehead was smooth, the left side of her face serene compared to her bullied right. Without warning, her eyes blazed wide and hands pounded the dining table before she bolted upright, her hands to her chest. "Eleph—, eleph—" She sputtered. "I can't,' she wheezed. "Elephant. Chest. Can't. Breat—"

Rodger lurched back like a caught thief.

Annabelle caught their patient's shoulders as her eyes locked with Thomas. He snatched his stethoscope from his bag and was by her side in an instant. Annabelle searched for her pulse; the refreshing pinkness drained from Miss Greville's face. Annabelle drummed her fingers over their patient's wrist, searching for life in the radial artery.

Rodger stepped back to his place without a word, his eyes darting, his mouth downturned.

No pulse resounded against Annabelle's fingertips. She had never seen a patient die on their operating table. She was totally unprepared for this. She had only wanted a preoccupation—not an occupation.

"No heartbeat."

Miss Greville slumped back, startling Rodger with her weight. The two men caught her and slowed her descent.

"Asystole."

Miss Greville was dead.

"Everything alright in there?" A man's voice trailed into the room beneath the heavy door, more affirmation than question.

"We're attending to a complication. . ." Thomas trailed off.

"Complication?"

"Remain calm, Lord Grenville. I'll be out in a few minutes to speak with you."

A flurry of caustic whispers ensued. "Let the doctor do his work," a woman's voice shrilled, presumable the Lady Greville.

Annabelle's eyes stretched wide. In their most absurd imaginings of how the surgery would unfold, they had never anticipated this. It was to avoid a living death they had pursued this undertaking.

Rodger moved away from the commotion as if he could dismiss his witness to their unfurling tragedy.

"As you wish, Dr. Christianson." Footsteps trailed away.

Annabelle was snared between panic for her patient and a desperate desire to be anywhere but this dining room in Green Park. "How could she? She was fine."

"Never a murmur. Nor angina. Or asthma." Thomas' tone escalated, his unflappable demeanor unraveling.

"But she's dead in front of us," Annabelle hissed. "We can't let her. . ." She was sinking into panicked despair as she realized she had exhausted her education which she had considered so extensive—until now.

"Sudden cessation of the heart. There's a technique." Thomas returned to their patient, running his hands along her ribs and sternum. "A happy accident. A fading patient. An unseen log on a country road. A violent rattle of carriage wheels. A life restored."

"Lord help me, I don't understand it but—" Thomas raised his right arm high.

Rodger yelped, then covered his hands to his mouth as if he hoped to swallow his doubt in Thomas' next move.

Thomas cast an arctic glance at Rodger, who shrank deeper into the corner, but not before sideswiping a side table. A heavy platter, painted with pagodas and cherry blossoms, rocked dangerously on its rest. Annabelle imagined she could hear the paneling and silver in the buffet rattle, as if a warning, rumbling thunder before a flood.

Thomas brought his fist down with all his might to meet Miss Greville's breastbone with a deafening crack.

It happened so quickly, and with such terrifying assurance, Annabelle could only narrow in on the still chest of their patient. Thomas' dramatic effort seemed uselessly idiotic.

A spread of silence counted their heartbeats—three—two—one.

Everyone hovered in hopeful anticipation, eyes peeled.

Nothing but stillness.

Thomas' chin fell to his chest, his hands covering his face.

Annabelle could hear his coarse whispers.

"Our Father who art in heaven, hallowed be thy name. Thy kingdom come, thy will be done."

Before she could join in, a soft, shivering moan wove above his prayer.

"Some water please?" Miss Greville greeted the world for the third time that day with her simple request.

It would have been impossible to describe the clatter of emotions thundering through Annabelle's body at Thomas' brute miracle. A direct force sustained to the tender cardiac muscle to evoke a fresh pace. Velocity. Kinesthetic energy. Displacement. Potential energy. Force. She splashed water from a side table into a glass and held it to her patient's lips, fighting to chain her tears of relief as Miss Greville took several hearty swallows.

"Is it gone?" The lady rocked her heft several times before righting herself with a gentle push from Rodger.

"The surgery was a complete success." Annabelle lied, unsure if she possessed the reserves to complete their charade.

Thomas stood in silence at the restoration.

Affording him a few moments to kiss the sky, Annabelle continued with a professional clip, hoping to assure not only Miss Greville, but herself. She glossed over the dramatic pinnacle to her procedure and plans for reconstruction in the coming weeks. But she felt at odds with her mind, ambitions, heart. She furtively wished she could remove herself from the corporal sensations as if stepping out of an evening dress, sewn too tight for effect. But she pressed on for the sake of Miss Greville and the trust she had bestowed in their hands. The line between savior and executioner was a narrow one.

Bandaged like a mummy, they ushered Miss Greville out to her waiting family's hushed cheers. Annabelle escorted her up to her bedroom and her convalescence. Thomas stayed behind to deliver his recommendations for Hoffmann's laudanum and brandy in moderate doses throughout the day. Mustard plasters over the chest and coals at the feet overnight would also be well-advised. When Annabelle returned to the drawing room, Thomas was concluding his remarks. A diet heavy with garlic and turmeric was imperative to thin the blood after the minor arterial injury.

Following their heartfelt farewells to the overjoyed Greville family, Annabelle and Thomas made their escape back to the dining room. Rodger had made himself useful and the long dining table was cleared, ready for the dinner service that evening.

Back in their carriage, a handsome having taken Rodger and their few boxes of equipment back to the College, Thomas turned to Annabelle. "What did you think of your first case as a real surgeon?"

Annabelle could hardly fathom the joviality in his voice.

Thomas kissed her heartily on the cheek. "Shall we try it again tomorrow?"

His cheer grated against Annabelle's battered nerves and threadbare confidence. She was grateful only she had not repeated her father's history. A torrent of depreciation rained down on Annabelle as the entire horrific episode replayed itself in a flash before her eyes.

Slice. Snip.

Death. Resurrection.

"I do not wish to do such a thing again," she declared bursting into tears, meaning every word of her defeat.

Chapter 24

It was one week after Annabelle returned to Berkeley Square following the curious case of Miss Greville's . So thorough was her defeat, she resorted to her lesser habits. These recent tantrums, confined to her bedcovers, were fueled by a gnawing sense of inadequacy, and shame at her fervent ego which had failed her (and almost Miss Greville.)

Despite Thomas' coaxings Annabelle remained below her duvet barricade for several days, before, with Simon and Kitty, dinner trays in tow, they invaded her bedroom. They ignored Annabelle's sputtered protests as they set up a lovely supper en pleine air.

Thomas and Simon made a great show of it, laughing uproariously at Punch's latest sketches drawing an unattractive, yet wholly accurate comparison of the latest bustle to a mollusk's shell. Simon knew Annabelle's weakness for comedy at the expense of inane ladies' fashions. As their voices drew suspiciously quiet after Annabelle picked out Simon's exclamation of a 'pretty lady doctor' gracing the cover of the month's issue, Annabelle acquiesced. Their aimable conspiracy had worked.

Flouncing down from her pillowed lair, Annabelle snatched the subscription from Simon's left hand, and the dangling salmon toast from his right. "Look here,' she eyed the drawing of a prim woman (the aforementioned pretty lady doctor) with a line of grubby scallywags stammering imagined maladies stretching before her. Annabelle elbowed between the two. "Men, useless articles if you ask me, have no regard for her time or education." Thomas and Simon did not spare Annabelle in their comically heated argument.

By the end, a smile had edged itself onto her face and Annabelle found herself agreeable to the notion of tea with her mother-in-law—pretty lady doctor indeed. It was as if Thomas knew any lingering haze clouding Annabelle's perspective was no match for Mrs. Christianson's bracing maternal influence.

And he was right. As he always was.

Beatrice Christianson with her bullish clatterings and cut-throat insight set to work expunging Annabelle's lingering misgivings over Miss Greville. "A mere scratch tidied up in the work of a moment," she declared, patting Annabelle's knee.

Thomas had obviously encrusted their tale with copious amounts of sugar, Annabelle thought to herself, though on reflection, it wasn't a totally incorrect assessment. Perhaps there was hope for a new kind of lady doctor?

"Dear Thomas, for all his worth in gold, has made his fool's share of errors, my dear."

In truth, Thomas had not been shy in disclosing the hard lessons he had learned in his years of practice at the butchering art . "But he always seems to land on his well-shod feet, Mrs. Christianson."

"Goodness me, Annabelle, do call me Bea. You make me feel thrice my age with that Mrs. nonsense." She aimed another hearty swipe at Annabelle's knee; its amiable intent almost sent Annabelle's teacup clattering to the floor.

Her mother-in-law appraised Annabelle for a moment, as a general might review a battle plan constructed by his newest sergeant colonel, whom he felt held both extraordinary potential and naivete.

Annabelle did not mind her matronly study, for there was not the slightest hint of disapproval, only curiosity and brightness. And there was that lingering question of the lady doctor. Annabelle found herself softening to the notion of the Apothecary Licentiate.

"As you have landed on your feet, Annabelle." Beatrice swiped an oatcake from the tea tray and crammed it into her mouth. "It's an act in faith indeed to reach into another human being in the hopes of saving them from whatever ill avails. There's no salvation without a risk. Part and parcel of your profession's manifesto." She washed down her declaration with a swill of her cooling tea.

"My profession?" Annabelle still clung to wells of self-pity. Was she part debutante, wife, and surgeon. Or was it surgeon, wife, debutante.

A spray of crumbs sprang from Mrs. Christian's upper lip as she crashed her cup to the slight table between them. "As you see, you must come of it, my sweet. You do me a great insult if you do not count yourself a true surgeon trained by the side of my dearest Thomas."

"Right. Surgeon. Lady Surgeon." Punch's title did not sit ill with her.

"Stuff and nonsense, Bella." The grand dame rose from her seat like a massive piece of ancient Greek artillery (Atilla surely would have quaked in his sandals.) "Leave a discussion of your skirts at the proverbial door. You are a surgeon. You have changed forever the fate of Lord Greville's cursed daughter. You cannot escape your talent, even if you choose to partake in this irritatingly human tendency to self-deprecation." She eyed the tempting tower of remaining biscuits wistfully, hesitated, then gave in. "For all your broad strokes and steps, Annabelle, you've folded so easily with one little bump in the road." Her smile was all kindness.

Annabelle found a refreshing course of energy reminded her of typical contrary preferences. "I resent your accusation, Bea."

"Now there's that good ol' British can-do spirit." Mrs. Christianson chortled. "Much more appropriate for a woman of your time and capacity." She crashed back into her chair, it squealed in response, and grabbed Annabelle's hands. "These are the times to be a woman. Change is in the wind and whether you want to be a part of it or not, you are a pioneer and must speak out."

Pioneering heart. Annabelle heard Thomas' whispered promise. On its heels with equal pull was Ben's open-hearted proposal to America. Perhaps more, if Annabelle admitted, for wasn't that unruly land built by pioneers?

"Would you speak at the amendment rally next month?"

Annabelle turned the idea round as her mother-in-law churned on about statics and ill-defined women's rights. She wondered where she stood in the settlement between her father and dear Uncle Horace, and at her inherent revulsion to anything political.

Before Annabelle could formulate a reply Beatrice trollied ahead with her usual steam-driven enthusiasm. "This latest Property Act is utter poppycock. Rich and poor women are defined as unrelated species—no true freedom in terms of personal property."

Annabelle had never formed much respect for suffrage, with fledgling efforts for the vote seeming woefully bound for failure. Until that day in Trafalgar Square. But her surgical studies had appropriated her attentions of late.

Beatrice's brassy tones broke through her thoughts. "We have the right to personal property. The same rights as men when we marry."

Annabelle's question still tickled her brain. Where did she stand in the accounts of her own marriage? For that matter, where did the formidable Bea? Annabelle was certain Uncle Horace would not permit certain freedoms to any woman. But then again, Beatrice Christianson was not just any woman.

"This act is woefully inadequate. Far too much power given to a man when he becomes a husband—and on paper and in flesh are two grossly different beasts."

Annabelle tipped her head in agreement. She wondered how much dearest Bea knew of her son, and his entanglements.

"You could address the crowd to counter our MP's stymied perspective that women's domestic duties will be neglected, should she be granted the same rights as her husband."

Annabelle thanked her stars she had long since finished her tea or she would have ravished Mrs. Christianson's rather fine afternoon dress with her disbelief. "Beresfield Sackville ?" Hadn't he been on the receiving end of a certain well-aimed ginger beer bottle?

"Yes, the idiot debases marriage as a covenant of financial security alone. He believes a husband to become a cast-off rag if a wife has sufficient resources. The Act needs to be radically re-written by the Lords. You could be at the forefront of commanding them to do just that."

"Why me?" Annabelle had no desire to experience the interior décor of Brixton prison, having so narrowly escaped once.

"You have an education, a voice, and a mission."

"My mission is a very personal one." Annabelle hadn't considered her recent education a bit political, but indeed it was. For wasn't she conspiring to ram through one such chauvinist loophole to pursue her Harley Street dreams? A quest for purpose had been polished quickly into one of political liberation—a stage she had no interest in entertaining. "I simply want to make the most of the mind I've been given."

"You shock me at your narrow-mindedness." Mrs. Christianson's look was both honey and venom. "You've never before considered what your accomplishments mean as a revolutionary? For all women?"

The afternoon was proving more taxing than Annabelle anticipated. Suffragette was not a word she ever intended to embody—there had been a paucity of glittering tiaras and ball gowns as of late. Though, since she had begun her bloody training with Thomas, her skin hadn't felt the kiss of satin. Worse still, she hadn't missed it until now.

Annabelle took the question as a condemnation. Affirmation she was indeed a fool. "I had not." Her reply rang hollow.

"Like it or not, my dear, you've become far more than a bejeweled mannequin. Have you not enjoyed this education? The opportunities it will open for you?"

Annabelle hung her head. "I have." As much as she enjoyed the intellectual gymnastics, she had equally loved sharing Thomas' time. Her heart squeezed—a tiny corner would not let her relinquish the fairytale she had strung together in her head. She swallowed her sentiment hard before lifting her head. Where was the old Annabelle? "Unfortunately, at present, there is only one ray of hope for me to practice medicine."

"Fiddlesticks, there's more than one way to skin a donkey. What a nasty expression. I adore the little creatures." Beatrice's expression brightened. "What way is that?"

"The Society of Apothecaries. There's never been a woman permitted to attend the medical college."

"More London idiots I see, it's becoming quite an epidemic."

Annabelle couldn't help herself and laughed.

"Legality is quite irrelevant, as thankfully, laws change. You've been quite the barber's hell cat, and you simply must find those stripes again. There is always a way." Her mother-in-law nodded as if she were the Archbishop of Canterbury, certain reality would yield to her authority.

With an unstoppable force such as Beatrice Christianson, and her own fresh questions, Annabelle found herself acquiescing, as her doubts were no match to her curiosity—and hope—a flicker of thanks fluttered in her heart for those small blessings. "I'm not quite ready, but I do plan to sit for their exam."

"That's the spirit my girl, you've got brains, ambition, and my Thomas in your court—you will pass, my dear, of that I am sure." Without another breath, she careened into Annabelle for a bullish embrace—almost throwing Annabelle's chair to the floor in submission. "You will write a new history for all women, like it or not."

Her senses both bruised and bolstered, Annabelle recovered her wits as her mother-in-law righted herself, looking as triumphant as if she had completed a hundred one-footed pirouettes at the Opera, and snatched up yet another tea biscuit.

"Heavens look at the time. I'm off to Millicent's to discuss the mission of Newton College." She took a great bite of her biscuit.

Annabelle thought she could make out an invitation to join her at the suffragette's home between chews. "I've bolsters to do on the piece on muscle flaps in the repair of vasculature dissection. We're submitting it to The Lancet next month. I'm first author." A skein of pride brought a bright note to her voice. It was a good article to be sure, though details of dissection versus accidental vascular injury had been massaged like a good pastel sketch into the background.

"That is an excuse I respect, my dear." Mrs. Christianson checked her mouth for lingering crumbs. "This won't be the last time I endeavor to convert your sentiments. You continue to pioneer in your own way, and I will in mine." She kissed Annabelle's cheek. "Stay as long as you like. Horace has just received some lovely new triple-deckers, Wilkie Collins and Harrison somebody or other. The binding's not been cracked, I'm sure you would enjoy the honors."

⚜

"Whose binding's not been cracked?" The door to the parlor swung open, as if propelled by a magician. Dr. Horace Christianson broke the feminine spell in the room as he strode in. His gazed fixed immediately on Annabelle.

Annabelle looked away, not missing his implication. Would he never let the past sleep in the graveyard of broken dreams?

"Those lovely new volumes you've let waste on that table. Delivered weeks ago. It's shameful how they've languished without your attentions. I've been simply too taken with my political essays to spare a second for fiction." Mrs. Christianson swept to her husband. "I'm off to Millicent's."

Horace Christianson exhaled like a stymied bull and shook his head.

Annabelle took it he disapproved of the good Millicent's works, making the suffragette appear slightly more hallowed.

"Do persuade Annabelle to crack at those books, and remind her how simply ravishing, in body and spirit she is . I've done what I can. To some success, I might add." Beatrice smiled at Annabelle, "But a good word from a man, in some instances, does smooth out the edges we have yet to smooth ourselves."

"Then I'll say no more on the matter of that irritating Mrs. Fawcett."

"As you should." Mrs. Christianson offered her husband a conciliatory pat on the shoulder. "If I'm a spot late this evening, so entertain yourself with a whiskey, as I do love to dine with you. I'm sure we'll have much to discuss."

"I do love my whiskey before a raring debate, my great thing. I will await your return with great eagerness, if not the latest news from the suffragette swells."

His wife smiled like the Cheshire cat. "I have faith in my powers of persuasion."

"As I do in mine," Horace countered. "Now leave me to my counsel." He tipped his head at Annabelle, 'as you've requested."

"Do mull over my proposal and your position, my dear. I believe there is a copy of The Vindication for the Rights of Women tucked cleverly between those volumes which you might find most stimulating." His wife propositioned over her shoulder to Annabelle. "Tea next Tuesday. Four o'clock sharp. Your position may have evolved by then." Her tone tinkled with mischievousness and she was gone.

"You're in need of ravishment?" Horace Christianson settled salaciously into the chair his wife had previously occupied.

Annabelle found it a depressive abdication. But a chord of Beatrice's pluck still strummed in her heart. She swallowed his hook, confident she could spew it back unscathed. "That is a topic of which you are all too familiar."

Dear Uncle Horace looked very pleased with her statement, though she had intended it as a slap rather than a compliment.

She considered their past, so long ago, and its tendrils which had suffocated her Fate. With so very little to lose, for wasn't that the purpose of a British marriage , Annabelle felt justified in casting her lure wide. "So well in fact, I gather you could approximate the very date I was last ravished as such."

Her father-in-law's face folded. He was no fool.

Anchoring into his brief uncertainty, Annabelle launched an attack she had not expected to make so soon. But the swell of lady surgeon made her steady on the deck of their battered warship. "My mother has made some very unkind remarks of late regarding the absence of a certain roundness about my person."

"Though I am never in need of reminding, I will fulfill my dear wife's request to reassure you the temptations of your person have never been as magnetic."

Annabelle never ceased to wonder at the depths of his conceit and deceit. "Time hasn't served your frontal cortex kindly." Her glace crystalized with intent. "I no longer need the paternalistic comforts of your company."

His eyes grew clear in innocent disappointment. "No?"

"Do you doubt your son's ability to offer solace between the sheets?"

As if remembering predatorial men do not typically marry off their prey to their prodigal offspring, brushstrokes of fetid peach crossed his cheeks. "Never. He has been well-educated in matters of both the head and the heart."

"You'll find yourself wrong there, Uncle Horace." Annabelle winced. It was so easy to slip back into old shorn paths. "Have you not found it unusual I have yet to announce my confinement?"

"No indeed, my dearest Annabelle. With a man like Thomas, so driven, so passionate, it is understandable he finds the trails of medical pursuits more exhilarating than the ritual of family life." He seemed taken away in reverie for a moment before he jolted back. "For now, that is,' he cleared his throat. "Give him another discovery, an invention, knighthood even. It won't be long. You'll have your swelling belly soon enough. Content yourself for now with the authorship he's given you."

"Have you forgotten who you're speaking to? Content myself?" She was sure Christianson knew Thomas' secret. She desperately wanted to travel down this hurtling track. "Getting back to the question of my ravishment, a favorite topic of yours." Annabelle would dare to ask the unaskable. It was beyond reason he didn't know of his son's proclivities. Otherwise why would he have thrown them together with such vigor and relative magnanimity, considering their former, clandestine pastimes.

"Your ravishment will always prove a highlight to my life."

His look, like a lusty executioner, hand on ax, almost took Annabelle back to those terrifying wonderful but horrible nights, as a Pierce. But she plunged forward with a kick of her crimson-stained skirts. "But it is his lack thereof which interests me most. Have you ever considered the fault may not be mine?"

"There has been no mention of fault. Only an observation and encouragement for what is in store for your long and happy marriage." His eyes danced over her form in a manner no good father-in-law would ever regard his prized daughter-in-law.

A prick of appreciation drove into her heart, like a thorn on poisoned bud. She hated her thirst for corporal approval had not waned. "But my question gets to the very crux of the matter. What is a marriage without its consummation?"

"How dare you suggest. . ."

"But I do." The words were as sweet as spun sugarplum. "And after my youthful,' she paused to search for the word, 'education.'" It stuck in her throat like other things forced too soon but it would do. "You know how well I can perform the mechanics involved in such consummation."

"Mechanics?"

"Mechanics." Annabelle repeated. Though she could more easily lie to him than herself. She had invited and taken her churlish pleasures too.

His face was awash with innocence. Annabelle wondered if he had ever registered such innocence in her face before he claimed it. Before she knew her worth.

She'd reclaim it now. "I learned of Thomas' preference for gentleman's company too late. I assume you were very well-aware and made me the perfect pawn."

Christianson's face rose and fell haphazardly, like an amnesiac mime caught under the spotlights. "He's a good boy—"

"I will not argue on that count. Your ploy was as perfect as a fairy tale." Annabelle's Queen's Gambit could not be refuted. Lady Doctor. "But we do not live on the tips of Anderson's quill. You have forgotten a passed pawn can promote to don a queen's robes. There's a truth to what they say about knowing no rage like love turn'd to hatred."

"Hate?" A flicker of goodness shuttered over his face again. As if their past had been smothered in whitewash.

"Or fury like a woman scorn'd ." She was pleased his face rippled and tore under her scalpel tongue.

"Fine robes cannot hide a whore."

His spitting retort left a welt on her cheek, but she weathered the whiplash. "You speak in lies as you always have. For you'd never have gifted your son with such a woman, though you have a nasty habit of turning women into such at your touch. Thank Christ I have survived your hand, with honey to salvage my wounds." She took a quick breath. "I was surprised to have so recently learned of your original fondness for Honey." Annabelle let her suggestion linger over the stickiness of the last word even as the sting still lingered on her face. She delighted his acknowledgement registered. Honey, Sarah's unfortunate mother.

"Take care on your climb, Annabelle, you aim for a crash."

"But climb I must." Annabelle rose as if lifted by her upper hand. "And thanks to Thomas, more of a husband than most, we have stretched the bars of my gilded cage wide. I will slip through and be my own woman." Her heart stepped in time with this ascension.

"You so easily forget your missteps, my pet. Assault. Adultery. Quite the deadly sins on which you so easily could hang your reputation." Christianson stood to meet her, his glare icy, his breath dragon hot.

"Would you so easily besmirch my name now it is Christianson?"

Christianson laughed cruelly. "Public denunciation would be too kind. I dare say your precious father's heart would break to know his only daughter is as common as. . ."

"Honey, a night flower?"

Christianson blinked, maintaining his stance.

"Or Sarah, an illegitimate fingersmith?"

His Adam's apple bobbed.

"Did any string in your heart break when you heard she had been murdered?" Check. "Her throat slit ear to ear?" Checkmate.

The wall clock chimed eerily as if to signal the beginning of the end.

Christianson's face puckered as if he had just taken a greedy bite of a fruit, only to discover it was a Seville orange rather than a Ribston Pippen . "What does your guttersnipe of a lady's maid have to do with Honey?"

Annabelle cheered at his admission. "You make no effort to deny it? Honey, dead from chloroform over-dripped, a baby orphaned."

"My appreciation for Honey was no crime. The crime was in your father's inept hand."

"A mistake for which he's paid dearly. You've never let him forget."

"A simple case of manslaughter."

"A daily error in London hospitals. Yet our prisons are not crammed with penitent doctors. Anesthesia is an inexact art now. Then it was a wild pursuit." Despite everything passed between them, she knew her father was a good man. Dearest Uncle Horace was not. "You've committed more crimes than King Henry, but they end with me."

"What crime have I committed against you?" Gone was his saccharine purr. "And what of your Sarah?" A skein of fear perhaps wove through his irises.

Annabelle promised herself she'd not weep at his lack of conscience. "You made me a woman before I was out of pantalettes."

"Do not fool yourself, my dear. You were a woman in your loose frocks. Or you'd have never posed invitations to me." His tone was all logic. Pathologic.

His denial was not worth her breath now. "As for Sarah, did you not know she was your daughter?"

His expression stiffened, as it would following a dram of arsenic. His left eyelid began to tremble uncontrollably.

Bullseye. That landed arrow was more satisfying than any ribbon at an archery tournament. "Perhaps you did not. Altogether too convenient."

As if indeed overcome by his own poisonings, Christianson staggered backwards.

Annabelle half-expected to hear an agonal death rattle as he fell into his chair.

But instead a simple protest escaped. "She was placed with a farming family in Dorchester. I imagined her living her days simply. Happily."

Annabelle could almost stomach pity for him. To Sarah's memory there was no need to resurrect the delicate point of her blackmail and slippery fingers. His continued delusions were making her weary. But the whisper of Lady Doctor kept her strong. "Obviously, your pastoral fantasy ended as an urbane nightmare." Should she go on? "But even her end—likely at the hand gangsters—was not in vain. I took my very first anatomy lessons from her. A rather charming recourse, don't you think?"

Christianson looked up at her like a pardoned criminal. "You spared Thomas your stories?"

"I am not cruel like you."

With his next inhalation, Christianson drew himself up to his full height like a wicked phoenix. The well-known flint having returned to his face. "I'll count on that. And on your love for your ridiculous father to keep you silent. You'd not want to tempt his disfavor if you force me to bring up your past misdemeanors."

Annabelle cursed Achilles and his heel. Her father was her own. "No,' she muttered bitterly. Christianson had tabled his trump card. It had been her father who had miscalculated the chloroform.

"Then you've kept quiet, for all your squabbling. I am glad." Christianson voice mellowed and he clamped his hands around her jaw and kissed Annabelle so violently she wondered if her lips might remain captured between her teeth. She fought the swirl of memories his touch raked to the surface. "Back to the beginning. Go home to Thomas, and content yourself with your home and husband."

Annabelle peeled her lips free, rattling her brain free from shock. "There's no going back. I'll sit for my apothecary's license in three months' time. You can't take away the education Thomas has given me."

"Like I said, my Thomas is a good boy, regardless of his tastes. Never forget that." Christianson loosened his grip, letting his hands fall to the curve of her breasts and linger. "You'll stay as you are, though my welcome will always be warm."

The flash of pleasure at his now kit touch, though any caress would have done, revolted Annabelle more than his actual violation. She lurched back, speechless.

"You're angry my pet, but here is a parting thought to cool your humors." He wiped a string of saliva from his chin. "That charming loophole through which you have aimed your ambitious arrows. . ."

"The Apothecary Licentiate?" Annabelle's stomach turned at the precipice his tone implied.

"That's the one." He replied with razorblades arched.

"What of it?" Annabelle clasped her hands to steady their shaking.

Christianson was at the door before he turned with a smile, not unlike the many he had shown her when he slipped from her chambers in the early morning light years ago. "Just yesterday it was neatly bricked closed." His eyes gleamed triumphant. "Puts the matter to rest quite nicely does it not?"

Annabelle imagined how the unfortunate Mrs. Karenina must have felt moments before she was overcome by steel and steam. In fact, that sensation might have proven infinitely more pleasurable to the despair wringing her soul tight.

"Like I said. Back to my Thomas. Back to your a cage. Back into the palm of my hand, where you belong."

And with an ill-winded chuckle, he was gone—victorious.

Chapter 25

Serendipity was a devilish thing, Annabelle decided. Still riveted to her chair in the Christianson's parlor, Cassius Larkin had just blown into her defeated reveries. She hadn't seen him in months, almost a year really, since Olivia. She was scornful then. He incapacitated by emotion, she fortified by it. It was with some chagrin she noticed he still made her breath catch. "You don't seem as terribly pleased to see me," she queried his ludicrous poker face with tepid anticipation.

After a few of her heartbeats skipped, Larkin recovered his graces. "Mrs. Christianson, of course I should expect to find you here." He brought his bowler over his chest and nodded with typical decorum. "How do you do?"

It was everything Annabelle could muster not to rush to him and pepper him with kisses.

"I came 'round after my private calls today to discuss a perplexing case with Dr. Christianson. The butler's gone to find him."

"Can you not see for yourself I'm rather well?" Annabelle slipped into her vixen frocks as easily as flipping one of those terrifying electric switches.

His eyes shot up from the top of his walking stick still in hand.

There it is, the old flame, so easily ignited. Perhaps this was where she was meant to be after all. Olivia had been right.

A faint twinge flicked the tops of his ears. "Rather well, indeed." He sputtered.

"Delightful we're back on the same stanza then." Annabelle hopped up from her seat. "I've no idea where my fa—Dr. Christianson has got to." No need to remind them of her vows at present. Nor court further adultery under this roof. "He's been called out unexpectedly." She looked out the long, street-facing window. The shine of the afternoon sun had dimmed, leaving a scatter of grey clouds corralled in the sky. "It threatens rain. Would you kindly escort me home?" A few moments alone in his carriage was all she'd need. "We could discuss your case on the way. There's likely a thing or two I could add."

"I, I—"

"You'd not deny me this simple request, for an old friend?" He'd need more coaxing in his widowed state. "Cassius?" How charming.

He was saved by a short knock at the door before Dr. Christianson strode into the room, breaking their awkward interlude. "Larkin my good man, what can I do for you?"

Annabelle's breath flared, but she did not retreat.

"Christianson." Larkin's tone retrieved its brisk metronome. "I've come to bash some ideas out regarding the use of medical batteries to ease pain from severed nerve fibers."

"Post-operatively, yes, it may have its place." Christianson appeared quite interested before he acknowledged Annabelle. "Annabelle my sweet," He looked her up and down. "You've made yourself comfortable, as I had hoped—"

"Not at all, we were just leaving. We'll be onto the finer points of treating phantom pain. Simply changes in the neurologic milieu, no need to bother yourself." She kept her tone as cooing as a turtle dove. "Cassius recalled how I've been spending my time and thought I might be of assistance." Though she hadn't the most ephemeral hypothesis to substantiate her claims.

"At Thomas' elbow," Christianson grinned. "Such wifely devotion I've never seen." His face fell theatrically. "Save for your dear Olivia."

Larkin nodded his head and thumped his hat to his breast in salute. There was a flicker of understanding between the two men. It smacked of chauvinistic rivalries as much as camaraderie—and of tongues kept silent in defense of primal pursuits.

Christianson retrieved a half-smile, declaring his second victory of the afternoon.

But Annabelle remained undeterred. She was counting on Larkin's amorous devastation, he'd succumb to her in moments. Carriages provided more than mere transportation. "Equivocality is not something to which I've ever aspired." Annabelle rallied before she cast Christianson her most beguiling siren smile.

The waver in his face gave her heart. Turning her attentions to Larkin, who remained in silent salute, she escalated her charms to their more angelic propensities. She knew her target too well. "Time is pressing, I must get back. Shall we, Cassius?"

A twitch of his nose expressed the younger doctor's telltale sign of displeasure.

Allowing a ladylike blush to grace her cheeks, Annabelle lowered her gaze. "Mrs. Mingle has been desperate for my guidance over the menu for a small regimental affair the week after next." She hoped her adoring look offered a decoy. "I simply couldn't fluster her if I run behind." Her spirit ached for the freedom, if not other corporal satisfactions, Thomas offered. Though Larkin's traditions were slightly stifling, these were the cards in hand, and she'd play them for all her worth.

Larkin regained his poise. "Happy to escort you home." He pressed his hat on his head and made for the door.

"And to discuss that perplexing case." Annabelle chorused as she swept by him into the front hall. She heard a muffled chuckle behind her.

"A snifter of Balmoral's finest awaits your eager return." Christianson declared. "You'll find I'll sort out your riddle before the second pour."

<hr />

Annabelle's quickened breaths echoed above the rumble of the carriage wheels. This was her chance. To rekindle a different future.

A subdued Larkin sat across from her unmoved.

Time was pressing so she dove in. "I've missed you."

"It has been quite a stretch that we've been removed from each other's company."

Annabelle pressed back into the jostling carriage seat and searched his face. Not a glimmer of their previous heat. She couldn't ever recall a time he hadn't looked at her with his passions fully exposed. This blank canvas completely unnerved her. Tick, tock. The clip of the horses' hooves reminded her of her mission. She looked out the carriage window, as if she held two figs of interest in the tumultuous swells of the London streets. Beggars, laborers, swells, pressed elbow to elbow at the end of the workday, forces united into a dichotomous army of filth and wealth. A well-outfitted hansom pulled by their side. The vehicles paused at a crossroads for a toppling double-decked bus to pass, passengers pulsating up top, its two thick harnessed Drafts huffing, dark with sweat. The sides of the carriages, inches apart, rocked, like steeplechasers seconds from the bell. Inside a woman slapped the seam of a tortoiseshell fan into the palm of her hand before it bloomed to full calico glory in front of her face. A gentleman appeared at her side, diving from the opposing seat.

A quiver, a kiss. Inspiration.

Annabelle yanked the cord of the carriage window shade with a vengeance. "A stretch of shear agony." She let her tone speak of quite the opposite, tempting emotion.

Without acknowledgement, Larkin began to rattle off the latest foibles and accomplishments of baby Olivia, who would indeed turn a year this coming June, as well as the rest of his children. Annabelle feigned interest. Since when had Larkin cared a crumb for his paternal responsibilities outside of producing handfuls of sugared sweets, marbles, and toy soldiers for brief delight?

Just when Annabelle's reserve of patience was quite tapped, the carriage took a sharp left turn. In other circumstances, she would have found it quite easy to maintain her seat But at this golden chance allowed herself to be flung, with all the melodrama of Sarah Bernhardt at the Odeon, into Larkin's unsuspecting arms.

Annabelle found a brief blush of victory as they shared a hint of their past amour. Everything about Larkin tempered, as if assuaged by Nature and Cupid. But a second later, he placed her back in her seat mechanically. As the carriage lurched forward, he jerked the blind up angrily, grunting softly.

Smarting at the rejection, Annabelle was grateful as the Curzon Street come into view.

"Annabel—." Larkin cleared his throat hoarsely. "Mrs. Christianson. We've shared our past moments. But that is precisely where they must stay. I am still very much in mourning."

"In all the splendor of Harris tweed?"

Larkin cast his sleeves a reproachful glare. "Private mourning."

"Funny how you seem to find more respect for your matrimonial commitments as a widower, than you ever did as a husband."

He winced, and Annabelle took heart.

"She knew, you know." He could take it as he would.

His brows pressed together in question.

"Before Thomas, she had a premonition." Annabelle for once hesitated to speak of the dead. "She had hoped you and I. . ."

"That you and I would. . ."

He shook his head violently before he retorted. "I am absolutely sure she had no knowledge of our sins."

"Our?" Annabelle set her lips in a thin line. Only a long block and a turn before 17 Berkeley Square. "Our sins? The only vows broken were yours. I was free to make my choices."

"Was. From a godless perspective, perhaps. But for a lifetime of offering temptation, you are as guilty as I."

Why the ecclesiastical facade now? She waded through a bog of heavy desire and despair among the scraps of her broken heart. Where was the Larkin who knew her better than anyone? And she likely him—for the precious times they shared. "Guilt or guiltless, I stand by us even now. With Olivia gone."

"Annabelle."

"Not Mrs. Christianson? Though I am that in name alone."

Something familiar took over his expression, but just as quickly, it vanished. "Oh?" The arc of his voice was at once both hopeful and cold.

"You must know as well as I." She could almost hear the off-chords her heartstrings strummed at her impending betrayal. But it wasn't a betrayal if the truth was commonly, uncommon knowledge. "Thomas has a preference for rather different bed partners. I seem to have been the last to know."

Beneath his momentarily raised brows, whether in surprise about Thomas himself, or Annabelle's privy wit. "Some topics are best left between men."

Annabelle's words severed the last tether of decorum. "Particularly when the fates of the poor women bound to them are at stake."

The clip of the carriage wheels and hooves slowed to a halt. 17 Berkeley Square.

This would be her only chance. "Vows and whatever dreadful game you're playing at aside, I know you love me. And I love you."

"You've left your husband out of this ridiculous equation," Larkin ran a fold of her skirt between his fingers and would not meet her gaze.

"Thomas prefers trousers to skirts. Life is too short to simply exist in a vacuum, praying for time to be kind, while I rot away from the inside out." Annabelle found no need to draw breath. "I'm trained. We can take on London, Europe, even America. Together, hearts and minds united."

He released her silk. "Dr. Christianson is a highly regarded surgeon and gentleman. His preferences outside the wards and Society have little to do with me." Larkin's tone was dismissive, but then turned ascorbic. "I've heard of your surgical dalliances. Thomas was altogether far too permissive. I warned him against it."

"Against it?" A chord of grief hit her soul.

"This education of yours is totally unfeminine. Far better to be a nurse or put your wiles to good use with charities. Or content yourself editing your father's work."

"Editing? I wrote every last article!"

Larkin's twitch returned.

Now there were only seconds, Annabelle kept her swell steady. "What was it that first attracted you to me? My mind, you've always said."

"Not exactly." He has the good grace to blush. "And it just isn't right. A woman's place is by her husband."

"Behind him you mean."

"You have no idea what you're playing at. The feminine constitution wasn't built for—"

"No human was built to play God, yet we do it anyway. And who is it to say men are superior? Who bears the brunt of creation?"

"Women,' he relied sulkily. "Olivia."

"She told me the truth which you deny yourself."

"The truth?"

"That you love me, always have, always will. Not that I ever doubted it."

"Doubt it now."

Annabelle grew cold—her offense was failing.

"Yours was an undeniable temptation."

Lies, all lies. Annabelle wanted to scream.

"But there was a softness, a gentleness to Olivia which won me over."

"What about our afternoon under Socrates at the College? You found me anything but repulsive then?"

"A moment of weakness."

"And your talk of unicorns and holy gates?"

"A ploy. You do not understand men."

"That is a falsehood and you know it. It wasn't over. It isn't over. Not for you." She sprang across the carriage, fangs open wide. "And not for me." She shouted into Larkin's chest, the scent of bergamot and hide taunting her raw affections. Her tears broke free as the carriage wheels halted and she sobbed without pretense into his overcoat.

To her surprise, Larkin wove his arms around her shoulders, letting them heave in her sorrows. He held her, wordless, for what seemed a comforting eternity. When every drop of misery had been tapped from her vessel, Annabelle released a final shudder before lifting her face. She found his steel eyes stared down at her muted as a dove.

"Annabelle," his voice was throaty before he cleared it.

"Mrs. Christianson to you." Annabelle could feel his heart pound against her side.

"Christ, Annabelle, don't look at me like that." Color washed his face before he turned away.

Annabelle's heart dangled on a frayed pendulum. Could she have broken through? Those eyes—her Larkin was back. She reached and tipped his reluctant head back to her.

"You mustn't—' his protest was weak before her lips found his.

As if brought to life with her touch, he pressed all of himself into her welcome advances. They surged and ebbed in brief ecstasy—Annabelle awhirl with joy.

Then just as his hands left the gentle curve of her jaw, one finding the slope of her breast, the other making quick work of her skirts, he drew back as if he had laid his palms atop Satan's furnace.

"Damn everything you are!" Larkin shrank against the opposite end of the carriage. "God had no right to create a creature like you."

In the cyclone of emotions, Annabelle spun the band of gold around and around her ring finger.

"No right." Larkin whimpered before his eyes steadied on the ring. His voice rose in strength, as a prosecutor's might, having found a critical piece of evidence. "You're bound by marriage."

"But I'm. . ."

"And I by the needs of my motherless children."

"Take them out of. . ."

"They will carry on my legacy. And what is a man if not for an enduring legacy?"

"Precisely, Cassius. You, we, could have had it all but for your damned pride. And an obscene loyalty to a family withering on ancient vines."

"Say no more of the Larkin name and my reasons for marriage. Your ambitions temper my desire." He ran his hands down his face. "Be so good as to recall your duties, as a Mrs. Christianson, to your husband and family." He kept shy of her as he reached for his hat, unlatched the carriage door, and kicked out into the whir of the street. Top hat in place, he offered his hand with great ceremony. "Let me at least escort you to your door before we say our goodbyes."

"Now you find it proper to act a gentleman?" Annabelle ignored his offer. "Though you besmirch my honest proclivity for expansion?" She swept from the carriage unassisted. "Your timing is absolutely disastrous." She stood in front of him, feeling every bit a chastised schoolgirl.

The stalwart lines of his face crumpled. "I wouldn't regard it in quite such an unforgiving light."

"You are content to stand here and lie, to us both, and betray not only your own heart but mine?" She could not let him go without one last rally.

"You have no idea what demons I wrestle to keep myself from you." The former huskiness in his voice returned.

"Why wrestle? You know of Thomas. He would allow me anything—even you."

"What would you become then? What would I call you? What would my children call you?"

"You could call such an arrangement many things, none of which are flattering."

He exhaled sharply as if he had caught a whiff of a distasteful, underworld scent. "What would Society call you?"

"Society could call me what it likes."

Saying nothing, Larkin offered his arm.

Annabelle took it. There was nothing to be gained by standing on the walk like a wayward homing pigeon. They proceeded with Larkin casting sideways glances at her every third pace.

Why couldn't he admit his happiness? When they reached the front door, Annabelle rang the bell before breaking the swirling silence, despite the busy streets. "You can't deny your flame still burns as brightly as mine. Do not chance that my wick proves shorter than yours."

In what she hoped he took as her glorious final words, Annabelle swept wordlessly past him and through the opening door, with Kitty offering blustering apologies for the butler's detainment. She pushed past her and pressed back into the heavy door, slamming it on Larkin. Then her tears erupted—vigorous and unchallenged.

Chapter 26

Annabelle spent the thawings of an early Spring (and their first anniversary) shuffling between the comforting folds of 17 Berkeley Square and her Aunt Maude's rooms at Mivart's Hotel, just around the corner on Brook Street. Thomas spared no expense in outfitting her with the latest fashions as Annabelle succumbed to her weakness for frothy bustled confections. He indulged her fragile moods by shepherding a carousel of tutors through their front door. Her interests were briefly peaked in turn by Japonisme, then miniature portraits in watercolor, and in a nod to her past profession—phrenology and expression of personality traits.

But for all her avoidant meanderings, Thomas never uttered a goading word or exasperated glance. Even Simon doted on her every whim. As a man of a conveniently sizable personal income, lively mind, and equally open heart, Annabelle found Thomas quite a forgivable character as he praised her talentless efforts in her pursuit of empty-headed domesticity.

With more time on her hands, they had not held a scalpel since the curious case of Miss Greville, Annabelle skipped from subject to subject like a water strider. She was, however, moved to inquire as to the success of Miss Greville's subsequent reconstruction. With genuine delight she learned all had gone well with the use of a nerve block of cocaine, rather than risk near disaster again with the unreliable chloroform. But when a ray of melancholy threatened, Annabelle found herself whisked off to Maude's lively quarters bright from the modern electric lights and vases of conservancy orchids and gardenias so garish in bloom they forced her mood to lift, however unwillingly.

Annabelle would remain just long enough for the veneer of superficial contentment to chip, and back she would land by Thomas' side to play the role of the reformed Mrs. Annabelle Christianson. Thus, Annabelle flew willingly back into the gilded cage she had beat her wings against for so long, though the exquisite interior provided quite a comfortable retreat. The countless nightly scheduled preoccupations with Society's crème were scintillating enough, so long as she did not bother to think too long or hard about her imprisonment.

One evening, after a particularly rousing performance of Aida at Covent Garden, followed by an intimate at-home hosted by the Lord and Lady Chatsworth, Annabelle felt herself quite light-hearted, bending and nodding in the approval of her peers, having forgotten how dearly she loved to do so, as a sunflower curtseys in shifting sunbeams.

Resplendent in a teal gown dripping with miles of gold-trimmed ruffles, Annabelle was with the doting attentions of a certain George Gosling, whose loyalty had not shifted from his adorations the season before. Only now, despite his undaunted lisp, he found it quite right to comment on Annabelle's abrupt shift in character.

Between polite coughs dearest Georgie noted her recent tempering made Annabelle all the more lovely, and Thomas, the absolute luckiest man in the British Isles.

Annabelle could not tell if the chocolate baron had shown unusual cleverness in the design of his barbs. Or if he remained a well-intentioned oaf in a china gallery. She stared dully at him, the ginger tines of his beard projecting like inquisitive porcupine quills.

"I see I've been under your lens, Georgie." She would never give him the credit of his due title and hated she had become the type of lacey specimen she loved to loathe not long ago.

"Rare creatures do s...s...s—spark great interest." He spattered cheerfully.

Presuming he was to continue down an unfettered path of idiocy Annabelle found herself unpleasantly without a retort.

"Rare creatures do only land for a moment." A clear voice trilled over Annabelle's shoulder. Saved. Annabelle allowed the poor man a smile. Aunt Maude really had the most delightful timing.

"Baroness Pearle." Georgie was all bowlegs and dimples as he arranged himself into a bow which would have made Louis XIV blush. "I was just remarking on the extraordinary t...t...transformation Mrs. Christianson has made." He swept his hand the length of Annabelle's silhouette. "Why I hadn't seen her much in S...society at all. Why it was only last s...s...season—"

"She finally declared her childish taste for confections ran its course. Or never begun rather." Maude railroaded the fop. "How is the chocolate business treating you?" She let a tinkling laugh ring out and appraised his generous belly before tapping the straining seams of his waistcoat. "Ridiculous question, I can well see you've outdone yourself."

Without waiting for comprehension to grace his daft skull, Maude linked her arm through Annabelle's and left poor Georgie to ponder his added inches since the Season last.

"Your dashing husband has been detained in a jaw-achingly dull conversation. With the last waltz of the evening at half past, you can extricate him from that trap and show yourself off with one last trip around the floor. You look simply ravishing, everyone says so."

Maude adjusted one of the tulle adornments bordering Annabelle's plunging neckline affectionately. "Is it really quite so unsatisfying to be the belle of the ball, night after night? Far less odious then playing at being a human tailor. Leave those brutish pastimes to the men. You'd only line your brows with too much bloodied thought."

Her recent terrors toyed with Annabelle's logic. Perhaps Aunt Maude was right. She'd always looked out for Annabelle in the face of her mother's sieges and ultimatums. And she understood men.

"Perhaps I'm far too young to crease my face with such involvements. Why shouldn't life be frivolous and simple?" With that rhetorical question careening around the ballroom, Annabelle allowed herself to be swept along the perimeter of the room, the glances of appreciation holding her in good stead, to a group of rather refined-looking men, Thomas of course, being one of them.

She hadn't broached the topic of Thomas with Maude—yet. Perhaps there was a way? Thomas looked up, his expression changed from solemnity to radiance in a flash. His metamorphosis, whose effects Annabelle has sworn herself against, made her heart skip a note in its own melody.

⚜

The last bars of the Waltz Madeline strummed in Annabelle's head the next morning but clattered into silence with a dissonant echo when she unfolded a presumed misplaced pair of pearl earrings. Finding their wrapping was made of a sheet of her old anatomy notes, she made out the five branches of the brachial plexus, before she ripped the paper to shreds in a shudder of self-disgust. Hadn't she planned on contenting herself with Society frivolities? Wondering at her fragile resolve as she made her way into the breakfast room. She hoped Thomas would not find it necessary to bring any of his academic pursuits to the conversation that morning.

With frivolity her purpose, she found particular appreciation for the Saturday shafts of sun cascading from the multitude of wall mirrors hung . The room captured all the beauty of a May day . Early indigo crocus and yolk yellow daffodils waved cheerily from foil-glass vases around the room.

Thomas sat at his usual place at the table, assaulting a journal with dashes and dots with his poised pencil. Annabelle braced herself, though she took no offense at his lack of acknowledgement to her entrance. Simon had gone off to visit his sister in Glouchester for a fortnight, without an invitation to Thomas. Annabelle found the exclusion quite understandable given Society was what it was. But Thomas had found the perceived slight as almost unforgivable and had hurled himself with new focus into the refinement of Dr. Pierce's disastrous prototype of a siphon recorder rather than sulk in private. Annabelle had steered clear of the device whose failure, or rather her father's she admitted, had cost her ultimately her freedom. But with ample funds and stretch of time to fill without Simon, Thomas was set on submitting a prototype of a portable oscilloscope to Smithfield's. He was delighted to not only give credit to her father's design, but to his own avant-garde ingenuity.

"Good morning, "

Thomas scratched at the paper before him with a brief frenzy. "Hallo my love." He pushed his work beneath his tea saucer, his morning glow was just as sweet as his radiance the previous evening.

"Wasn't last night grand?" She bounced merrily over the memory. "Now things are settled, we should really begin hosting ourselves, I'm eager to cultivate my reputation as a consummate hostess." For what else was a woman of means to do now all other dreams had been obsolete by Fate or by deluded choice?

"I believe you prefer to serve as the sun around which Society's sweethearts orbit." He reached for his teacup and took a sip. "Cold." He let an impish question shade his face before his smile cracked.

He had a point. The stress of pulling off a flawless evening to be discussed for weeks to come shouldn't be overlooked. "Let me get you a fresh cup of tea. After breakfast we can revisit the subject." She retrieved his cup, unable to catch a glimpse of Thomas' shelved notes. As she filled it to the brim and swirled the exact drizzle of amber honey he preferred into its depths, she was unable to relieve herself of her urging curiosity.

Sitting down with her own lemon-laced Oolong, Annabelle settled into a pleasant daydream of a fancy-dress ball. She wondered if she would look more astonishing dressed as the Empress Theodora, Marie Antoinette, or as a young Queen Victoria (sans sausage fingers and bursting gut). Before she could properly tease of the benefits of Byzantine, form-skimming stola over the hallway blocking panniers of the ill-fated Austrian, Thomas cleared his throat.

"I say." There was hint of a questionable crescendo.

Annabelle popped from her reverie. He sounded very much like her father—which she was surprised to find she resented. "What is it my dear man?"

"Now you're flying high on the wings of last night's success and you've named your own prize, I'll state my affairs quite plainly."

What was he playing at?

"Your avoidance of any kind of mental floss worries me deeply."

It took a moment for his accusation to register, but he continued before Annabelle could give her mouth shape.

"These dalliances served their purpose beautifully. I am glad you are not the shuddering mess I brought home after your ultimate success with Miss Greville." He reached to take Annabelle's hand in his.

The warmth of his touch confirmed her descent back to Earth. "What are you saying?" Annabelle knew the truth however painful it was to acknowledge. For Christ's sake, even dimwitted Georgie (or was he quite so dimwitted) had called her a fraud in so many words?

"I have a proposition for you." Thomas let her hand go, then slapped his knees with his hands, like a schoolboy anticipating a refreshing game of lunch-time rugby. "The complexities of the oscillograph are devilish. To Penwood House. The fresh country air would do us good. Bolster our creativity. Long walks, hacks, a hunt. I'd arrange it all, whomever you'd like. A first call to my beautiful wife's hospitality."

Annabelle quite liked the sound of his proposal. A Saturday to Monday house party. It would require a bit of social calculation to pull off a weekend of recuperative puttering with the hunt as its pinnacle. A country holiday to remember indeed. "It would be just the thing. There'll be absolutely heaps to organize. Who's to come, what to serve, the hounds, the mounts."

"Invite whomever you please. Mrs. Mingle could entertain the entire Royal Family in style at a moment's notice with her right hand tied behind her back, so she'll have the rest of it."

Annabelle laughed at the truth of his remark. He remembered her cherished protector's handedness. Dear heart.

"Leave the hounds and mounts to me. Our man Briggs is an absolute genius arranging these things. It's been ages since we've had a bit of a retreat."

Not since their ill-fated honeymoon, Annabelle thought to herself. But the memory could not extinguish her smile. "When shall it be? The fortnight after next?"

Annabelle caught Thomas as he held a loaded fork of buttered eggs and flaked kipper aloft. He gave her a closed mouth grin and shook his head before he swallowed. "No, no, Simon will be back by then. The weekend next."

"But I won't have the time."

"I have every faith in your capabilities, my dear."

Finding she could find no solid argument with his request, as her calendar and commitments were few, she conceded.

"We'll organize our research here. We're bound to come up with the necessary fixes for that confounding contraption over a few days of heady meandering over meadows and hills. The weekend hunt will be our carrot to keep our scientific work minds plowing steadily."

"Work minds?" Annabelle shook her head, dazed, as if she sniffed too strongly at Aunt Maude's powdered laudanum. "I shouldn't call the delightful arranging of persons for their greatest enjoyment work?" Her heart was as light as a bright red balloon at a county fair.

Thomas waved his empty fork. "You have worn your selective ears today, my dearest wife."

The edge to his last word was not unpleasant, like biting brightness a squeeze of citrus lent to a bracing cup of black morning tea.

"There is to be a bit of an exchange here, my darling. I need your mind. And not the rather sizeable portion devoted to superfluous pursuits as of late."

"What are you implying, Dr. Christianson. " Damn him, he was right, as always. It had been an effort to keep her eyes from attempting to make sense of his scrawlings. He had likely reversed a square and square root, she frowned deeper.

Thomas snagged his papers an inch closer to him.

Annabelle craned her neck more acutely to follow.

"I knew it!" He shoved the manuscripts towards her. They crumpled into her plate, making her coddled eggs tremble in their pots. With an irritating gusto, Thomas shoved back from the table, stretching his arms long before letting them fall behind his head. "I feared your fright with Miss Greville really did your ambitions in." He looked at Annabelle as if he'd just been awarded a top place at Scotland Yard. "But I knew you were made of sterner stuff."

"You find yourself in sore need of a trophy, do you?" This constant teeter-totter between afront and amusement made Annabelle queasy. All of her own doing she admitted silently.

"Perhaps." His expression became only slightly less bemused. "You could very well say the same of yourself with the siege you've laid on London Society these past weeks."

"I thought you were quite pleased with my successes." She dove into her eggs and felt a brief contentment as the yolks ran gold over the just set whites. "Any acclaim I have earned, I've taken in both our names. Don't forget outside these walls, as a wife, nothing belongs to me. It certainly hasn't harmed your reputation by having a ravishing wife capable of the most brilliant conversation and angelic turns on the dance floor."

"Agreed. But I've found myself missing the bristled belle who scoffed at monocle penguins and aerated coiffures so wonderfully at the Opera."

"Society does not share your sentiment. I have never been held in such high regard as I have been these last months. Even Aunt Maude has taken to wearing a green veil in my presence."

Thomas bit his lip in a manner. "You find the envy of a courtesan, albeit a good-hearted one, an endorsement of the pompous Ten Percent preferable above all else?"

"What if I do? I adore being adored. And I can't get that from you—not in the way I want."

Thomas's lips tightened. The only outward sign of anger he ever allowed himself.

Annabelle took note, a healing heart was a confounding thing, in the same way the slightest slice the wrong way across a sheet of letter paper evoked great yelps of pain. "You sound as if you are going to launch into a particularly tiresome tirade."

"There's no need to ride that tired nag. I've apologized again and again for my wrongs and am doing everything in my power to atone. I'm offering you the chance for something crystal chandeliers and marble floors could never give you. A future as a captain of your own vessel."

"I suffer from sea sickness on any kind of open waters."

"Anything larger than the boating lake in Greenwich Park?"

Annabelle fired a cannoned look at Thomas. "What do you know about the boating lake on Greenwich Park?" Chestnut trees and champagne, Keats and stolen kisses. Surely Larkin had kept his silence. If not as a gentleman—for Olivia's sake.

"I've simply come to understand it was a place where you found great happiness for a time with a certain colleague of mine." Thomas' lips grew full, his eyes bright.

Damn him and his propriety, she couldn't justify an attack now.

"You forgot happiness has not always been within my reach either, Annabelle."

Annabelle saw a mist lace his eyes. They were so much alike, in situation, if not humors.

"A confidence between gentlemen. There'll be no more word of it." Thomas, teacup in hand, came around to Annabelle . "We're allies, Annabelle." He leant and kissed her forehead. "More tea?" As if he hadn't just stolen Annabelle' s remaining secret.

"So where do we go from here? I fear my crystal and marble hopes will be dashed."

"I thought you'd never ask." Thomas strode back to the table, the acrid warmth of the tea bringing a coziness to their tete-a-tete . He drew his chair close. "It's a roundabout story, but it will explain a few things, and my point today." Work had become his supper, his lover, and his salvation. A daily devotion of purification for his shame and sins. He had lived this way until he found himself in conversations with a different God than the one he had known under the dictates of the Church of England and (holy) Society.

These conversations began in St. George's Cathedral on a songbird and soft sunshine kind of day, when a man, his man, abandoned Thomas for a life of utter normalcy. "Depravity more like it. What could be less normal than a man like him bound to a woman with traditional expectations?"

Only then, when the gentleman in question looked at Thomas, a tear brushed away in feigned joy, did Thomas admit how utterly his profession had failed him. How he had failed himself. He could lie to himself no longer even in a time when such thoughts and acts were strictly policed and even language to name such intimate behaviors did not exist. Thomas made no effort to hide a soul-deep sadness as he recounted his tale. But his intrinsic brightness prevailed, and he plunged into the next chapter of his tale. India. Thomas believed the expanse of geography would ease his broken heart and quiet Society's whispers. He had no other choice. A nd hadn't wanted one in any case. Though when he was promoted to Major General, he found the home call strong.

When the wind carried news Thomas' gentleman had taken over his wife's family business in New York, Thomas accepted the sign. "Then there was you." He smiled winningly at Annabelle. "I believed with your strength, and mind, we would be strong medicine for one another."

"Perhaps we are. Just not in the way either of us imagined." She found it quite easy to squeeze another drop of forgiveness from her heart—it felt oddly full for having been thought damaged beyond all repair. She moved to Thomas and draped her arms around him.

He reached his hands over her forearm and dropped his head into the crook of her elbow. They held each other, Annabelle hovering over him like an archangel. Their breaths met in unison and in the unawkward minutes of silence which followed, Annabelle found her perception of Thomas shifted. He no longer being an unattainable object of subtle torture, but a lesson in sympatico—a kindred spirit. A pressure in her heart released like a locomotive letting off its final exhales of steam as it pulls into its home station.

Eventually, Thomas gave Annabelle's silked forearm a kiss. "We both needed that." He sighed, a sound full of sweet satisfaction. "Come sit, I've not finished my scolding."

Annabelle seated herself with her best look of cheeky expectancy.

"A real profession would offer you another form of self-expression and service." He reached to tap his crumpled notes with his fingers. "Women have been denied this pleasure for so long and it is the greatest possible thing I can find to give you. A gift that will outlast the latest Paris gowns and glittering bobbles ."

"But you just said medicine wasn't enough. Love. What about love?"

"Love is nothing if you cannot find love for yourself first." Thomas leaned forward and traced her cheek with his fingertip. "Life has taught me that. The moment I accepted that, Simon appeared. I had made room, so to speak."

He could have been plucking her heartstrings as the rush of emotion at the veracity of his words sunk into her soul.

"Medicine can give you an independence, a self-sufficiency I know you crave. Become your own woman first. Then you will have the choice of any man you like. On your own terms—free from the trappings of bank accounts and decorum."

Since her history with Cupid had been checkered, Annabelle found autonomy an appealing priority.

"In the spirit of your new-found battle cry, would you give me an hour on this capillary electrometer? You'll have plenty of time before tea to assemble a guest list for our hunting weekend?"

"I believe I have just an hour to spare."

"It will be a splendid thing, our work and play. I have already invited one guest whose company you will enjoy immensely."

"Who may that be?" As if the morning's developments could be improved upon.

"Our mutual friend, Cassius Larkin." An almost imperceptible reflection of intrigue graced Thomas' lips—filled with the glee of Father Christmas as clocks tick midnight on December twenty-fourth.

Chapter 27

It was one of the moments Annabelle liked best. Just before the master of hounds sounded his bugle and hooves made short work of the ground beneath. The etiquette of the hunt field was as intricate and strict as that of the ballroom. Thankfully Annabelle found herself quite content she was equally skilled in both arenas. Annabelle's velvet train swept behind her as she paraded down the front steps of Penwood House. The spray of country dust from the milling riders hung heavy like evening fog, though the sun was high in its roost. Those weekend guests inclined to hunt were already mounted, busy fortifying themselves with nibbles of handcake and port, though not an hour had passed since breakfast. Lady Somersville was taking Dexter through his paces, tilling the top of the poor hedges into oblivion. Annabelle decided to ignore the insufferable suffragette until the fox had been cornered.

Annabelle had been startled by an introduction to Lord Somersville by an embarrassingly appreciative Lord Greville. He was a last-minute addition of a certain member of Parliament, as Lady Greville remained (with kind regrets) at home with a chill. As the MP complimented Annabelle on her stunning estate, she feared he could hear her heartbeat as loud as the clatter of her protesting ginger beer bottle which had narrowly missing his egghead in Trafalgar Square. His new wife had been the Somersville's governess and it hadn't been two months after the unmentionable death of his wife (who had hurled herself from the estate's clock tower) before Lord Somersville had taken the young woman to a small country church. But they seemed happy enough and with her own past dubious ethics, Annabelle had been inclined to write the couple a moral pass.

The evening before, Lady Somersville met Annabelle's attentions with a fiercer gaze than Annabelle expected from a newly minted Cinderella. "Perhaps we can begin our own steeplechase, I believe I will prove to be a suitable rival." Her eyes, the color of the English Chanel, laughed about the rim of glass, her expression all feigned innocence.

There was nothing sweeter to Annabelle's ear then the metallic sear of a sword swept from its sheath to meet a challenge. At first blush, a governess should be no match for a well-schooled socialite, but with another moment's consideration, she found there was a calculated edge to Lady Somersville which she believed she admired, if not quite liked.

Lady Somersville raised her glass to a speechless Annabelle. "To the hunt. And the best woman." Leaving Annabelle feeling very much outranked, not only in title, but in feminine prowess, on her home grounds, nonetheless.

To worsen the matter, that morning, Ben had taken the gross liberty of lending Lady Somersville the skilled Dexter as her mount for the hunt, rather than one of the spare warmbloods brought up especially for that purpose. Annabelle hoped she any traces of anger remained tucked beneath her corset as she digested the treachery to which she had just been subject. She had never considered another woman would ever tempt Ben's ever-steady adoration—and it seemed to have done in an instant. She caught her breath, even more determined to best Lady Somersville (the cheeky tarte) on the hunt today. How much time could have a governess spent astride to acquire any kind of estimable equestrian skills?

Annabelle, in the mood to give him good scolding was a touch disappointed when she saw the dappled gelding trot into view with Ben, an elbow pressed into the beast's chest to contain him. Perfect to best that little governess. She laid the handle of her hunting whip in the palm of her hand with a satisfying thwack.

Ben brought Aberdeen to a standstill as Annabelle continued down the stairs to meet him. He patted Aberdeen's neck—already a darker shade of grey from his excited sweat. "He's nothing short of inspired this morning, m'Lady. It'll be a grand hunt." He pulled her stirrups down with a slap. "With you at the lead."

"So you say now?" Annabelle swept her train in hand, preparing to mount. "I'd dare say you've been plotting something sinister the way you gave my Dexter away to that horrid Lady Sackville."

Ben snorted. "Jealously doesn't look good on you, Bella. Take the reins."

Before she could retort, Ben boosted her into the saddle where she landed heavily, startling Aberdeen.

"Whoa now, son," Ben jiggled the gelding's reins. "You were saying about Lady Sackville?" The edges of his mouth quivered.

Annabelle clicked her tongue in disgust. Mrs. Christianson, astride her chocolate brown beast, reins in one hand, handcake in the other, saw Annabelle, and waved her elbow in greeting.

"If you have nothing to say on the matter—shall the best woman win."

Annabelle snapped her head back and glared at him.

"Take up your reins before ye hurt yerself." Ben released Aberdeen from his grip.

Annabelle ran the braided leather into her gloved hands. "Why did you let her choose?"

"To see you aflutter like a hen caught in a storm. You're a right picture, m'Lady."

"You're absolutely cracked, Ben Fulbright." Annabelle flicked her riding crop just shy of his left ear. "To provoke me for utterly no reason, I should have you dismissed." Even though she meant the jab, her threat was utterly hollow.

"There's reason, alright."

"And what reason is that? Oher than sheer meanness?"

"The way I sees it, it is sheer meanness to keep a good bloke waiting on a promise he's given with a clean heart."

Annabelle narrowed her eyes.

"Just a poor man's way of getting your goat," Ben admitted with a wry shrug.

"Kentucky then?" But she could never quite admit to herself, how she felt about him in return. Ben's working-class strata kept her heart safe from his total taking.

Ben dropped his chin, a sweep of hair falling into his eyes. "Consider me first. Kentucky second."

"Ahh." His proposal in the stables.

"The Great Western sails in two months' time. I've two tickets on me mantle. I mean to sail, with you by my side." His look told Annabelle he was serious. "Or if I'm meant to find another, I am resourceful."

"Annabelle, dearest." Annabelle heard Thomas's tenor above the clatter of the preparing hunt. She turned in her saddle to see her husband break away from a grove of mounted gentleman. "Your mother wants a word." He bowed his head at Mrs. Pierce as she marched into the front yard from the side garden, wearing an obscene bonnet more suitable for a ladies' afternoon of tea and croquette rather than a mid-October hunting weekend in Yorkshire.

It had been such a lovely weekend avoiding her mother. But her stomach backfliped when Dr. Christianson sauntered through the garden gate. A place where his brilliant pinks had no right to be with the hunt about set to be off .

She swallowed as heat rushed to her cheeks. "This isn't the place for this conversation, Mr. Fulbright. "Just a minute, mamma," she trilled over her shoulder.

Thomas spurred his mount to intercept her mother and began an amorous monologue on what Annabelle could only assume were the fetching qualities of her millinery.

Bless him.

"There's never a right time or place for you, m'L ady." Ben pressed on. "You have a month. If the answer is no, there'll be time for other plans."

"Other plans?" Annabelle, though she couldn't ever reasonably accept him, did very definitely not want him to make other plans. But what could she want from him?

"I've plenty of resources, I'll not find meself lonely for long." Ben's good nature won over.

Annabelle cursed his unnerving dimples. Could she? Certainly not. But? It was all too much for her heart, which she had begun to discover was not nearly as nimble as her mind. She remained, like an acrobat, straddling her high wire of indecision.

"Devious, more like it." Annabelle wondered what other lady he had stuffed up his sleeve. "Don't change your grand plans on my account." Though she meant anything but.

"A month. I'll not wait for ye to draw breath."

She hated to hurt him, down deep, in that secret part of her soul, but she'd not have her hand forced on his terms. "Very well then, we'll let Fate take the reins." Annabelle declared as she tightened hers and swung Aberdeen around to meet what she presumed was the approaching hunt. Instead she ran Aberdeen inches from her mother's disapproving glare and almost decapitated a silk chickadee slung merrily through the ribboned band of her gargantuan hat.

Mrs. Pierce held her ground. "I've had a revelation among the azaleas." She kept her hand held protectively to the brim of her bonnet, sounding very much like she had just realized fairy tales were indeed fairy tales, not realities from neighboring counties.

"Do tell mamma?" Annabelle relaxed the grip on her reins, she had imagined a far worse accusation would have spewed from her mother's mouth. "I do believe it's a first—this revelation of yours."

"You look so well this weekend. Don't you think it best, for the family, if you did not hunt today?"

Leading with a compliment—a first in her twenty-four years. "I commend you on your new tactic, mamma."

"Dearest," Thomas broke in again. "I'm afraid the hounds can't be kept at our feet much longer." He trotted up on his mount—a solid black affair.

"Nonsense, mamma." Annabelle laughed. "If I'm looking so well, all the more reason to ride, don't you think?"

Mrs. Pierce offered Thomas a shy smile. "This ladies' talk will bore you, Thomas."

Thomas kept his smile broad, as if ignorant to her hint.

Seeing he had no intention of leaving them together, Mrs. Pierce clasped her hands in front of her. "I can see you are driving Thomas to distraction." She glanced at him with motherly approval.

Thomas widened his eyes but shook his head emphatically.

What was she playing at? Annabelle poorly disguised her mirth.

"You should think of the family." Mrs. Pierce tiptoed closer to Annabelle, eyeing Aberdeen as though he were a Nubian giraffe. "And planning." She strummed over the last word with heaving meaning. "My true thoughts are unmentionable in mixed company."

The hounds announced the time with their whines.

Annabelle looked to Thomas for reprieve.

"I'll tell Briggs to sound the horn in two minutes."

"But should she not. . ." Mrs. Pierce voice trailed after him, but he was already beckoning the party to gather for the first bugle cry. "You have been childless thus far. No doubt of your own doing. With Thomas' attentions at their peak, you cannot afford an injury that would compromise your abilities to carry a child."

Annabelle gathered the slack in her reins. "You have already referenced my suspect abilities at motherhood, mamma, why should a brisk gallop change that now? Perhaps a good tumble might knock things about. Improve the odds?" It was times like this she wished she could slap her mother broadly across the face with the truth.

The clear trill of the Master's horn provided excuse to conclude their idiotic conversation, but Annabelle's ire was up. *Good, a little ruffle will see me to the fox.*

"Enjoy the hunt on solid ground, I vastly prefer my vantage point." And with her blood reaching Phlegethontic temperatures, she spun Aberdeen about on his haunches, and spurred him into a startled canter, intent on her kill—of he fox, but more importantly, Lady Sackville's ego.

⊱❦⊰

The Hunt was in full cry, wholly dangerous and utterly exhilarating. The spectators, left to follow in carriages on the roadway, clamored for a glimpse of the excitement through bronzed binoculars.

Taking the crest of a hill, Annabelle let Aberdeen flush into a gallop. The huntsmen ahead recast the hounds in hopes the fox scent would be discovered. Keeping her hands soft and her weight off his back, she instilled confidence to forge ahead in his equine wisdom.

The bracing slap of the autumn air on her cheeks almost hypnotizing, Annabelle, lost the herd of huntsman and the enviable Lady Sackville over the last fence half a field back. The faces of their well-turned-out group glowed in wholesome recreation as the Master trumpeted the hunt to life. The black and red coats, the polished boots and soaped leather, the dustless horses before the bugle note were a far cry from the truth of the hunt—muddied mounts, disheveled—and even wounded riders. But it was the black notes of the hunt which made the terrifying glory of the spectacle rest on hallowed ground. Splashing through a stream, icy sprays glancing her cheeks, Annabelle wondered if today would be the day nothing would go wrong.

The shrill of the hounds' tongue ratcheted Annabelle from her pleasant daze—they had caught wind of the fox. She slowed Aberdeen and swiveled her head for a glimpse of the hounds, a thunder of hooves rattled behind her right ear. Turning in her saddle, she saw Dr. Christianson on his thin Thoroughbred, a wicked grin plastered on his face. Before Annabelle could gather her reins and spur Aberdeen back to full speed, he was upon her.

"You shouldn't be riding,' he shouted, edging his mount's nose into her thigh.

Annabelle sank into her saddle to avoid an upset as Aberdeen recoiled a quiver away from the Thoroughbred. Despite Annabelle's inclination to do the same, she steadied him with her whip laid firmly across his hip. "Must you still insist on getting into my skirts?"

"Don't forget you've accused me before of such originality." He pushed his dark beast up so they were nose to nose, the horses' hooves beating the earth in time.

Annabelle jammed her thigh well between the pommels and pressed her hips off her seat, digging her heel into Aberdeen's flank, already at his top speed. "I can't imagine why you've imbibed your primitive view on my mother. I have every right to this hunt," she cried, wishing she could take her whip to his face. "There isn't a chance I'm in the very way you imply. With Thomas." Speech was proving trying at their breakneck pace across the coverts. She kept her eyes peeled for the fox.

"That kind of talk will land you in an asylum,' Christianson retorted, head craning too for a red tail.

Then she saw the white-tippled plume of tail and ruddy coat flying in an arch over a log. The hounds had lost him, still milling about a field ahead. Without the Master in earshot, Annabelle broke code. "Tally-ho!" The word almost felt like a declaration of her sure victory as she seesawed the reins, and sank heavily back into the saddle, collecting Aberdeen. Annabelle veered, delighted as Aberdeen complied, leaving her father-in-law sputtering behind. Aiming Aberdeen at a four-foot stone fence with a winking barbed wire laced over the lined fieldstones, she glanced behind her. Christianson was in pursuit, coming in at a wide angle, elbows flopping, face hardened. His speed and disarray flashed certain warning through Annabelle's head, but she dismissed it and returned her focus to the fence. On a new mount it was too large to really be taken safely. But he was a seasoned rider. He'd certainly seen the barbed wire which added another half a foot to their handicap. He was wiser than to attempt the impossible—through impossibilities Annabelle considered her specialty.

The fence was all she could see.
She shouldn't.
Couldn't.
But the fox. Besting Mrs. Sommersville.
Both wild and beautiful. What she wanted to be.

Christianson was gaining ground. His Thoroughbred's head wagged in protest—two beasts at odds. In horror, she tried to shout a warning over her shoulder, but he took no notice. She turned back to the fence. The difference between a good jump and a poor one was like the difference between playing in tune and playing out of tune and there were so many ways to break one's neck on a hunt. She was too close to slow Aberdeen without a certain accident. She swiveled in her saddle and waved her whip at Christianson, screaming at him to have some sense. But she was only met with his wicked intent.

With Aberdeen's hooves demolishing the remaining ground before the fence, Annabelle commanded her attention ahead of her.

She'd take it. She must. Now she had no choice.

Giving Aberdeen the reins, she slung her hands to either side of his neck and rose out of the saddle to free his haunches for the leap. Another stride. Annabelle swallowed hard and rose a bit more in her stirrup.

Three. She flung a silent prayer to Christianson.

Two. She said another for herself. Every man for himself.

One. Soar.

She and Aberdeen left the ground, moving in perfect parabola, defying Newton's first law; two hearts—one goal. Hooves returned from the heavens. Annabelle caught herself against Aberdeen's bobbing neck and fought to regain her view of the fox.

But he was gone. A breath of relief washed over her, as the fox was free, before despair at her defeat came in like the tide.

Annabelle pulled Aberdeen to a halt, his sides heaving against her leg. Despite her thick skirts she could feel his sweat seeping through. She heard a rustling behind her and the chink of metal against metal. She shifted in the saddle. To her horror, Christianson's Thoroughbred was trotting amiably towards them. His reins were free, looping within inches of his flicking hooves; empty stirrups swung eerily. Swallowing her gasp, Annabelle squeezed her leg to Aberdeen's side and he came to life. The Thoroughbred gave in easily to Annabelle's tuttings as she snatched his reins, noticing his fine forelegs were ripped and bloody. When she looked back to the fence, a gaping cavern greeted her; illegal barbed wire dropped to meet the meadow grass. Fear seared her heart as her stare moved to the lone ash tree—its thick trunk—a strip of crimson coat and top hat at its base.

Chapter 28

Annabelle's feet had not hit the ground before she was certain Horace Christianson was dead. With his top hat crushed by his side, a devilish gash opening his forehead obliquely, and no semblance of a quivering breath, Annabelle left the horses to their own devices as she approached what she feared was the second corpse to be thrown unceremoniously across her path. With the horses grazing behind her, she collected her skirts and fell to her knees beside the fallen man. The vault from his mount, who had wisely refused the taut barbed wire, might not have ended fatally if the stalwart ash had been another foot aside. A sliver of repulsion—an impulse to run, to defect—came over her, just as it had when she hovered over Miss Greville's bloodied throat. But there was something that kept her rooted. Horace Christianson, torso twisted ungainly against his strewn legs, eyelids at half-mast, simply was not a man—notorious doings and all—to meet his demise in so ordinary of a way, and without an audience.

Annabelle held her breath her fingers slid over his neck in search of a life pulse. She hung in an absurd balance, hoping the truth wasn't so but finding a lack of sorrow if it were. Her fingertips found the jugular groove and were met instantly with a bounding throb. She almost lurched back in surprise, but an almost magnetic force kept her connected to her Uncle Horace.

He let in a shivering inhale, his eyes widening as his breathy exhale inflated a collection of pink bubbles between his parted lips. "I suppose you intended to bring me down like this?" His clear eyes, despite his battered body, met hers, amused.

Annabelle's hand softened around his neck. He looked, for the first time, helpless and small.

"You know I won't go down without a fight—or at least a final kiss." He continued past his unanswered accusation.

Feeling unusually safe, the murmur of the hunt behind them, Annabelle saw him as she had when he'd first cast a look of unadulterated desire over her frame; her immediate recognition of it for what it was, despite her thirteen years.

Christianson reached for her face, almost in a trance. Annabelle leaned towards him, revisiting his old spell. But his icy fingers speared her senses back and a quiver of something more amiss traced her consciousness. His jugular vein bulged, waxing and waning with his heartbeat, pacing double time.

Before her next thought, he brought his fingers down to her shoulder and hauled himself up—wincing. With his face inches from hers, Annabelle could appreciate his quickened breath and the soft wheeze of his exhales.

His expression veiled, looking as if he had just been set behind museum glass. "I've always loved you, Philippa."

Annabelle jerked, taken aback. "Philippa?" His tone implied an intimacy to the subject which heightened the color in her cheeks. "I'm Annabelle." Her pride almost deflated the urgency of his rattling breath.

He continued on. His gaze, piercing yet superficial, did not appear to see her any longer. "Pippa, come back to me."

Her memory flickered. Honey. Sarah's wayward, unfortunate mother. Freezing extremities. Bounding heartrate. Racing breath. Confusion. Annabelle's breath caught in her chest. She gave into kindness as she caressed Christianson's cheek and gently pressed him back into a pillow of dried meadow grass, visions of Olivia on her deathbed crucifying her conscience.

He complied without resistance, after his face relaxed with eerie contentment following a wave of pain.

Annabelle pushed back. If what the state of his insides was indeed as she imagined— he'd not last another two hours. How easy would it be to rejoin the hunt? To leave him forgotten, to take his last breaths under the craggy branches of the old ash? A sharp pang bolted her heart right and she took his hand.

As she did, Christianson mumbled the one word that sealed his fate. "Thomas" wove from his stained lips before he succumbed to gravity and his hemorrhaging belly; a cherub's smile replacing every single leer and smirk he had ever proffered.

Annabelle pushed to her feet. "I'll find Thomas." She strode to the gamboling horses and swung herself back into Aberdeen's saddle, the Thoroughbred reined in by his side. "Hold on,' she pleaded, meaning her imploration, if not for her own sake, for Thomas' before she took her heel to her gelding's flank, spurring into him to a gallop in search of Thomas and the Master of the Hunt.

⚜

Annabelle had been shocked when after meeting Thomas one field over, and returning to his fallen father, Thomas went to pieces in a panic, elephant tears rolling down his face. His typically astute faculties departed instantaneously, leaving him a helpless little boy.

Annabelle blessed Beatrice as she thundered up to their woebegone party. Tumbling from her wooly mount, a cyclone of sweaty tweed and sweat, her soul was stuffed with a sterner batting. Beatrice took stock of the disaster and with a practicality which would have made all wives and mothers the world over swoon with pride she queried, "What's to be done?" Shoving her hands on her hips she questioned, "Dare I touch him?"

Annabelle had been the one to take that dare and now she raced into the front hall of Penwood house. She had only minutes before the carriage escorted by Beatrice and the Master would fly with the fallen Christianson in tow, through Penwood's front gates.

"A woman never looks so well as when she comes in dirty from hunting." Lord Sackville bellowed as Annabelle crossed into the front hall. They collided as he strode towards her, all whiskered joviality, and she caught herself (and her breath) against his barrel chest for a moment.

"There, there my girl. What in heavens is the matter?" He patted her back with one hand; the other held aloft protecting a snifter of Madeira. "I was feeling peckish and have found a bit of fortification." He brought the glass back into view. "But you seem to be in greater need of it."

Annabelle shied away from the glass, although nothing could have tasted sweeter in this instant. "There's been an accident, Lord Sackville. My father-in-law, Dr. Christianson."

"Not good ol' Horace," Sackville bumbled. "Where's he now?" He drained his glass and looked rather uselessly around for a place to rest it.

"Into the drawing room." Annabelle commanded as she searched for words. "Your renowned wit will come very much necessary to keep the guests entertained while we see to Dr. Christianson."

The Lord blustered. "I say—shall I run and fetch a doctor?"

The idea of Lord Sackville running anywhere struck Annabelle as preposterous as her next admission. "I've trained as a doctor, Lord Sackville . A surgeon. Exactly what he needs right now."

Between his confused blunderings of calling for a real surgeon, of the masculine variety, Annabelle turned the Lord in the direction of the drawing room and gave him an encouraging shove. "Your wit, Lord Sackville , for the guests, please." Then ignoring his protests, she picked up her feet and raced to the end of the hall and down the stairs to the kitchens, her heart pounding with a curious mixture of giddiness and terror.

With all kitchens in great houses being as they were quite similar in terms of the general velocity of persons and volume of chaos, Annabelle let the hubbub of the mid-day preparations for the hunt luncheon offer her a temporary calm before the unavoidable, brewing storm.

The clamor of serving trays, flustered kitchen maids, and the jokings of squirrely footmen, ground to a silent halt as Annabelle made her entrance. The countless pairs of eyes on her as the younger Dr. Christianson's still new wife, felt like miniscule daggers of judgement . Annabelle readjusted her hat which had fallen askew in her race and lifted the veil before she addressed the room. "Dr. Christianson's had an accident." She wondered if honesty would fare well now, and decided it would. "He can't be moved far; the dining room must be cleared, and the guests kept to the front of the house." She swallowed—fear and pride intermingling with a nasty trace. It was Miss Greville's case all over again but magnified a hundred-fold. "And boiling water for my instruments and to wash. Keep a steady flow up to the dining room. Make sure whomever brings it has a strong stomach." Annabelle expected the kitchen to roar to life at her wishes, but the Penwood staff gawked back at her. "I have under an hour and a half to prevent him from expiring—look sharp," she commanded. And though she didn't know if the urgency of her crazed request or simply fear of the fevered woman in front of them—the kitchen sprang into action with affirmatives meeting the trail of Annabelle's skirts hustling back up the stairs.

Bounding back to the main hall, Beatrice Christianson was comforting Thomas who had collapsed into a highbacked chair. His mother was in turn offering him sips of something Annabelle hoped was stronger than sherry and caressing his back.

Beatrice gave Annabelle a rally-cry of a smile. "You have all your necessary preparations then?"

"Yes, the staff think I'm one step closer to an institution, but they don't need explanations now." Annabelle locked eyes with Thomas. His initial attempts to pull himself together had been overtaken by the white shock of fear. She'd have to face the dining room and its bloody bath alone. There was no need for explanation. He cast his eyes down and held out his hand, the last swill sloshed angrily in the glass responding to his shaking hands' rough tides.

Her heart cracked open, in the way only Thomas could allow, like a fresh laid egg, shuttered against the edge of a glass bowel . Annabelle pressed her lips to his forehead and whispered her reassurances. "Larkin can run the chloroform, ' she had no one else to ask, 'only you would keep a stock in a country manor." She smiled, the discovery of enough anesthetic to repair the wounded from a small battle in his Penwood study had been most opportune indeed.

At the mention of the impending operation, the snifter took a last shutter and flew from Thomas' grasp as his tremor increased until it seemed to take over the better part of his body. "I'm sorry, I'm sorry," Thomas implored for her forgiveness and he looked at her helplessly.

"You have every right to be distraught, no need for forgiveness. You've taught me well. I'll not always have you by my side in the theatre." She nodded with an assurance she did not feel before she leaned into offer the comfort of her entire body to this man. Not a husband—but so many things far greater—better. "We'll see this through. I from the battlefield and you a safe distance from the cannons."

Thomas' face spread with relief and gave Annabelle a feeling she would never forget.

"Hear, hear!" Beatrice offered her hearty approval as if she were in parliamentary chambers and not championing her daughter-in-law's surgical prowess.

This was an altogether new pleasure. To offer hope in the face of despair. In that moment, Annabelle believed she just might be able to face the nightmare of Horace Christianson's insides.

※

Despite their wretched history, Annabelle had no desire to add dear Uncle Horace to her short list of surgical disasters—as the first headstone in that cemetery Thomas had once said every surgeon tows on their soul's back all lifelong .

She assessed the dining room turned surgical suite—her mouth as dry as Moorish sands, her heart clamoring against her sternum. But the panic she was expecting had been called away on other pursuits. Instead, the neural troops of her frontal cortex turned out with pressed uniforms and polished brass. "Right."

Everything was just as it would be in the College's operating theatres. Thomas' instruments were boiled and set out on towels on a side table pushed to meet the walnut dining table—that in other circumstances would have preferred to host a scintillating dinner party of twenty. Masses of starched sheets surrounded her unconscious father in law, Larkin manning the chloroform cone covering his face. Her humble request for his assistance had slipped easily and was met with an equally easy affirmation from Larkin. For a moment, it had almost felt like old times.

"Is he deep enough to begin?" Annabelle approached them. When Christianson remained in his unworldly state as she ran her knuckles briskly over his stripped shin.

Wrapping herself in the rough, bleached cook's apron, she wondered, was this exhilaration she was feeling? Power? The unabashed thill of capability? Her fingers deftly double knotted the ties behind her.

The ridiculousness of her mission struck her as she thumbed through the step by step approach for Surgical Exploration of the Abdomen from the Council's guide. Though the caveat of Proceeding Blunt Trauma had been conveniently left out—leaving Annabelle to short memories of battlefield surgeries from the Crimean reported as Lancet case studies. Even more absurd, was the charade Larkin had heartily endorsed as he coaxed Christianson to sleep. Without the waver of untruth in his voice, he reassured the man it would be his son, the genius surgeon, Dr. Thomas Christianson, to save his wounded father, rather than the patient's forsaken child-mistress and daughter-in-law.

"Excellent." Annabelle smiled—appreciative of Larkin's compliance. "Can you manage the anesthesia and offer a spare hand if I need it?"

To her vexation, a look of ultimate adoration won over Larkin's features. "Nerves of steel, heart of a lion, hands of a woman. That is what is required for the surgical arts. I have none of these—you possess them all, my Angel."

Their makeshift operating theatre was no place for Cupid's protests. "Not now,' Annabelle snapped.

Larkin bit his lip in retreat. A solemn promise of something—yet unvoiced—hung in the air.

Annabelle allowed herself an amorous flutter before steeling herself for the task ahead. "One more examination before I make the first cut." She whisked a binaural stethoscope from Thomas' bag—peaking from beneath the low-slung tablecloth like a watchful archangel and pressed it to Christianson's chest. All lobes of his lungs echoed as they inflated with air—likely no seeping of blood into his respiratory organs. But she sighed when she faced his protuberant abdomen, hemorrhage. If it were his liver—aside from suturing the lacerated organ back to right—the odds were he'd succumb to infection or further bleeding. But the spleen. That could be removed, leaving a stubbly vesseled frontline. And his insides were bathed in saline and diluted carbolic wash—Dr. Horace Christianson might just stand the chance of seeing another sunrise. Though how Annabelle would view her father-in-law when next she set eyes on him was a question she was unable to answer.

"No hemithorax?" Larkin questioned, more student than teacher. Annabelle looked at him with open eyes and realized she indeed was the relative expert in the room. "Doubtful, lung fields are clear."

He nodded as she imagined Napoleon would have to his Josephine, in respectful capitulation. "Then the abdomen." He looked to Annabelle's current nemesis.

Uncertainty kept Annabelle from replying as she soaped her hands in the basin with a shard of carbolic soap. There'd certainly have been a funeral if Lister hadn't brought light on microbes and the putrification they brought in their wake. And something so simple as saponification. She bought herself several additional moments of planning as she lathered a second time and wondered if she should have pursued the mortuary arts instead.

Her surgical safari called for an upper midline incision to access the deep peritoneal cavity. "Knife up." Annabelle took her scalpel in hand. Christianson's skin was dull and tacky from the film of dried carbolic she'd scrubbed over his torso. A shaft of crystalized sunlight—as though she were being supervised by the gods—leaving a golden orb over Christianson's lower left ribs. Annabelle prayed fervently there was a force greater than her to guide her—as it seemed as if the Heavens were pointing directly at the offending organ—the spleen.

Minutes later, Annabelle was occupied, deep in her patient's abdomen. Larkin kept a protective plate pressed against the pancreas with his free hand as she tied off the gastric arteries with waxed catgut. Divine forces had been correct. The spleen, a horrific, stellate split having fractured the organ almost in two, was the source of Christianson's hemorrhage. Annabelle wove between a thrill of the chase and relief she had a small odds of saving Christianson. Double ligating the splenic artery and vein with a vicious throw of her suture, Annabelle wondered if she could be a truly vengeful person. Almost up to her shoulders in bits and blood, she could see an easy nick (with a deliberate intent this time,) and a life could be ended under the guise of a medical mishap. Easy retribution and avoidance of the gallows for murder. What kind of charges might be invoked in her name if the truth of today's surgical dalliances were to made known? But she dismissed that worry to be trifled with another day, when Christianson would be safely tucked into his convalescent bed.

Annabelle removed the soaked linens from Christianson's belly and clamped her fingers at juncture of the spleen's vessels and the securing ligament, separating the organ from its physiologic garden plot. The battered mass gave way easily and she pulled it through the incision with the same thrill as a Highland's miner who had just panned an enormous gold nugget in the Kildonan Rush. With the spleen safely tucked into a pan on her makeshift instrument table, Annabelle made another sweep of the abdomen. Diaphragm, left liver lobe, left kidney, all intact.

"You've done it." Larkin smiled winningly. "Shall I set the pancreas free now?"

Annabelle was too relieved to appreciate his attempt at humor. "Yes, do. Saline lavage. A hint of carbolic. Drain. Close. Then we wait." A feeling of contentment began to ease the tension from her shoulders and jaw as she secured a length of commandeered gas lamp tubing through a slit oblique to the umbilicus. With each subsequent step, nearing the finish line of her first, seemingly successful, solo surgery, Larkin interjected with clucks of praise, so different than the solid reassurances of Thomas' brand of guidance. Though Annabelle enjoyed a wind of superiority, she yearned for Thomas' egalitarian repartee. She wondered if that ache would ever dull.

As she ran a final sweep of sutures down the belly long incision, a sneaking dose of reality brought Annabelle back down to Earth. The hard truth was that despite all her precautions, Christian faced a higher chance of demise in Penwood's varnished rooms than on the Queen's battlefields.

But there was nothing else to be done save for the paste of turmeric and garlic to stave off the risk of a vessel-choking clot, flush the drain morning and night, and leave Christianson to his fate. Though as she sponged off the cranberry-colored flecks of dried blood from his abdomen, and Larkin slowed the chloroform, Annabelle began to question where the roads of fate and human intervention intersected. And what that far-away land was called.

Chapter 29

With the hunting guests gone home, the cadence of Penwood returned to its gentle sophistication as the weeks ticked towards the ivy and mistletoe of Christmas. The climbing holiday anticipation was heightened by the recovery of its master.

While no one seemed surprised Horace Christianson took on his ruptured spleen with his typical bullish lack of compromise, Annabelle waited with bated breath for updates from Thomas, whom his father roaringly credited with his unprecedented recovery. Infection and embolism were shockingly avoided; Annabelle smilingly had already begun a case study she intended to submit to The Lancet. And with a not so gentle nudge from her husband, Annabelle neatly rewrote the first page with her solo byline. A tiptoeing step but finally she had turned her gaze in the direction of the ever-hopeful, rising sun.

Late in the week Annabelle trotted up Penwood's front stairs full force from the stables. A fine dew highlighted her exertions from a gallop after a morning pouring over final toyings with their electrocardiogram. Thomas had been back to London to collect his father's papers and notebooks. Now Dr. Christianson regularly made his way to the drawing room, carried down the main staircase in a whickered wheelchair by Bleeker and his valet. There he would occupy himself with a brisk review of his most unusual cases, intent on a grand presentation at an upcoming medical conference. No one had been bold enough to mention the relatively idiocy of Christianson's notion with his recent flirtation with an untimely demise.

Clapping her boots against the final stair, Annabelle paused to release the ribbon from her wool topper. The release of heat from her head against the sharp December air was sublime. With her stomach rumbling like a woken bear, Annabelle decided to pilfer a nubbin of Somerset cheddar and a crisp Cox before she'd peek in on Christianson. Just to ensure he was back in all his evil spirits. With her attentions occupied, she almost screamed when her left hand was snatched up as she entered the house and she twirled into Cassius Larkin's square chest.

With one arm keeping her to him, Larkin pressed his finger to her lips, a beaming smile lighting his face. "I considered finding a mount and playing a bit of cat and mouse on the moors if you weren't to return in another quarter of an hour."

With her shock blooming into a more enticing emotion, Annabelle returned his warm expression. "Good morning,' she considered his address, 'Dr. Larkin. You've been waiting?" In the moment she thought it cruel to remind him to call her Mrs. Christianson. She made no effort to free herself from his embrace.

Larkin maintained his smile. "Your formality pains me, Annabelle. And yes, I've been waiting all morning. But I've the children to present to Horace as requested, they'll lift his spirits immensely."

Annabelle wondered at Larkin's real motives for his visit, despite the pleasure of his company. Horace Christianson was his antithesis in more ways than one, and was known to poorly disguise his dislike of human varietals under at least twelve years. For what conversation could be held with a being without the semblance of a fully formed brain? Regardless she donned a joyful trill. "You've brought the children. They'd love to tromp around the grounds, it's been ages since I've seen—' She couldn't honestly recall their names Her late reconciliation with Olivia gave her an excuse for this lapse, 'them."

On perfect cue, a miniature version of her aforementioned friend, presented herself from behind the morning room door. Annabelle's heart quaked at the resemblance. Not being more than eight years old, her brow was furrowed like a school marm just sprung upon a pupil's rude sketch.

"They're anxious to meet you." Larkin reluctantly released Annabelle. "Adelaide, come say hello to Annabelle."

Adelaide shot him a sharp look that almost made Annabelle jump. "Father, I know who she is. Adelaide Larkin, the pleasure is mine." She curtsied low and murmured, "Mrs. Christianson."

Annabelle balked at her current title. "Lovely to make your acquaintance, Adelaide. You comport yourself rather well for a child so young."

Adelaide wrinkled her nose. "I am not so very young. I'll be ten in four months' time and have already read the Brontës and mastered the French past perfect. I daren't call you Annabelle when I know you to be Mrs. Thomas Christianson. Father has spoken often of you since the hunt."

Annabelle forgave the situation its awkwardness and swept forward, crouching down to level her gaze into the Adelaide's cornflower blue eyes. "The Brontës are absolute genius, if you had to choose, which is your favorite? Charlotte, Emily, or Anne?"

They were well into the weeds of a debate on the superior qualities of Wuthering Heights over Jane Eyre, before Larkin cleared his throat gently. With the interruption, Annabelle gave Adelaide a conspiratorial wink. "I believe your papa has other aims for us this morning."

The girl wriggled; her tiny pearl earrings trembled in her ear lobes like a puppy wagging the entirety of his body upon its master's return. "I'd like that very much." She gave Annabelle a restrained but true smile, then looked to her father. "The others are waiting to meet Annabelle." She turned her head in the direction of the morning room. "And you were right, I do like her very much."

The whispers of engineered theatrics pricked at Annabelle as she stood, but she Adelaide's hand a squeeze. But those momentary bristles were shorn to their roots when Annabelle found herself locked in Larkin's orbit. Their magnetism remained constant, and undeniable, as gravity.

As if guided by an inner knowing, and perhaps mischievousness, a smaller girl poked her head around the morning room door, her eyes curious. "Father, the boys are beginning to pinch the baby. All they want is to play horse and rider in the lovely leaves."

Her whine cracked the force between the two adults. "The sergeant of the troops." Larkin took Annabelle's hand and paraded her a few steps forward to meet the informant.

"Luella Larkin, I'd like to present,' he paused mid-dramatics, his hand closed reassuringly over Annabelle's. "Mrs. Annabelle Christianson, a dear friend of the family."

"Why have I not met her before then?" Larkin's second daughter protested without the propriety of a curtsey. "If she's a dear. . ."

Adelaide rushed to her sister; her face pinched in rebuke. "We like her." She yanked her younger sister into a curtsey. "This is my sister, Luella Larkin." An impish grin erased her grown-up pretenses. "She's not quite right most days."

Delighted she was indeed still dealing with a child rather than a tiny woman, Annabelle laughed. "Never you mind, Luella, if what your sister says is true, you haven't a worry. None of are really right most days anyway."

The morning room felt shockingly empty, now the clamoring introductions of the remaining Larkins were completed (namely one Reuben, a sturdy boy of five, Thaddeus, drooling on his teething amber necklace, and baby Ottilie, none the worse for the alleged pinchings.) They paraded out to the gardens, led by the fearless Adelaide, for a thrashing game of horse and rider. Annabelle was left to wonder exactly who would be riding who.

Settling into the emptied settee, Annabelle ignored the tumult of her empty stomach, and appraised Larkin, across from her in an overstuffed armchair. He leaned forward, his head cradled in his cupped hands, elbows balanced on his knees—showcasing his almost idiotic expression of contentment.

"Rather ambitious to descend on us without the nursemaid?" Annabelle arched her brow. She wondered he had never seemed so passionate a parent when they had known each other in a very different manner. Before Sarah. Before Thomas. Before she had wrapped her fingers around a scalpel. She wondered too, why other children seemed so perverse. But Larkin troops were altogether charming, in the manner of a traveling circus, all jangling caravans and roaring lions.

"They're really no trouble, outside of being very sure of their own opinions. They make me smile more often than not. I figured a day off for nanny and an outing to the country was just the thing. They've heard so much about you as of late. I couldn't stave off their pesterings to meet you."

"I thought they were to provide cheer to the recuperating good doctor?" Annabelle questioned, mirth dancing along every syllable.

Caught, Larkin cast his eyes down momentarily, before looking up at Annabelle—his grey pools full of longing.

So contrary to the last time they had been alone in one another's company—Annabelle's horrific rejection in Larkin's carriage—she found herself what felt like solid ground rather than one resembling the fading sands beneath the ocean's evening tide.

With his tone a little desperate, which Annabelle found very much to her liking, Larkin sprang from his chair and came to her side on the settee, grasping her hands between his. "You have bewitched me in a manner most unexpected."

But Annabelle had gone through the anguish of having him wrenched from her so many years ago by a cunning Olivia, then sharing his bed (all pleasures aside.) And for the utmost in humiliation, having him throw her aside for having shed her feminine appeal for intellectual garments. And yet, he had returned, making Annabelle question the simpering artifice of a Society darling she had trying to fervently to cultivate. "Bewitched? You are a rake indeed. I recall you threw me from your carriage as an unfeminine wretch. Made unwholesome and repulsive by the roaring flames I stoked over my textbooks?"

Annabelle saw a shiver of emotion trace the side of his face—exposing him without apology—making her hope even more he was true.

"Go on." There was no goading or laughter in her voice, only reassurance now, with her heart hanging so tenderly on a hook.

"I've been a fool. Since the beginning. And then you took me back." He looked at her. "Those secret days of ours have been the happiest of my life thus far."

Annabelle nodded. Their stolen bliss had just been thrown on the balance next to the thrill of the knife. With the promise of autonomy on future horizons, those moments with Larkin turned fragile, like the aging autumn leaves, threatening to disintegrate into her dead past with the next December gust. But what of her heart? She wondered if that winning thrill pleasured her head or her heart—or perhaps both? Neither? Her heart seized in indecision.

"You were right in the carriage."

"I was?" Annabelle could barely remember their conversation; she had been so occupied with the bleeding of her heart .

"I've been ruled by family and Society obligations, and never by my own heart. " He pulled their hands to his chest.

Annabelle could feel his heart clap against her palm—the duet only adding to the tumultuous state of her sentiments.

"And now, with the children, I've had no choice but to re-examine my options—and the only one I want is you."

"How have the children turned your opinion?"

Larkin shook his head. "They did not. But the house is empty without the life a woman gives it. It no longer is a home. That is what they—I—really want. I want that woman to be you."

Though Annabelle had found Adelaide most charming, and Larkin even more so—until now—she curled her fingers into his coat to cool her palms and disappointment. "I don't believe you've—" As sweet as the children were, she had to admit, there was no room in her professional future for motherhood.

"You're wrong Annabelle," Larkin cut her off. "Never mind the children. When I saw you, just like the Annabelle I fell for in your father's library so many years ago, take Christianson's life into your own." He returned their hands between them though his grip renewed. "Your spirit is at once terrifying and admirable. Your flame drawsx me in. I've been reduced to a moth in your presence."

"Come now." Looking at the pleading man in front of her, Annabelle found she held his arrogant, assured counterpart in far greater esteem, but reformation had not detracted from his upfront handsomeness in the slightest. Though her heart was alight from a match lit in the past, Annabelle lead with the toying note of her recent introspections. "I've won over your distaste for a woman of substance?"

"There was never any distaste for your substance, my Angel. But in that moment, in the carriage, the idea of a woman sullying herself in surgical butchery and finding herself a wife and mother was imposturous, and my heart closed to the idea."

"Your enthusiasms have changed then, having spoken so highly of me to your children." It seemed too much a fairy tale. And who had been the author?

A renewed look of prospect came over Larkin. "Yes, I have, very much indeed. And they are ready, I am ready, with open arms."

"But what will you welcome and truly, what are you even proposing? Have you forgotten I am not just Annabelle, but Mrs. Thomas Christianson?"

"As you said, that is an arrangement in name alone?"

"Abinding arrangement, nevertheless."

"You led me to believe Thomas would very much allow. . ."

"To spend my life as your mistress, I have no desire to return under that crown."

"Then a dissolution of sorts, there must be something?"

"Even if our marriage could be disbanded, I wish to be more than an object whose sole purpose is to love and adorn. To mother and obey. I have a talent and I intend to pursue it, regardless of the state of my ring finger." She contemplated her gold band, and how it had been bent to form her cage. Would she really be so eager to exchange it? Her fingers really were quite pretty unadorned.

"Of course, my darling. You could see patients in the sitting room on your afternoons." Larkin ecstatically leaned forward and kissed her. "And the papers we could write. I could dearly use your insight on the workings of a paper on the post-operative management of pain by the physician. We'll be unstoppable, Angel." He stole another kiss.

A flicker of hesitation made his lingering warmth on her lips less sweet. Annabelle's pattering heart slowed, regaining its senses. Still soaring on the wings of her private triumph with Christianson, Annabelle had been steadily crafting her professional future. Apothecary Licentiate aside, she'd take on the surgical field on her own terms, even outside Thomas' guiding hand. She recognized no matter of the heart could quiet this new drumbeat in her soul. Perhaps she could not slam that draw gate aloud, but her decision was made.

Larkin took left hand in his and regained his habitual, regal posture. At once, the Larkin of old returned. "I'll speak with your Dr. Christianson as soon as I can. Arrangements will be made. In no time before you're settled by my side in Park Lane."

Annabelle opened her mouth to protest, the notion of being settled by anyone's side seeming as hollow as the gaping belly of the hundred-year hollowed oak standing watch over the Penwood gardens.

But she was saved the argument as the door handle to the morning room jangled savagely before the door blew open. The Larkin brood flooded into the room in a storm of whoops and hollers.

Sergeant Luella was stern as she marched over to her father. Adelaide rounded the gaggle up at the back, her curls coming unpinned. Baby Ottilie grinned wildly in her arms, several crisp leaves stuck to her fine blond hair. "Reuben is abominable!"

The accused stood with his younger brother in hand, looking very defiant as he toyed with Thaddeus' amber necklace, split in two, with the other.

"I taught her that word." Adelaide gave Annabelle a pointed expression.

Annabelle tucked her chin to quell her chuckle before she gave the girl a congratulatory nod.

"Chaos ensues," Larkin swept Luella onto his lap. "What did you do to deserve such treatment?"

"He was the horse. I was the rider. Being in a very bad humor this morning, he threw me. So I beat him."

"Then I beat you." Reuben gloated.

A slice of what her life would entail in all the domestic glory of the Larkin's. Annabelle held her breath to stave off a shudder.

Heavy heeled footsteps echoed in the hall. "Yoo-hoo, do I see the Larkin Adorables?" Beatrice Christianson bellowed with her robust joviality.

Larkin and Annabelle pushed apart to the respectable opposing corners of the settee. Annabelle wondered if this would be a recurring situation in any future of theirs.

A moment later, the lady strode into the room, offering the stabilizing presence of Gothic nanny to the helter-skelter of the room. Her face blazed with joy as she registered the Adorables. "There you are my lovelies, do give Auntie Bea a kiss." She swooped down on her haunches and opened her arms ready for the welcomed assault.

The children blinked at one another before Bea's magnetism overtook their skepticism and they ran to her with a slurry of yelps, nearly toppling her.

"They've only met her once, but she's been so kind this past year." Larkin confessed.

Annabelle was glad he didn't mention Olivia.

"Right, Adorables, let your father and Mrs. Christianson finish their business. No doubt discussing her surgical brilliance and we'll be off to the kitchens." She tapped the side of her nose. "I know where there is a trove of sugar biscuits."

The children cried out in delight.

"They'll go exceptionally well with a cup of tea to take the chill off. Then up to your rooms for some clean things before luncheon."

Nodding in agreement, the Adorables joined hands and the merry bunch headed to the door—the tenacious leaves finally losing their grip, scattered behind the baby, perched on Adelaide's hip.

"I'll meet you in the drawing room, I have some developments to go over with you and Horace." Beatrice trilled over her shoulder. "You'll find them very much to your liking."

Feeling slightly battered, but energized from the events in the morning room, Annabelle made her escape, after aiming a kiss at the top of Larkin's head. She noted the particular lack of regret she felt as she turned her back to him. It felt good to close that chapter, she'd tell him of her decision that afternoon. Heading for the drawing room, and her convalescing patient, she wondered how ecstatic it would feel when she cracked open her first headlining case study in The Lancet. It would certainly only be the beginning of things to come for Doctor Annabelle Christianson.

Chapter 30

Horace Christianson inhabited a plump easy chair, surrounded by pillows, feet propped on an ottoman, in Penwood's well-furnished drawing room. To Annabelle he appeared every inch a modern-day Caligula surrounded by his subjects.

Her father sat on a low stool, papers and scribbles strewn at his feet, within arm's reach of Horace. Thomas, still with the chill of the outdoors on him, top hat and overcoat undisposed, was on his knees, unloading more texts and notebooks from a small chest.

Very well then , she thought to herself, there's to be an audience for my demands . In days past, she would have postponed the damages for the sake of her father. Then there was Thomas. But today, the truth would fly, her claims would be known, and her ears would ring deaf to anything but an affirmative from Christianson.

On her entrance, Thomas sprang to his feet, his grin ever-present, now. He has played his role as bedside physician perfectly, never breaking Annabelle's confidence over the events in the dining room after his father's fall, soothing his father's pandering remarks when Annabelle insisted on at least a brief view of the surgical incision and tubes. He rushed to her side and spun her around, whispering into her ear as he did so, "Your brilliant, no infection. He'll most certainly recover thanks to you."

Annabelle allowed herself the pleasure of a blush before Thomas leaned in and kissed her cheek.

"You ready for this?" His smile stretched to his ears, smacking of well-intentioned mischief. "It's about time."

Annabelle glared at him behind her smile—she did not know which of her most recent secrets he was about to expose—her entrepreneurial aspirations the least of her worries. Never mind she would relish a bit of a fight and reveal—like a magician—revealing his sequined assistant—sawn in half moments before—was whole—body and soul . Holding back, slowing Thomas' stride, she protested between gritted teeth, "I really would like to—"

But he met her resistance with his most charming of winks and pressed on to his father, Annabelle reluctantly in tow behind him.

"My dearest," Dr. Pierce hastened to relieve himself of his lapful of dogeared medical journals before he could right himself.

Annabelle offered him her other hand and pulled him to his feet for a quick kiss on the cheek. "Morning Father."

"Did you enjoy your ride?"

"Quite exhilarating certainly, Papa, h ow have you been occupying yourself this morning?"

"He has been occupying himself, as you say,' Dear Uncle Horace scowled at Annabelle, 'with me." He kicked his afghaned foot between her father's haphazard piles, his expression easing as they cascaded into disarray.

Her father dove to save the semblance of his filing system.

Her father-in-law's ill humor cheered Annabelle immensely, as she released herself from Thomas' grasp and bent to help her father. Let the secrets spew then.

"Father,' Thomas, obviously accustomed to his father's temperament, continued with the intensity of a jolly town Mayor, just announcing his win on his fourth, consecutive re-election. "There's something I must tell you. We must tell you." He reached for Annabelle and drew her to him—the very picture of marital bliss.

Christianson's scowl dissolved. "Well this sounds like a cheerful announcement."

"I really do think I should be the one—and I've had other ideas we haven't—" Annabelle argued as Thomas pressed her closer to him. But he was caught on those incredibly kind wings of his—intent as much on his atonement as his sincere enthusiasm for her future.

"It's bound to come up, no time better than the present." Thomas pressed on—as if he could taste his relief (and pride) on the divulgence.

Christianson pushed himself up in the chair, casting a look at Annabelle. "Would this news bring any father supreme happiness? An extension of the family, perhaps?"

Before Annabelle could scoff at the notion, Thomas broke in. "Nothing of that sort father, yet." He did have the grace to offer her a soft smile of acknowledgement. "But there's something we haven't told you. Since your fall."

Christianson's patriarchal anticipation was replaced with a stern arch of his brows. "What then? Something about my injuries?"

"No, no, nothing like that." Thomas dropped by his father's side and patted his leg, dropping into his practiced bedside tones.

Annabelle stood uneasily, looking between the two men. Here it goes—perhaps she'd chime in with her demands in the wake of Christianson's likely shock—perhaps he's acquiesced more easily than anticipated?

"You're recuperating spectacularly well— we anticipate a full recovery—y ou've been supremely lucky."

A light tapping at the drawing room door made Thomas pause as Larkin stepped cautiously into the room. "Am I intruding? Brought the children up—" He appraised the scene he had interrupted after he closed the door. "A social call." He smiled cautiously and clasped his hands behind his back, his eyes shot to Annabelle for a beat before he ducked his head to await an invitation.

Curiously his eagerness and projected dreams of domestic divinity made her heart's earlier pitter patter shy in its beams.

"Good man, good man." Christianson huffed, obviously pleased at the added attentions. "My wife will be very glad to see your brood." He cocked his head—his expression worried. "You've left them to their own terrifying devices?"

Larkin relaxed and laughed. "No, no, Mrs. Christianson is busy procuring them some mid-morning tea—she does seem to enjoy them rather."

"She does—we'll leave them with her." Christianson looked relieved—as if he'd been spared an embrace with a boa constrictor. "You've come just in time for the grand news—my Thomas has been up to something apparently."

Larkin nodded at Thomas and came fully into the room. "Do go on, Christianson, I'm all ears." His eyes flicked again to Annabelle.

Annabelle considered Larkin's response to Christianson, when he knew the truth, to be a test—if his profession of love had been heartfelt—or simply another ploy.

"Perfect, our accomplice joins the party." Thomas beamed. "You'll have to fill in the glorious details."

Annabelle wondered how many additional superlatives her dear husband could stuff into the upcoming assertion.

"Out with it, boy." Christianson barked, though his underlying affection was obvious.

As Annabelle jumped at his tone, she appreciated Thomas stood fast and met his father with an even broader grin.

"As you wish."

Annabelle was certain this moment rivaled any past or future Christmas morning for Thomas—she supposed everything he had done for her surpassed his betrayal (although just) and she'd allow him the spotlight. Perhaps a natural opening for her demands would present itself and the entire proposal would only seem quite natural.

"It's Annabelle who you must thank for your current health."

Christianson pursed his lips—her father allowed himself a soft, but triumphant smile.

"She's your surgeon." He swept Annabelle forward like a little boy as he were presenting her at court.

His grimace was part spoilt child as Christianson spat, "Impossible. Why would you frighten me like that?"

"It's the truth, Father, and its anything but frightening." Thomas grew serious. "I simply couldn't face puttering about with my father's insides. Thank Christ she's been a gloriously quick study this past year."

Christianson turned his displeasure to Annabelle. "You,' he accused.

"Yes." Annabelle admitted sweetly.

"My dear girl!" Her father was on his feet.

"Sit down, Pierce." Christianson shot his leg out to corral his colleague. "This is some mad hoax."

"Anything but, Father." Thomas returned to his former amusement at his father's predicament—the least worrisome being his offending belly-long incision. "Annabelle has quite a bit more head for the medical arts than even her articles would bely . Save for the idiotic restrictions on women, she'd have set up with me at the College months ago."

At this confirmation, Pierce jauntily hopped (if one could say he made like a robin) over Christianson's shin and swept Annabelle into his arms. "You are a credit to your mother and me ." He looked over to Thomas. "You've cultivated something I never had the courage to imagine."

His praise brought a patter to Annabelle's heart—perhaps old dogs could learn?

"It was the next natural step, really." Thomas admitted. "It would be a shame to let talent like hers go to dust in a ball gown. "

"You're having me on," Dr. Christianson sputtered.

Annabelle kept her smile—he hadn't roared—the truth was sinking in.

"I wouldn't do that to you, Father." Thomas picked himself up—as if he were certain the argument would soon come to an end. "Simple truth is—you would have expired by teatime if we hadn't gone into stop the hemorrhage. But you, being a father, and I, a son, made me choke. I couldn't have held a scalpel my hands were shaking so badly. But Annabelle knew she had the nerve and ability, so came to your rescue. You owe her everything." Though his words were sincere, his voice hinted at the pleasure of his disclosure.

"And the anesthesia?"

"Me. Sir." Larkin cleared his throat—coming alive like he was called to speak in front of a magistrate. "That was my small contribution."

Christianson's face lost the last dregs of disbelief at Larkin's confirmation.

Annabelle looked to Larkin, hoping he was not too daft to appreciate her disdain. He'd not add more accolades than that? Only minutes before he'd lauded her abilities as beguiling as the rest of her. She was very much afraid she had been a fool to believe he could have reformed against his inclinations to conform in the face of opposition.

"And I thank you, Larkin—though I am surprised you kept this from me—though I am grateful you took on anesthesia—as you knew how I have a great distaste for the stuff."

Larkin saluted like the good pupil he had been. "Just a bit closer to training is all." He commendably took the high route—Annabelle could give him that—for the sake of her father. But no mention of her, again.

"Doesn't surprise me, Pierce, you've never had the stomach for anything but your drawing room consults." Christianson jabbed.

"Come now Horace, we were all students once, were we not?" Dr. Pierce gave Annabelle's hand a squeeze as he released her. "But as evidenced by your very breath, Annabelle's taken to the surgical arts quite expertly. With far more natural proclivity than either you or I ever did to medicine." His face hardened. "You remember those days of Honey, no doubt?"

The two men—friends, colleagues, rivals—locked eyes, the air in the room tightened—each seeming to teeter between the past and present.

"I'll never forget, nor should you, if you give a care for anything you hold dear!" Christianson's prickled displeasure turned to brutal fury as he attempted to leap from his repose.

Annabelle's stomach curled as she held her breath. She was certain she was the only other person in the room who knew of Honey's terrible death—that would forever seal her father's, in debt, to Horace Christianson for his silence. But her father had paid dearly, and in more ways than he would ever be aware.

But Christianson was thankfully hobbled from murderous intent by his still-healing incisions and deconditioning. Clutching his belly, he rocked with a loud moan back into his armchair, looking like a bull, though speared, unwilling to retreat.

A clattering of hasty footsteps and tousled commotion in the great hall announced a visitor. The group broke from the scene as the drawing room door swung wide and Mrs. Pierce flew into room, looking for all appearances as if she had just escaped the rabid jaws of the hounds from hell—feathers waving wildly in her hat— pushed back on her head from her exertions. Her face, typically so pinched from her own sufferings, was drawn smooth as risen cream.

Annabelle could not readily classify the entirely new expression she wore—though she was torn between comedy and concern—until her mother spoke.

"Horace, my darling, I came as soon as I was right myself!" Mrs. Pierce trilled before stopping stone still in her path to this chair. She brought her hand to her chest and uttered a soft exclamation of shock. "You're not alone,' before she twittered a nervous laugh as she acknowledged the rest of the party, all of whom looked as though they had been caught attempting to pilfer the Crown jewels.

Annabelle was sure she was the only member of these theatrics who was privy to their history, her father, Larkin, and Thomas only likely aware of the implication of an intimacy uncustomary between in-laws. So she decided to take pity on her mother— her embarrassment and dashed hopes—a rare bird about to be gunned down on a Central African safari (though conveniently right in the Yorkshire dales.) "Uncle Horace has been a darling of a patient, mamma , he's going to make a full recovery—as you are— considering how well you look." Annabelle wanted to gag on her taffy-coated words.

But considering the fits of hysterics Mrs. Pierce had reached after she was told of Horace's presumed fatal accident, requiring yet another psychiatric sojourn, Annabelle felt she could spare the kindness.

She looked to her father—who seemed to have mislaid the implications of his wife's exclamations, then caught her mother's eye squarely. Finding an intimacy in their shared lie, she continued as she swept to her mother, taking her by the arm and bringing her into their folds. "Yes, ma'am, we've just let dear Uncle Horace and Father in on my secret." The temptation to goad her mother was too rich to resist.

The pinchedness returned and darkened Mrs. Pierce's thin face. "Secret?" Her voice trembled.

Annabelle replied after a rush of laughter. "Yes. That Thomas has trained me most excellently as a surgeon. Horace's misfortune has perhaps changed mine foreseeable —and substantially—for the better."

Her mother's head quivered. "Surgeon? How?" She darted her eyes to her husband. "Did you—?"

"Dearest Mrs. Pierce, Annabelle has saved my father. In a rush of emotion, I was ill-suited to wield a scalpel, and so she put her merit to the test—to her supreme triumph." Thomas explained in a manner fitting the simple arithmetic equating one plus one makes two.

"You?" She drew in her breath, with almost as much emotion as when she realized there had been an audience to her affections minutes before. "You—operated?" She scanned her daughter as if her laser-beam focus could identify any telltale signs of this wayward talent. "And what misfortunes have you anyway?" She shook her head. The momentary connection between mother and daughter vanished.

Dr. Pierce seized his chance—moving to his wife—and wrapping her protectively in one arm. "Don't you see, my dear, our fireside lectures and admittedly haphazard education has paid off—with great dividends." He grinned and hugged her closer to him, though Mrs. Pierce certainly did not seem to reciprocate his joy. "Our Annabelle is a surgeon, and a damn fine one if I can judge by our Horace's miraculous recovery."

"Far from miraculous with my constitution," Christianson growled.

"Father,' Thomas half-groaned in protest, half-laughed at his recalcitrance. "You must admit this does approach the miraculous—your spleen had ruptured from the fall—you would have bleed to death in hours had she not operated. And you know how fatal post-operative infections can be."

Realization dawned over Mrs. Pierce, unshrouding rather than cloaking her tighter. "You?" She repeated, though her tone was tempered. "A woman?" Looking back to Christianson, she studied him for several beats.

He regarded her with silent retaliation—she with an evolving smile persuading her features to a semblance of beauty.

"Yes," Christianson chortled. "Ridiculous pursuit—even if she really had done as you say, Thomas—nothing will ever become of it—I will have been her first and last experiment."

"Hardly her first, Father." Thomas countered, 'and you will certainly not be her last success."

As Thomas moved to put his arm around Annabelle—much like her father had to her mother—Annabelle wove wide— finding the feel of solid ground beneath her own two feet quite liberating. Ignoring his daunted look, and not giving herself another moment of doubt, she plunged ahead with her ask. "And on the topic of my successes—the downscaling of the mercury electrometer and the addition of the vibrating pen to the syphon recorder were my suggestions—proving the electrogram to be more than an exhibit piece. With a few more months of work—we'll have the first successful prototype of a mobile unit well on its way to production and—"

"And? We?" Christianson laughed harshly.

"Yes." Annabelle and Thomas both chimed.

"She's always been the force behind my latest work, Horace." Dr. Pierce acknowledged.

Annabelle savored his sweet admission and gave her father an appreciative smile.

Thomas reclaimed his place at her side, and quietly slid his hand into hers. Its persistent warmth made Annabelle turn to look at him. The solidarity and affection shining from his eyes made Annabelle's eyes well with tears. She had been right to love him—in every sense of the word—in spite he'd never love her quite the same. Though she found the texture of what she felt for him to have changed—less the desire of bergamot-scented silk, and more the familiarity of cedar-cloaked tweed.

With a renewed confidence, Annabelle faced Christianson—lover, father-in-law, nemesis, sure that sooner than later, she would find herself whole. With or without Thomas (though she preferred with in any measure,) and likely without Larkin (it was delicious to be almost free of that twisted attraction.) She'd come this far. Even with doors to be shoved in, minds to be persuaded, laws to be changed, she'd not give up now.

As if harkened by the sound of Annabelle tightening her bootstraps, Mrs. Christianson made her heavy-footed entrance into the room—like Mrs. Pierce—looking a little worse for wear—save for the telltale half-eaten scone in her hand and a very merry smile on her face. "Quite the audience you've found yourself, Horace." She boomed. "Hallo everyone," she nodded at the group as she made her way to her husband. "I'm sure you've had them make you quite comfortable." She patted his head affectionately, spattering him with crumbs as she broke off another bit of scone and popped it into her mouth. Christianson hunkered down in his chair, as if he were about to be mauled by a pack of African wild dogs,

Beatrice poked and prodded, stretching his eye lids wide to expose their whites, and commanding he open his mouth wide and holler into her face. Satisfied, she finished the last of her scone, straightened, and put her hands to her hips. "I'd say our girl Annabelle, here. ' she looked over to Annabelle a military bob of her head, 'has a mighty fine talent and should be given anything—nay, everything—she asks for."

Realizing no blood had been shed, Christianson quickly brushed himself off. "She has some ludicrous notions about that damn ' cardiogram, Pierce has concocted. Patents. . . royalties. . . income." He sputtered.

"And as she should, my dear, if she's put her nose in that game—and likely won it if not for the both of you,' she nodded (a bit disapprovingly Annabelle believed) at Dr. Pierce after giving her husband a hard look.

"Ehhh,' Christianson dismissed her logic. "And with these silly surgical dealings, Thomas,' he kept his eyes on his son, 'you've had your fun playing teacher with your pretty wife, but it has proven a waste."

"A waste?" Thomas frowned.

"I suppose you may have had naïve notions or promises made but—' Christianson slapped his thighs—in great enjoyment of his next declaration, 'no woman can practice medication in Great Britain."

"But the Licentiate—" Thomas protested.

"Closed—a few months ago—I found some vague wording. It clarified to its proper meaning. There'll be no lady doctors stepping their slippered feet into a man's ring for the foreseeable future."

"You?" Annabelle stepped forward. He had purposely had it closed—he had been so much more than a messenger but a malicious instigator.

"You had the laws rewritten?" Thomas cried. "How could you—knowing all we had—all Annabelle has—"

Christianson leaned back, folding his hands deftly in his lap. "Never mind the who's or how's,' he added with relish, 'if you put a pen in your hand—she could record your notes—ledgers—and things—"

"She'll do nothing of the sort—" A shrill bark hit the ceiling as Mrs. Pierce took the stage.

"Here, here!" Beatrice chorused, always in favor of a political row—especially if it involved members of her own family—and were to prove her husband wrong.

Mrs. Pierce, likely for the very first time Annabelle surmised, looked to Beatrice as an ally, rather than a lumbering, elephantine nuisance, to be avoided and if unable, merely tolerated. "I think some choice words from the two of us will convince Horace to take up his wicked pen to right his wrongs."

Mrs. Pierce looked past Beatrice to find her daughter's gaze—her intent most shocking—and as clear as the waters of the Malham Tarn.

Chapter 31

Nestled back in 17 Berkeley Square, Annabelle thought of her mother's parting words in the drawing room at Penwood. She could hardly imagine her mother confronting Horace, certainly not with Beatrice nearby; her mother would not be that cruel. And why now? Why after the tired protests and screechings would her tides change? Each morning in the window seat, admiring the crystalline icicles adorning the disrobed branches of the horse chestnut tree, Annabelle would toy with the various scenarios where the tiny Mrs. Pierce would topple their Goliath. She knew it was a childish pursuit to sit and dream of sugarplums, snow angels, and vindication. It had been too long since she had known that simple pleasure. But there she was, a week before Christmas, counting down the days as if she were a child of seven and her greatest wish was for a French china doll with ringlets and a button nose. And that workbook on The Geometry of Shapes.

Annabelle smiled at the memory. On their return from Penwood, she had busied herself in the Season's merriment, putting her thoughts of bending to Beatrice's implorations on ice. Joining the fledgling suffrage movement, horrid Lady Sackville aside, might be the chance she needed. Though her mother had made it seem as if there might be more to the matter. Annabelle sighed at the solitary cherry-bright robin perched at the tip of a waving branch. Annabelle wondered if metaphorical wings might sprout from her shoulder blades just when all seemed so dire.

Leaving these cares at the sill, Annabelle went to her dressing table to await Kitty's nimble hands to finish her bows and buttons before heading down to start her day. She was glad of the stack of half-finished articles her father had delivered yesterday. And the engineer had delivered the blueprints of the electrogram. Plenty to keep her evening worries of the future at bay if her mother's efforts proved futile. If her mind strayed, there were always gifts to be wrapped and sugared almonds to be dipped (and snitched.) Mrs. Mingle had managed to find an in with their new cook, Mrs. Homesley. The two got on like melted butter and clover honey, ensuring her frequent visits would continue.

In the growing twilight that evening, the roaring, drawing room fire reflected husky rainbows in the glass bulbs strung across the branches of the fir tree. It seemed some sort of Christmas magic staved off anything but the best of the world. Annabelle was amusing herself with alternating between the fantastical absurdities (and poignant observations of life' truths) of Carroll's Through the Looking Glass and fiddling with her father's latest article on the treatment of keloid scars with iodide of potassium. Though her fiddling involved more staring lovingly at the byline rather than correcting the article's contents. The idea of the new treatment, injected into the thick scar tissue, had been hers. And while not a ground-breaking title to have been crowned first author on, for Annabelle, it suited her quite nicely.

An eruption of laughter broke through her reveries. Annabelle looked up. Thomas was seated, shirtless, with a heavy velvet curtain draped lovingly over his form, teasing at a full reveal to Simon's complete delight. Seated in the window seat, with a sunset view over the London Park planes, he looked timeless and inexplicably beautiful. Simon had chosen his setting well, and was stretched out on the settee, letting his pencil worship the man he loved. But these were only preliminary sketches. He planned a far grander oil painting in the Spring and had promised to paint Annabelle by the seaside in Brighton that summer.

Annabelle had recovered from her original unease, or was it curiosity, over the two men and what ran so deep between them. Since she had first encountered the besheeted Simon, the patinaed pain of Thomas' betrayal had been buffed by the men's kindness and the new sheen of an understanding of love, in its many forms, had replaced her rage. For now, she was content, in their sheltered globe, and with her precious work, the smell of pine and the promise of festivities.

A gentle knock at the door reminded Annabelle gingersnaps and cocoa had been ordered. "Do bring them in, Kitty."

The door creaked open and Kitty skittered in and shut the door, clapping her back to it as if it were a gargantuan magnet and her spine made of steel. "Yer mother's 'ere ." She gasped, all Irish worry and melodrama. "M 'lady."

"My mother?" Annabelle's eyes jumped to Thomas, then to Simon, her heart pounding unpleasurably. There would be no explaining this. Simon had been sold as a friend from India, staying on indefinitely with the new Christianson's , making himself scarce as decorum commanded. But this would be far too unusual to explain. "My mother's here, heaven knows why."

"She's waiting in the hall. Nearly 'ad me knickers when I asked her to 'ave a seat."

"As long as she hasn't kept yer knickers from you,' Simon chuckled. "No harm here—though perhaps,' he paused, eyeing Thomas.

"Perhaps a shirt would do,' Simon wadded up Thomas's tunic he had been using as a pillow and threw it him. "No need to put the glorious Mrs. Pierce in a tizzy." He laughed as he looked to Annabelle who thought there was no linen large enough to cloak the truth of their arrangement from her mother's prying eyes. With her mother's loose lips, Thomas' secret would be a thing of the past if her faculties were even minimally intact.

Annabelle rolled her eyes back at Simon, trying to smother her brewing panic. Her mother's notoriously frail nerves had always proved quite comedic. But there was neither room for comedy, nor need to risk toppling their Atlas now; his footing so recently having been regained after Penwood.

"I 'ear her, she's coming." Kitty's croaked. "Whaddo I do?"

A sharp rapping sounded on the door. "Annabelle." Mrs. Pierce singsonged.

Interest halted Annabelle's dread in its tracks. It took her a heartbeat to recognize the tone. Her mother sounded— pleasant, happy even. And when did she ever follow decorum and knock on doors with her penchant for grand entrances?

Thomas finished buttoning his shirt. "Let her in for some cocoa by the fire, t his will be a very merry evening indeed."

Annabelle gave him a jovial glare before nodding at Kitty.

Kitty hung her head, obviously doubting her mistress' sanity, but obeyed.

Mrs. Pierce stepped in, without her natural flurry. She looked flushed, but happily so, rather than from hysteria. She looked Kitty up, shook her head, as if to free herself from any short remarks, before scanning the room.

Annabelle's heart decrescendoed.

Her eyes lingered on Simon and Thomas, before she came to Annabelle. "Ahh, my dear." She chirped. "I wanted to have a word with you, or I would not sleep a wink tonight."

"We can't have that, Mrs. Pierce." Simon was on his feet with a smile so radiant, it would have charmed the keys from the warden at Newgate. "Seeing you are looking rather well indeed,' he gave her a once over to make dear Uncle Horace blush.

Annabelle breathed easier. Flattery would get one anywhere—including out of a sticky situation. Simon played her mother brilliantly. Mrs. Pierce's melting look told her there would be no need for contrived falsehoods and awkward explanations.

Simon looked back at the now unfortunately shirted Thomas. "I believe I'll take you up on that sherry and game of whist, Tom. The study or the club, your choice?" He shot Annabelle a hooded look.

She returned it with one full of good-natured venom. Whist was the quiet euphemism for other gentlemanly pursuits the pair had used in the early days when Annabelle's sensitivities were raw with the newness of their truth.

The side of Simon's face quivered against his own humor.

"It's a shame for you to rush off,' Mrs. Pierce regarded the men with a longing out of place for a mother-in-law. "But a word alone with Annabelle would be best."

"More gripping than The Morning Post to be sure,' Simon didn't miss a beat, striding to her and offering her a solemn bow before he kissed her a hand. "And with your news unveiled, I hope your forty-winks tonight are bliss."

Thomas was at his heels, pecking Mrs. Pierce's cheek, before they made their exit with a crisis nimbly averted. Kitty ran off behind them with her persuasions of cocoa and gingersnaps. With a crisis narrowly averted, Annabelle thanked the heavens for her mother's vainglorious nature. Sheathing her saber, she readied herself to indulge her mother's whims, as she settled back into the settee. Annabelle patted the cushion next to her.

"You'd better sit down and divulge your story before you do yourself a harm, mamma ." Mrs. Pierce complied, smiling sweetly, although Annabelle detected a distinct flavor of mischief. After she undid the strings of her bonnet, as if she sensed the newness of their dynamic, Mrs. Pierce began to toy with her fur-lined sleeves, her eyes flicking back and forth. "I don't know quite how to start." She let out a nervous laugh. "I've never been good at things like this".

Annabelle tipped her head. There were so many things to fill that blank.

Another nervous tinkle before her mother went for the chase. "I've not always been a good mother."

The pain of the sentiment—both on the offering and receiving ends—seared through the following silence.

Torture notwithstanding, Annabelle broke it. "You've done your best m amma." She almost believed it. W ith Mrs. Pierce's last break after Horace's fall. After she was carted off to a sanitorium in a locked and barred carriage, Annabelle finally admitted her mother's cards had not been stacked in resilience's favor. Though whether heredity alone, or their damning social milieu, were to blame, Annabelle would never be sure.

"It's a difficult thing for a lady to admit." A regretful hesitation made her mother's features tighten. "To carry that regret." Her eyes were searching, imploring for a reprieve without a drawn-out exposition of past shames and words unkind. "Even more difficult a thing to discuss in any great detail." She looked away, as if her prim (and frail) mores would shatter at any rehashing.

"Mamma, you were at fault, but not in the way you think." Annabelle swallowed. "You used me to keep Horace for a bit. Then found me despicable when he left your chambers for mine."

Her mother's eyes swam, the tiny muscles around her mouth tensed.

"One could say I did not understand such things at my age, but I wonder if I knew precisely what I was doing." Annabelle admitted. "It was the first time I felt powerful, when I was with Horace. He was so afflicted with his desires, he sat in the palm of my hand. And knowing I could take something away from you brought me a contrary pleasure indeed." She took her mother's hands. Mrs. Pierce gave no resistance. "Perhaps we are more alike than we care to admit. I have not always been a good daughter."

Mrs. Pierce took a heaving sigh, "I would have done so many things differently. But cannot take them back now."

There was no arguing that.

"True." Annabelle dipped her head. In her darkest moments, Annabelle felt like damaged goods, and her mother had taken every opportunity to confirm it. But in a grand book, The Exotic Orient and Our Empire, which Thomas had laid knowingly by her bed on their return from Penwood, she had made a discovery. Kintsugi, the repair of something broken by filling its cracks with gold.

Wabi sabi followed. The practice of celebrating imperfections. Those foreign concepts had touched Annabelle, precious gold-filled scars—more brilliant with, than without them. Annabelle was who she was each day, because of the preceding one. No looking back.

"But it is never too late to make amends." The declaration had been easy and Annabelle meant it.

With that generous proposition, Mrs. Pierce seemed to unload the weights of her cares. "Oh goodness, yes,' she squeezed Annabelle's hands. "I'd like that very much."

Annabelle painted on a sly grin. "With one caveat."

"Oh?"

"No more talk of the state of my belly. It's something I am tired of defending."

"But it would really be so wonderful for your father and I—"

"No. No more. Or no amends." Annabelle commanded. She was torn between amusement and irritation that her mother still would push the topic of grandchildren.

Mrs. Pierce conceded. "No more talk of that then."

"Right." Annabelle drew breath. "On to these much-anticipated amends."

Her mother's glowed even brighter. "Which is precisely why I've come tonight. After a week's toils, I've finally done it." Her announcement rang with the achievement Annabelle imagined Christopher Columbus must have felt when he announced his discovery of America to the Spanish Court.

"What have you done, mamma?" She hoped her mother had used her manipulative powers for good rather than her habitual evil.

"I,' Mrs. Pierce sat up straighter, 'have had words with Horace."

Annabelle frowned and fiddled with her earring. Her mother having it out with dear Uncle Horace was not exactly what she had in mind in terms of amends. She had hoped for something more self-serving in nature. Perhaps the patent and a royalty portion for the electrogram? But that would have been beyond her mother's imagination.

"You see dear, after some reflection, I do see what you were trying to do, fiddling with all your surgical notions." She fluttered her hands as if Annabelle had seriously pursued a career as a candy floss purveyor rather than a valid, scientific profession. "It would offer you a bit more interest than designing balls and talking about all those Society topics I know you feel are nonsense."

Annabelle nodded. "It would and does." Far more than that, but now was not the time to argue.

"So, I've had it out with Horace, who had not forgotten the influence of my charms and," she paused, holding her hands out dramatically. "You'll never guess what I've done." She grinned maddeningly.

"I couldn't possibly." Her mother seemed to sincerely wish her well, but how on Earth could she have possibly altered anything for the better?

"He was to go before the Queen. He's the one who had that line reworded, the one about ladies not being specifically disallowed from medicine in one form or the other."

"I gathered that." Annabelle's heart hardened briefly. One wicked whim and her hopes had been dashed. "But the Queen?"

"Yes, dear." Mrs. Pierce seemed to take a distinct, if benign, pleasure at her upper hand. "You know she can be rather sympathetic on the right day."

Annabelle certainly was not aware of Victoria's temperament. Nor should her mother.

"But then that stupid man thought he could put me off and refused to speak with her. But I had him." She cried as her plot thickened. "You remember Lord Sackville , that very nice political man from the hunt?"

Annabelle nodded. She very well recalled the MP's unsullied egg head which had narrowly escaped her ginger beer bottle. Though with her careful avoidance of Sackville over the weekend hunt, she had avoided a whiff of recognition. And his very irritating wife.

"I remembered him mentioning a certain acquaintance with her Majesty through his mother. I called on him Saturday past and told him exactly what I was up to."

Annabelle's jaw gaped. Her mother had never been the resourceful type. Had her umpteenth fit of hysteria rearranged her faculties back to right? "But you always hated my interest in med—"

"Hate is really too strong of a word, dear." Mrs. Pierce blustered over her past, ascorbic sentiments. "I simply do not have any academic proclivities and did not understand yours as such. But in my time away, our Mrs. Mingle brought me to see your side of things."

"Mrs. Mingle?" Annabelle's heart expanded. The darling woman always had her fingers on the pulse of the Pierce family.

"Yes. She really is quite persuasive when it comes down to it." Mrs. Pierce looked slightly abashed. "As are her almond petit fours."

Annabelle fought to maintain a solemn expression as she imagined the kind-hearted manipulations of the housekeeper on her behalf.

"Then it really was quite simple. Tea with the Queen. She really is quite a dear and I spelled things out for her. On hearing of your story, she was quite happy to have things set right."

"Meaning she took pity on my barren, loveless marriage?" Annabelle bristled. "As I assume that is the tale you spun?" She found solace in the Queen's unearned mercy as she wondered how things would ever be set right.

Mrs. Pierce shrugged. "I may have told her of your heart-breaking story. No children, an active mind, and a disparate husband." Mrs. Pierce shrugged before she added airily. "The great woman took pity. Though she does have rather strong objections to women's medical training otherwise."

"What?" Annabelle felt sick—how could her mother know about Thomas? Did this explain her easy acceptance of Simon just moments before? What had she done? They had taken such care—discretion.

"There, there, dear, just a few inflated white lies. Necessary when she put her back up at the idea of a lady doctor. Surprising from a kingless Queen."

"White lies about Thomas?"

"Thomas? Heavens no. Just a sterile but brilliant daughter; sure to come to no good if she could find no fruitful preoccupation."

Excitement flooded over Annabelle's relief. Thomas was safe. "So I can sit for the Apothecary's Licentiate?"

"Even better—an exemption. You will be allowed to sit for the medical licensing exams. You my dear, when you pass, will be the first lady medical doctor in Britain."

"An exemption?" Annabelle sputtered. "Pass?" It was more than she could have ever hoped. For herself. For other women. If she could prove a success. . .an example.

"Quite simple really. Writing one of those dreary bills to allow all women to sit if they chose, then pushing it through Parliament would be quite a thing. An exception for you was just the thing." Her mother leaned back obviously quite aware of the weight of her gift.

"And Horace?"

"Oh, him." Her mother sounded as if she was being cruelly reminded of a delinquent third cousin twice removed quietly shipped off to Western Australia. "At first I thought I could convince him to change his mind. He said he would do as I asked when I threatened telling poor Beatrice everything. But I didn't quite trust him so I took matters into my own hands as I've said. I've done quite well, haven't I?"

"You know you have, mamma ." The admission was not nearly as terrible as it might once have been. "Thank you, you know how much this will mean for me."

"I believe I do now." Mrs. Pierce smiled and patted Annabelle on the arm.

An overwhelming urge to be held by her mother came over Annabelle and she leaned into her shoulder. She had half-expected a stiffness of silk and sinew. Instead Mrs. Pierce wrapped Annabelle in aa warm embrace, the newness of the sensation made her feel complete and yet want to shatter into a thousand pieces.

"The exam will be in late January, I believe. The letter from the College should arrive quite soon." Plenty of time for holiday merry making before a month of review.

"I've told the Times." Her mother tucked her in closer. "They may want to interview us. You."

Annabelle looked up, marveling at how quickly her mother's need for recognition attempted to usurp her reformation and laughed. "Likely tucked in a back corner near the adverts for Moseley's health corsets and Beake's moustache wax.

Chapter 32

But news of one Mrs. Annabelle Christianson being allowed to sit for the Medical Officers' Examination did not play a wallflower to Moseley's health corsets and Beake's moustache wax next month's Times.

Annabelle's original exhilaration dampened. The original paper's snippet on the Queen's exemption had been diminutive enough. Annabelle conceded to her mother's pleas for a few minutes in the spotlight. Her hand in the matter was included quite pointedly to the young journalist who scrawled his notes in a furious (and blatantly disapproving) hand.

Then the article in Monday's The Lancet shattered a delicious afternoon pouring over manuscripts in the library at Harley Street. Her father had desperately tried to keep the reel from her. But Annabelle snatched it. A litigious column calling her a 'traitess to her sex' who would come to harm if she were not reined in against her own 'eccentric longings' ensued. The ascorbic type was signed by none other than the acclaimed physician to the Queen, Dr. Horace Christianson. Aside from his sweeping lambastations, he used the press for a bit of literary ingratiation as he commended the Queen's favor for the care of women's health and her staunch opposition to the Woman Question in general. With a final flourish, he announced he would do everything in his power to keep the Board's ruling in line with Royal opinions, saving the repute of the wayward lady in question.

Annabelle's protests brought Kitty and her mother running. But her mother pointed out that if she were not meant to best dear Uncle Horace, he would have neatly expired under her blade at Penwood. With raised eyebrows at the honesty of his wife's statement, Dr. Pierce reminded Annabelle the rest of his colleagues on the Board were sound, reasonable men. If she were to bring all she had learned to their table, and express herself eloquently, they would have no choice but to crown her as she wished. And with great satisfaction, he made his way to his afternoon calls. Though he left Annabelle to wonder if he secretly feared for his reputation—and hers— regardless if she were to pass or fail—a double-edged scalpel.

Left to themselves, her mother asked if Annabelle would like her to present the tawdry history between Dr. Christianson and a certain mother and daughter, right on Beatrice Christianson's stoop, to be aired out in any way she chose.

Annabelle's heart nearly flew out of her mouth as she imagined the catastrophic heartbreak such a move would cost both their families. Then there was the woeful double standard between the sexes which not even Athena's thunderbolts could shatter. No need to bring each down like sinking battleships. Who was to say she would not pass? After that Annabelle reread the article on the hour as each day ticked away until her Independence Day. Reliving her anger only served to fuel Annabelle's flames of purpose.

⚜

Annabelle hung back a moment after Kitty left her room. She had given her mistress a posy of hot house edelweiss, humbling Annabelle as it was given so shyly. Aan Irish prayer of luck sung sweetly as Kitty pinned it to Annabelle's lofty millinery from Madame Victorine's.

Not long ago, she thought to herself, she might have contented herself with the cards cast in front of her. But having waged against life's game of Whist , so close to victory now, she was reminded of the history she hoped to write that morning. The first—albeit by the Queen's condescension and exception—lady to be granted the privilege of a seat before the Medical Examining Board.

Annabelle recalled Fate's keen twist and her recent reconciliation with her mother. Her long-held sentiments had softened against a private preference to institutionalize her mother at Salpetriere , and for now, she's bow to the favor bestowed.

For that was then, and today was shockingly today.

⥊⥋

The throaty clang from the bell of St. Stephen's startled Annabelle as she alighted from their carriage on Fleet Street. The gritty January smog slapped her cheeks and the dense smell of ammonia seared her nostrils. Annabelle stood, Thomas' grip firm on her arm, on the path leading to the dispassionate columns of the Royal College of Medicine.

A throng of pulsing cloaked bodies lined the path from the road thick with manure to the steps of the main hall at the Royal College of Medicine—pearly white by comparison. There must be hundreds of people here. Despite recent publications, she hadn't anticipated an audience. A solitary walk to her execution would have been far preferable. But she reminded herself of her repulsion to a Society who preferred its ladies jailed by whalebone cages and men's desires. Dr. Annabelle Christianson.

Annabelle loved the trill of the title of her chosen profession in her ear. In a few hours, the title, which she had childishly scribed over blank paper as a necessary distraction that morning, would be hers. Her father and Larkin stepped down behind them, insisting on escorting her to the door of the examination room. Annabelle protested, preferring to walk her plank alone. But they rallied until she gave way, anxious for another pass at the compendium of microscopic anatomy in the latest edition of Grey's rather than an hour wasted in petulant argument. And of course, then there was Ben.

Sending his second and third coaches off on a wild chase for new, worsted reins that morning, leaving him, the duty of driving them to the College. "Gotta keep me eye on ye, m'Lady,' he joked as he had helped her first into the carriage. He made her lot of chaperones chuckle as he found it in his place to declare, "It'll take the lot of us to keep ye straight." Annabelle had wished he was in arm's length so she could offer him a proper cuff of thanks. On the short trip to the College, the troops pulled every stop in the book to make her smile. And they did. Irritations aside—their intentions were good.

"Oy, there she is!" Several of the onlookers cried above the street noise, righting Annabelle's thoughts to the present.

A sure smile slid across Annabelle's face as she drew herself a bit taller. They've come for me. The public knows I am right. To do this. To want this. A lady surgeon. The very first to qualify elbow to elbow with the gentleman. Though gentleman was a term to be loosely used.

"There's the vazey tart!"

To Annabelle's horror, guffaws erupted from the crowd before a low din of booing ensued, making her stomach heave. She almost damned her mother and her incendiary tongue, having started the fires in the Times. But in the same breath she remembered the door that tongue had just swatted open.

Thomas's face contracted into expression so rare it proved more startling than the raucous insult.

A jolt of fear coursed down her spine and snaked itself thickly around her calves, shackling her in space. Insignificance might be preferable to notoriety.

"I was afraid of this." Thomas announced to the smog before he turned to Annabelle, his grip tightening on her arm. "Never you mind their ignorant guff, we'll get you to your exam. We'll wait for you."

"It'll be hours—" Annabelle objected though the chaos was beyond her wild imaginings, the crowd's tangible hatred speared her skin.

Her father and Larkin clustered behind them, muttering their disbelief at the scene as they moved close, their protection reassuring in a way Annabelle could not have anticipated she would appreciate.

Every muscle of Annabelle's body tensed as she saw angry mouths moving in protest. Her eyes darted to the front gates of the College not more than one hundred yards away. Annabelle considered bolting with a prayer on her lips. But prayers never seemed to get her very far.

"They can't have read your father's piece in The Lancet,' Dr. Pierce sputtered, 'or that side piece in The Times."

Thomas looked as if he had been aboard an ocean bard for months. But he shook his head. "Of course mother's taken full advantage of the strife with her ladies."

Her father's face softened. "Never mind that now. Ignore the lot of them, my dear. You know who you are, and what you have done to deserve this chance."

"When a whiff of changes strikes a chord, it's a cigar stub in a dry forest apparently." Larkin hand found the small of Annabelle's back as he appraised the protestors with the same view he might use to appraise a cartful of week old corpses in high summer.

Annabelle heard the swirl of skirts at her side. The scent of an unwashed body and mildew hit her senses before she made eye contact with a disheveled mess of a woman.

"She's nottin' but a dirty puzzle!"

"Watch your mouth, madam!" Larkin raised his arm.

The ingrate ducked, grinning up at them with bloodshot eyes.

Annabelle wished she could implode into a heap of crinoline, s he had never been under such attack, though the catty lashings of debs, vying for the spotlight under eligible young men ran a close second.

"We've treated women like you at the infirmary,' Thomas reached for reason as he estimated the woman's unfortunate career. "She's trying to help you. . . all women."

The unfortunate's brow furrowed into a scowl. "Straining against yer rank, lovey. We don't want, ner need yer help, git back to yer fine drawing room and pearls. Let our kind take care of ourselves."

The woman's grit and black-toothed snear made Sarah's flash through Annabelle's mind. Her great gift. Annabelle moved to protest.

Thomas held her back. "Say nothing. Don't give her the satisfaction."

"Oh-oh, satisfaction indeed,' the woman quipped. "I can you a bit o' satisfaction, as you say. And with the face, lovey, special price. "

Before they could retort, the woman hacked a lipful of tobacco—its soaring arch ending with a sickening splat on Annabelle's shoulder. "No use for you, Bridget."

"I say," Her father barked before he reached for his handkerchief.

Tears stung the corners of Annabelle's eyes at the irony, but managed to glare at her attacker as she swept her satin coat clean.

Larkin, restraining himself, put his back to the women, allowing Annabelle to pass.

"Suit yourself,' slipped from her lips before Annabelle swept past the woman. Who was that pathetic creature to pass judgement over what she could or could not do, who she could, or could not be?

With their first hurdle passed, the troop continued down the path. The clappers of St. Stephan's bells struck against their bronze ribs a split second before a muddy clod struck Annabelle squarely in her chest. Her breath soared from her mouth and she rocked back from the impact. Her father and Larkin broke her fall. Icy tendrils wove around her nerves as Annabelle swallowed hard and righted her hat. She had never minded a bit of a tousle of wits. But they wanted a fight.

"Where's the leaky sapper who threw that?"

Annabelle heard Ben's voice bellow. She looked over her shoulder to see him bobbling along the front lines, giving as much insult to the picketers as they were offering. His face flushed with a fury that would have made the any Whitechapel gangster think twice.

Knowing he'd not be afraid to throw himself into a scuffle on her behalf, Annabelle thrust her shoulders back.

"Go back to your sitting room and Beeton's," a tall young man scoffed. A crunch and a burst of choking sulfur followed the insult. "It's not right, Professor Pierce."

Annabelle ignored the bits of rotting egg clinging to her sleeve.

But her father had his handkerchief out and swiped angrily at her arm as he barked. "Archebold Havishtash, I wouldn't expect this kind of behavior." The dismay of the disloyalty was obvious. One of her father's second year students. He'd locked Annabelle from the early morning anatomy lab once or twice in the early days before Thomas pinched Annabelle her own key.

"You'd best confine your ineptitude to the expired souls, in city morgues, Archie," Annabelle spat before continuing without a second glance.

"He's an absolute fool, turn a deaf ear." Larkin took her elbow as her father held back to give said fool an earful. "Let's get you inside and to your exam, Angel."

Behind them Annabelle heard her father's voice crack above Archie's disgruntled protestations. Annabelle's feet struck the pavement with new determination as a righteous anger surged up her spine.

Thomas and Larkin met each other's stride, their faces grim.

Boots scraping dangerously over the gravel called Annabelle to snap her head over her shoulder. She met with the horrific sight of her father, her father, red-faced in his overcoat, suspended between two high-hatted bobbies, like a criminal on a rack. Overtaken with rage at his predicament, Annabelle was unable to meet his eyes before they forcibly escorted back down the path to the gates, as he commanded Ben hold his stead behind her.

"Go to him. By the carriage." Thomas directed Larkin.

Larkin worried his brows but slowed his pace. "Ben's behind me. We'll get her inside."

Larkin acquiesced, releasing Annabelle. "This is only the beginning for you. If not for us." His smile was bittersweet before he jogged back to her father by their abandoned carriage. For once, us did not sound sweet in the least. Annabelle was glad she had firmly buried his proposal in the cemetery of her past. Her future began today.

With Thomas solo at her side, it all came back. Those hard first days, following Thomas around in nursing whites. From those days when prayed for grace. Annabelle viewed the pulsating crowd. Her steps were cut short as a handful of rotting mashed peas struck Annabelle in the chest. She looked down at the mess, cascading down her lovely velvet coat as if it were not her own. She was almost inside the gates. Chin high. Ignore them. Say nothing. You have a mind and a voice. Now you know when to use one and when the other.

Then Douglas Haddock bellowed from behind Annabelle. She knew that hog's ass's squelchy baritone too well from his impotent efforts to simultaneously impress Thomas during his guest lectures and demean her, seated quietly to the side in the process.

"Ye've got a slit fer a brain, Madame, I'd take yer head to me stalk and teach ye the right way of things." A Cockney falsetto hung over his crass declaration.

Thomas dropped Annabelle's elbow, and lunged at his student. "Have you lost your bloody mind, man? You are addressing my wife!"

Haddock wriggled in his sinewy grip.

Wife. The word cut as sharp as a saber.

Ben was at his side in an instant. "'Ave a crack at 'im, Tom, feckin' blighter, deserves to meet 'is Maker fer that wit."

298

The gleeful proposal fueled a rage within Annabelle she didn't think existed. She stopped and brushed her front clear of the vegetal assault. "Do have a go, Thomas."

As Ben grabbed Haddock's neck, detaining the taller man, the angry throng drew venom, their voices rising in anticipation of what was to come.

Beneath the flames of her rage festered a cauldron of fear gurgled . Annabelle wondered if it could be contained with an iron-clad lid.

"I'd prefer a bayonet." Thomas scowled and looked to the Hall. "Keep him here, I'll get her inside first."

"Have yer bugger way, then lad." Haddock gave Thomas a smug grin. "Afraid you'll break your precious hands?"

The implication of the insult struck more fear into Annabelle than any of his prior invectives. He was grasping for a jab. A feeling of furious injustice erupted within. She thought she had been down as deep as one could go to speak with the Devil. She spun on her heel and locked eyes with Haddock, the crowd hooting and jeering. She sensed a delicate fierceness clinging to her expression. A wounded tigress, protecting a dying cub from a vengeful pack.

Thomas grabbed for her. "Don't Annabelle, he means nothing."

But she flung him off.

"Let m'Lady 'ave some fun, Tom, she's earned it." Ben protested as he nestled his fingers tighter around Haddock's windpipe.

"Don't give them any grounds to disqual—"

Thomas' protests rang hollow, for Annabelle had already made her mind up.

Her feet crunched the gravel as she neared the suspended Haddock. She slipped the enormous emerald engagement ring from her ring finger and placed over her long finger.

"That's right. Left hook—just like I taught ya when we were ten."

Annabelle met Ben's eyes and grinned. She never dreamed their breathless children's pastime would ever be put to its proper use.

Haddock let out a loud, cat-call whistle between his teeth.

The crowd cheered at the innuendo.

"Coming to take me up on me offer, lassie?" He jiggled his hips suggestively.

Ben gave him a solid keep in the shins. "Shut yer pie hole!"

"It'll be good fer her!" An anonymous cry echoed.

"That's enough!" Thomas roared, outpacing Annabelle. He grabbed Haddock by the shoulder and wound his right fist back, right into the outstretched arms of another policeman who seemed to have materialized from the London haze.

Growling in defeat, a gargantuan constable carted Thomas off like her father.

"I've got 'er ," Ben reassured him as he tightened his hold on Haddock.

"Give us a lay, lassie, give ye a sense of yer real place in the world." Haddock pushed Annabelle roughly, spinning her away from him. Before Annabelle could react, he dove for her skirt, lifting a handful high. She shrieked and as he yanked her back to him, she heard the rustle of his belt buckle.

"Like hell you do. Have yer go, m'Lady."

Haddock squirmed like his namesake on a hook.

"Sock it to him if you must!" A familiar voice trilled loudly.

Beatrice Christianson and a band of women pressed to the tall iron posts surrounding the Hall, striking picture with wide white sashes slicing across their coats.

"If you must!" Beatrice hollered again. The white sashes fluttered as her flock locked elbows much to the distress of the constables.

Haddock sneered at the intrusion. "You wouldn't dare."

Ben dug his fingers tighter into his neck. "A bettin' man we 'ave here." He nodded at Annabelle, like a starter at a steeplechase.

Without another thought, Annabelle drew her bejeweled arm back and sent her mighty rage into Haddock's astounded face. The sound was like an orange ending its short life in smithereens against a brick wall. The smack of contact was so satisfying, it took a moment for the fiery pain in her hand to register.

The crowd let out a collective cry of affront.

Ben threw the crumpled Haddock to the ground. "Bastard!"

Annabelle appraised the moaning mass at her feet. "You'll remember me, you swine," shocked by how refreshed she felt.

Countless arms waved high and the group united, tightening the communal noose around Annabelle. More police emerged from their midst, as if given wings of righteous anger, and swarmed them. It took three coppers to remove Ben, kicking and spitting, from the grounds.

An officer dragged Annabelle from Haddock. "I could arrest you."

Annabelle took one last look at her victory. To her horror, Haddock swiped the coursing blood from his nose completely over his face and winked before he threw himself prostrate, committed to playing the piteous victim.

"Have you gone mad, woman? Anyone else would take ye right to the prison where ye can kiss yer fine learnin' and bobbles goodbye." The officer shook Annabelle as if searching for loose change.

A ginger-bearded constable joined their quarrel. "To be sure." His colleague, a wire-whiskered oaf, agreed. "We should leave 'er to her proper punishment by the broken-faced gent." He sneered at Annabelle; fumes of stale ale wafted in her face.

He never would have dared speak to her like that in any other circumstance. Annabelle raged. "You ignorant—" She struggled to free herself from the first man's grasp, but it only tightened like a Chinese finger trap.

"Squirm as ye may, ye little cunt,' the little copper crooned, 'just a word from me and Billie here and ye'll meet yer worth at Hollings Gate. Plenty of our comrades aching to put ye in yer place."

Her captor came to life. "Cut that talk now."

"You've gone soft, Fred."

Blazes. She hadn't set out to cause this raucous, to start a movement, a cause. Revolution had never been her aim.

"Aye, I might 'ave." His fingers relaxed against Annabelle's silk sleeve. "Me youngest's 'bout yer age. And just as pretty. I've got about five seconds in these bones to hold 'em off. Get gone, if ye don't, ye're on yer own."

With an inspiration rooted in the desperation of a Bengalize tiger, having spent its lifetime pacing in a glittering cage, Annabelle found her heels and made her escape. A few strides down the path, the throng constricted, narrowing her route to the Hall's entrance. as she calculated the number of dives and dodges from thrashing arms and stomping feet required to reach her destination, a hand took her arm and pulled her through.

Beatrice Christianson, thick walking stick raised, bludgeoned through the protestors. "Nothing like a bit of a riot to get the blood flowing." She looked quite exhilarated from the chaos. With a few light cracks of her stick, the mob gave way to her mother-in-law.

A trickle of relief lightened Annabelle's breath as she wrapped her sweaty palm around the icy steel of the hall's gates. Sanctuary. She leaned her forehead against the parallel bars to gather herself, hoping their steel would transfer into her soul. Preparation for the task at hand.

"Nothing to it, you see." Mrs. Christianson railed her stick as the masses gained ground again, her eyes darting to the front door of the Hall as a steward loped down the stairs to meet them.

He fumbled with the gates, mumbling his apologies, but never looking into their faces.

Once safely on the other side of the front gate, Beatrice prodded the steward with her stick as they continued up the walk. "Gawking at the unlawful accosting of two gentlewomen behind lock and key. There's a special seat in Newgate for men like you."

He didn't acknowledge the rib.

"Never mind him." Beatrice cried, exasperated. "It's that lot inside who'll have to deal with me. Sitting on their duffs behind the examination table while we are assaulted for the simple right available to every man."

Annabelle swept her hat from her head as they entered the College. Kitty's stellate poesy a cheerful reminder of her abilities—and of her purpose. She wanted a man's respect, a man's profession. Not only for herself, but for Olivia, Sarah, Beatrice. All women.

"There will be words between Horace and I this evening, my dear." Beatrice's voice echoed in the large entryway. "He's had to have seen the crowds. And that wretched paper of his." She took Annabelle by the shoulder. "I nearly broke his neck with I saw The Lancet turned to his hateful soliloquy. But the damage was done."

Annabelle shook her head to dismiss any bubbles of resentment. They had never served but to derail her plans.

Beatrice smiled. "He will pay for his malice." Her face grew quizzical. "So out of character for him." She took Annabelle's other shoulder. "But he will right his wrong my dear and you will have a neat little sum from machine and with patent royalties." Her expression grew dreamy. "It will have been worth this tiny scuffle." She kissed Annabelle on the forehead. "Off you go, I'm back to my girls to make any kind of stink we can. That'll really get to Horace tonight."

The icy cool of the marble columns looming in the entryway steadied her tense nerves. Annabelle wondered if some of the woman's steam could carry her through to the end of the day. Should she have prayed for ignorance in the end?

Chapter 33

The mantle clock's dancing pendulum and scrolled hands taunted Annabelle, scribing the present into the past, as she paced the expanse of the library at 17 Berkeley Square. Its frenetic, even melody grabbed each of her nerves and plucked them cruelly. Her fate should have been signed and stamped by noon. But it was 1:17pm. Still no word. Leave it to dear Uncle Horace to make her wait for now what seemed more like a pardon than a triumph.

Her examination had been no triumph. Walking through the College halls, which had borne witness to her affairs (intellectual and otherwise,) had felt like walking into the embrace of an old friend. Her feet slapped the marble floors with renewed confidence as she headed towards the conference room where she would face the Medical Board. To be gutted and fileted by twenty of the most senior physicians in London. She had found grim humor in the paucity of her odds, searching the rows of whiskered faces as she had removed her hat, coat, and gloves, thankful for their midnight blue hues, disguised her recent trials in the gauntlet leading up to the College.

As she got on with their rapid-fire examination, fielding her replies with equal ferocity, Annabelle relaxed and even began to enjoy herself as she collected nods of agreement at every turn. She flew through their bulleted questions on anatomical intricacies and the technical challenges of anesthesia and amputation, which lead her into a defiant defense of Pasteur's germ theory. Which was her first mistake.

The examiners were not sympathetic to this practice-altering theory and stood by the accepted 'cleanliness and cold-water' practiced for over a decade. The idea of carbolic sprays for what Annabelle claimed was true antisepsis versus a mere laundering of instruments and organs stoked their prejudices to a boiling point. After spelling out her argument plainly, Annabelle stilled her tongue, fully expecting yet another chorus of nods and another line of questioning.

Instead she was met with a great bellow from the Royal physician, without the benefit of disclosing his very conflicted interests—considering the examinee was his daughter-in-law and former lover. Irritatingly pesky trivialities.

Then the war broke out. Christianson began to spew his disparaging thoughts on Pasteur, Lister, and lady surgeons, championing his colleagues to rise in their ranks against the hearsay echoing in that morning's arena. Finding no fault in taking up uncivilized arms in the face of their opponents civilized pursuits, Annabelle sympathized with those poor scientific pioneers as the room exploded in debate, dousing the walls with their lambasting lava.

When the thrill of war had gone on for several minutes—the Board having left Annabelle at her post like a witness halted mid cross-examination on the stand—she decided to let caution sift through her fingers. "Enough,' she had cried. "I find your views rather shocking considering you, Dr. Christianson, have so recently benefited not only from the work of those two, great men, but from the hand of a lady surgeon."

The room clanked into silence, like a train quiet after barreling late into King's Cross Station. Pleased to have gotten hold of their cyclone by the tail, Annabelle continued. It had been easy enough to look earnestly into the quizzical eyes of the Board members while Horace pouted fiercely, his surprisehaving come to her aid, silencing his wrath. Christianson's face pinching with every sentence, Annabelle outlined how she successfully performed an emergent splenectomy on her expiring patient. The details of the case delightfully disclosed her familial ties to the physician-turned-patient.

She finished with a great flourish and wrapped her hands behind her back, daring any one to counter with an unanswerable counterargument. But judging from the expressions on the Board's faces, her tale would have been suitable not only for a case study in The Lancet, but a penny dreadful serial. Silence encapsulated the room as Annabelle studied her examiners for any sign of life, never mind approval.

Finally, a gentleman who had a special interest in malaria, could have doubled for a British installment of Rip Van Winkle, and appeared somnolent during the morning's lively exchanges, came to life with a guffaw. "She's got you there, Horace. How does it feel to be eternally indebted to a skirted scalpel?" The mirth in his eyes belied more respect than his words.

Heads turned to await Christianson's volley. But being a man of good intelligence, though without a soul as far as Annabelle could tell, he acknowledged the corner he inhabited with grunt and a twirl of his pointed beard. "Divine intervention more like it." His protest lacked the heat of his previous ardor.

Dr. Van Winkle, whom Annabelle believed had been the former royal physician before a disagreement in fundamentals with the Queen compelled him to resign, laughed fully. "Nothing divine about this young lady going a few bare-knuckled rounds with Death to save your hide." He slammed his hand on the table, making the scattered ink pots and spectacles jump to attention on the long table. "You must give her that." He gave Annabelle another inquiring look. "Granted the notion of a lady doctor on many levels seems absurd. Though there is a certain novelty, at least in her case, that appeals."

His tone might have been more aptly used to discuss the purchase of Bengalese tigers for the London Zoo. Annabelle could not smother her offense. "There is absolutely no novelty in the idea of a woman pursuing a medical degree. What of Lucey Sewall in Boston? Elizabeth Blackwell in New York?" She was grateful to Thomas for schooling her in the history of her cause—though even stateside those women remained the exception and met with resistance at every turn.

"Then perhaps you should be off to America? That country is too young to understand its mistakes," Christian countered.

"Considering your particularly hateful tongue, I have no doubt my husband would support that venture." Though the very idea of running from British soil seemed to smack of defeat before the journey was begun. "I expect you would not fare well without his company."

Before their exchange could spiral into a domestic argument, Van Winkle broke in. "Horace, you don't acknowledge the possibility of curious youth, advances from so-called mistakes." He tipped his head back and forth, as if calibrating his mental balancing scales before turning to the other members. "I must say the idea of holding this woman from the profession does make us seem rather archaic." He looked back to Annabelle. "I'd not like to give the Americans the satisfaction." He shot Horace a triumphant look before adjusting his monocle and clearing his throat. "Young lady, you support some rather unusual ideas regarding antiseptic. Let's move on to some less—inflammatory—topics."

Annabelle easily outlined the proper techniques for gall bladder removal and delivering a breach birth, as the clock ticked towards the end of her allotted time. Though they nodded their heads at the correctness of her answers, the view of the remaining examiners seemed still skeptical as to her capacity. But Annabelle's spirits remained high until a staunch physician threw the question of hysteria onto the floorboards, quite detached from the implication as he looked at her with an expression as clear as the blue North Sea.

While there was a litany of subjects on which Annabelle had many opinions—female hysteria—and the asinine foibles by medical men attempting to cure the condition—was her top irritant. With no regard for her current position, Annabelle castigated the patriarchal itch to cut. The masculine questto relieve women of their troublesome ovaries and clitorisesso they could settle into a steady existence, devoid of emotion and pleasure. Allfor the sake of their husband's (and Society's) convenience.

Driven by her past pleasures and pains under the fingertips of men Annabelle dove into her theories on feminine insanity and its perpetuation by the masculine species. Her lips took on a life of their own. She was helpless to still them, before the stunned faces of the nineteen medical men before her.

Only one expression varied.

As Annabelle plunged into female freedoms and desire with the ferocity of a parched man finding water in the middle of the Mojave, Dr. Christianson cackled. "The inescapable fact is women cannot be as such without the attentions of men to bring her into full bloom."

The inference lacing his final word brought her rushing to the table, the tumblings of her past loves and current hates hobbling her reason. "Do you take credit for my early bloom?" As soon as the accusation sprang from her mouth, she staggered back from the table as the room stood in weighty silence. The personal chords of the past had woven tightly to the professional ones of the present—forming a deadly slipknot.

Christianson, undeterred, stretched long in his chair. "Without putting too fine a point on things—yes." He rose from his seat and stood at the end of the table. Wrapping his hands over its wood edges, he adopted a face softened with concern. "Dear colleagues, you must admit a woman is defined as she relates to the men surrounding her. And do we not owe these cherished creatures the respect to show care in educating them well, for their health and happiness, as to the roles which suit their English spirits best?"

"Educating—"

"The wildness of those American ladies speaks to a depravity of character which debases their feminine wiles which are the cherished attributes of their sex." The quiet that followed was broken by the whir of the clock before it struck the hour. Glancing at its face, he rounded the table. "Just in time gentleman, I believe we've had enough of this."

He took Annabelle by the elbow—too firmly for her escape gracefully. "I'll escort the lady out and we'll reconvene to discuss her score." He steered Annabelle back to her own seat. "Gather your things." He looked back to the Board. "A decision within a week. Is that reasonable, gentleman ?"

The wrinkled Board toggled their heads in agreement, though they still seemed to be recovering from the scene they had just witnessed.

A prime example of female hysteria indeed, Annabelle thought to herself as she rammed her hatpin so viciously through the crown of her bonnet she nearly impaled her thumb.

When she had buttoned her coat, Christianson again took her elbow and turned her to the Board. "May we offer a round of congratulations to the young lady for her efforts this morning. Perhaps she may well indeed be able to offer her talents in the realm of female maladies? Her temperament may be less-suited for the surgical arts, no?"

His rebuff was met with a few chuckles as Annabelle jerked from his grasp.

Before Annabelle could remind dear Horace of his unfortunate spleen she had unrooted only a few months before, Dr. Van Winkle again came to her aide. "I can't imagine Mrs. Christianson would have carried on quite as she did when she was elbow deep in your innards—or you would not have fared quite so well."

The other examiners, not quite off the proverbial hook yet, nodded at his logic.

Annabelle was unwilling to have her destiny chartered for her—despite her volcanic humors. "You haven't even examined my extensive work in research and cardioelectrics."

A few brows flickered and she took heart.

But before she could break into an altogether different kind of monologue, Christianson wielded his opinion like a shillelagh. "Perhaps then you better keep to your pen and pages? Rather than risk your unsexing at the operating table?"

In a flash, Annabelle was trundled down a back corridor, on Dr. Van Winkle's insistence, to a side wing of the College to avoid the protestors, though their numbers had dwindled during her examination hours. The steward, sent ahead to hail a hansom, ran square into Thomas, propped against a column, arms crossed, a gleeful expression akin to an upper crust Texas outlaw plastered across his face.

Settling into the carriage, which had remained unharmed, as had Thomas after his forceable removal hours before, Annabelle released a shuddering sigh. She hated to let Thomas' obvious thrill at her presumed success deflate with the real tale. Holding his gaze with hers as they bumped along the high street back to Berkeley Square, she recounted the disastrous morning. Thomas listened with quite good humor until his father's misbehaviors (Annabelle had held back on the exact degree) surfaced.

Then his face grew hard before his eyes watered, charming Annabelle at his loyalties. If she were to have failed, to not have gained the distinction of medical doctor, she had certainly gained his friendly heart for a lifetime. Of that she was certain. Leaving Thomas to stew, despite her attempts to assuage the hurt of his father's recent betrayals, she let his comfort cloak her in a few moments of much needed contentment. But as Thomas returned his arm around her, she allowed herself the reprieve of not thinking of the thing called tomorrow.

The incessant metallic pendulum of the clock had kept in time with Annabelle's racing pulse for the last quarter of an hour; the pages of The Woman in White having failed miserably to distract her tumbling thoughts. Logic was locked in mortal combat with her eternal flame of hope against hope. Jumping up from her seat, Annabelle paced behind the settee, worrying Thomas would arrive home from the wards before his father could parlay the news and make his escape. As dearly as she would love to see the two go head to head, she feared for Thomas' own precious heart, and wished he would be detained long enough for some pardon to come to his father.

The tapping at the door was so quiet, Annabelle at first mistook it for her own heartbeat. Kitty's brogue won over the room with her question. "Dr. Christianson to see you m'lady." There was more question than statement to her introduction.

This is it. Annabelle wondered if she never turned around if she could possibly stop time—if the eternal echo of an unanswered question would be preferable to the truth. She steeled herself and sat stiffly back onto the settee. "Do bring him through." The tremor in her hands made its way into her voice.

Kitty pushed her head around the door. "Ye sure, m'lady? I'll take the broom to 'im if ye'd rather?"

Her loyalty stilled Annabelle's hands and brought a smile to her face, as she questioned the tenacity of Christianson's rages against Kitty's Irish temper. "No, no, best be on with it."

Kitty looked vaguely disappointed. "Suit yerself." She curtsied. She never curtsied.

"Might be no need for violence. He's as meek as a lamb 'tis afternoon." Mischief washed over her face. "But I'm just a shout away if ye change yer mind. I bet it was my posy that done it." With a laugh washed with visions of shamrocks and sunbeams she closed the door.

Moments later, she showed Dr. Christianson into the library. Annabelle swore Kitty kicked up her heels like a Connemara lamb as she flounced out of the room, leaving the door open more than a crack. Christianson stood awkwardly in the middle of the room. Pressing his hat to his chest, he looked at her expectantly. An original expression from a man who preferred to communicate with hellfire and brimstone.

Annabelle found him unreadable, unusual for her, and almost as vulnerable as when she had found him under the ash tree the day of the fateful hunt. What had Kitty said about her posy having done it? She nodded at the clock. "I expected you would have shown me the curtesy of coming straight away after meetings with the Board concluded."

Christianson ducked his gaze to the carpet. "The decision proved to be much more sordid than anticipated." He looked up and smiled, almost sweetly, then shook his head. "Not sordid, exactly. But provocative. Unprecedented rather."

"You best take a seat and have it out before we both are asphyxiated by this suspense." Annabelle found his perplexing nervousness both irritating and emboldening.

Her father-in-law spent an inordinate amount of time arranging his hat and walking stick beside him. Apparently, Kitty had wanted to avoid any unnecessary lingering as she troubled to retrieve his belongings on his exit—particularly if she held a broom in one hand. When he finally pushed back, he looked as though he expected a cannon to go off at any moment.

"Well, have I or haven't I?"

"Right to the point then. But first, I do want you to know my sentiments the other day—"

"The ones where you suggested I would sacrifice my femininity for my ambitions, talentless as I may be?"

"Those are the ones." He had the unusual grace to redden. "They've tempered. Thanks to Beatrice mostly."

Annabelle had expected Bea to take up arms on her account but feared what truths had been necessarily (or un) uncloaked in the process. "She can be a hard woman to refuse."

"She is. Particularly when her reason is clearer than mine. I owe her some exchange for my past wrongs." He looked to his lap and rolled his thumbs, looking as if he was preparing to meet with the Archbishop.

Annabelle bolted forward. "You've not told her of our—"

"Heavens no! What good would that do anyone now?"

Annabelle rested back in her seat; relieved Beatrice's certain ignorance remained intact. "So where does that put me— in terms of the Board's decision?"

"Though there were several sympathies, the majority, while they found you remarkably bright, could not see the application of a medical woman outside the maternity wards."

"And you? In your position, you hold the most sway in their opinions."

"Having found myself indebted to you for my life—I have allowed my persuasions to shift. Dr. Hendrickson as well was a staunch supporter."

Dr. Van Winkle. The darling.

"We really gave the Board no choice. The Queen would take quite an offense if her exemption were to be overturned by the Board, left them with precious few options to the contrary."

Despite her continued chagrin that her Fate rested heavily on the grace of a royal whim, however kindly influenced by her mother, Annabelle began to see a redeeming shaft of light. "And so?"

"And so,' Christianson swept in, tucking his hand under her chin, 'my darling."

The suspense of his answer kept her from flinching at his touch, though his eyes held none of the sharpness she hated (and woefully feared.)

"I must congratulate you on your successful examination and hope you find the ring of Dr. Annabelle Christianson to your liking."

To Annabelle's mortification, she felt the weight of the last year swell from her heart, rivulets of vindication coursing down her face. She had hoped for a more triumphant release, but she held no power to plug her dams. Annabelle pushed past Christianson, striding to the window as the room had suddenly become tight. Park Lane at that hour, before the pulse of the city quickened as the evening hours approached, was quite still and provided little distraction.

She pressed her hands into the chilled glass and found the shock of it cooled her, allowing her tears to ebb. She heard Christianson sigh far behind her and was thankful for the distance to regain her dignity. She had done it. The first lady physician. An exception—but a medical doctor nevertheless. Where would she go from here? Annabelle had focused so much on the striving—the end result—she hadn't given serious thought to what should we do if her dreams rested neatly in the palm of her hand. Dabbing at her eyes with her fingertips, she gave herself a moment more before returning to the settee. "Heavens, after our performance in front of the Board, I hadn't held out much hope." She laughed to relieve the uncertainties already beginning to percolate.

"That's the other reason I wanted to deliver these tidings." Christianson ran his finger beneath the corner tip of his starched collar. "Some apologies are long overdue."

Annabelle credited him. A humility pervaded his manner—the arch of his shoulders, his dew-soft voice, his clear expression. She believed his sincerity. "I'm to have two shocks of a lifetime this afternoon, then?" There was no elegant way to open his pardons. But pardon she must. For herself. For Thomas.

"Perhaps more. But your recent triumph should carry you through quite safely."

Annabelle hoped he was right. "Go on then. I'm happy to hear you out, but you've wounded Thomas fiercely, you know." She let the statement sink into Horace's soft flesh. His wince was satisfying.

"He's been my redemption since the day he was born."

"He does have a way about him." It was funny how the mere mention of Thomas always seemed to soften animosities and cheer dulled hearts. "Even with our story, that never seems to end, I wish things with Thomas could have been different."

"I had held out hope, with your arrangement, he might be persuaded to return from trousered pastures. But not even you can redeem a carnality woven so deep." A nostalgic sadness outlined his words.

"Redeem? He needs no redemption! He and Simon lov—"

"A poorly chosen word, my dear." Christianson alighted next to her.

Annabelle leaned away from him—into her habitual distrust.

Christianson preserved the space between them. "We'll come back to Thomas, but I must explain a thing about myself to you. Not to excuse things, but to offer an explanation. We can find an understanding between us. A fresh start." He reached to put his hand on her shoulder in his plea.

Annabelle shot him a warning glance. Christianson instantly retreated uncharacteristically. "I'm not sure." Though their constant waltz between their past and present—affections, hatreds, and otherwise—had grown so tiresome and destructive— it whetted Annabelle's appetite for clemency.

Christianson worried his upper lip between his teeth, as if steadying his nerves for the confession to come. "It began before you. Before Honey. When I was very young. We would summer in Brighton. There, I met a girl, nymph really, Thomasina."

Annabelle's attention flicked at the name—recognition of something deep-woven.

"We were too young. But summer after summer we became more smitten until finally, in August 1825, we confessed our love, and planned to marry."

Annabelle found it an effort to imagine a juvenile Horace; his heart pinned to his sleeve.

"Our families forbade us. Quite rightly. It was a disastrous idea. But with our childish ardor we swore to be together whatever the cost."

It sounded as if he were painting a Montague and Capulet scenario set among a British landscape. Annabelle could not see him ever having embraced the world with an open heart, but for his ever-saddening expression as the seconds ticked by.

"One night we stole away in a chaise to a midnight ceremony with a sympathetic minister in Hove. But the rain and the black roads proved too much. In a flash, I lost control of the chaise. My world ended with a crash and a snap." His chest heaved. "Her neck was broken."

Sympathy for an Uncle Horace she never knew ate at the rind around Annabelle's heart.

"I offer this not for your pity, but so I may actively work to look at you without those young eyes."

"Look at me?"

"You see, the inescapable appeal of youth. That forbidden fairy child. The great promise of perfection. It began and ended with Thomasina. I found it with Honey. And even more so with you. The eternal Magdalene."

"What would you have me do with this confession?" Annabelle found her sympathies rising even as she recalled his first persuasions.

"Absolutely nothing. It's what I will do with it that matters to you."

Annabelle felt if she were standing in the rolling waves at Brighton, watching them ebb away leaving a dizzying terrain of sand and shells beneath her feet with the Mingle sisters. "What have you done then?"

"I hope to have purchased your pardon, if not your absolution."

"Purchased my pardon?"

"Your name on the patent and future royalties for the portable electrogram. Ink's just dried." Christianson's beam made him regain the transitory idealism of his early years.

It wasn't only the due credit, but the possibility of an independent income that brought a real smile to Annabelle's heart. Then a wicked wicket blew open. "It wouldn't be mine, really." Not that she believed Thomas would withhold a thruppence from her.

"That's where you're wrong. Bea had her hand in this plotting. Have you forgotten the amended Acts? Any income is yours. From the electrogram, surgeries, all of it."

The headiness of the proposed freedoms brought Annabelle to her feet her mind twirling with all kinds of possibilities as she bounded about the room.

Christianson laughed, breaking her stride as he met her between the world history and geography collections. "I've not even arrived at the best of it yet."

Breathless from her exhilarations, Annabelle swallowed, feeling her cheeks warm as if she had just finished a glorious afternoon hack. "Out with it then."

"Your run of loopholes and exceptions continues. I consulted one of the MP's who owed me a favor. Turns out, there's something to be done about your marriage."

Chapter 34

Thomas showed up in force just as his father was spelling out the formula for a very happy dissolution of their marriage. One Parliament's Marriage Act, plus a short, veiled trip to the divorce courts, and Annabelle would be free as a lark with rights to her own property and income—faring far better than her singleton brethren. Gossip and snubs would assuredly follow as the London winds blew word into Society's leant ear, but that was a small price to pay. Professional rivalry could be named as the stake which drove the darling couple apart, though likely Annabelle's childless state would bear the brunt of the remarks. Blame she was only too happy to bear to protect Thomas.

It was time a bit of righteous anger burned in his crucible. Thomas' Fate having been manipulated as much as hers—though Fate had seemed to favor him— as a man—until now. She sincerely hoped the quiet arrangement at Berkeley Square would continue to sustain his private passions with Simon. On a whim she wondered if there would ever be a time the two men could walk arm in arm down an avenue like the proper couple they were.

Unaccustomed to any emotion from his son outside of adoration, Christianson beamed and strode to meet Thomas, who brushed past him with a curt nod and positioned himself behind Annabelle, his hands on her shoulders, stronger than banded mail. "You've taken your time. Knowing full well I was out on the wards this time of the afternoon. Typical scheming."

"Scheming perhaps, but I've made things right."

"Doubtful."

Annabelle placed her hand over Thomas'. "Let him say his piece. I've passed and your father's given me rights to the electrogram."

At this news, Thomas' rocky facade crumbled. He leapt over the back of the settee before he took Annabelle in his arms with a schoolboy yip. "You've done it, my girl!" He pushed her away from him, holding her at arm's length. "Never mind, my girl ,' he paused as reality seemed to dawn bright. "I do beg your pardon, Dr. Christianson."

"Yes, yes, it's simply wonderful." But there was a pang. Christianson. Pierce. Who was she now to Thomas? Who would she be without him? She didn't know why she looked to her father-in-law in the moment, but the good news she presumed Thomas would believe t as such too should come from him . Or would Thomas be quite as elated as she at a full-fledged divorce?

"I indeed have had a change of heart." Christianson let the statement settle on his affronted son as he sat back in the chair across from them. "I'll be writing a second article in The Lancet—an amendment to my first piece written quite out of turn."

"I'll say, Father. I've never known you to be cruel, but you've been nothing but these past few weeks. It's been an awful mess, defending Annabelle's brilliance and not completely disowning you at the club and the College."

"Let me care for that now, Thomas, those are not your wrongs to make right."

"I should say not."

Annabelle could see the flinch at the edge of her father-in-law's mouth.

"Medical Board and colleagues aside, we were just discussing the more important matter at hand."

"Pray tell what that is?" Thomas cut in.

Christianson answered him with a sharp glance, as he could not raise his hand in warning.

Thomas tucked his chin, scolded back into propriety.

"I was just discussing your impending divorce." Christianson's final word rang around the room like a hawk, freed from a trap.

At once Thomas's expression became grim. Annabelle reached to put a comforting hand on his knee. As much as she loved him for exactly who he was, the idea of a boundless future had sounded overwhelmingly lovely. But he jerked his leg away and cast her a look as if she had just led a coup against the SS Thomas made black despair cloud her hopes.

"Divorce?" Thomas' eyes darted between his father and Annabelle—the sole surviving prisoner in now enemy camps.

"Yes." Christianson was matter of fact. "To give Annabelle the freedom we were so quick deny her. I had held some hope that she might have swayed you—"

"But she has not father, nor will she ever."

Annabelle cursed that still sharp sting of her failure, though she knew it was illogical. Thomas had told her that time and time again—as had Simon—but still.

"I know that now, Tom, but we cannot expect her to—"

"Expect her to remain my wife in name alone?" Thomas sprang from the settee. "It's something we've discussed, and she's agreed to. She knows I would condone any other arrangement she prefers." His glare at Annabelle was as beseeching as it was accusatory. "I've encouraged it, practically pushing her into Larkin's ready arms." He strode about the room, his anxious energy building.

Annabelle looked at Christianson, wishing they hadn't kicked the hornet's nest.

"It will set you free as well."

Thomas squared off against them. "A divorce? Just when things have settled, suspicions have been choked down, and you propose a divorce? We'll be right back to India and I can't go through that again!"

"But things have been righted. Professional differences have frayed a childless marriage. A palatable explanation."

"Unlikely to last. Simon and I could never have a life outside of our marriage. Annabelle understands that She'd never agree. After everything I've done for her."

Annabelle saw a crack in Thomas' shining knighthood—forced by a chord of self-preservation. Her stores of forgiveness had been sapped for Horace's reprieve this afternoon, she regretted having nothing left for Thomas but outrage. "I've earned my honors!"

"But you would not have without my tutelage. Or that royal exemption. Those blessings simply fell from the heavens into your satined lap." Thomas was her match. "And your father would have been a guest at the union workhouse with his gross misestimations in his research ventures."

"You'd throw that in my face?" His refusal absolved her of any lingering hesitations. She briefly entertained the idea of exposing her twisted past with his father—but she was beyond brutality now. "After what we've accomplished together?" Annabelle's eyes stung as huge tears erupted. "You expect me to live my life as a lie, no better hope than to be another man's mistress while you go on living on a cloud?"

"It wouldn't have been like that."

"You know that's a lie. There's no other way for a woman, with the hateful gemini standards to which women are held compared to men." All the pain of the past year and a half boiled over. "Our marriage provided you with a cloak. With my reputation and word, even with a divorce, no tongues will wag with uncloistered truths about you."

"She's right my boy." Christianson chimed in. "She'll not let you down—it's not in her nature. With a few whispers and another congratulatory article from me,' he produced a handkerchief and went to her.

Annabelle snatched the cloth from his hand and blotted her face.

Christianson continued unphased . "No one will question your equally fierce ambitions forced you two apart. You'll have your choice of suitors even as a divorcee. Most women would not be so lucky."

"Most women would not have found themselves in a predicament as unpredictable as this. Until this afternoon, I was useless to charter the waters of my destiny. Now at least, thanks to the last person on Earth I would have looked to for aide , I found myself with an oar and boat." Annabelle looked to her new ally with slight apology. She couldn't risk a retraction of his earlier promises.

※

It had been weeks since the mention of divorce had deftly chiseled a chasm between Annabelle and Thomas. They had gone about their quotidian activities with icy civility—surprisingly mostly on Thomas' part. But Annabelle decided to allow him his mood with some encouragement from Simon who had the patience of a saint. And it was Simon who eventually cracked the arctic air one evening after a particularly painful dinner full of knife scratching and clattering wine goblets. "Enough!" He roared before draining his port and bursting to his feet in the middle of the drawing room. His usually unalterable pleasantness tufted like a wet cat's fur. "Tom, I beg you. Give this beauty her freedom. You have no need of her protection any longer. It will be easy enough to sort out a very pleasant arrangement with two houses side by side. Like the one Victor and Andrew have in Hanover Square. You know very well they are quite happy, virile, yet raise no suspicions to the fools who would care."

A flash of revelation brought a smile to Annabelle's lips. The retired Major-General, medaled in the Crimean, and the slightly younger and very flamboyant architect who neighbored him were just like her Tom and Simon. And they were always on the top of Society's preferred guest lists so desirable was their conversation and compliments.

The wordless air crinkled with the current of crisscrossed objectives—redemption, sovereignty, normalcy.

Thomas averted his eyes from Simon's direct stare.

"Tommy, dearest, we cannot maintain this warzone when it is so counter to who we are. Give her the divorce. We are at no risk, truly." Simon lowered his tone and crossed to Thomas who was halfway to his feet in protest. "If you love me, as I know you do, you'll sign the papers with a flourish. I'll not have our happiness tarnished by the poor belle's misery." Simon reached to his lover, pulling him close, and kissed him with unchecked passion.

Despite being the sympathetic object of the conversation, Annabelle felt as if she were a an voyeur, intruding on the raw intimacy between them men.

After Simon released Thomas, he held his face in his hands for a moment. "Do it for us, my love."

"Alright." Thomas collapsed into an upholstered chair, his head in his hands. "I don't know who I thought I was fooling. I would have done to you what I was trying to avoid myself, my love."

Annabelle rushed to him, kneeling in a mass of indigo skirts, she pushed his head up from his hands. Remorse flooded her veins as she saw his handsome face was blotchy and wet, his cheeks like waterlogged lily pads. She sent Simon a look full of a lifetime of gratitude which he returned with a proper bow and kind smile. Returning her attention to Thomas, his tears cooling, Annabelle steeled herself against her instinctive amicability and her debt to their friendship. "Things will be different now. With some careful considerations and bleached half-truths, we'll both end up with the cards we've fought so hard to keep."

Chapter 35

In the first week of March 1872, after a flurry of house calls from the solicitor, a blessedly quiet Court session, and a magnanimous grant from Parliament, the Doctors Christianson found the ink drying rather nicely on their divorce papers.

Not that there hadn't been a few tears shed by both parties at the gavel's final echo, but the cautious anticipation of their new respective chapters overwhelmed any last twinges of regret. In the following weeks, the two delighted in benign collusion at various dinner parties and public appearances—letting the shuffled cards fly. While professional differences had worried their marriage vows to threads, a general amiability remained between the very eligible divorcees, much to Annabelle's delight.

✥

"Leave your bloomin' ascot alone,' Mrs. Mingle swatted at Ben's hand as he fiddled with the oversized cravat. She seemed in high humors that evening at Berkeley Square, particularly after her second glass of Madeira.

The gathered party of Annabelle, Thomas, and Simon unanimously smirked into their glasses at her mothering—and Ben's appropriate blush. But as he did not wisely take to her command, Mrs. Mingle brushed his fingers aside, tugged at one end of the silk, and whisked the offending item from his neck with a snap.

Shoulders shaking, their roars filled the oak-paneled dining room as the audience returned their glasses to the table. Annabelle felt no qualms that her laughter rang out the loudest. Ben replaced his surprised expression with an impish grin as he unbuttoned his collar, yanking it wide before he took a gulp of his own Madeira. "You know what I've been thinking?"

Annabelle let her eyes pop open wide. "Lord save us all." Despite all that had passed between them, their natural repartee remained engard . Ben's flicker of adoration before he dismissed her jab strained her heartstrings. Annabelle was torn between the happiness evoked by his familiarity, and horror at the ease with which he could still tip her emotions.

"I was only going in for a compliment, Dr. Christianson. Keep yer skirts down." Ben scoffed. "I were only going to thank ye for a splendid evening where I can loosen me stays so to speak and speak plainly without fear of embarrassment—"

"Now, now,' Mrs. Mingle waggled her empty glass and cast Simon a silent request for continued libations. He responded with the promptness of a royal footman. "That's the stuff,' she cried as the sweet wine flowed. "I think you did your family quite proud at Dr. Pierce's evening for you."

"Aye know, I know. ' T'wasn't all bad." Ben gently shrugged off Mrs. Mingle. "I'm right grateful for his kindnesses. But ye know I'm not in for that sort of pomp and bow ties."

Annabelle remembered the evening with fondness. Ben and his father, Mrs. Mingle, Thomas, and her parents had indeed spent a lovely dinner in conversation; her father sparing no expense. But her ever class-conscious father and her just-tempered mother had made formality rule the occasion at Fernhead House. An aura which thankfully did not carry over to tonight. The highlight of the evening had been the sweet blushes shared between Mrs. Mingle and Matthew Fulbright and she sincerely hoped something would come of these early sparks. Annabelle was relieved for the amorous spotlight to have shifted, at least for that night, from her and Ben. After several weeks of space between them, tonight she was determined to rid her soul of the lingering webs of attachment to her faithful coachman.

"We wouldn't have you any other way." Annabelle was in more than a generous spirit tonight, certain this was the only tact to effectively rid her passions of one Benjamin Fulbright She took up her glass and scanned the group and they followed suit. But not before Simon and Thomas shared a mischievous look.

Thomas shifted and met Annabelle's eyes before they turned to Ben, "I second that." They raised their glasses. "Here's to a bright future in new worlds and a fond farewell to the old ones. Here's to the things yet to come, and to the sweet memories we hold. May the Lord light the way to heaven on Earth." He reached across Mrs. Mingle's tempting currant and orange pavlova to touch his glass to Ben's. "You're pure gold, Ben Fulbright, and I'd like to hope this'll not be the last we'll see of you."

All eyes darted to Annabelle. Her task might prove more difficult than anticipated. Tthere weren't many men like Ben. Any perhaps? Only Thomas could rival him. Mrs. Mingle boldly raised her eyebrow. Annabelle's heart jumped as if the housekeeper could read her thoughts. She couldn't repress a blushed glance at Ben as she struggled to cobble together an innocuous reply. And with the constant panache which far eclipsed his social strata, Ben steered the conversation away from unchartered waters of their beating hearts. "With the way Pa and this one 'ere ,' he gave Mrs. Mingle a loving nudge, 'were carryin' on, I'll hafta be saving some coin for a return sail for a weddin' ."

Mrs. Mingle promptly turned the shade of an early summer beet. Catching sight of her pavlova , she sprang from her chair and grabbed the unsuspecting confection as if it were a life vest. "Now, now, none of this foolish talk, when we've not finished our beautiful meal. You're your father your dallying on about."

"I'll give 'im a year to court you, Mrs. Mingle. Should be enough time to raise funds." Ben gave her a peck on the cheek. "Ma."

Now a feverish ruby, Mrs. Mingle let out a robust 'pshaw' as she ruffled Ben's untamable hair. Her audience seemed temporarily detained from their loving persecution of the housekeeper by mouthfuls of meringue and cream, leaving the room silent save for the gentle tick of the wall clock and the clatter of forks on china.

Annabelle allowed herself the ridiculous pleasure of a momentary daydream—Mrs. Mingle and Mr. Fulbright, side by side with Ben and her, both couples hand in hand—before she cleaned all traces of sugared life from her plate. "That was an absolute delight, Mrs. Mingle."

Caught with her own mouth quite full, Mrs. Mingle murmured her appreciation at the compliment, though her cheeks again grew bright.

"Father reminded me the other night you've been with our family for fifty years. Have you given more consideration to your own sweet shop? I can only imagine you'd like to put your glorious efforts to use for your own pleasures." She kept her words as gentle as lamb's wool.

Mrs. Mingle's lips switched ; her fork hung midair as she seemed to digest the blissful morsel Annabelle proffered.

Annabelle was unable to ascertain whether a quick retraction was in order as Mrs. Mingle looked as if she could easily burst into tears. Without a thought she flicked her eyes to Thomas who softly nodded in encouragement. "You've worked so hard in service, since you were thirteen, am I right?"

Mrs. Mingle looked down to her empty plate and nodded as she set her fork across it. "And all those years have been my pleasure."

Annabelle wanted to laugh at the housekeeper's lovable bondage but knew that would have been the ultimate rudeness. If only the woman would admit her hopes. She again looked to Thomas who could be counted on for his ethereal footsteps in delicate territories.

Without missing a note, Thomas broke in. "Dear Mrs. Mingle, Annabelle and I have had your welfare on our minds for some time now and we've a proposition for you."

Annabelle returned his gleeful expression, his blanched lie so perfect for the occasion, before Thomas launched into an improvised business plan to set Mrs. Mingle up with the confection and bake shop of her dreams, funded by a generous investment from the Drs. Christianson. Thus she could live out her days doing what she loved best, and have a tidy income to boot.

All that, Annabelle thought to herself, from some brief remark she had made during their courtship. Even with their marriage dissolved, Annabelle rejoiced that their almost primordial bond remained strong.

Ben pounced as soon as Thomas had concluded. "And you must stock your ginger cakes, you know they're father's favorite." He said, helping himself to another wedge of pavlova .

"Ohhh,' Mrs. Mingle scoffed—a devilish dalliance taking over her expression. "Do ye not think I've not considered his weaknesses? Why else do ye think I've been keeping him in mincemeat pies and chocolate kisses for the years since your kind mamma passed on?" She cocked her head saucily at Ben. "I'm not quite as daft as this crowd takes me for. And Thomas here has done the gentlemanly thing and put the roaringly impolite topic of money on the table."

She winked at Thomas who straightened with pleasure. "So I'll not make his breath for naught. I'll accept that kind offer but need some time to set some affairs in order." She grinned madly, as if she had just won her fortune at the gaming tables at a Monte Carlo casino. "And if you gentleman would be so kind as to entertain a cigar in the other parlor, I do have some words to have with our Annabelle before the evening's out."

The men dutifully took to her suggestion with much enthusiasm; Thomas being quite delighted to break open a new shipment of Havana Coronas and Demerara rum.

※

A few moments later, more comfortable in the drawing room, arm chairs drawn close to the fire, Mrs. Mingle pressed back in her chair and let a slow, wide smile cross her face as she appraised Annabelle. "I'd say things are wrapping up nicely for you, lass."

Annabelle had no argument with the sentiment but, as she was in a teasing mood, pressed the housekeeper. "How so exactly?" She did have the grace to look humbly in her lap with the query.

"Always in for a bit of praise, aren't you, love?" Mrs. Mingle's motherly chuckle overtook the paneling and wallpaper. "Knowing I wouldn't begrudge you a thing, I'll pontificate on the matter as you request." She set her head to the side, "To use one of your highfaluting words,' she grinned. "you see I've always got me wits and memory."

Annabelle smiled sheepishly—certain any airs she held for the rest of the world were lost on the dear woman before her.

"And it's your wits that've righted things and now your set to every advantage—a free woman with an income, profession, and reputation."

"You could be describing my Aunt Maude."

"Dawww,' Mrs. Mingle pressed her hand to her heart in what seemed real distress before she backpedaled. "Now I don't mean that in truth, she's your blood, and has been a real ally since the beginning. But her charms won't last. Yours on the other hand will not whither with the passing seasons."

A feeling of superiority washing over Annabelle, though it made her feel at once both delightful and horridly disloyal to her good-hearted, if slightly tarnished relation.

"You must have felt like Queen of the Empire after you hacked and sewed that devil, Christianson, back to life." Mrs. Mingle looked both pleased and exasperated. "Though to your ever-lasting credit, I can't say I'd have not let me knife slip and called it a rightful execution." As soon as the last, damning left her lips, she crossed herself, 'Lord forgive me."

"I can't say I didn't consider it—but my ambitions won over any lingering wish for vengeance I had. And now I'm presenting his case in Paris—with his blessing, might I add."

Mrs. Mingle shook her head, as if she had come face to face with King Arthur and found he was a woman. "Gads, girl, you speakin' in front of all those men. The British army could use a bit of your brass."

Annabelle hopped the bustled midnight blue velvet masterpiece from Worth, edged with popping bits of gold satin would well-contain her nerves the night of her presentation which would open the conference's ceremonies.

"I know you'd hate to admit it, you've your mamma's fire, though of a slightly less hysterical flavor." The housekeeper shifted into a more relaxed position in her chair. "And that face of yours. That's hers too."

A lifelong instinct to protest against this benevolent accusation surged through Annabelle, but her good sense reminded her of her mother's recent favors which should really have purchased Annabelle's full gratitude and forgiveness. For hadn't the grit between the two women, lodged early, as if in a Whitstable oyster, provided the essential contrast for her current state of evolution? "I suppose that's true, and we are thankfully on new, solid footing."

"It does my heart good to know those things have been sorted before I take my leave of Fernhead House—though in person alone. I would quite like the chance to set up my own shops ." Mrs. Mingle's expression was priceless—full of the joy of youth—untampered by the tyranny of daily life and routine heartbreak. "But there is one last string that's yet to be tidied." She looked to Annabelle suggestively, as if the topic needed no introduction.

In the space the following silence allowed, as Annabelle wondered how she could avoid the question, a scattering of feet, slightly unsteady on polished hardwood, and rum-laced hoots came into earshot.

"They'll be back in a flash." Mrs. Mingle hissed. "What are you planning with Ben, my dear. There's no one else, and never has been. Now he's off to America. And you to Paris. But I just can't paint a picture of a future without you two together in it eventually."

Annabelle had known Mrs. Mingle was bound to voice her preferred amour once she had the precise arrangement between Thomas and Simon spelled out for her. And she had failed at dismission the notion of Ben from her psyche. Miserably in fact as even his name made her pulse quicken in exquisite anticipation. But even with all that had transpired, with Annabelle's plans and aspirations stretching out before her like a constellation of steppingstones in the heavens, Ben's magnetism kept her stars tethered in the same galaxy.

Though a constant from the very beginning, his brightness not dulled by class or bank books, Annabelle told herself it was foolish to cling to inflated daydreams. Not now since she was Dr. Annabelle Christianson, who could hold the attentions of the Continent's medical men—whether for scientific or novelty's sake, she was unsure. But she'd ride this wave of notoriety as far as it would carry her. Despite where she now stood, despite the confidence she now felt in this new skin, that old chord made her wonder if she too could imagine a future without Ben strummed in its major key.

Giving herself the luxury of a brief splash in a pool of sadness and indecision, Annabelle's eyes stung of regret before the reality of her aspirations snapped her back to her typical senses. There was no future with Ben. Their worlds were too different. And always would be. She shuddered horribly as she envisioned herself being announced to address an assembly of her peers on her breakthrough electrocardiogram as the Dr. Pierce (or would she take his name and become Dr. Fulbright,) accompanied by her faithful coachman and husband. Shaking off the last droplets of her wallow, Annabelle replied. "I can't either."

Those three words might have been the Bishop's blessing to Mrs. Mingle. A radiance far surpassing any Annabelle had seen that evening beamed from her every pore. Now her hands clasped to her heart like the Blessed Mary. "Oy, I can't tell you my love how long I've waited for you to admit that with full force." And with a contentment to rival the Virgin she cooed, "I can't tell you how much I'll miss your sweet face, but I know you'll write and tell me all about Kentucky."

Annabelle opened her mouth to protest at Mrs. Mingle's dabbles into fiction--or was it fantasy , but there was no stopping her. The kerfuffle from the hall approached the drawing room followed by a barrage of knocks on its door.

"I imagine the wedding'll be a simple do with such short notice, and with your reputation, you'll be able to gather a ticket to sail next week in a flash."

"There'll be no wedding." Annabelle snapped, immensely irritated she could not shake Ben's grasp on her affections. Was she ever going to be allowed to take up her own pen to write her future without the constant edits from others?

But Mrs. Mingle did not deflate like one of her perfect popovers, but instead offered one of the most irritating, all-knowing smiles Annabelle had ever encountered. "We shall see."

Without further invitation, the door blew open as if it had been holding back the Shetland gales, and the troubadours crashed into the room, fracturing the tension which had begun to mount.

"Have you finished with your gorgeous chatter?" Thomas lisped gently. "We would like to extend a formal invitation to The Star, for the last London toast to this fine horseman—the Americans won't know what hit 'em." He clapped Ben brotherly on the back.

"' Right, right, you win, Tom. I'll go for another round. But—" Ben's eyes settled on Annabelle.

With an infuriating astuteness, Mrs. Mingle jumped at her chance to play fairy godmother. "Well I best be off to get my forty winks or I'll never be up to the task of planning for the sweet shop." She gave Annabelle a meaningful look cloaked in good cheer. "Now I'm sure Ben's got a few words to say to our lady here. So—" She rose. "Yer father's made space in the carriage to Dover as Maude'll be meeting you there from Paris. Then we'll have a nice cozy picnic as an umpteenth sendoff." Giving Annabelle a firm kiss on the forehead, she whispered, "Do give the boy a chance, I know he's got somethin' to say."

Annabelle wanted to do anything but nod as she did. She could begrudge neither Ben nor Mrs. Mingle at least that civility.

Smiling with her convictions , Mrs. Mingle marched from the drawing room with Thomas and Simon, linking their arms in hers and the three of them breaking into the final stanza of Ta-ra-ra Boom-de-ay .

⁂

Ben and Annabelle studied each other for a moment, but neither spoke.

Finally Ben broke the quiet. "Seeing as I can hear the steam whistle of the Great Western marking the turn of the clock hands, I best say my piece." He looked so very earnest from his seat on the hearth, his one leg sprawled before him.

"Are you sure, considering the copious amounts of alcohol you've consumed tonight? I'd not want you to regret a thing in the morning." Annabelle offered one last open window as an out to avoid the inevitable conversation. Ground floor of course—from which he could jump unscathed. But Annabelle wondered if it would pain her greater to leave things unsaid between them.

"Ahh, this,' he poked at his half-full snifter by his side, 'I've been cheekin' it all night, haven't swallowed more than a thimbleful. Clever, no?"

"Go ahead, then. Your piece, Mr. Fulbright." As Annabelle settled back in her chair, she found she was fairly certain her will was strong, but when faced with those imploring sky eyes and puckish dimples, she could not say she was sure.

"Ahhh, Bella," Ben growled, without displeasure. "It's a tired song I sing, but nonetheless it remains true for its refrain." He rocked on to his hip and scrounged in his pocket for a moment before he retrieved a tiny scarlet pouch and untied it. "With me sailin' on the 'morrow, I've held me breath long enough." He cast a quick look at Annabelle as a plain gold ring fell into his palm.

Though her tight stomach had pounced into her throat, Annabelle could not hide the smile that touched her lips. It was the first time he had brought a ring. Damn him. They might prove as ridiculous as coupled dove and donkey. The sense of the familiar and good fought fiercely against her soul's pressing need for exploration and freedom as she regarded the dull metal. After so many months of considering such jewelry worse than the hangman's noose, Annabelle now saw the completeness it could offer.

The promise of a true union. The sensation was made all the more penetrating as there were no secrets between them. Unlike her and Thomas— at the beginning. And most unlike Annabelle and Larkin. She shuddered as she recalled his vehement declaration in the drawing room at Penwood House and the infinite expanse in which she considered trading her spirit over for the familiar discomfort of wifely servitude. That refusal had been quite sweet. But this one, if she could hold her wits steady, would sting, as if the edge of a sheet of stationary had been drawn quick over a fingertip, then plunged readily into lemon juice.

But instead of rolling dutifully onto one knee in the manner of King Arthur for a formal declaration, Ben kept to his seat on the hearth, and offered his upturned palm, crowned by the ring, to Annabelle. "You know my heart, Bella. It's yours for the taking."

His sincerity made Annabelle's heart tilt. She leaned forward as her mouth fought to form a protest.

Annabelle caught the flicker of her expression in Ben's eyes before he looked to her feet. He met her again with a determined expression. "Just as I thought. Ye need yer bit of liberty now, and I want ye to have it. Surest way of catching a cantankerous filly is to show her the sugar, then turn yer back." His easy grin returned— but with an effort. "And there it is. I'll write with my address when I arrive. And if I don't hear word, I'll know your decision and learn to forget you."

The wound forged by his suggestion of her becoming a part of his past was deep. Annabelle sprang from the chair. "But I don't want you to forget me!"

In an instant Ben's eyes were level with hers and they stood in a stalemate, as a Catalan matador and his bull might meet before their final round—both parties exhausted but eager to hold the trophy aloft. "But if you're not by my side, I must, for the sake of the precious few threads of sanity I've left after a lifetime of lovin' you."

Annabelle stood before Ben speechless as she could not argue with his plea.

Now his smile came into full humor. "Now if I could haul you off to America like this, all compliant and tongue-tied, 'twould be a treat." Laughing, he let the ring slip from his fingers as he wrapped his strong hands behind Annabelle's head. "I love you, Belle. And with or without you, always will I reckon."

His kiss, full of more than gentle intent, was as pleasurable and pure as the reassuring summer rays on a Cornwall beach. Annabelle returned the pleasure in turn as they explored each other as familiar passions took on new, corporal forms. As Ben drew up her skirts and pressed her to him, Annabelle was thrust back to the ecstasies she had known beneath Socrates' paternal eye at the College, and wondered if she could not board the Great Western if she were to indulge in a farewell parting encore that evening.

Her pounding heart stopped quick as the first chorus of Ta-ra-ra Boom-de-ay swelled behind the drawing room door before the trills of Thomas and Simon sounded and Annabelle and Ben tore themselves from one another, leaving Annabelle feeling as unsatisfied as a grenade whose fuse had extinguished prematurely. "We've come to collect Lord Ben for a final round, Annabelle. Are you decent?" The men erupted into hysterics as they hurtled into the room. "I hope not, ' Simon echoed as he heaved into Thomas.

Sweeping his hand over his mouth to clear any incriminations, Ben cleared his throat.

"I presume you two have been discussing a possible appointment for Annabelle at Harvard and the train scheduled between Boston and Louisville?" Thomas quipped as his s's smeared from both his good-intent and continued libations.

"Precisely."

"Hardly."

Ben and Annabelle chimed in unison.

"Has all needed been said?" Thomas questioned. "I've one last parting gift for the Master here and I'd not want to cut him off."

Annabelle wished she could take a holiday in a snow globe to preserve the past moments alone with Ben without concern for the future. Or more precisely, finish the act which had been so unkindly interrupted. To hell with talk of class, reputation, and opinion.

"To be sure, Tom. A chat with our Bella always gives me a great thirst. You'll have me for a pint?"

"There's a booth with our name on it down at the Arms. One last round as a sendoff." Thomas declared.

"Right." Ben nodded at his comrades. He swept to the floor and collected the ring which lay glinting by the grate. Returning it to safety in its pouch, he stuffed it back into his pocket before he took Annabelle's hand. "Like I said, show 'er the sugar, then turn yer back. That's how it's done." His lips landed steadily on her skin and a glimmer of what might have been blazed bright. "Knock 'em dead in Paris, Bella. I'll look out for yer letter."

And with that, he took on his usual swagger and was ushered out of the room between Thomas and Simon as he bellowed out, "I'm not too young, I'm not too old. Not too timid, not too bold. Just the kind you'd like to hold." Annabelle caught Thomas' amused backwards glance as he grabbed the door handle. "I'll tell him you'll leave your door open tonight, if you'd like?"

But Annabelle shook her head sadly. "Not tonight."

"Suit yourself, my sweet. This means he's fair game." Thomas cackled before he closed the door.

As their voices receded into the night, Annabelle fell back into her chair, allowing her thoughts to still as she focused them on the lapping rusty peach-colored flames in the grate. Perhaps she should warm to Thomas' proposition? Heaven, if only for a night. No. For if she slipped between the sheets with Ben, she'd likely never leave, and what would become of Dr. Annabelle Pierce? She was grateful she could postpone a decision, for what treasures might Paris and her knifed profession hold? What harm would it do if she were to be taken to the States and Harvard? Right then she promised Ben silently she'd write.

Chapter 36

Annabelle rose from her seat to the thrills of applause at Dr. Christianson's introduction in Le Grand Hotel at 2, Rue Scribe, in the inimitable Paris. The very occasion of the conference invited a thrilling electricity into her bones—full of joviality, hopefulness, and excitement. She had taken long walks before. To the debutante spotlight, to Thomas, to Sarah's anatomic mausoleum, to her medical examination, but there was a sureness to her steps now which she would not trade for all the heartache she had endured. Annabelle wondered if Mrs. Gertrude Fawcett had felt the way she did now when she had addressed her amorous crowd in Trafalgar Square.

"It is with my utmost pleasure, I give to you, Dr. Annabelle Christianson, savior, colleague, and I dare say, friend." Horace Christianson shook Annabelle's hand with supreme ceremony as their eyes met. His smile was as clear as a country brook and Annabelle returned his new expression with an open heart. It was good to be free of the old Uncle Horace. To her even greater pleasure, he made no effort to kiss her hand as he positioned her at the podium.

Surveying the riveted crowd, Annabelle soaked in their attentions which were so richly rewarding as they had been hard won. Her days as a Society ornament were over, much to her surprising relief. This was what she had come for. She was met with another round of palms before she rose her arm graciously to silence them. She combed the crowd to find her father's beaming face. Dr. Pierce sat with his top hat, held over his heart. Their eyes locked. He looked as if he were to burst from his dashing black suit from joy. Annabelle feared she very well might do the same. At her father's side, her Aunt Maude fluttered her fan madly before Annabelle shifted her gaze. With her niece's attention arrested, Maude threw her shoulders back and gave the teardrop pearl dangling precariously in her décolletage a tap. Annabelle ignored the ill-concealed reminder of her Aunt's professional preferences before she dove into her case study on her successful emergent splenectomy in the setting of intrabdominal hemorrhage and shock.

The ball following the closing ceremonies had just begun when Annabelle came down the staircase, the glow from electric lights flickering in the chandeliers, making the contrast of the rich gold trim against her cobalt satin gown all the more brilliant. The rustle of the attendants was reminiscent of beehives. Flashes of colors caught in the mirrors lining the room—flowery pastels and bold primary hues. The orchestra's strings began to pluck out the very first waltz as she reached the landing.

Her heart squeezed sharply as her hand went to reach for Thomas and did not find him. She wished he had come, so he could privately revel in her success, which he had taken such a careful turn to cultivate. But she knew at the heart of his refusal, he wanted her to stand alone, confident, without a crutch. A wizened old man slicked his beard to a point as he stepped aside, obviously admiring Annabelle—but for what qualities she was unsure. A man only slightly older than herself stepped aside as he rebuttoned his glove and smiled openly at Annabelle's neckline.

Perfectly transparent attentions there. Annabelle found great pleasure in pushing past him before he could stammer out an invitation to dance. Another perk of her slightly mysterious situation as both a closeted divorcee and lady surgeon. Despite the hours she had spent with Kitty (who could not contain her glee at her afternoon exploration of the city) to set her coiffure and skirts at supreme attention, Annabelle knew she looked as if she had awoken as effortless and dewy as Sleeping Beauty from her hundred-year sleep. T hough the breath-rising kiss had been none other than her own. She smiled at the thought and decided she would take admiration in whatever form it came but need not indulge the giver.

Making her way over to a group of laced ladies and pomaded men, Annabelle allowed the newness of the experience to lift her even higher. All the sights and sounds blend into one magical experience she hoped she would remember for a lifetime.

"Always the belle of the ball, my darling." Her father swept her into his arms to begin a tour of the dance floor to the notes of Voices of Spring .

There was no need for words as the pair dove and dipped, both grinning like children set free to run on the plains of Kensington Garden, their pace increasing to chase the beats of their hearts. The timpani drumroll and brass flourish brought their flight back to Earth. They landed, rosy-cheeked next to an equally exuberant Maude whose dashing, young partner was making a beeline for the tower of champagne coupes filled to the brim with honey-colored charms.

Catching sight of the two, she chortled, "You-hoo , Vic, be a dear, two more glasses if you would?" She whipped back to her brother and niece; a devil may care look glossing her pretty features. Even on the shy side of fifty, even a sightless fool would have been powerless against Maude Pearle's intrinsic allure. Tonight she was a picture in nude taffeta. "Have you heard the whispers tonight?" Dr. Pierce gave his sister a look of only mildly disapproving brotherly affection. "And I say, gloves off this one,' she nodded at her companion. "An academic from Harvard and a captain in the army. I've never had an American and am quite looking forward to it." She sent Annabelle a loving, if warning glance. "I hope that all their revolutionary spirit and ingenuity just spills over into everything they do."

Now Annabelle felt free to chuckle and put her hands up in surrender as she looked to the returning gentleman. For a split second, Annabelle thought Thomas had surprised her, as the man could have been his double at a glance. Though her heart did not slow as she took in his perfectly proportioned frame and softly contoured face. But the conduction of her heart nearly stopped when the jolt of his stark sea moss green eyes captured hers. He seemed to hold her fixed as he delivered the champagne without spilling a drop. It took everything in Annabelle's power to bring the glass to her lips without a quiver.

"Dr. Christianson, Dr. Vic Buckley at your service."

Annabelle could almost hear his heels click to attention, now relieved of his cargo.

"Your aunt has been telling me how your incredible medical ventures began."

"I have done no such—' Maude sputtered as she moved between Annabelle and Dr. Buckley. "Vic, let's have another turn." She eyed the orchestra, as if she could compel them to break into song.

She downed her glass and tugged at his arm. But Maude was met with a permissive smile before the American stepped forward to Annabelle's father and extended his hand.

"Dr. Pierce, I presume? You hold the enviable position of having both an intellectual and beautiful daughter."

Needing no encouragement, her father broke into a loving monologue on Annabelle's triumphs. Annabelle wished her father would still his lips and sent Vic a look imploring forgiveness for her father's demonstrative praises. She was met with a gracious smile gliding across the rim of his half-full glass and returned his manners with a ladylike blush. Perhaps Aunt Maude had a point about Americans? Annabelle looked sideways at the Grande Pearle and almost jumped at the piercing glare which had replaced her Aunt's typical bemused expression.

Dr. Buckley volleyed his stare between the two women and his smile grew wider.

Conveniently, her father paused for breath just at that moment.

"You are the luckiest of men to have such charming feminine representation in the family." Buckley clinked his glass with Dr. Pierce's who nodded heartily.

As if she were a parched rose in the afternoon sun given a pitcher-full of water, the Baroness bloomed to her full brightness at the compliment.

"And I would count myself that lucky if I could—" the dashing doctor took Maude's hand and kissed her ungloved wrist, his lips lingering too pressingly for politeness. "A divine pleasure, Pearle,' he added quietly, before he completed his Fool's Mate. The whisper of an impending waltz sounded with the crinkle of sheet music and the wrap of the conductor's baton sounded. Turning on his heel, he faced Annabelle.

"May I have the honor, Dr. Buckley?" Annabelle offered her hand without a glance of apology at her aunt.

"Boldness in a woman is an excessively attractive quality, I must say. It would certainly be my honor, Dr. Christianson." Without pause, Dr. Buckley took Annabelle's glass and the two paraded onto the floor elbow to elbow, leaving her feeling light and only a bit chagrined by her fuming aunt cooling her embers. Brains over pearls this evening.

Depositing their glasses on a side table, Vic looked back at Annabelle, his smile both sure and questioning, making her heart drum double-time. He wasted no time and caught one arm around her waist and pulled Annabelle to him, making her think of new beginnings.

Resting in his embrace as the strings brought the ensemble to life, Annabelle let her hand fall to his shoulder—slimmer under her touch than his appearance belied. "You are quite mysterious, Dr. Buckley. Tell me more of yourself,' she requested as he carried her over the varnished floor with ease.

"I have little to tell, and I would much rather spend our time together learning your story."

So Annabelle indulged him, though she glossed over the details which could reopen wounds if not treated with care. Buckley's ear was intrigued and sympathetic.

"A sundry, pioneering tale, complete with dark alleys I hope you'll allow me to explore with you some day?" Buckley's hand tightened around her waist.

"Dark alleys?" Annabelle protested beneath a flutter of her eyelids.

Buckley ignored her coy reply as they continued their three-time step, gliding between the other couples, without an obvious care. "Come now, Dr. Christianson, we all have our secrets. How dull life would be without them?"

His piercing gaze pried her eyes wide. There was a familiarity in his arms she could not quite articulate. She avoided an answer as she focused on the perfect knot of Duponi on his smooth, white neck. Smooth. Too smooth.

Annabelle eyes climbed up his kind face. His angleless jawline and ridgeless brows.

Suddenly Dr. Buckley released her left hand abruptly and let her unreel, then pushed her under his arm in a daring spin, before whirling her back to him to the crash of a diabolically triumphant bass. "Don't you agree?" He grinned deeply as they continued their tour.

With Buckley's other hand pressed deep between her shoulder blades and the spell the doctor had conjured over Annabelle, belief, or the lack there of, was suspended for a few notes as Annabelle enjoyed this novel enchantment. They slowed to a standstill on cue from a melancholic oboe, as if it too were despondent they could not stay as they were for eternity.

Annabelle's fingers brushed against Buckley's throat, confirming a lack of prominent cartilage. Buckley flinched but his gaze did not flicker. Annabelle smiled in mutual understanding.

This was proving to be a very interesting evening indeed. "Back to the topic of secrets, I find them most stimulating, but prefer to call them puzzles on which I whet my wit." What would have dear Aunt Maude have done if she knew? Annabelle beamed at the American doctor, finding Vic's ambiguous intrigue supremely tantalizing. She hoped she might find herself a pioneer in more lush fields than medicine.

A subtle softness took over Buckley's entire frame as Annabelle remained content in their embrace. As if remembering propriety, Vic cleared his throat, releasing the matched polarity between them. "Very well then. I may soon call myself your puzzle and have the chance to whet more than your wit."

Her experience with masculine liaisons had not prepared Annabelle for the jolt of Vic's suggestion. It had been too long since the person's attentions made her cheeks burn so wonderfully.

Laughing, Vic retreated. "Forgive me, Dr. Christianson, your charms have made me speak out of turn. Shall we cool ourselves with a bit more champagne?"

Libatious effervesce was just what her thumping heart needed.

Slipping from the ball room, bubbling coupes in hand, Buckley lead Annabelle to a secluded corner, before offering her a toast. "Like water from the river Lethe."

"Let us forget the past and embrace our future." She tapped her glass to Buckley's. "Like water from the Lethe." The promise of the request shown as golden as the rising sun highlighting the divide between earth and sky. She quite liked the sound of that.

The End

After completing a PhD in Animal Science, I fed my Peter Pan syndrome by attending PA school shortly after meeting my now wife.

While credentialing for my first job, staring into the bowl of my Kitchen-Aid as I churned my own butter, I realized I needed another hobby–apart from my regular hot yoga habit and my perpetual culinary tinkerings.

With the greatest arrogance I have, or will ever, muster, I decided to write a novel. Fast-forward six years later and I'm rolling up my sleeves for my next literary project (a children's book or another historical novel, TBD,) while I juggle being a new mom, a bustling practice in Hepatology, and teaching yoga–deeply in love with my crazy beautiful life.

The Three Little Sisters

The Three Little Sisters is an indie publisher that puts authors first. We specalize in the strange and unusual. From titles about pagan and heathen spirituality to traditional fiction we bring books to life.

https://the3littlesisters.com

Milton Keynes UK
Ingram Content Group UK Ltd.
UKHW031617231124
451036UK00003B/32